Karen from the Mill

A novel from the golden age of sail

Anne Ipsen

To Heidi,

Karen from the Mill

A novel from the golden age of sail

Anne Ipsen

Enjoy your stay on Fanø

Anne Ipsen

Beaver's Pond Press Inc.
Edina, Minnesota

The drawing of the Sønderho mill and Millfarm on the cover is by Jørgen Lind. The thumbnail images for chapters 1, 3, 5, 7-10, 12, 14, 16-19, 21-23, 25, 28, 33, 36, 37, and 39 were derived from xylographs reproduced in Gunnar Knudsen, *Dansk bondeliv i forrige århundrede*, Chr. Erichsens Forlag, Copenhagen, 1975. Used by permission.

ISBN 10: 1-59298-107-0
ISBN 13: 978-1-59298-107-6

Library of Congress Catalog Number: 2005902836

Book design and typesetting: Mori Studio
Cover design: Mori Studio

Printed in the United States of America

First Printing: April 2005

08 07 06 05 6 5 4 3 2 1

Beaver's Pond Press, Inc.
7104 Ohms Lane, Suite 216
Edina, MN 55439
(952) 829-8818
www.BeaversPondPress.com

For more infromation or to order, visit *www.ibusgroup.com* or *www.BookHouseFulfillment.com* or call 1-800-901-3480. Reseller and special sales discounts available.

To my family whose hospitality and paintings inspired my love of Fanø:
Grandparents Emilie and Johannes Ipsen at Sydhuset,
Margrethe and Einar Lind, Else and Jørgen Lind at Møllegården;
To my father Johannes Ipsen,
who planted the seed for Karen's story over a half-century ago;
And to Jay, always.

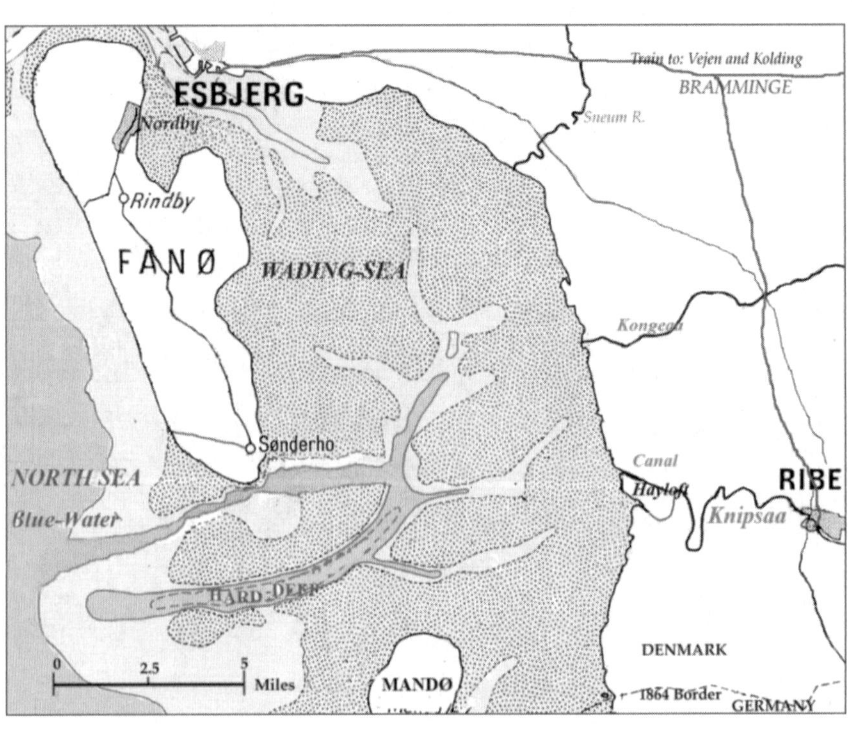

Train to: Vejen and Kolding
BRAMMINGE
ESBJERG
Nordby
Sneum R.
Rindby
FANØ
WADING-SEA
Kongeaa
Sønderho
Canal
NORTH SEA
Hayloft
RIBE
Blue-Water
Knipsaa
HARD-DEEP
DENMARK
0
2.5
5
Miles
MANDØ
1864 Border
GERMANY

One

Sønderho

Denmark, May 1874

May has come to the island. The west wind is still icy as it chases white clouds across the sky, but the sun comes out often and birds chirp in the heather. Long fingers of sand stretch into the churning waves of the North Sea and give a resting-place for logs washed up by the stormy night. A lark spirals up towards the clouds and the blue vault beyond, his endless song greeting the arrival of spring after a night of storm and a morning of drenching rain. Sønderho stretches below the soaring bird like a toy town of blocks scattered among the dunes by the whimsy of a child. The red brick walls peek out from under the gray thatched roofs; the narrow streets, most hardly more than foot paths, meander as they will from door to door. Yet each house is carefully placed with its long sides facing north and south so the narrow west end-gable can take the brunt of the winter storms from the sea.

The town of Sønderho—Southbay—has lain here at the southern end of the island of Fanø since the end of the Middle Ages, protected from the sea by the western dunes and separated from mainland Denmark by a strip of water so shallow it is called the Wading Sea. During the winter months, tall masts forested the waters of the 'Hard-deep' outside the harbor, but the proud sailing ships of the town departed at the end of February to roam the seven seas during the summer sailing season, not to return until fall.

Early in the afternoon, the town usually naps after the morning's labor and noontime dinner, but today eager spring voices mingle with the sounds of work. The clanking from the smithy of hammer striking anvil is echoed from the other side of town by the whine from the sawmill biting into wooden planks. A group of women cluster in the street between the new telegraph office and the sole grocery store. Scarves tied in turban-like peaks on heads that bob up and down as they gossip cover their hair. They all wear flowered long-sleeved bodices and matching aprons, alike except for subtle differences in color. Two mothers with toddlers on their hips leave to return home; the heavy pleats at the back of their identical green wool skirts sway artfully as they walk down the street. Excited young children mill about, the barefoot boys in workpants and shirts, the girls clad like their mothers except for their red skirts and lace-trimmed bonnets. The retired sea captains drift towards the bench that overlooks the empty harbor to smoke their pipes and settle affairs of town and world.

The older children are in school at the southern edge of town, their spring fever barely contained by Teacher's stern frown and hinting glances towards the switch in the corner. A map of Denmark hangs on the wall; Fanø is a speck just large enough to show that the northern and southern ends of the island wrap protecting arms around the harbors of the two towns of Sønderho and Nordby. The constant wind gave *Fan-ø* its name of 'Fan-Island' and the natural deep-water harbors are among Denmark's most important seaports.

Teacher is from the mainland with little appreciation of the sea. He accuses the children of being like their island home with their arms to the world but their backs to Denmark; they are much more interested in the distant lands across the oceans than in their own country only a few miles to the east. On this fine afternoon, even the more attentive girls grumble that the mundane history of wars and kings is boring compared to exotic tales of adventures in Asia, Africa, and the Americas, told by seamen during dark winter evenings.

On the edge of town where a dirt road winds towards the northern end of the island, the windmill stands watch on top of a tall dune. Its silhouette against the white clouds and blue sky is imprinted on the soul of every Sønderhoning, a landmark eagerly sighted far out at sea by homebound seamen. At the foot of the hill lies a red brick farmhouse with a thatched roof. Here lives the miller with his family, and here, on this fine spring day of 1874, begins our tale of Karen, his eldest child, who would fly with the lark but whose heart can never forget the mill.

The door on the north side of the house opened and Miller stepped out, his wooden shoes clomping on the cobblestones. He glanced at the racing clouds and, noting a change in the wind, called to his son to help him mount the sails on the wings and pivot the mill into the wind. In the courtyard, his wife and the servant girl struggled against the strong breeze to hang wet laundry on the line.

At almost the same time, Karen strode purposefully through the south garden to where the sheep were tethered on the heath. Twice each day she had to water and move them. "I don't see why they can't graze on the inland meadows with the rest of the town sheep," she had grumbled at dinner, as usual. But her mother had said, "Nevertheless," and repeated, as usual, that there was no point in paying the town shepherd when they had Karen. She didn't really mind because she would rather be in the dunes than help with the laundry.

One of the lambs was missing. It had probably not wandered far but Karen decided to use its truancy as an excuse to cross the heath and climb her favorite dune. Not that even a lamb would be stupid enough to go this far where there was nothing but sand and prickly dune grass. If her mother questioned her lateness, she could tell her that from the top of the hill she was able to see if it was stuck in a boggy ditch somewhere.

Karen looked around to make sure that this part of the island was deserted, so she could take off the mask that protected her face from unfashionable sunburn. She tucked it under a tuft of heather out of the wind and added her wooden clogs and long black stockings to the pile. She would have liked to remove her headscarf to feel the wind in her hair, but feared she would never be able to retie it neatly enough to satisfy her mother's inspection. She picked up the front of her green skirt and ran to the foot of the dune, relishing her relative freedom yet feeling guilty for playing hooky. The heavy wool skirt made it hard to run, but at sixteen she was too old to be cavorting around in her underskirt like a child. That's why she was really here, to read the birthday letter Papa had handed her this morning. Not until next week would the family celebrate her name-day, the anniversary of her baptism, but today she was sixteen years old.

You'd think Mam would let me have a few minutes to read my letter, Karen thought resentfully, anticipating an argument with her mother that had not yet taken place.

The climb, up the steep wind-formed ravine to the top of the sandy hill, was slow. Her bare feet slid in the soft white sand and the stiff breeze swirled her apron around her head. There was a firmer path along the ridge but it was covered with razor-sharp lyme grass. The coarse grass was planted on the outer dunes in the continual struggle against erosion, its deep roots controlling the drifting sand.

Karen sat down on the grassy top of Kangaroo Dune, as she had named it, the pleated back of her green skirt bunching up behind her. Dangling her bare white feet over the edge, she extracted a thick letter from the bodice of her blouse. It was addressed to her aunt Kirsten, but in big letters on the front it said: "Hold until Karen's Birthday." She turned it over and slid her finger across the stiff paper to loosen the wax of the old-fashioned seal. A little package dropped into her lap but she was more anxious to read what her friend Peter had to say. He was sailing around the world as first mate on her uncle's ship, the *Marianne,* and had promised to write.

Horta, March 21, 1874

Dear Miss Andersen,

I found the enclosed pin in a funny little shop in the whaling town of Horta in the Azores. It was carved by an American harpooner from whalebone and is called scrimshaw. I hope your mother will allow you to accept this small token and that you will wear it occasionally in memory of our time together.

This was our first port of call after Rotterdam and when I saw the little pin I was reminded of you and my promise to write. I have been very busy learning my duties on a long voyage. It is very different standing watch as an officer on the open sea compared to our short trips to Norway and England last summer. Most of the sailors have not been this far from home before and certainly not this far into the Atlantic, almost a thousand miles from Portugal.

We have had good passage up to now although the Channel and the Bay of Biscay lived up to their reputations. Fortunately, I always gain my sea legs quickly. Horta is on Faial, in the middle group of the islands of the Azores. It isn't anything like Fanø, being much larger (almost as wide as Fanø is long) with high volcanic mountains in the middle covered with tropical forests.

Ah! Three bells, so I have to go eat and then to the bridge for the second dogwatch while Captain has his dinner. More later. . . .

Karen let the letter drop into her lap for a moment and looked out to the little strip of sea barely visible between the tops of the dunes to the west. She thought of the day at the end of February when the *Marianne* had sailed with Uncle Paul on the quarterdeck, his new first mate standing tall at his side. The three-masted bark was an impressive sight, as she ran before the light northwest breeze with all of her sails unfurled. Karen had watched until the mainmast sank slowly over the horizon of the North Sea wishing she could be on board and away from her mother's domination. She now mentally traced their route: to Holland for cargo, down through the English channel, past France, and down along the Portuguese Gold Coast where they would have caught the trade winds west to the Azores and on towards the Virgin Islands.

She smiled at the 'Miss Andersen' salutation—Peter's joke. Since her confirmation, she was supposed to be addressed as an adult, but only he called her that! Peter Larsen was from the other end of the island, from Nordby—Northtown, where he had attended the Navigation School in winter. Often he came to get help from her uncle, the Captain, striding the seven miles down the length of the island, sometimes getting a ride from a passing wagon. If the weather were bad or the night late, he slept in Uncle's loft. He claimed seamen could sleep anywhere, any time.

Peter and Karen had been friends since she was a child, she showing off her part of the island and he telling stories of strange lands. Karen sometimes sat in on his tutoring sessions with Uncle Paul, fascinated by the navigation instruments. In good weather they wandered on the heath or climbed this very dune where she helped him memorize long lists of terms and formulas. He in turn listened to her recite the catechism on which she had been tested for her confirmation at the end of February. After that, her mother had not allowed them to be alone in the dunes and Peter had started to call her 'Miss Andersen,' mostly as a tease about Mam's new strictness.

Karen sighed. Confirmation was supposed to be when children became adults and no longer went to school. However, instead of letting Karen decide things for herself, it seemed that Mam had used her being out of school as an excuse for piling on chores during every waking hour. *It's not fair*, she grumbled. *The boys get to go to sea, but girls just get to stay home and work.*

Karen picked up the letter again and read on. She rushed to finish, suddenly anxious to see how he signed the letter.

> *We leave tomorrow for the Virgin Islands. We will sail south for 1000 miles, almost to the 15th latitude, just east of Cape Verde. Then we will follow the current west to St. Thomas. Please write. You can address it: c/o Harbormaster, Charlotte Amalie. We will use that as a base during the summer while we transport goods around the Caribbean. In the fall, we will tack down the coast of South America in order to arrive in the Southern Hemisphere after its winter storms.*
>
> *Your friend,*
> *Peter*

Karen's dreamy sigh gave no hint that the letter might not be quite as ardent as she had hoped. She carefully refolded it and tucked it in her bodice, intending to read it over and over until the next one came. As she refastened the amber buttons, her hand hesitated at one in the middle. It was traditional for a woman to leave this undone so she could reread her latest letter from the sea whenever she had a rare free moment, but only if she were a *married* woman. She quickly finished closing her blouse. She sighed once more, admired the little scrimshaw brooch and pinned it so that the scarf around her neck hid it. She would wait until Mam was in a good mood to tell her about it. She probably wouldn't let her wear it; she was so old-fashioned.

Perhaps someday Karen too would sail around the world. That would have to be as the wife of a captain because only the Master of the ship could bring a woman on board. Granmam had done that when Granpapa first received his command, before Mam was born. Even her aunt, stick-in-the-mud Kirsten-Mos sailed with Uncle Paul last summer on the *Marianne* on her shakedown voyages in the North Sea. Perhaps someday Peter would become captain and she could sail with him—that is…if…blushing, Karen came back to the present.

She had always thought that when she was grown up she would be able to do as she wished, but even at sixteen, everyone still treated her as if she were a child; especially Mam. All day long it was: go there, do that, do it this way, that's not right, that's not tradition….

The angle of the sun reminded her that it must be four o'clock already and she needed to hurry home before Mam yelled at her for dawdling. Standing up, she automatically checked the blue horizon for tall masts and then turned slightly to admire the 'Alps,' the tallest dunes to the north. She continued to inspect her domain, her eyes quickly passing over the scrubby trees in the middle of the island where the sea gulls circled incessantly, past the meadow on the inland side, and on to home. From here, she could barely see Millfarm under its steep thatched roof, hiding behind the protecting dunes, but the mill stood tall. Papa must have finished turning it into the wind because the wings were rotating merrily.

Recalling her original errand, she cursorily checked the whereabouts of the wandering lamb. Sure enough, it had ambled back towards the flock by itself and she would only have to stake it on her way back.

As if she were still a child with no concern for propriety, Karen hiked her skirts up around her hips, gathered them loosely in her hands, and jumped straight out from the edge of the dune. In two gigantic leaps she reached the bottom, barely sliding as she landed with practiced balance in the soft sand. This was the best part of going to Kangaroo Dune, sailing off the edge of the world, feeling she would never land. If only the rest of life could be like that.

Back down at the bottom of the dune, she replaced the hated mask and slung her stockings over her shoulder. Slipping bare feet into the wooden clogs, she half-ran down the path towards the mill. Soon, from the top of the dune, only a scarf-covered head and the swaying pleats of a green skirt could be seen hurrying across the heath.

Two

Peter

The Danish Virgin Islands, April 1874

While Karen was dreaming of adventure, First Mate Peter Larsen was having the time of his life on the bridge of the *Marianne*. They were nearing the end of their 2,000-mile trip from the Azores and passing through the archipelago of islands strung out from the U.S. possession of Puerto Rico. The *Marianne* approached the Danish Virgin Islands from the southeast, running fully rigged before the great scoop of prevailing wind and ocean currents that had carried her across the Atlantic. It was the evening before their expected landfall at Charlotte Amalie on St. Thomas and Peter was on watch.

Bark

As the bark sailed between St. Croix to port and the smaller St John and St. Thomas to starboard, the wind shifted to the south, carrying tropical scents across the Caribbean from Venezuela. Peter glanced up at the huge spread of the square sails on the main and fore masts and then at the smaller fore-and-aft sails on the mizzen. He would have to slow their headway or they would be at the harbor entrance too early in the morning for a pilot.

He leaned over the railing of the poop deck and called down, "Mr. Hansen, trim the topsails; furl the topgallants and lower the jibs and stays. Helmsman, north-by-northwest, if you please."

The second mate responded with a loud, "All hands," and the men scrambled aloft. The sails came down and the 680-ton *Marianne* slowed majestically and swung towards the new heading.

Satisfied with the completion of the maneuver, Peter went forward to stand on the beakhead. He bent over the rail, mesmerized by the phosphorescent curl of water at the prow and felt the power of the ocean in his body as the bark rolled with the swells. Intoxicated by the white wings of the sails against the purple velvet of the night, he dreamt of himself as Master. A handsome and hard-working young man, he knew that ladies found him charming, men enjoyed his company, and sailors responded to his command. After this voyage, he felt he would be ready to become Captain. He was conscious of the potential of his friendship with Karen to help forward that ambition. He enjoyed her company, found her intelligence and imagination stimulating. Although he doubted she would be the docile Fanø wife, content to stay at home to raise children and wave goodbye from shore, the companionship of a wife on board appealed to him.

Yet, it was hard to visualize her sharing his bunk in the main cabin. She was still too young and he felt guilty unclothing her innocence, even in his thoughts. In his memory, Karen was still the child with whom he had roamed the dunes, but last winter he had felt the promise of her lithe figure when they partnered at the Sunday dances. Her face had not yet the mature beauty of her mother, but she would soon bloom and easily rival any girl on the island. Her impudent smile and sunny nature already contrasted favorably with the typical stolid Fanø woman. However, he would be away for a long time. Meanwhile, he was a healthy young male, as celibate as a hermit in the desert, with no control over his erotic dreams.

The cabin boy interrupted his thoughts, "Sir, Capt'n wants you. 'At your convenience,' he says."

Peter looked up once again to check the set of the sails. "Thanks, Jeppe. Tell him, I'll be right there."

Captain Paul Fredriksen had taken the fatherless Peter under his wing since he had first signed him on as a common sailor. The newly confirmed fourteen-year-old was a likely lad and he himself was a freshly minted first mate. Over the years, Paul had arranged for the young man to sail with him whenever possible and had watched his protégé mature. Last spring, when he had become the proud master of the brand new *Marianne*, Peter had passed his navigation exam just in time to become first mate on the bark's maiden voyage to Norway. Her Captain had been happy to see that Peter fulfilled every expectation; authority sat easily on his shoulders and he had a comfortable rapport with the men.

Now, during the Atlantic crossing, Paul relied on him more and more, confident that he could trust him to do his job without much supervision. Fredriksen also favored First Mate's developing relationship with his niece Karen. He planned to help assure the young man's future on the sea, especially if he were to become a member of the family. The *Marianne*'s Master would give up the sea before long and his yet-to-be-born children would be too young. Paul was therefore looking for someone to fill his place and, by Fanø tradition, family ship companies often passed along the distaff side.

Peter crossed the waist to climb to the quarterdeck and then the poop deck. Checking the compass one last time, he shrugged into his jacket and, with a "steady as you go" to the helmsman, he went below, trusting that it would continue to be a quiet watch. At home, Captain Fredriksen treated him like a younger brother but on board ship their relationship was more formal. They exchanged favorite books from small personal collections and had lively discussions about the finer points of navigation, but that was usually as far as it went. Occasionally during quiet watches, Captain unbent enough to challenge Peter to a game of chess, but only seldom did the conversation turn to home and personal matters. Peter therefore knocked on the door of the main cabin expecting to play chess and was surprised when he was invited to sit down but not to take off his jacket. The ivory chess set was not in evidence and Fredriksen looked uncomfortable.

The Captain's cabin was the most spacious on the ship. Its large windows ran between decks, the full width of the semi-ellipse of the stern. Except for the bunk built into the bulkhead, the German furniture was the latest fashion. The chairs and couch were upholstered in red plush and festooned with velvet tassels while the large table in the center of the carpeted floor was of dark mahogany.

Clearing his throat and staring at his hands, Paul Fredriksen said, "Please have a talk with the men before we dock. Chalotte Amalie may look like a Danish town, but it is about as wild a port as any we have yet visited. Although the brick government buildings and the red uniform of the postman may remind of home, this is the Caribbean. The bars are wild and the women not-so-virgin." He barely smiled at his own joke and his voice remained solemn. "Tell the men to watch out. They should pick their company carefully, women as well as men, and not linger outside after dark. If thugs don't get them the night air will. Tropical diseases are deadly."

"Yes, sir. I can do that," Peter replied, mopping the sweat from his face and wondering why Fredriksen seemed so embarrassed. "But don't you think it would come better from you? You have so much more experience."

"The men respect you and are more apt to listen to a young man than a married old fuddy-duddy like me." Again he grimaced to signal his attempt at humor. "Hansen and Pedersen have been here before so you can depend on them to back you up with the new hands."

Then, looking even more embarrassed, he continued, "Ahem, you too should take care." He pushed his engraved calling card across the table, an address handwritten on the back. "If you wish to avail yourself of island hospitality, ahem, this house is clean and the Quadroons beautiful. Tell *Madame Prouste* that I sent you."

Captain Fredriksen finally raised his eyes and looked straight into those of his first mate, "It is understood, of course, that youthful indiscretions remain confidential."

Peter shifted uncomfortably in his seat. Captain seemed not just to be reassuring Peter that he would tell no tales about him to the family, but was proposing mutual silence. Rising from behind the table, Fredriksen extended his right hand and the two sealed the bargain.

Changing to a lighter tone, Fredriksen affectionately patted the younger man's back. "You need some cooler clothes. There's a good tailor up on

Sneglegade, near the Jewish Synagogue. If you are short of funds, charge them to my account against your next paycheck."

"Do you think they can make something quickly? I don't have anything to wear to call on the Governor," Peter confessed gratefully.

"Abrams is very efficient and may even be able to make you some evening clothes before we sail to St. Croix. Henningsen, the owner of the sugar plantation there, lives rather grandly and will probably invite us to a formal party. We won't call on the Governor until we return to St. Thomas, so you have time to have a morning coat made, as well."

Hoping that his blushing cheeks were not visible in the low light, Peter bowed slightly. "Thank you, Captain Fredriksen. I will certainly take your advice to heart—all of it," he said and hastily left the stuffy cabin for the fresher air of the deck.

The pilot guided the *Marianne* into the bay of the natural deep-water harbor without incidence, and by late morning they were docked at King's Wharf. The Captain disembarked with the pilot and immediately reported to the harbormaster. He returned with a heavy mailbag. Peter looked in vain for a letter from Karen, though he had little hope. Since her birthday was still two weeks away, he could not expect her to write until she had heard from him—even Karen would not be that careless with convention. He had to be content with a chatty letter from his mother and a scribbled note from his sister.

The Captain spent most of the next several days on shore. He paid toll on their non-Danish goods, sold the cargo, and arranged to transport supplies to St. Croix the following week. Opening a bank account to handle their funds during their stay in the Caribbean, he returned to the ship to pay the crew. Sailors' contracts specified the shares of profit that each was to receive by the end of the voyage, but Fredriksen liked to dole out a little spending money at each landfall because it was good for morale. Contrary to usual ship-policy that actually encouraged sailors to defect so they would forfeit their pay, this captain liked the security of a familiar crew and treated his men well. In the evenings, Fredriksen dined with friends on shore, usually spending the night. Peter guessed how to reach him in an emergency, but the subject was not discussed.

Meanwhile, Peter supervised the off-loading of cargo, emptying the hold of all but a few barrels destined for St. Croix. The tanks were refilled with fresh water, and he disembarked briefly to buy provisions of fresh fruits and vegetables at *Torvet*—the market. On the way back, he made a detour to visit the recommended tailor.

Abrams, a tiny wizened man who spoke English with a heavy Yiddish accent, inspected the lean frame of his tall customer. Pursing his lips, he nodded slightly and declared, "Beige linen trousers with a buff jacket and brown satin reverses. As luck would have it, we have such an outfit ready for fitting."

He gestured for Peter to try on the providential suit. Peter looked at himself in the mirror, amazed at the transformation. Though the trousers sagged over his hips, and the unhemmed sleeves of the jacket covered his hands, the colors complemented his sun-bleached hair and the fabric hugged his broad shoulders without a wrinkle. The assistant emerged from the backroom, measuring tape around his neck, chalk and pins at the ready. The jacket was removed. The two men jabbered in Yiddish while the assistant made chalk lines at the back of the trousers and down the sides with rapid strokes. After inserting a few pins at the hemlines, he helped Peter on with the jacket. More lines to nip the waist and pins to shorten the sleeves completed the fitting.

Reassured that the suit would be ready by the end of the week and that a formal morning coat would be waiting when he returned from St. Croix, Peter left the store with a supply of thin cotton workshirts and two pair of duck workpants. These readymade trousers were a little too short for his long legs, but were better in the tropical heat than the wool he had worn at sea.

By the end of the first day, the *Marianne* was towed to her mooring in the bay where fresh breezes would protect the crew from the disease-laden night-miasma. There, the hull was checked and even the smallest leak caulked. The hold was scrubbed and prepared for new cargo, most of which would serve as ballast until replaced with sugar and molasses in St. Croix. Peter set up skeleton watches to guard the ship so that each member of the seven-man crew could rotate shore leave.

In the evenings, Peter stayed on board and wrote letters to his family at home. If he wanted to receive word from Karen, he realized that he would have to write her and he resolved to write often, even if he could only manage a few lines. That way a letter could be ready to send whenever they chanced to meet a ship heading for home. He wrote his first impressions of Charlotte Amalie, explaining that it looked just like a Danish town from its houses to its postman, except the postman was a Negro and the trees were tall palms. He described the colors and smells of the market place and recounted his experience at the tailor shop. To his surprise, he enjoyed reliving his day and discovered a gift for describing sights and people. He was vaguely conscious that his vignettes would add to Karen's restlessness, but little did he know that they would take on a life of their own.

Peter's turn to explore the diversions of the town did not come until Saturday when Captain took the skeleton watch. It was with a light heart and a bounce in his step that Peter climbed down into the tender that transported him and three of the crew to shore. He could have sworn that Fredriksen winked at him at the end of breakfast, which he had been invited to share in the main cabin. The cabin boy had left for the galley with their dirty dishes when Captain had dismissed Peter, saying, "I'll see you in Church tomorrow morning. I noticed you have Mr. Hansen and seaman Skovby on skeleton watch tomorrow and have given the rest permission to attend Church—well done. I'll take Jeppe in hand and make sure he doesn't stray elsewhere. Enjoy your day on the town," he had added. That's when he had winked—or perhaps Peter had only imagined it.

There was plenty to see in the old town. He walked up Drake's Passage to Droningens Gade. Along this palm tree-lined main street was a funny mixture of Danish baroque brick buildings and tropical gardens. Dark-skinned women in colorful sarongs carried baskets on their heads and hawked exotic fruits, their gaudy turbans matching the plumage of the tropical birds flitting between the flowering bushes. By comparison, the headscarves of Fanø women were as drab as the Danish nightingale.

Peter sat down at a sidewalk café and ordered lunch by pointing to an appetizing dish that had just been delivered to the customer at the next table. The meat looked like pork but the exotic aroma was unfamiliar. He took a bite and almost choked as spices burned their way down his throat.

"First time on the Virgins?" his neighbor laughed. "Hotter than in Denmark, is it? But the beer is good and the women better!" The man's oily voice insinuated more than his literal words. "If you wish a guide after your long sea voyage...."

Peter shrugged good-naturedly, downed half the beer, and took another mouthful. "What's the point of traveling if everywhere were like home?" he answered. He finished the savory dish and extracted himself from the man's clutches by claiming an urgent appointment.

Peter made his way north towards the synagogue hoping that his clothes might be ready at the tailors. The sign on the door announced that they were closed for the Sabbath. *Of course,* he thought, realizing he would have to find time Monday morning before they set sail for St. Croix. Extracting Captain's card from his pocket, he lectured himself, *If you're going to do it, now is the time.* Seeking help from the nearest policeman, he was directed towards the street named on the back. The officer replied in a Danish inflected with a pleasant singsong, "Turn left at the top of the hill. Madame Prouste's house is on the right half-way down." There was no hint of censure on his friendly black face.

The house was located on a pleasant residential street, its conventional exterior giving no hint of its unconventional occupants. Entering through a bougainvillea-covered arch and walking up the hibiscus-lined path, Peter wondered if he was at the right place. He knocked uncertainly and the door was opened a crack by a massive black butler who scowled at him suspiciously.

"I'm here to see *Madame Prouste*?" Peter croaked, his voice rising to a squeak, as if he were an adolescent asking a question rather than a man of the world announcing his presence.

The butler-cum-guard glanced at the stripes on the sleeves of Peter's uniform. His expression changed to a welcoming grin and ushered Peter into a large reception room.

Having spent most of his teenage years at sea, Peter had visited other houses of "ill-repute" in dark alleys of seamy ports, but never one as elegant as this. He glanced around the room in awe. It was dimly lit by the candles of a chandelier suspended from the ceiling, its crystal pendants tinkling softly in the sea breeze that came through the slats of the closed shutters.

The hostess approached with a rustle of silk and outstretched hands. "*Je suis Madame Prouste*," she purred in French, continuing in slightly accented Danish, "Le Capitaine said to expect his tall first mate, but he not say 'ow 'andsome."

Peter's mouth open like a beached fish gasping for air and he started to stammer his name. *Madame* shook her head and murmured, "Not with ze names, just le First Mate." She sat down on a red plush settee and patted the space beside her. "Jericho, *Champagne, s'il vous plait*," she called to the butler who instantly appeared and offered Peter a glass.

Being used to having to pay ahead of time, Peter fumbled for his wallet. "*Mais, non!*" *Madame* exclaimed. "*Demain*—in the morning, *c'est d'accord*."

Giving the nerves of her flustered guest time to mellow, she indicated the various ladies scattered decorously about the room, naming each and sketching her particular accomplishments.

Peter heard someone mumble, "Such ladies!" and realized it was himself. "I'm just a sailor and not used to such elegance," he confessed more loudly.

Madame's light laugh tinkled like the crystals overhead. "Janette," she called softly to a plump girl dressed in a lemon-colored skirt and white peasant blouse. With her black wavy hair, brown eyes, and tawny skin, the quadroon looked friendly. As the plump girl approached, *Madame* whispered to Peter, "Janette is not so *formidable, non?* She has no Danish but a little Eenglish. *Le conversation*, he is not necessary, *non?*"

Discreetly relinquishing her seat to the girl, *Madame* went to greet another guest in a flood of liquid Spanish.

Janette was exactly as promised; while no challenge to anyone's intellect, she was expert at putting her customer at ease. Peter forgot his self-consciousness and started to tell the girl how beautiful she was. She responded with uncomprehending giggles. Pointing to the ceiling, she queried, "En haut?"

Peter stumbled up the staircase after his companion. He disappeared behind a closing door, not to be seen until morning when he walked into the Frederick Lutheran Church, looking tired but content.

Three

Nameday Coffee

SØNDERHO

A week later on the day of her nameday, Karen was again late returning from checking on the sheep. When she came around the west end of the house into the courtyard, her mother was sitting on a boulder by the north door. She was a handsome woman, her worn but graceful hands automatically matching and rolling the socks piled in the basket at her feet.

Karen was about to take off her clogs when Mam started complaining, "Where've you been? How long does it take to move a few sheep? Look at you; your hair is coming out everywhere. And wipe that sand off before you bring it in the house!"

"Yeah, yeah," Karen grumbled as she went to the middle of the yard to shake out her skirts. Balancing on one leg then the other, she emptied her clogs onto the cobblestones and wiped the sand off her feet. Defending herself with last week's excuse she said, "One of the lambs strayed and I went to look for it." Handing her mother a metal bucket, she added, "Here's Granmam's milk." She hardly thought it worth the effort to milk the sheep since they had plenty from their cows, but Granmam was from the old days when they only

had sheep and traditions die hard. It was now considered a delicacy to be served in coffee.

Mollified, Mam smiled, transforming her face. Large blue eyes twinkling, she joked, "It seems to me you're the lamb that strayed." Then more briskly she said, "Hurry and change so we won't be late for your nameday party—you know how Granmam is. Help Lil-Anne with her bonnet. Your brother will meet us there."

She picked up the basket of clean socks and followed Karen through the low wooden door into the hall known as *æ frankel.* This stone-paved passageway ran crossways through the house between the north and south doors and separated the house into the family rooms on the west and the scullery and stable on the east.

Karen sat down on a chair to put on her stockings and high-top shoes. Deciding that this was as good a time as any, she took off the scrimshaw pin that Peter had sent and displayed it in her hand. "Look what Peter sent me," she said.

"It's lovely dear," Mam said absently as she bent down to line up Karen's wooden clogs with the others along the wall. "But you know you can't accept anything that personal from a young man. Everyone would talk."

"But Mam, it's just a little old pin. It's not like it's gold or anything. Can't we just say Uncle Paul sent it to me?" She bent her head over the laces so that Mam wouldn't see the tears in her eyes.

"Certainly not. I knew it was a mistake to let him pay so much attention to you this winter. You're getting too old to roam around the dunes with a young man and he's not to be depended on."

"You know that's not true. He's very responsible, Uncle says so, and Papa likes him too. Besides, I only saw him at dances or at Granmam's."

"Nevertheless...."

Karen sighed. 'Nevertheless' seemed to be Mam's favorite word these days, except maybe for 'certainly not.' There was no point in arguing with her when she used those words.

Gloomily, she went through the kitchen and the northroom into the little bedroom she shared with her younger sister at the west end of the house. Sounding just like her mother, she grumbled, "Come here Lil-Anne, let me fix your bonnet. Can't you ever keep it on straight? And look at your hair coming out everywhere. We'll have to completely redo it."

Everyone called her little sister Lil-Anne to distinguish her from Mam who was named Anne too. Granmam was also an Anne, but everyone called her Big-Anne although she was tiny, like many of the old people. Mam had once been Lil-Anne. Then she got taller than Big-Anne and the family switched to calling her just plain Anne or Lars-Anne because her father's name was Lars. But the older woman remained 'Big-Anne.'

Karen often wondered why she herself wasn't named for anyone. In some ways this made her feel unique and that she could be her own person. Other times she felt like a stranger in the family and wondered if she belonged in Sønderho at all. Then there was her nameday; no one else was born in May, or even April or June. Maybe she was a changeling and trolls had stolen Mam's real daughter. Everyone said she looked like Mam except for being tall like Papa, but what did they know? Perhaps they were just trying to make her feel better about her gangly body and ugly face. Mam was so beautiful and graceful; Karen couldn't possibly look like her.

This morning, as they did the breakfast dishes, Karen had asked Mam why she wasn't an Anne, since she was the eldest daughter. Mam had mumbled something about it was time. Time for what? A new name? Getting away from Anne? Mam was very good at explaining how to do things, but a wall of mumbled words met Karen's questions about anything other than the practical. Talk of the past just made her grumpy. Why wouldn't she ever answer Karen's *real* questions?

Mam wasn't the only one absorbed in the everyday; this was characteristic of most Sønderhoning women who worked long days, especially during months when the men were away and they were alone with all the responsibilities of family and land. Until a hundred years ago, when the men started being skippers and owners of the great sailing fleet, survival had been marginal and life very hard. Frugality was so ingrained that now, in a time of relative prosperity, the island character was set and the work ethic fixed. Only during the long winter evenings, known as the 'darknin,' when most of the men were home from the sea, families and friends gathered and told stories of the past.

Karen was wakened from her reverie by Lil-Anne's giggles. She was shaking her short curly hair now that it was free of her bonnet. At barely seven, she did not wear the intricately tied turban of her older sister and mother, although she had started practicing tying a scarf on the post of her parent's big bed.

Other than their head coverings and Lil-Anne's skirt, which was red rather than the adult green, the two girls were dressed much alike. Their felted wool skirts had heavy kilted pleats in back and the bottom hems were bound with green ribbon to protect against dirt and wear. Aprons of dark-flowered calico covered their skirts. The short blouse, called a "nightshirt" for reasons long forgotten, was of the same material. Down the front were two rows of amber buttons, two pairs at the top, three below the ribs, and the edges were trimmed with embroidered black velvet. Karen's shirt buttoned on the left but Lil-Anne's was reversed because it was a hand-me-down and the right front was worn.

Lil-Anne wriggled where she stood clamped between Karen's legs while her unruly curls were being combed. "Ouch" and "Keep still," the two sisters said at the same time. Karen placed a piece of white linen edged with lace across her sister's forehead and tied the ends at the back of her head. She then added the bonnet, also tied at the back. A clean white muslin scarf went around her neck and was covered with a larger plaid scarf, fastened with an amber pin on the shoulder.

"There, now," Karen said, thinking that Lil-Anne really looked sweet with her freckled face framed by lace and her velvet-trimmed bonnet coming to an elfish peak. She gave the child a hug and kissed the enchanting little velvet bow on the top of her head.

Karen undid her own headscarf and re-braided her long blond hair, pinning it up. "If only Mam would let me cut my hair short like yours, it would be so much easier," Karen grumbled. Like her sister's, her hair was secured by a triangular scarf. She also had a peaked bonnet; it was just of muslin and had no lace, as it was not meant to be seen but merely to give shape to the covering headscarf. She folded the large square into a triangle and draped it over the peak. Wrapping the ends down and around the back of her head, she tied them on top. Lest Mam find something to criticize, she felt around her face and neck to make sure that there were no stray hairs and that the folds of the scarf came down straight along the back of her head. Then she pulled on the scarf ends, *pjeggerne,* that had to be knotted just so at the top and made sure they draped properly. She checked that the point of the triangle-folded neckscarf scarf was exactly in the center and halfway down her back before she re-wrapped it around her neck.

As was the custom, her neck and headscarves were identical generous squares of dark cotton with lighter blue and red stripes, woven in a large plaid pattern. For everyday, mother and daughter wore similar cotton scarves but Mam had some of iridescent purple silk that she wore on special occasions to go with her fancy silk blouse and apron. Karen admired the flair with which her mother tied her scarf and how it set off her beautiful oval face. She despaired of her own skill; she thought her square head was the wrong shape and that was why her scarf was always slipping. And the dark colors made her face look pasty, emphasizing her nose and chin.

Peter used to tease her about how she tied her headscarf, claiming that *his* mother's way was right. But then they were from Nordby and what did they know about tying *pjegger*? The two towns had a silly rivalry, not the least of their disagreements being about how to tie their scarves. Papa said it was all nonsense and the difference was too minute to be discerned; but then he was a man.

Thinking of Peter reminded Karen to take off his scrimshaw pin and replace it with her old amber pin. "Look what Peter sent," she said to her little sister. "Isn't it pretty? It's made of whalebone. But you mustn't talk about it or Mam will take it away." Lil-Anne reached out a pudgy finger and traced the black ink pattern on the white ivory.

Karen unbuttoned her blouse to extract Peter's letter and tuck it on the little shelf by her pillow. She and her sister shared an alcove bed that was built into the partitioning wall between their room and their brother's. Called a tightbed, it was well named and looked much like a shipboard bunk, as if designed by the same carpenters that built the Sønderho ships on the harbor beach. She was going put the pin on the shelf, but thought better of it and rebelliously put it back under her neckscarf.

"Coming," Karen called in answer to her mother's voice from the other end of the house. She hurriedly undid her worn work apron, exchanging it for a newer one that matched her nightshirt. After fastening the silver clasp of her belt she was dressed to go visiting. Gently pushing Lil-Anne in front of her, she went through the northroom and kitchen, then out the door.

"Hello Loves," the girls' father greeted them. He was waiting in the afternoon sun with one arm around Mam's shoulder and the callused hand of the other cradling the bowl of his unlit clay pipe. Tall and broad-shouldered, he stood as solidly planted on his cobblestones as the mill on its stump behind him. Lars-Anne was nestled comfortably under his arm and smiling. She didn't permit signs of intimacy in public but Anders had made it very clear that the children were not the public and the mill wasn't either. Karen marveled how Mam always seemed to melt when Papa put his arm around her, as if he alone had the magic that could soften her spine.

Anders Andersen had been called 'Anders-Miller' or simply 'Miller' by the townspeople ever since his bride had brought him home to her island. They had moved in with Lars-Anne's aging maternal grandfather, Anders gradually taking over running the mill and quietly settling into the life of the village. Although he was born on the Danish mainland less than fifteen miles from where he now stood and had earned the respect of the island with his honesty and hard work, he would always be considered a foreigner. His children, however, were true Sønderhonings, born at the house by the mill: first Karen, then Christian three years later, and finally Lil-Anne.

"Here, carry Granmam's milk," Lars-Anne said, handing her eldest daughter the metal bucket. The four of them walked down the rutted road that ran by the house, but instead of following it around the church and into the center of town they chose the Westerlands footpath which curved between tall thorn hedges towards Big-Anne's house at the southern edge of the village. The parents walked ahead, their arms linked, followed by the two girls holding hands. Mam took a few steps, her left stride shorter than the right until the pleats of her green shirt started to sway gently from side to side. Once they were properly swishing, she evened her steps to match Papa's shortened stride and tipped her face up towards his to say something. The top of her scarf barely reached his ear. Karen half-consciously tried to copy her mother's seductive movements while swinging the little bucket in one hand and restraining her bouncy sister with the other.

The grandfather clock tolled four inside the house just as Lars-Anne opened the door. Looking fleetingly relieved that they were on time, she called, "Hello! Mam and Kirsten, we're here!"

Big-Anne's house, called Southhouse, was built in the same style as Millfarm, a long oblong of red brick with an overhanging thatch roof. Because of its age it was lower, smaller and settled into the ground. There was no front yard, just a narrow strip of sandy grass and a low picket fence between it and the dirt road. Over the door, a dormer broke the trim edge of the foot-thick thatch of the roof. The dormer had green shutters and was topped by a rounded arch, decorated with alternating black, white and green stripes. The windows also had these "colored eyelashes" over the eyes of the house to symbolize the cycle of life: white for birth, green for hope and life, black for death.

Inside, as at the mill, *æ frankel* separated the house into the family rooms on the west and what had been the stable but was now an additional room at the east. A long supporting wall ran right down the middle of the east-west length, dividing it almost in half. On the north side of *æ frankel* was the entrance into the kitchen and the northroom that served as dining room and summer sitting room. South of the wall were the southroom and master bedroom.

"Anders went around to the garden," Lars-Anne said quietly as her tiny mother bounced through the kitchen door to greet her guests. "We figured it's warm enough to be outside."

"Well then, come in, come in. Let me look at you, Karen-child. My goodness, you're taller every time I see you. Go on with you, out to the garden. Kirsten-Mos is already there with her feet up; she's a little tired. There's a bottle of cold beer for Miller in the well."

Big-Anne was a lively woman whose commanding presence more than compensated for her diminutive stature. While her black clothes and blue-striped scarves proclaimed her a widow, her manner left no doubt who was captain of the family. In her youth she had been one of the town beauties, a role she had gracefully passed on to her namesake daughter together with her oval face, but her lively mouth and sparkling eyes contrasted with Lars-Anne's serious, sometimes severe demeanor.

As Sønderho's midwife, there was hardly a house where she had not helped bring a baby into the world. It was not possible to walk through town without seeing a small black figure darting in or out of the door, like one of the busy sandpipers running up and down the Fanø beach. Young and old alike readily sought her advice. Boys showed up on her doorstep to have fishing hooks removed from their clumsy hands, and housewives struggling with the latest weaving or knitting pattern dropped by in the afternoon to gossip and sip coffee.

Big-Anne took the milk bucket and looked up at her daughter. "It's that giant husband of yours that makes such big children. And I know why he went into the garden, he hates coming into my little old house, complaining there's no place where he can stand up straight without hitting his head." Then in a lower voice, "How can you let her look like that? Her skirt is half-way up her leg and soon the cuffs of the sleeves will be above her elbows. And the freckles on her nose…."

"She won't wear her mask when she works in the fields. As you said, she's growing all the time and with her nameday and all, I thought…," Lars-Anne protested, her voice and body shrinking as if she were still her mother's Lil-Anne.

"I saw her coming down the road and swishing her skirts; most unsuitable at her age," Granmam continued uninterruptibly. "You need to speak to her about such provocative behavior."

I wish they wouldn't talk about me as if I'm not here, Karen thought. *Doesn't it ever end? She yells at Mam just like Mam yells at me. Scolding, scolding all the time.*

But apparently the diminutive black-clad figure wasn't really cross because she turned to Lil-Anne and wagging her head from side to side exclaimed, "Here's someone more my size. Give me a big hug and come help me carry."

As the three Annes disappeared into the kitchen to bring out the food, Karen heard, "And where's that son of yours?"

"Isn't Christian here yet? He's been at Pastor's studying Latin, but he was supposed to come straight here afterwards. He's totally undependable these days, always running off with his friends."

Karen's younger brother was thirteen and a gifted but reluctant scholar. Mam had plans for him; he was destined for big things—on dry land. In the fall he was to go to the Latin School in the cathedral town of Ribe, just across the water on the mainland. This summer he was preparing by taking lessons from Doctor and Pastor. If he graduated from Latin School, he would be able to go to the University in Copenhagen and become a lawyer or a doctor. Mam was afraid that if he stayed in Sønderho he would run off to sea as soon as he was confirmed.

Maybe I could cut my hair, dress like a boy and run off to sea, Karen thought but then dismissed the idea with a shake of her head.

She walked into the garden and greeted her aunt, Kirsten-Mos, 'Mos' being short for 'Mother's sister.' Big-Anne's younger daughter was shy and serene, a peaceful contrast to her sister and mother's domineering personalities. The only time she had been away from home, other than short trips to the nearby coast, was last summer when she had joined her husband on the *Marianne's* maiden voyage to Bergen. She had proven a poor sailor, spending most of her time in her bunk, wretchedly seasick. Overwhelmed by the brooding mountains along Bergen Fjord and depressed by the rain-shrouded town, she declared with unusual firmness and much to her husband's disappointment that henceforth she would stay at home.

Kirsten-Mos was sitting in the shade of a gnarled apple tree, her hand holding a letter and resting on her bulging stomach. Karen went up to her aunt and, studiously avoiding mention of the obviously coming event, she received her kiss of congratulations. "You got a letter too?" she asked. "Peter wrote me also—from the Azores."

"Yes, I know. He sent it to me and asked me to hold it for your birthday," Kirsten-Mos replied. "Mine's from St. Thomas so you'll probably get another one from there soon. I'll read mine aloud later—he sent a photograph of the whole crew!"

Karen walked over to the well. At home, they had a deeper well with a boring winch; the one at Southhouse was a "tilt-well" with a long pole supported in the middle, fastened at one end to a rod holding the bucket, and at the other to a counterweight. Right now the counterweight was up in the air because the bucket was deep in the well. Karen pulled lightly on the pole to retrieve her father's cold beer, Big-Anne's concession to her son-in-law. She never drank herself and disapproved of alcohol. Everyone knew that to be invited to coffee at Big-Anne's meant just that, and that they would not be offered the traditional 'coffee-punch,' spiked with brandy. However, Big-Anne knew from experience that in a battle of wills with Miller she could only lose and, despite initial doubts, had to admit he was a hard-working man who was not going to be led astray by an afternoon beer.

"Here's the errant scholar," teased Anders as Christian appeared around the end of the house. "You're tardy," he chuckled. He seldom said much but liked fancy words.

Lars-Anne started to cross-examine her son about the Latin lesson and why he was late. Christian was very like Papa, tall even at thirteen, taciturn but with the same good nature and even temper. However, at his mother's nagging, he became sullen and mumbled something about boring parties.

Anders interrupted the looming argument with a cheerful, "Never mind, you're here now. Come and help."

The man and boy went into the shed and came out carrying a large basket covered with a worn cloth. "Karen, don't look," Papa said. She pretended to be fascinated by a spider walking across the table.

Just then Lars-Anne came out carrying the coffeepot; Lil-Anne was right behind her with the sugar and sheep milk. Big-Anne followed, triumphantly carrying a platter with a fragrant pretzel-shaped pastry that she put down right on top of the spider. She bustled around, telling everyone where to sit, making sure they all had their coffee, and handing Anders a glass for his beer. Miller ignored her, grabbed the bottle in one hand, scooped his youngest daughter onto his knee with the other, and settled down to watch his women at their best.

Christian slumped into another chair looking bored while Lars-Anne sat down next to her sister. "How're you feeling?" Karen heard her whisper. "Mam said you're tired."

"I'm fine, but you know how Mam is, so I came out here to get out of her way."

Like mother, like daughter, Karen thought. *I'll never treat my children that way!*

Lil-Anne, bouncing up and down on Papa's lap, patted the basket and demanded, "Karen, open your surprise now."

Karen had not expected nameday presents—they were not an island tradition. Papa always claimed, "I'm a foreigner and do as I wish. My girls should have a few fripperies."

The whole family seemed to be in on the surprise. "What do you suppose is under that old shawl?" Granmam joked.

Karen took the hint, pulled off the cloth and exclaimed at the pile of fabrics in the basket.

"Material to make new clothes. I'll help you," her mother said. Lest she sound too generous, she added, "You're getting so tall that your confirmation clothes are already too short."

Big-Anne pulled out a little bag and showed her granddaughter the silver filigree buttons for her new nightshirt. These buttons were imported and prized more than the everyday buttons that were made from local amber, collected on the beach.

Karen took out the treasures one by one. "And a new red skirt for harvest," she exclaimed, running her hand over the soft flannel. The red skirt was tied like a sausage and wrapped with wide ribbons. The pleats were neatly basted with long running threads to keep the folds pressed.

"Thank you, thank you everyone."

"I basted all the pleats on the skirt. I did them all by myself," Lil-Anne bragged.

"Well almost," Big-Anne mumbled, as usual insisting on the exact truth.

"Here's a present from your uncle and me," said Kirsten handing her a bag shaped like an envelope. "Uncle Paul bought this in India, but it was made in Persia. We know how you admire beautiful things."

Karen opened the little bag and found a wool shawl, as fine as a spider web. She draped it admiringly over her shoulders and stroked the soft threads. So engrossed was she that she forgot to say thank you, but no one said a word of reprimand, since her pleasure was obvious.

"You should put it in your hope chest, for when you have your own home," Mam suggested, as if such an exotic piece of clothing was not suitable for her plain daughter.

Kirsten-Mos passed around a photograph of the crew of the *Marianne* that had arrived with her letter from Paul. The Captain was seated stiffly on a chair perched on the deck, his first mate proudly at his side and the small crew arranged with studied casualness, their eyes squinting into the tropical sun.

"Look, Peter has grown a mustache, " Karen exclaimed. "He didn't tell me that in his letter. They look like pirates!" Then, glancing at her aunt, she hastily added, "All except Uncle Paul."

While the photograph was reverently passed around, Kirsten read her letter aloud, except for the very end, which she blushingly skipped. She replaced the precious letter inside her bodice, leaving the middle button unfastened.

While the women chatted, Karen carefully repacked her presents in the basket, the refolded shawl on top. Quietly, she only half-listened to the latest gossip about Girl-Gerda, the current maid at Millfarm, and Little-Klaus. During the winter, the two had been constant dance partners and he had called frequently at Gerda's home. They were discussing whether there would be an engagement, called a Yes-party, when he returned from the sea in the fall.

"I wonder if a Yes-party is already too late." Lars-Anne said. "I think she said yes this winter, she seems to be a little big around the middle."

"How could she say yes, without a party?" Lil-Anne piped up. "And what does being fat have to do with it?"

"Never mind. And don't interrupt and make personal comments about your elders," her mother reprimanded.

Miller leaned back in his chair, stretched his long legs in front, and contentedly puffed on his pipe. He winked at Karen, laughing with her at the gossiping older women. Next to him, Christian rolled his eyes and squirmed impatiently. Papa suggested that the boy could be excused since it was time for him to pick up the cows at the meadow and bring them home to be milked.

"And take Lil-Anne with you," he added. "Little pitchers have big ears."

"I do *not* have big ears," Lil-Anne protested indignantly as her brother dragged her out of the garden. "You always say that but you can't even see them."

"No," Kirsten-Mos protested, ignoring the children. "Gerda's smarter than that. She told me she ate too much at the parties before the men sailed."

"You always think the best of everyone," her sister accused. "But she's too young. They would have to get a King's Permission Letter in order to marry even next winter," she added, looking meaningfully at Karen.

"Well, if she is, I'll find out soon enough," Big-Anne said from the depths of a lawn chair where she had finally relaxed with her coffee and a big Havana cigar.

Karen thought about Mam's warning about Peter's pin. The town really was full of gossips—even in her own family. It wasn't anyone's business whether Gerda was pregnant. Kirsten-Mos had it right, though; Gerda wasn't stupid. Everyone knew you had to wait until after the Yes-party—and get married before the man went to sea, in case he never came back. They didn't talk about that. Imagine being left with a child and not even married. Last winter had been bad; thirteen men had died at sea—Niels, one of her classmates, was only fifteen.

Karen thoughtfully removed Peter's pin and hid it in the bag with the shawl. Two years before she would be old enough to marry and escape! What was she going to do with herself all that time? Could she and Peter possibly get permission earlier—when he returned? That is, if he... if they... if she....

Four

Wise and Foolish Maidens

Karen's daydream of marrying Peter when he returned from the Warm was not substantial enough to fill her life. He was to be her dashing hero on a white ship that would whisk her beyond the narrow boundaries of her island existence. Yet, coming back to reality, she realized the foolishness of depending entirely on him and his eventual captaincy for adventure. Even if he shared her dream and the family could be persuaded to let her marry at seventeen when he returned, what was she going to do with herself until then? To passively wait for a year and a half, was not in her nature. She began to cast about for a way of life that would suit her better than housework and farming. The seed planted by that chance gossip at afternoon coffee sprouted in the spring rain of another minor event, a Sunday sermon. The young plant would be buffeted throughout the summer by periodic thunderstorms and take the remainder of the year to mature as Karen took control of her own future and no longer just drifted with the whims of her mother and the rest of the family.

Since her confirmation two years ago, Karen had not attended school. She missed learning new ideas but at least during the winter, when the men were home from the sea, there were the Sunday evening dance parties with the adults, albeit under her mother's watchful eye. She was still too young for the young men of the town to call in a courting ritual, known as 'Counseling,' when they would gather at a girl's house, ostensibly to seek advice from her parents and elders. However, Karen was allowed go to the community dance hall with her parents and although Mam always chased her home by ten o'clock, she enthusiastically paired with any man or boy who invited her onto the floor. She was particularly radiant when Peter came to visit and thoroughly enjoyed showing him the intricacies of Sønderhoning dancing—steps that he had not learned properly, having grown up at the northern end of the island.

Peter's occasional weekend visits were always a joy. Every two or three Sundays, he would attend church at home in Nordby and then set out for Sønderho after dinner, ostensibly to visit his mentor, the Captain. Although Karen was no longer allowed to roam the dunes with him, she needed no one's permission to visit her grandmother on a Sunday and hang around while the men talked.

Therefore, each Sunday after dinner, Karen would meander up the hill by the mill so she could see Peter's long legs in case he came striding around the bend in the road. Each would acknowledge the presence of the other with a brief wave, Karen never sure whether his apparent casualness was as studied as her own. After giving him enough time to reach Southhouse, Karen would invent an urgent need to consult Granmam about her knitting and hurry along the back path to Big-Anne's house for afternoon coffee. Lars-Anne, of course, was perfectly capable of helping with any knitting problem but as much as she disapproved of the young people's continuing friendship, she would only watch her daughter's animated departure with a jaundiced eye. Even Lars-Anne could not invent an urgent household chore for her daughter on Sunday afternoon. Peter usually stayed for supper at Big-Anne's and then went to the dance, returning to Captain Paul's in the early hours of the morning for a few hours sleep in the loft before setting out for home.

That Karen's company was the chief inducement for this young man to embark on a seven-mile walk from Nordby to Sønderho and then back was obvious to everyone but the object of his attention. The town gossips assumed that only consciousness of Karen's youth and his own imminent departure on a long sea voyage kept him from expressing his sentiments more overtly. The gossiping elders nodded their approval at his forbearance and thought him a fine young man, even if he were from Nordby. Only Lars-Anne disapproved, but other than scowling at the sight of the two of them together and making sure that they were never alone, she kept her reasons to herself. She breathed a visible sigh of relief when it came time for the *Marianne* to depart with the other ships at the beginning of March and, unconscious of the contradiction, settled in to do her traditional duty and ensure that her daughter would become the epitome of a well-trained wife.

Accordingly, now that she was sixteen, Karen was expected to go to the spring Ribe Hiring Market with the other unmarried women. There they would hire out to mainland farms for the summer, as had their mothers and their mothers before them. It was accepted that away from home and under the guidance of a good mistress, not her own mother, a girl would be prepared for the marriage market as an ideal wife, proficient in all demanded of a Sønderho woman with a husband at sea. If a girl saved her money carefully, she would also have a nice little nest egg to help her future husband become a shipmaster.

Karen's mother had, of course, chosen a different life for herself in marrying the miller, a man who was not going to drown at sea and with whom she could share everyday joys and hardships. She was hoping for a similar, safe marriage for her daughter, but Karen thought her mother's days were full of dull, hard work without time to feed the mind or soul. *There must be something better somewhere.*

Karen was therefore partly relieved and partly resentful when, a few weeks after her nameday, they were discussing the subject of the fair and Mam had said, "Certainly not."

Girl-Gerda's mother had come to call that afternoon, her fourteen-year-old Ellen in tow. Apparently rumors of the older girl's pregnancy were false and Saturday-week she was sailing to Ribe with the other young girls of the town. The mother came, hoping that her Ellen could take Gerda's place as the new girl at Millfarm. Ellen, prompted by her anxious mother, shyly mumbled that she would count herself lucky since everyone said Lars-Anne was the best mistress in town. This was not just flattery; Lars-Anne had the reputation of being an excellent housekeeper, a patient if demanding teacher, and fair in dealing with those under her tutelage.

Karen had a different view of her mother. *She's persistently perfectionist and constantly critical,* she mumbled to herself. She liked the sound of the double alliteration. *Let her have Girl-Ellen to yell at.*

The family was sitting around the table after supper when Mam announced that Ellen was to replace Girl-Gerda next week.

Christian, who usually paid no attention to the comings-and-goings of mere girls, had turned to Karen and asked, "Are you going to Ribe Market?"

That was when Mam said, "Certainly not, she's too young."

Karen resentfully pointed out that she was also sixteen just like Gerda, but Mam's answer was a tiresome, "Nevertheless."

Karen didn't insist because she really didn't want to slave on a farm all summer—at least at home she was free in the afternoons. However, she resented Mam keeping her a prisoner at home and wondered if she thought her too young or just too dumb. She was certainly ten times smarter than Gerda.

She was still stewing Sunday during the sermon. *She doesn't trust me out of her sight*, she thought resentfully. Karen liked Pastor Engel and was usually stimulated by his intellectual approach to everyday problems, but only later would she recall today's sermon. Her attention wandered from Pastor's waving arms and bushy eyebrows that he raised at the end of each sentence as if asking a question. Instead, she imagined that the white ship model hanging from the ceiling beam in the center of the nave between her and the pulpit was Peter's ship and that she had escaped Sønderho to sail with him for adventures in Lagos on the African coast.

Pastor Johannes Engel was a much beloved, tall, mast-thin man with a flowing mane of snowy hair. His bushy eyebrows were so long that his parishioners wondered how he could see and the town matrons had to restrain their hands from brushing them out of harm's way. Since his arrival in Sønderho ten years ago, he had tried to understand and respond to the needs of his stubborn flock and their strange ways. He was a devoted pupil of Bishop N.S.F. Grundtvig in whose extensive writings he sought assiduously for guidance and whose death the previous year he still mourned deeply. Like this charismatic reformer of Danish religion and education, the good pastor believed in the virtues of the Living Word and inflicted long, rambling, but invariably cheerful sermons on his nodding congregation. During the short winter months that the town's seamen were home and under his wing, he tried earnestly to convince them of God's love. However, their closed faces hinted that they related to their Heavenly Father in their own way and that no landlubber could teach them anything they hadn't discovered in the stormier moments of their risky existence nor tell them how to behave on foreign soil.

"Lord, only Thou knowest what they'll be up to all those months away," their shepherd would mumble each spring as he sonorously blessed the men going down to the sea in ships.

On the other hand, Pastor Engel had the ears of the women year-round and he strove mightily to find pearls of scripture with which to inspire their hard lives. This particular Sunday, anticipating the coming departure of the young girls for their mainland summer jobs, he deviated from the lectionary and chose the parable of the five wise and five foolish maidens from *Matthew 25* as his text. He reminded the girls that they should emulate the prudence of the wise maidens and fill their lamps with God's oil to prepare for their futures. Thus, they would not foolishly run out of oil and be locked out of the Kingdom of Heaven but be ready for the feast. Karen's mind was so far away in the tropics of Africa that she almost missed what he was saying but something about the good man's message penetrated and the next day she could not get the parable off her mind.

Monday, the wind shifted from the usual fresh western breezes to a sultry breath from the Russian steppes to the east; uncommonly hot weather that made everyone irritable. It was great-washday. Once a month or so, weather permitting, accumulated household linens were boiled in a big kettle on the scullery stove and then hung on lines or laid on the field in back of the barn to be dried and bleached by the sun. Karen was helping her mother wring out wet sheets while Lil-Anne drooped over a tub, half-heartedly rubbing neckscarves against a washboard.

Karen went to the basket to fetch the next sheet but accidentally dragged one wet corner on the dirty cobblestones. "Don't just brush it off; rinse it, rinse it out," scolded her mother.

"Yeah, yeah," Karen muttered and growled at Lil-Anne to get out of her way.

The child looked up at her sister in surprise. She was about to growl back but instead took out her resentment at the hens clustered around her in the vain hope that it was feeding time. "Scat," Lil-Anne yelled, snapping a wet scarf at the clucking birds.

The hens cackled, the gander honked, and the dog, which had been sleeping in the shade under the kitchen window, started to bark and pull on his chain. Lars-Anne watched the cascade of tempers in dismay. Although she was too hot and irritated to realize that Karen was at the edge of rebellion, she merely sent the sisters inside to put dinner on the table. "Ellen, come help me with the last few sheets," she called to the girl in the scullery. Girl-Ellen, eager to impress her new mistress, came immediately.

As did most Sønderhonings, the Andersens had the main meal at noon. Usually it was a hot dinner of potatoes and fish or meat, but on laundry days the cold leftovers from Sunday's fare sufficed. The sisters therefore had little to do to prepare the meal. Lil-Anne set the table in the north-room and Karen added platters of cold lamb, potatoes, cheese, bread, crackers, and pitchers of fresh milk and home-brewed ale before ringing the dinner bell.

"Now, can I go see Mette?" Karen asked as she was drying the dishes. Mette was her best friend, the town carpenter's daughter, and Mam had promised that Karen could visit her this afternoon.

"Just stack the dishes and Girl-Ellen will put them away," Mam agreed. "Take Lil-Anne with you. And find Christian in town and send him home, he's supposed to study math with Doctor this afternoon. Then take the milk to Granmam and see if they need anything." The heat hadn't slowed her at all.

"Aw, it's too hot to do all that," Karen protested for form's sake, though she was anxious to see how Kirsten-Mos was. She wasn't too sure when the unmentionable baby was due. Maybe Kirsten-Mos would tell her. Or she could ask Granmam; she'd tell her.

"Nevertheless...," was Mam's predictable reply.

Anders was skipping his usual after-dinner nap to putter outside. He now came out of the stable at the east end of the house, pulling their horse across the cobblestoned yard. As he passed the open kitchen window he called to his daughter, "Help me hitch up and I'll give you a lift. I'm delivering flour to the baker and picking up peat at the harbor. The *Lene* just brought in a big load. I'll take the milk to Southhouse when I bring them their peat, so you don't have to bother."

He looked in vain for Christian who had escaped before anyone could find something for him to do. Miller grumbled, "Now where did that boy go? Always running off when I need him most."

Karen backed the horse towards the open doors of the barn, a thatched brick building that lay parallel to the main house. While she hitched up the mare, Miller loaded several sacks of fresh-ground flour into the back of the wagon. Lil-Anne climbed up on the high seat next to a sleeping cat and the rooster perched on the back. She held the reigns and pretended that she was riding through a dark forest chased by wolves, while the rooster bobbed his head up and down as if the wagon were indeed racing down the road. Considering that she had never seen a forest and there had been no wolves in Denmark for centuries, child and rooster had lively imaginations.

Karen climbed up, shooing away the animals. Miller joined the children, pretending to push them off the end of the seat with his sturdy bottom to make room for himself. Laughing and waving to Lars-Anne in the kitchen, they swung out of the yard onto the main road towards town.

The water between Fanø and the Danish mainland of Jylland is so shallow it is called "the Wading-Sea." At low tide, it appears that one can walk all the way across; the deep tidal channels with their strong currents are not visible from land. At the Sønderho end of the island, land lies along the horizon, only eight miles to the east. An additional four miles inland, on the banks of the twisting Nipsaa river, lies the market town of Ribe but only the top of the massive square cathedral tower is visible from Fanø.

This afternoon, the low tide had turned and was starting to come in but there was so little wind that the sea was as flat as the land behind it and the cathedral tower shimmered and danced in the heat.

"Why does the tower look funny?" Lil-Anne asked.

"It's like a desert mirage," the Miller said, putting a hard 'g' at the end since he was not sure how to pronounce this wonderful French word. Then he had to explain to Lil-Anne what he had read in yesterday's newspaper about the Sahara desert and how it was like a sea of sand.

"Let us off at Carpenter's," Karen said. "I'm meeting Mette and Lil-Anne is supposed to go with me. Mam said."

"You mean at the Cockeyed House?" Papa teased. This was a joke. The solid house wasn't crooked at all, just a little different and Papa knew full well where Karen's best friend lived. Carpenter's grandfather had been a successful sea captain who, at the turn of the century, had built this substantial house for his family on the east side of Sønderho. Because the site was well protected from the western storms, he broke tradition and built his house so the long walls instead of the gabled ends faced east and west.

Karen jumped off the wagon, flashing her long bare legs and almost losing her clogs. As she was lifting Lil-Anne down, Papa said, "I almost forgot, here's a letter for you from St. Thomas."

Karen hurriedly tucked the letter behind the third button of her blouse for later. Mette, who had just finished her chores, suggested, "Let's go to the harbor. They've laid the keel for a new bark."

The two older girls walked hand in hand, giggling and chattering while Lil-Anne trailed behind, lost in her own fantasy. They started talking about the Ribe hiring-fair.

"Are you going?" Mette asked—she was six months younger than Karen and would not go until next year.

"Mam won't let me go this time," Karen answered. "One minute she can't wait to get rid of me, the next she says she can teach me anything I need to know. But she's so fussy; I can't ever seem to get it right. I suppose she'll let me next year, but I can't see myself slaving on a farm all summer—I get enough of that at home." Karen stopped. Looking sideways down at her friend, she grinned. "What I'd really like to do is go to the Skipper School in Nordby. Peter learned such interesting stuff."

Mette was shocked. "They'd never let you!" She glanced up at her friend. "You're terrible. I never know when you're kidding." Then she tried a safer topic. "My Mam went to the island of Sylt for three summers. She says that you can learn a lot on one of those big farms."

"That's where Gerda wants to go, but when I mentioned it at dinner, Papa pounded the table with his fist and yelled, 'No daughter of mine is going to work for a bunch of Germans.' Only he used a dirty word and Mam made him apologize. You know he never yells but ever since the Battle of Kolding he hates Germany."

The disastrous war of 1864 was still fresh in everyone's memory. Only ten years ago, the German army had marched across the border, through Holstein and Slesvig on the mainland peninsula of Jylland. They met hardly any resistance and slaughtered the ill-equipped and unprepared Danish army near the ancient fortress of Sønderborg. Another terrible battle followed further north at Kolding on the east coast. Anders Miller had been slightly wounded in that battle. Finally, the Danish navy won a decisive victory by the island of Helgoland near the mouth of the Elbe and the army stopped the land invasion just north of Kolding. Mette's father had been in the battle of Helgoland. In final peace negotiations, the border between Denmark and Germany was shifted ninety miles north of the ancient dirt fortification wall that had protected the country from military invasion for a thousand years. Forty percent of Denmark's most fertile land was lost when the new boundary line was drawn across the peninsula, from just below Kolding on the east, to just south of Ribe in the west. Needless to say, the Danes were bitter, especially those who lived near the new border. Formerly Danish Sylt, one of the string of Fresian islands of which Fanø was the furthest north, had therefore suddenly become German.

Mette said, "According to Papa, many of the farmers on Sylt are just as Danish as us and the war wasn't their fault."

"Nevertheless," said Karen. "If I go to a farm, it'll be Danish, but I'd rather go someplace far away and exciting."

"It'll be bad enough to be away from Sønderho for six months. My sister says she was so homesick for the first half of the summer. How can you even think about going further away?"

While they talked, the girls slowly walked down the main road through town and towards the southern harbor. They passed the sawmill, perched on top of a square shed. There was no wind today so it was blessedly quiet, but freshly cut planks were stacked near the road waiting to be carried down to the harbor for the new ship's hull. The original owners of the mill had refused to buy a license from the Ribe council so they built their illegal mill only tall enough to reach the wind but not so tall that it could be seen from the mainland. The Sønderhonings felt it cost enough to fetch timber from Norway for shipbuilding, why should they pay more good money to the Ribe burghers for cutting it into lumber? After all, the wind was God's gift to Fanø, for them to use without government interference.

The girls reached the bustling harbor, its wide beach revealed by the low tide. A small dock reached out to the deep sailing channel that flowed right by the town. The island was blessed with these deep natural tidal flows whose swift currents carried water and ships back and forth from the Blue-Water of the sea, around the southern tip of Fanø. They could sail right up to the town, the water deep enough to accommodate even the largest three-masted barks of the Sønderho fleet. Some of the channels also flowed towards the mainland and carried shallower boats up the Nipsaa to Ribe.

Above the high-tide line of the beach, work crews were busy on the new keel in its cradle blocks. It was to be a three-masted bark, almost as large as Uncle Paul's *Marianne*. Next to it lay an almost completed schooner whose deep keel made it appear much larger than it would when launched into the water. Mette went up to the scaffolding and hailed her father who was installing storage cabinets on the captain's bridge way above her head.

Karen sat down on a stack of lumber to read her letter. Hungrily, she scanned Peter's description of Charlotte Amalie. He wrote so vividly that she could almost see the colorful market and smell the fruit and flowers ripening in the sun. All too soon she reached the last paragraph.

Sunday

At church this morning, I ran into my old friend, Mate Hansen from the "Julie." They have just come from Dutch Guyana and are on their way home, so I am finishing this hurriedly for him to take. We leave for St. Croix tomorrow and then on to New Orleans with a hold full of sugar. Please write; still to St. Thomas as we will return here again.

Your friend,
Peter

"Listen to this; it's really funny," she said to the returning Mette. They had a good laugh about his story about the funny tailor and choking on the spicy food.

"What should we wear to the ball on St. Croix?" Karen asked.

"Do you think my mam would lend me her silk scarves?" Mette countered, her limited experience struggling to follow her friend's imagination.

"You can't dress as a Fanniker at a ball!" Karen retorted.

Three smaller, single-masted sailboats, called *everts*, were beached below them. Their design was probably originally from Holland where the shallow *schouw* had long been used on the canals. They were well suited to hauling supplies from the mainland since their flat bottoms allowing them to navigate in the shallow Wading-sea. They could sail right onto the harbor beach at high tide. When the water ebbed, they remained upright on the sand, wagons pulling alongside to offload cargo. Under sail, leeboards, that could be raised and lowered at the side of the boat, prevented sideways drifting, functioning much like a keel on deepwater ship.

The *Lene*, an evert whose main owner was Mette's father, was manned by a crew of two young men. She was piled high with peat for the Sønderho ovens and the center of a milling crowd. The Andersen wagon had pulled up next to it, Miller re-stacking the blocks being pitched to him by a sailor on the ship.

The twin sisters, Hanne and Ane-Marie, had just finished loading peat onto their wheelbarrow. These maiden ladies lived with their older widowed sister in a tiny house just down the road from Granmam. No one could tell the younger sisters apart except by the colors of their nightshirts and aprons so Karen and her friends called them Tante-Brown and Tante-Blue, while the widow was Tante-Black. Rumor told that in their youth they had both been in love with a hapless sailor who had *stayed out there*—that is, had drowned. Another story denied this tragedy and claimed there had been two faithless beaus, brothers who had decided to try their fortune in the gold fields and warmer climates of South America. While Tante-Black always had sweet zwiebacks called 'chamberboys' for the children, the embittered old maids were more likely to use the sharp edge of their tongues. The town's children usually stayed clear of their path.

Karen pulled her skirts up above her knees to catch a cooling breeze on her bare legs. Just then the sisters walked by, pushing their barrow over the wet sand and frowned at her. Mette, sitting next to her on the makeshift bench, would also have hiked up her skirts if she hadn't seen Karen hastily pull hers down.

The frowning maiden ladies reminded Karen of last Sunday's sermon and she said to her friend, "I've been thinking about Papa Angel's sermon and those silly maidens running out of oil waiting for the bridegroom." Then pointing with the peak of her turbaned head towards the departing wheelbarrow, she added, "Those two dried-up apples certainly ran out of oil a long time ago."

Mette giggled, "You're mean. And you shouldn't call Pastor that. He's such a dear, bushy eyebrows and all, but it's not respectful."

"These days I feel like one of those stupid girls in the parable, not planning ahead," Karen sighed.

"Not you," Mette protested. "You're always so organized; I'm the one who would forget."

"My mam would remind me though. She'd make sure *all* the girls in town had enough oil even if the bridegroom were walking from Nordby in a snowstorm and it took him all night to get here. At least, I wouldn't be dumb enough to go rushing around town trying to find oil in the middle of the night and miss the party."

Now Mette was really shocked. "That's blasphemy; you can't put yourself in the Bible like that and change the story to suit you. The bridegroom is Christ, not your Peter. And they didn't miss a party but the Kingdom of Heaven."

"We're suppose to think about the parables to fit them to our own lives; else what're they for? No, the bridegroom couldn't be Christ. He was really mean to those girls, locking them out of a house that wasn't even his. Besides, it was all his fault—they only fell asleep and ran out of oil because he was late," Karen insisted firmly.

Then she added, "And I don't intend to sleep while I wait for my bridegroom. I may not be wise, but neither am I stupid."

"What are you talking about? You're so odd these days," said her friend. "It must be this terrible Russian wind. It always puts everybody in a strange mood."

"Maybe so." Karen sighed and rebelliously hiked her skirt up again.

Five

Christian's Rebellion

Karen and Mette sat in silence for a few minutes looking out over the bustling harbor. The *Fortuna* was floating high, her cargo of wood from Norway having just been off-loaded. Captain Nielsen stood on the quarterdeck supervising the crew carrying provisions up the gangplank into the hold, wheelbarrows shuttling back and forth to the pile of foodstuffs on the beach. Christian and his friend Karl had snuck on board and were climbing the ratlines in a precarious race for the crow's-nest. Lil-Anne watched from the beach, jumping up and down.

"Oh, well, I better get Christian on his way home before Papa catches him climbing the rigging," Karen sighed. "Somehow I'll get blamed."

She was too late. Christian had reached the crow's-nest and Lil-Anne rushed to tell the world of his triumph. "He won, he won!" she yelled to anyone who would listen. She ran along the beach to Miller's wagon. "Papa, look at him way up there! He got there first."

Papa reached the edge of the dock in a few giant strides, his face a thundercloud. Christian slid down the ratlines, hand over hand, and hit the deck running. He reached the top of the gangplank just in time to be picked up by the scruff of his shirt and the seat of his pants, as if he were a sack of flour, and thrown off the dock in the general direction of land. The boy barely avoided falling into the water, scraping his shin in his scramble to find footing. Then he had to face a towering Papa.

At the top of the dune by the Inn sat three retired captains on the bench known as the *Exchange.* From there they kept a watchful eye on all the comings and goings up and down the beach. One was knitting on a sock, a pass-time from years at sea, and the other two were puffing on their pipes. One elder called out, "Give'm a good hiding," but another yelled, "Nah, he won the race didn't he?" And the knitter said, "He's pretty good in the rigging for a miller's kid."

Papa ignored the advice and merely said, "I'll deal with you later, you're late for your lesson." The boy ran off looking relieved to escape.

"Let's get out of here before Papa starts blaming us," Karen said hastily. "Just wait until Mam hears about this. She'll be too busy yelling at Christian to pay attention to my foolishness."

When Christian finally returned home from his lesson, it was past the usual milking time and threatening to rain. The boy came striding towards the stable, hardly slowed by a slight limp from when he had fallen on the beach. He had his math book under one arm and was pulling their lead cow with his free hand, his belt looped over her horns to hurry her along. He set such a pace to get home ahead of the storm that the protesting cow's neck was stretched out and her full udders swung from side to side. Her bellowing calf trailed forlornly far behind while the other two cows took their own sweet time. The little procession almost collided with Girl-Ellen who had been dismissed early because of the impending storm. She was running home, the back of her skirt thrown over her head against the first few drops.

Because he was late, he had to do the milking, usually Ellen's task, and the family was half-way through supper before a subdued Christian slid into his place at the end of the bench.

"I gotta talk to you," he whispered to Karen but was interrupted by his mother.

"Enough from you young man. Eat your supper and Papa will settle with you afterwards."

"The thermometer at the Inn read 84° today," Papa said to no one in particular. "I can't remember the last time it was that hot, especially so early in the summer."

While the women did the dishes, the man and boy went into Papa's study, a tiny room squeezed between the southroom and the back hall. The door was firmly closed so Karen could only hear the sound of Papa's voice rising and falling for a surprisingly long time, surprisingly long because he was usually a man of few words. Then a hangdog boy emerged and slunk into his room to ruminate on his sins.

Karen wondered at all the fuss. The boys of Sønderho were often in trouble because of their wild adventures, but since most lacked a father's hand, at least for half the year, they were seldom disciplined other than with a mother's tearful lecture. Papa kept a firmer rein but climbing ship's rigging and avoiding chores seemed pretty normal. Karen doubted that Christian had been whipped, because Papa believed in punishment that fit the crime. He often said that his belt was for keeping up his pants not for destroying his son's spirit. Mam, however, always acted as if the end of the world was at hand and Christian doomed whenever he rebelled even a little.

Papa explained his son's punishment. "The *Fortuna* is sailing with the tide tomorrow morning. I've arranged for Christian to meet her at the Hen to help load sand for ballast. So I sent him to bed 'cause I'll have to wake him at four-thirty." Lars-Anne looked furious, but bit her lip—she never criticized Papa in front of the children.

Sønderho and its harbor were protected from the North Sea by a point of steep dunes called "the Hen" and outgoing ships usually stopped at this headland for a ballast of sand. Because of the thick local dialect, the word "Head-land" had sounded to government cartographers like "Hen," so thus it appeared on official maps. It amused the townspeople to let the foreigners be confused about the true name.

The rest of the family passed the evening quietly in the relative coolness of the garden. The promised rain had not yet materialized, the ominous clouds still hovering on the horizon in the sultry air. The undaunted nightingale trilled his endless song to his nesting ladylove in the long light summer evening. The two women were knitting. Karen had only recently mastered the art of making socks using five needles, and the tip of her tongue made a bulge in the side of her cheek to help her concentrate. Lars-Anne, her needles moving as if they were extensions of her fingers, gave her undivided attention to Lil-Anne's reading lesson from Hans Christian Andersen's *Fairy Tales*. She took special pride in sharing a last name with her favorite writer whom she called "Uncle Hans."

Finally, Papa sighed, folded his newspaper, and went into the house to hang his long pipe on its hook next to the ticking clock on the wall. Reaching overhead to the top of a beam over the table, he lifted the heavy Bible down and returned to the garden. He found his place and read aloud, as was his wont before bedtime. Finally peace descended, soothed by the cadence of the familiar words.

Karen, relieved that the family storm had apparently passed, helped Lil-Anne to bed and then undressed herself. She gratefully uncovered her hair, loosely re-braided it and slipped her cotton nightgown over her head. Despite its long sleeves and high neck, it felt blessedly cool compared to her heavy daytime clothes. She walked through the house towards the east end to visit the little room discreetly tucked between the scullery and the stable, the room that Lil-Anne called the 'smelly place.' When she emerged, she heard her parents' voices coming from the garden. She was about to join them to enjoy a little more of the cooler outdoors, but stopped in surprise inside the door when she realized they were having an argument.

"How could you? Especially letting him on board the *Fortuna*." Mam was furious and actually yelling. "That will just make him want to go to sea more than ever!"

Papa was much calmer, "You're making too much of this little escapade."

"He could have broken his neck, climbing like that!"

"He's a boy with saltwater in his blood, you have to let him be around ships. But, since he shirked his chores and was late for his lesson, I think he should atone like this. Captain Nielsen is a good man. His own son was the one who dared Christian to race and he'll keep both boys working hard."

"Nevertheless, I don't like it. Couldn't you just have him do extra work around the mill?" Mam protested. "I won't have him going to sea."

Karen could barely hear Papa's next words, "I have to discipline the boy as I think best. Would you have me beat him as my papa beat me? Or do you want him chained in the yard, like the dog, to keep him away from the ships?"

Like she chains me, Karen thought, for once in sympathy with her brother.

Then in an attempt to lighten the mood, Papa chuckled and added, "Having to get up before the birds and sweating in the pouring rain will do him good. You'll see; he'll come back wet, tired and chastened."

Papa put his arm around Mam who relaxed at the magic of his touch. Ashamed to have eavesdropped on her parents' privacy, Karen closed the door quietly and tiptoed back to her room. She crept into the tightbed next to Lil-Anne but tossed and turned, unable to sleep with thoughts that whirled and creaked, like the wings of the mill. *Will this strange day never end?*

Finally, she heard the rain against the windowpane. *The wind must have changed,* she thought, relieved that the Russian weather was gone at last.

Karen thought she had been asleep for only a few minutes when Christian shook her awake. "I have to talk to you," he insisted.

"Shh, let's go into the kitchen or you'll wake Lil-Anne," Karen said.

She followed him through the house into *æ frankel*. "So what's so important that you have to wake me before dawn?" she demanded, watching him put on his oilskins. "It can't be much after midnight, it's not even light yet."

"I don't have much time. Papa just woke me up so I can meet the *Fortuna* at the Hen by 4:30. We sail on the morning tide." Christian sat down on the chair to pull on his boots.

"What d'you mean, we sail? Are you crazy? Mam'll have a fit," Karen yelled, forgetting to be quiet. "Just because Papa's mad, you run away?"

"Papa has nothing to do with this. Mam's driving me crazy with all this studying. It's summer, for heaven's sake. Karl's no older'n me, and he's going to be cabin boy, so I'm going with him. We've planned this for a long time."

"What about Latin School? Don't you know I'd give anything to be going to a serious school and learning real stuff? Don't you want to make something of yourself?"

"Being captain of a ship is being someone, but I do care about school and I'll be back before it starts. This is my last chance to go to sea. Explain it all to Mam and Papa, you c'n do it better'n me."

"Mam'll kill me when she finds out that I didn't stop you," Karen protested.

"I don't care. If Karl can go, why can't I? If you stop me this time, I'll just go on the next ship."

Karen could no more resist her brother's imploring freckled face than she could Lil-Anne's. She wanted to hug him but instead she made sure he had extra socks. He tucked his little bundle of clothes under his coat as he went out the door into the rain.

I'll get it now, she thought as she listened to his wooden shoes clomping across the cobblestones before tiptoeing back to bed. *I haven't even done anything but I'll be blamed.*

She had barely closed her eyes when, once again, she was being shaken. This time it was light out and Lil-Anne was whispering right into her ear, "Something terrible is going on. Mam and Papa are yelling at Christian."

There were indeed loud voices coming from the southroom, but they were yelling for Christian, not at him. Karen heard Papa's solid step going into Christian's room.

"Be quiet, so I can hear," Karen said, putting her ear against the crack in their door.

Grandmam had arrived, contributing to the din and asking about Christian. "He's not here," Miller said. "He even left his tightbed neat and his extra shirt is missing."

Big-Anne said that she had walked by way of the Hen, on her way home from Else Oledatter's confinement. "Another girl," she said, as if anyone cared, "their fifth." She had seen Christian struggling with a heavy wheelbarrow full of sand, the rain and sweat pouring down his face. Captain

Nielsen explained the situation. He said that Christian was almost finished and the *Fortuna* ready to sail. When her grandson came off the gangplank, Granmam invited him to stop at her house for a hot breakfast and he mumbled something that she took for assent. Big-Anne went home to change out of her wet clothes. When Christian did not appear, she went to the mill to find out what happened.

"He's stowed away," Lars-Anne shrieked. "I knew it! Now look what you've done!"

"What did I do?" Miller protested. "I gave him strict orders to come back in time to take the cows to the meadow."

"Maybe if you didn't push him so hard about going away to school and let him be a regular boy, he wouldn't need to run away," Big-Anne grumbled unhelpfully.

"He can't go to sea. I won't lose him too," Lars-Anne sobbed and mumbled something about Karen and Peter.

Karen couldn't believe what she was hearing. Mam not just yelling but crying! She was completely coming apart and just because her precious boy was having an adventure. It made no sense. Besides, Karen wasn't lost; she was right here. And why would Mam care a hoot if Peter never came back?

Momentarily forgetting that she was hiding, Karen opened the door and walked into the northroom. Lil-Anne was right behind her, clinging to her sister's nightgown. Trying to restore some sanity, Karen said, "I'm right here and Christian'll be back in a few weeks; they're only going to Liverpool for coal."

If Karen thought her mother would be relieved that her daughter was still at home, she was soon disabused as her mother's wrath immediately turned on her. "You knew!" she bellowed and slapped her hard across her face.

Karen was too stunned to duck. "I only found out this morning. I couldn't talk him out of leaving," she protested, putting her hand to her burning cheek. "He says not to worry, he'll be back soon and loves everyone."

"It's not Karen's fault," Miller said, grabbing his distraught wife's arm. "Christian will be fine; his biggest danger is a whipping from the Captain.

He runs a tight ship and will be angry at having a stowaway. He's a good captain and they'll come home safely."

"That's easy for you to say; what does a foreigner know about the dangers of the sea?" Lars-Anne cried, pulling away.

Miller growled, "He's my son too." He stomped off to his mill, slamming the outer door.

Big-Anne took charge, her diminutive figure growing to fill the room. Turning to Karen she said, "Leave Mam to me. You take care of Lil-Anne and the animals." She took her daughter by the hand and led her away, making soothing noises. As the door to the southroom closed behind them, Karen thought she heard, "It'll be all right, Lil-Anne. I miss them too but that was a long time ago. Christian isn't Peter and Kirsten isn't Karen."

Karen caught sight of Lil-Anne still hesitating in the doorway, looking like a lost angel in her white nightgown. Her tangled blond curls made a halo around her crumpled face and fat tears crept from her eyes, down her pudgy cheeks, and into the corners of her open mouth. She shook her head back and forth, looking first at the kitchen door through which her father had stormed, and then towards the southroom which had swallowed her agitated mother.

Karen rallied and murmured in an unconscious echo of her grandmother, "It'll be all right, Lil-Anne. She's just sad because Christian went to sea. He'll be all right. You'll see, he'll be back in just a few weeks to tell us all about it." 'Sad' was such an understatement that she almost choked on the word. *Today is even worse than yesterday,* she thought. *Everything is topsy-turvy.*

Six

Running the Gauntlet of the Gossips

Feigning cheerfulness while she and Lil-Anne dressed, Karen made up a story about their brother's adventures at sea. Soon they were caught up in the rhythm of their morning chores, Lil-Anne collecting eggs and Karen feeding the animals. Girl-Ellen milked the cows and put oatmeal, cheese, and smoked fish on the breakfast table. If she found the absence of her mistress strange, she made no comment.

When Karen returned from taking the cows to the meadow and moving the sheep, Mam was back in command, dry-eyed and composed, and Granmam had left for Southhouse. No one said much, but by mid-morning apparent normalcy was restored. The people in this family did not drag out their fights but buried resentments under a facade of activity. The only overt sign of lingering distress was Lil-Anne, who shadowed her elder sister for the rest of the morning, unable to pretend that all was well. Karen almost tripped over her several times and would have been irritated except that she too was more bothered by the events than she let on. The good summer weather was back and white fluffy clouds chased across a blue sky in a

Eric Henningsen, 1883

pleasant west wind, but even a cleansing rain and a shift in wind could not wash away Karen's questions nor resolve her growing suspicion that there was a mystery in Mam's past that was somehow related to her hysteria over Christian going to sea.

Just before noon, Else Oledatter's four older girls appeared at the door to announce birth of their baby sister. The eldest child was carrying the youngest and the other two girls shyly held hands as they chorused the traditional invitation for Lars-Anne and Karen to walk to church with their mother for the baptism on Sunday. Girl-Ellen found some sweet crackers as a treat and the children scampered away to repeat their singsong message at the farmhouse next-door.

At dinner, Papa said that he had made up his mind to go to Ribe to find an apprentice, as he had talked about all spring. "With Christian going to school as soon as he comes home, I need the help," he said. "Even when he's here, he's not much use. He'll never make a miller."

"What about me? I'll stay here with you forever," Lil-Anne piped up. "I'm a good miller."

"Maybe when you grow a bit," Papa said, a smile finally playing at his mouth. His youngest child had already appropriated her brother's place at Papa's end of the table.

Karen glanced at Mam to see how she was going to react, but Mam was back to being the practical housewife. "The apprentice can sleep in the extra tightbed here in the house until we have a chance to fix up the barn." Before Anders had become miller, the journeyman had lived in the barn loft. Since then it had stood empty.

After mentioning some supplies that she needed in Ribe, Mam turned to Karen and told her to go and explain to Schoolmaster, Doctor, and Pastor that there would be no tutoring sessions for the next few weeks. "Just give them the message and don't stop to gossip with anyone."

The whole town will know by now, Karen thought. *Everyone will pounce on me the minute I appear.* Although she resented being the one to face the gossips, she pressed her lips together, fearing another scolding if she protested. When Lil-Anne looked as if she were going to tag along, she managed to persuade her that Papa needed her help.

Striding off alone to carry out her unpleasant assignment as quickly as possible, she stopped first at Doctor Munck's house. The waiting room was full, but the buzz of conversation stopped when she stepped in. Tante-Brown was perched at the edge of her seat as close to Tante-Blue as the chairs allowed. Their eyes followed her to the only empty chair in the corner. "Busy times at your house, I hear," sniffed Tante-Brown. Karen bit back a rude retort. Everyone knew that the twin sisters went to Munck's office hours at least once a week; it was the best place for them to hear the latest news.

Fortunately, just then Doctor came out of his consultation room. He was about to call for his next patient when he saw Karen and waved her over. She whispered her message and quickly left before anyone else could confront her.

She walked into town and past the unusually large group of gossips outside Brinch's store. As if on an errand that could not wait, she marched towards the Inn with eyes straight, conscious of the turned heads and whispers behind her. Since it was summer, she knew Schoolmaster would be lingering over his dinner. Here too, heads turned when Karen entered the smoke-filled room. Fortunately, the local diners had retired to the *Exchange* bench on the beach and only Schoolmaster and a table of foreign visitors remained. The serving girl bent down and whispered something to the visitors, who stared curiously in her direction.

Schoolmaster Madsen sat alone at his usual corner table with his pipe and the paper. He was a foreigner like Papa but not popular. He was already in a bad mood because he had been subjected to a barrage of barbed jokes from the retired captains about his star pupil having run off. Not that they disapproved; rather, they felt the boy had shown spunk and was living up to his distaff heritage. Many of them had had similar adventures at his age, with or without parental approval. Schoolmaster felt otherwise, sharing Lars-Anne's pride in the boy's potential and her ambition for future University studies in Copenhagen. Here was finally a lad on whom his teaching would not be wasted and drown in the North Sea.

Karen tried to deliver her message and leave, but it was impossible to dodge Madsen's worried questions and she tried to answer them as briefly as she could without being rude. Karen disliked the teacher; he had never accepted that she had the same fine mind as her brother. He made no secret of the fact that he preferred the education of girls be left to their mothers, as in the old days. He felt his obligations to the law fulfilled if they could read the Bible well enough to teach their eventual children the rudiments and could add well enough to settle their bills with the grocer. He allowed the girls to listen while he taught geography and mathematics to the boys, as long as they kept quiet, but Karen had annoyed him with her constant questions about subjects that she had no need to know.

Niels Madsen's disdain was not lost on the town nor its children. Except for Karen, he usually managed to cow the girls well before they were confirmed and escaped his clutches. He was so fixed in his narrow view of the world that despite his twenty years as Sønderho's schoolmaster, he never understood that Fanniker women ran town affairs six months of the year while their men were gone. If there were no retired captain in the family, the absent shipmaster's mother or wife managed their shipping business as well as home, farm, and children, even traveling to the mainland to sell shares in the company. Women took care of the correspondence, banked the profits sent home, and distributed the interest to the shareholders. They sold the products of their hands and their farms and competently sailed their small boats to buy and sell goods at Ribe market. These women were not merely housewives any more than their seamen husbands were ordinary sailors.

Karen finally escaped the Inn and doubled back through the town to rerun the gauntlet of gossips and go to the parsonage. When at last she knocked on Pastor Engel's door, she was close to tears. Pastor Engel took one look at her pale face and called to Mrs. Engel to bring them tea and cookies. He led her into his cluttered study and lifted a stack of books from his easy chair so she could sit down.

He turned his desk chair towards her and sat down, folding up his long frame as if it were a carpenter's ruler. Resting his elbows on his bony knees and his chin in his hands, he looked straight into her eyes from under his bushy brows and said, "Now tell me child, what is wrong?"

Karen burst into tears. This was the only sympathetic voice she had heard all day. The Pastor fished a huge crumpled handkerchief out of the pocket of his frock coat and patiently waited for her to recover sufficiently to relate the events of the morning. He did not interrupt when she repeated the tale of Christian's defection to the sea, which he had heard about many times already—in many versions. He paid close attention when Karen went on to tell of Lars-Anne's hysteria and her peculiar outburst about losing not just Christian but also, seemingly, Karen and Peter.

"It was as if she couldn't see me but I was right there," Karen sobbed. "Yet later, she pretended that all was normal and she was back to bossing me around like a slave."

Pastor unwound from his chair and started to pace back and forth, stepping adroitly around several stacks of books on the floor. Karen was used to his absent-mindedness from confirmation class. He had always been kind to each of them, no matter how stupid their questions, but Karen thought he had encouraged her particularly. She waited patiently for him to remember her presence.

He picked up the sermon whose composition she had interrupted, and frowned at the scrawled sentences. They seemed to help him focus and he turned back to face his guest. "Could she be worried about losing you when you eventually marry? Would she think that you and Peter Larsen have plans and he will take you away?"

"Peter is just a friend and we have no plans," Karen insisted firmly but added a silent *yet*. "She talked about us as if we were in the past—and Granmam compared us to Kirsten and Christian. That makes no sense."

Pastor resumed his pacing finally stopping directly in front of Karen's chair. "I don't think your mother was talking about you at all," he said, raising his eyebrows to emphasize the 'at all'. Then he swept out his arm as if to solicit the opinions of the scholars littering his floor, "Perhaps there was another Karen and another Peter in her youth."

"I never heard of anyone in the family called Karen or Peter," Karen said, puzzled. "But she never tells me anything about when she was young. Granpapa's ship went down and he stayed out there, but he was called Lars, so who is she talking about?"

"I'll see what I can find out from the church records," Pastor promised just as his wife appeared with a tray. "Ah, there you are Angel, did you bring a cup for yourself?"

Karen smiled to hear Pastor Engel call his wife by her own nickname for him. Then she remembered her manners and jumped up from her comfortable seat so her hostess could sit. The two conspirators told Mrs. Engel of the puzzle they had been discussing, though Karen noticed that Papa Angel didn't mention Lars-Anne's hysteria.

Ellen Engel, usually called Pastor's Ellen, could contribute nothing to the resolution of the mystery since she too was new to Sønderho. She was as short as her husband was tall, plump where he was skinny. A childless woman, she lavished her motherly instincts on the parish. In turn, the town respected her and appreciated her efforts to fit in and blend with her surroundings. Recognizing that wearing a Fanø headscarf was not acceptable in an off-islander, a foreigner, she wore her hair in a neat bun, covered with a modest bonnet when venturing out and with an outmoded mobcap when at home. It was evident to all that both Pastor and wife were sincere in their admiration for the uniqueness of the town and devoted in their calling to what some might have considered an unimportant backwater church.

Soon the conversation took a more general turn and Karen's ambitions finally found sympathetic ears. She was fascinated to learn that her hosts had traveled to Berlin, Paris, and even London, before Pastor Engel had been called to his first parish, near Copenhagen.

"England is the future," the Pastor said expansively, knocking several books off his desk in his excitement. "Here, read these, and tell me what you think," he added, as if Karen were a fellow scholar.

"But I can't read English," she protested.

"We'll have to take care of that," said the Pastor. "Who knows where you might end up. Stop by any afternoon and we can study together." Retrieving a thick volume from under several others on his desk, he added, "Meanwhile, here are some of Bishop Grundtvig's sermons. You'll like what he has to say about the education of women. Great man, great loss to the world when he died last year," he mumbled mournfully.

"Johannes dear, don't you think Grundtvig is a little heavy for her to start with?" Mrs. Engel suggested.

"She'll do just fine and we'll be here to answer any questions," her husband said grandly, waving his arms and endangering the precarious perch of several books.

Mrs. Angel extracted a slim volume from a corner of the bookcase behind her and handed it to her young guest saying, "Just in case you don't find Grundtvig to your liking, try this novel by Thomasine Gyllembourg. She often expressed doubts about being a writer, worrying that it was too masculine a role and an insult to her femininity."

Karen opened the flyleaf and was surprised to read the title: *Little Karen.*

"Lars-Anne might object to her daughter reading a book by a divorced woman," her husband protested.

"Nonsense," Pastor's Ellen replied. "P. A. Heiberg was a wonderful writer but he was a scoundrel of a husband. He deserved to have her divorce him. Her book is a perfectly suitable and uplifting novel about a young girl's spiritual development and eventual happiness as a wife. I still find it inspiring."

All too soon, the study clock chimed, reminding Karen that she must leave.

"Come back soon, dear child," Pastor Engel said as he courteously escorted his bemused visitor to the door. "We usually have tea about four o'clock and read aloud for a while. You are always welcome to join us."

Karen stumbled home under her load of scholarly books and jumble of new ideas. She marveled, *He calls me a child but treats me like an equal. Everyone else says I'm an adult but talks to me as if I have no mind and no feelings.*

Seven

News from Peter

To all appearances, life at the mill-farm settled back to its normal pace and the summer went its usual way. In early July, Papa went to Ribe and returned with fourteen-year-old Erik, the new miller's apprentice. He declared Erik a willing pupil, if overanxious to please. Mam seemed disappointed at his youth but Papa said, "What did you expect? He's just a beginning apprentice, he'll learn." Karen thought him a clumsy oaf, not worthy of serious attention. Surely, Mam hadn't planned anything silly?

Christian's abrupt departure was not discussed; indeed, his name was hardly mentioned, as if his defection were to be buried with other unhappy events of the past. However, Lars-Anne's anxiety about her son and resentment at Karen's growing independence spurred tension between mother and daughter. The rest of the family seemed to have adjusted to Christian's absence, having been reassured by a telegram from Liverpool:

> *Christian fine* Stop *Working hard* Stop
> *Home mid-August after Rotterdam* Stop
> *Captain Nielsen.*

"*Working hard*," Papa mimicked in English after asking Karen to translate the only phrase that wasn't so close to Danish that it was obvious. "That's more than he ever does at home. I suppose it's all in the motivation."

Mam was obviously unhappy that the *Fortuna* would not return directly from Liverpool as Karen had said, but she pressed her lips together as if to prevent the escape of an *I told you so*.

Meanwhile, Karen lived in two worlds. She automatically went about her chores in a dreamy fog, trying to ignore her mother's constant criticism, but snatched spare moments to write a long sequential letter to Peter or study the steady stream of books supplied by Pastor and his wife. She did indeed find the going heavy in some of the tomes lent by her new mentors, but treasured the occasional afternoons when she could slip away and join them for tea.

English lessons with Papa Angel started with him reading aloud from an English novel called *Great Expectations*. It was his theory that to learn a foreign language one merely needed to be immersed in its sound and eventually one would catch on. When Karen seemed to make no headway, he started over and began reading one sentence at a time in English then repeating it in Danish. This worked a little better and Karen began to recognize a few words. Best of all, they discussed the story, all three disregarding that Pip was a boy with expectations very different from what Karen could reasonably achieve. It was enough for her that her opinions and feelings were taken seriously.

One misty morning, Karen was sent into town to buy coffee beans and then deliver Granmam's milk. When she came out of Brinch's store it was raining and she pulled her outer skirt over her head to keep dry and almost collided with the postman emerging from the post-and-telegraph office across the street. "I'll take Big-Anne's mail," she offered. "I'm on my way there."

"Thanks. There's one for you too. From America," he said with a wink as he handed her two letters, the top covered with wonderfully strange stamps and addressed to *Miss Karen Andersen*, *Millfarm, Sønderho, Fanø, Denmark.*

Karen blushed and worried that even if the postman wasn't supposed to gossip about the mail, the whole town would soon know that she'd had a letter from Peter.

She ran most of the way along the back path to Southhouse in the dreary drizzle. "Did you get one too, a letter?" she asked Kirsten-Mos breathlessly.

Her aunt was knitting in front of the window. "Did you hear from Peter? Maybe mine'll come tomorrow. Go on into the northroom where you can read it in peace. Where's it from?"

"New Orleans—I think that's in the United States."

Peter had sent several thick letters from various ports on the southern coast of the United States, Mexico and the Caribbean. They picked up whatever cargo they could and, according to Kirsten-Mos, were doing a brisk business in sugar cane from the Caribbean and manufactured goods from the States. Karen often had to consult Papa's atlas—the geography was very confusing. The West Indies were not anywhere near India and still belonged to France, but some of the Virgin Islands were Danish, New Orleans was in the USA but really French, Miami had been Spanish but was now in one of the States, Cuba was still Spanish but constantly fighting for independence, as had French Haiti over fifty years ago.

Peter wrote wonderful descriptions of these fascinating places and all the strange peoples he met. His letters were filled with stories of black slaves and ex-slaves; silent Indians, who weren't from India but the original Americans; loquacious plantation owners from Louisiana, Florida and Cuba; stern New Englanders, not from England but from the northern United States; and graceful senoritas with black eyes and watchful mothers.

Wonderful as his letters were and much as Karen treasured each one, she longed for something else that she couldn't quite explain. At first she thought it was because she was jealous and wanted to go to all these marvelous places herself. Her own letters were so ordinary compared to his great adventures, but Kirsten-Mos told her, "Paul tells me just to describe my day. He says that men at sea are so homesick that they long to read familiar stories about people they know. Tell him what you see and feel and he'll be pleased."

That was the problem. Peter's letters were full of what he saw but never how he felt. Karen recalled their long walks on the beach when they first knew each other and his warm hands holding hers when they had danced last winter. Then they had been able to share all their thoughts. Where had that Peter gone? She could not find him in his stilted words on paper. Her own letters were no better. She longed to tell him of her tumultuous thoughts of the summer, but was afraid to be too personal since Peter seemed to have put more than geographical distance between them.

Karen sensed that today's letter was different even as she slid open the unusually thin envelope. Her hand started to shake with fear that there would be bad news, but surely a telegram would have warned if something dreadful had happened. She moved over to the bench and held the letter up to the window to read in the dim light.

The Caribbean, June 20, 1874

Dearest Friend,

Today I had to arrange my first burial at sea. Young Klaus Holgersen from Varde died last night of yellow fever. We watched helplessly as he burned up, out of his mind with fever during his last few days. He could keep no food down and even the clear soup that Cook prepared went right through him. We took turns dripping liquid into his mouth, one teaspoon at a time and sponging his wasting body. It was all in vain. Through the long dreadful nights, I kept thinking how hopeless it was and what a waste of such a young life. He was no older than you.

He should never have become sick to begin with; if only he had listened. We were anchored in Havana harbor. The men had been given shore leave but with strict orders to be back on board by 10 o'clock when Captain moved the "Marianne" further out in the bay to get away from the night air. Boatswain, Captain, and I had all lectured the men on the dangers of the night-miasma in the tropics, but Klaus did not listen. He went to a bar and they threw him out on the street at closing time. Being too drunk he lacked the sense to go to the seamen's mission and slept in the gutter. A few days later when we were at sea, he turned feverish and yellow. There was nothing we could do.

I keep thinking about the white sands and cool breezes of home and wonder what I'm doing here. I long to wrap my arms around you and dance the night away. I want to hold your hand and climb Kangaroo Dune and sing songs while the lark spirals up to the blue sky. There is no else with whom I can share these thoughts. The crew looks to me for leadership and I cannot be their friend. Captain Paul is kind but distant; he too must be lonely.

I will end now and seal this letter before I lose the nerve to send it.

Yours,

Peter

P.S. Please continue to write; your wonderful letters are my greatest joy. Our next port will be back in St. Thomas.

Tears ran down Karen's face and dripped onto her already wet apron. She closed her eyes so she could see Peter's dear face and hear his familiar voice tell her again of his loneliness and pain, every word of his letter already memorized.

Big-Anne came into the northroom to hear the news from the *Marianne* but stopped with her hand still on the knob when she saw Karen. Fearing the worst, she quietly closed the door and went back to the kitchen to pour her granddaughter a cup of hot coffee. Soon she would have to get her out of those wet clothes and hear what was surely bad news.

Big-Anne and Kirsten were therefore puzzled when Karen emerged a few minutes later, composed and dry-eyed. When asked about the news she merely said that one of the crew, whom they didn't know, had died of yellow fever but all was otherwise well. They were even more surprised to hear Karen humming to herself out in *æ frankel* when she was leaving. They decided that the tears must have been of joy and the letter a declaration of love.

Karen was indeed joyful, even if they were wrong about the reason. *I'm his dearest friend,* her heart sang. Love would surely come.

On her way home, she called on Pastor and his wife and, as usual they read aloud. Although they were still spelling their way through Dickens, Papa Angel wanted to try Wordsworth. The poetic English was too difficult for Karen and Pastor's attempt at translation into Danish sounded silly rather than lyrical, so they turned to their tea and conversation. Karen wanted badly to share Peter's last letter with her friends, but felt it had to stay where it was, safely buttoned next to her heart. Pastor's Ellen, as if sensing she had thoughts too personal to talk about, asked her if she had ever thought of keeping a journal. "I've kept a diary since before my marriage," she said. "I find it's such a good way to straighten out my thoughts. Better than prayer because my mind keeps wandering, but when I write it down, I focus better."

"I can't ever seem to get around to it," Karen complained. That gave her an idea. Now that Peter had re-opened the door to sharing their feelings, she could share her worries about her mother's past and her own future. The Engels were sympathetic listeners but Peter would better understand her determination to find a fulfilling life. Tomorrow, she would seal the long sequential letter that she had already written and mail it to St. Thomas, but then she would then start the next one fresh and tell what had really happened when Christian ran away. It would be weeks before she would know the next mail stop of the *Marianne* so there would be plenty of time to find out more by then.

Karen was so full of her plans that she found it hard to listen to Papa Angel's rambling monologue, but fortunately he was so engrossed in the point he was making that he didn't notice his young guest's distraction. Just then the French column clock in the corner chimed the hour and Karen had her excuse to say a hasty thank-you, I-gotta-run, I'm-so-late.

That evening, Karen went to Papa's office to write by the window. She took out a clean piece of her favorite cream paper, a new steel nib for her penholder, and the bottle of blue ink that she reserved for writing to Peter.

Sønderho (where else?), July 15, 1874

Dearest Peter,

Your sad, sad letter from New Orleans made me weep but brought your dear voice right to me. In my last letter, I told you about Christian stowing away on the "Fortuna," but I didn't tell you what happened when Mam discovered he was gone...

No longer did she have to search for funny stories to share with her friend; the words flowed by themselves, forming in her mind faster than she could transfer them to paper. She was so immersed in her tale that she didn't notice Papa coming in and looking over her shoulder. Karen tried to cover her letter with her hand, but it was too late.

Papa apologized, "I didn't mean to read your letter to your young man. I just wondered what you were so busy doing." He didn't seem cross at finding her in his office but gave her shoulder a friendly squeeze. He continued, "Don't hide it, friendship is nothing to be ashamed of. He and I had a long talk last winter about how special you are to both of us."

"So that's why he never...? You made him promise, didn't you?" Karen accused.

Papa, for once, looked flustered. "He did promise not to speak to you before he left, but letters seem safe enough. You can hardly get in trouble when he's ten thousand miles away. I really like him; he's one of the good ones. Just don't commit yourself until you have a chance to grow up a little more and find out what you want."

"If you like him so much, why doesn't Mam?"

"Just give her time, she'll come 'round eventually," he assured her and left her to her writing.

Eight

A Grubby Little Place

At supper a few days later in July, Papa announced, "I'm going to Nordby tomorrow." Then he turned to Karen and asked if she wanted to come with him. "I also have an errand in Esbjerg so we'll finally get to ride the steam-ferry."

Lil-Anne said eagerly, "Me too, me too."

"Certainly not," said Mam. "It's much too dirty and noisy."

Only a mile-wide channel separated Nordby, at the northern end of the island, from the mainland and the new town of Esbjerg. This port city had been created in 1865, after the war with Germany, to compete with Hamburg and spur the nascent trade with England. After nine years, it had already become an important center of commerce, its harbor being the only deep-water port on the west coast of Denmark large enough to accommodate the ironclad hulls and steamships of the growing merchant marine. The development of steamships, which had barely begun to transport people and goods across the North Sea, would have a long-range impact, but the third quarter of the nineteenth century was still the golden age of sail for the island. The great ships still carried most of the grain from Danish farms to England and returned with cargoes of coal for the factories of the industrial age.

A steamship did regularly make the overnight trip across the North Sea between Esbjerg and Harwich, England and just last year, a steam-driven ferry had begun to bring passengers and supplies the short distance between Esbjerg and Nordby. The whole family had made an excursion to see the sight. Karen wanted to try the ferry, but it was obvious that they were there only to disapprove.

Granmam had sniffed. "Anne Sørensen says it looks like a dirty old stove that got carried out to sea." Timid Kirsten-Mos had shuddered at this belching monster that had none of the grace of the *Marianne*. "Who wants to go to Esbjerg anyway?" Mam had argued. "Such a grubby little place." Even Lil-Anne, adventurous as she usually was, didn't know what to make of this noisy beast.

This evening, Mam seemed about to protest Karen's going, but Papa silenced her with a look, as if to remind her that they had talked about this. Instead, Mam said, "While you're gone, we can clean the bedrooms. Lil-Anne can help change the straw in the tightbeds." Then she turned to Apprentice-Erik and added, "We'll need to move your stuff to the barn, now that your room is finished."

"What a treat, more cleaning!" Karen muttered sarcastically but fortunately Mam tacitly seemed to be agreeing to let her go.

Early the next morning, Papa hitched the horse to the wagon and, as well supplied with food and drink as if they were traversing the Sahara instead of a mere seven miles of heath, father and daughter set out for the neighboring town. For the first mile out of town, the road was crudely paved with broken sea shells and discarded bricks, then only sandy ruts, made by generations of wagon wheels, led the way north. Someone had dumped salt hay in the most exposed place, lest wagon wheels become mired.

At first both were quiet, Anders from habit and Karen enjoying the unusual outing alone with her father. A few miles down the road, Karen tried to find out how Papa felt about Mam's plans for Christian to go on with school, but Anders seemed not to hear. Then he surprised her by saying, "This trip isn't about him. I've been wanting to talk to you. You argue with Mam all the time, are you unhappy about something?"

"Mam's always yelling at me to do things her way. She's already planned my future. Christian too. But it's all right for him; at least he can become something important like a doctor or a lawyer. I'm to stay home and be a good housewife."

"Mam only wants the best for you; for both of you."

"Yeah, but why can't she let me do what *I* think is best?"

"And what's that?"

"I don't *know*!" Karen wailed. "That's the problem. I just know it's not endless housework. I'll just have to become rich and then someone else can do all that."

"Did you ever think that no matter where you live and no matter how rich you are, you would still have to know how to manage a household?"

"That's what Mam says, but she's already made sure I could be housekeeper at King Christian's palace. How hard can it be to tell someone else what to do?"

They rode on in silence until Anders said, as casually as if this were a sudden inspiration, "How would you like to help me with the accounts and records? You write a fair hand and you'd be good at the math too. There's too much for me to do with the mill and all."

"How can a few bills for grinding grain be so much work?" Karen asked.

"Not just for the mill, also the shipping company. Who do you think keeps the books, writes letters, organizes association meetings, and sells shares when Paul is at sea? Did you think Kirsten did it? Or Granmam?"

They both smiled at the picture of shy Kirsten running a company or Granmam writing letters between delivering babies. "I guess I never thought about it," Karen admitted and suddenly realized that this was why Papa asked her to come along. He was actually offering her a challenging job, away from Mam.

By this time they were passing the farms on the outskirts of Nordby and could see the town perched on its hill by the northern bay, so instead she asked where they were going.

"First we'll go to the grocer's, Mam wants some cardamom that Brinch's doesn't carry. Then we'll stop by the Inn for a meeting of shareholders. After lunch we'll take the ferry to Esbjerg, inspect a new warehouse, and then go home."

"Can we stop at Peter Larsen's house? Kirsten-Mos lent me the photograph that Uncle Paul sent. I thought Peter's mam would like to see his new mustache."

"Sure. I need to talk to Bodil anyway."

Karen thought she had sounded casual enough, but he seemed to sense her nervousness and gave her hand a comforting pat. "It'll be all right, you'll see," he reassured.

Whatever can Papa mean? Did he read my thoughts?

They turned left away from the harbor road onto the main street into the substantial town of Nordby, about twice the size of Sønderho. They swung into a little side street and stopped in front of the Larsen house. The red brick, thatch-covered house was like any standard Fanø house. Except for the rose-covered fence around the front yard, they could have been at the door of Millfarm or Southhouse. It was a little early for a social call and Karen had never met Peter's mother so she was afraid she would be thought forward for showing up uninvited. Papa confidently knocked on the front door.

The delighted Bodil Larsen made them welcome. Karen remembered just in time not to curtsy like a child when she shook hands with the older woman. Bodil was a trim attractive woman, but slightly older and not as beautiful as Lars-Anne. Like Granmam, she wore widow's black, but as Peter had bragged, she did tie *æ pjegger* of her blue-striped scarf with a flair that complemented her proud carriage. Graciously she led her guests into her cool northroom, and then disappeared into the kitchen for refreshments despite their polite protestations. Soon she returned with coffee punch and 'chamberboys.' Peter's curious younger siblings were chased outside with their own plate of sweet biscuits so she could entertain her guests in peace.

This northroom was similar in shape and function to the one at Millfarm, but the furniture was more modern. Karen silently took in its funny one-handed wall clock and the knickknacks from around the world that covered every surface other than the dining table. Mam would have hated the clutter, but Karen was enchanted. She smiled at the two white porcelain poodles that had pride of place on the windowsill, flanked by pots of bright red geraniums and clearly visible to all that walked by on the street. Peter had told her that he had brought home these popular Staffordshire figurines from England last summer because his mam had always been envious of her neighbor's. They had chuckled over how ugly they were, despite their popularity.

At first, Bodil and Papa chatted about association business and the latest news from the *Marianne*. Karen was half relieved to have her presence taken for granted and half upset that her hostess was ignoring her. Didn't she know about her and Peter? How was she ever going to be able to interrupt Mrs. Larsen to show her the photograph? Finally, Papa came to her rescue. "Karen has something she wants to show you."

"It's a photograph of the crew of the *Marianne* that Captain sent to Kirsten-Mos," she managed to say, relieved that her voice sounded modest and natural.

"My word, look't Peter's mustache! Don't 'e look a pirate, but a right 'andsome pirate," exclaimed the proud mother, clapping her hands together and reverting to the dialect of south Jylland. Karen suddenly realized that Peter's mam had been just as nervous as she and only propriety had kept her from cross-examining her young guest.

"I see you noticed my dogs. They were a present from my son," the older woman now said proudly.

Karen mumbled her polite admiration, refraining from telling her hostess that she knew about them already. Papa took the opportunity to drain his cup, rise from his chair and edge towards the door while mumbling gratitude and farewell. All the while their hostess was urging him to have more punch and chamberboys. Even at the door, between more farewells and a final round of handshakes, she managed to tuck some extra biscuits into Karen's hand.

Back in the wagon, Papa lightly flicked the reins and clicked his tongue at the patiently waiting horse. "So how did you like your prospective mother-in-law?" he teased.

Karen looked at him in shock and blushed beet red. "Please don't tell Mam we saw her."

"I won't, if you don't tell her that we didn't eat her carefully prepared provisions," laughed Miller. "We can feed the evidence to the birds on the ferry."

After a brief stop at the grocer's, one of several such stores in the center of town, they went on to the Inn. Anders tossed the reins to the stable boy and, with a rare show of formality, he jumped off the wagon in time to gallantly lift his daughter down. She slipped her hand over his proffered arm, pulled back her shoulders, and allowed herself to be escorted into the Inn, hoping no one would realize that she had never eaten at a restaurant before—the Sønderho Inn didn't count.

Papa introduced her to several farmers and two retired captains with whom they were to dine. After a round of handshakes, they were seated at a long table. Papa whispered to Karen to pay attention and he would explain later. Awed at her new responsibilities, she tried to follow the conversation but soon became lost in the intricacies of shares to be traded, ships to be bought, the advantage of iron clad over wooden hulls, and the impact on trade of the railroad extension that was coming to Esbjerg. The discussion seemed endless. Papa suggested the importance of steamships for the future but was good-naturedly dismissed as an impractical dreamer too easily impressed by the latest mechanical marvels. The debate finally turned to the wisdom of investing in a warehouse in Esbjerg. The captains were reluctant to put money into anything other than ships and cargo, but the farmers liked the security of property that couldn't sink in a storm.

Karen was so busy listening that she barely had a chance to savor the succession of marvelous dishes placed on the table before them. A nervous waitress, no older than Karen, served them soup, followed by platters of carrots, cauliflower, sliced braised beef, and steaming bowls of potatoes and gravy. How could anyone eat so much? Finally, dessert of sweet melons from the Mediterranean appeared, chilled on beds of ice. Karen discreetely removed a small piece of straw from the ice, not wishing to embarrass the novice waitress. Karen might not be an experienced diner, but she certainly knew that straw did not belong with the dessert.

Finally coffee was poured and the cigars passed. Karen declined with a nervous giggle but no one paid attention. She could have smoked one, as Granmam liked to do after Sunday dinner, and no one would have said a thing. Papa summed up the meeting, "Well, we're in agreement then."

In agreement about what? They had done nothing but disagree. Papa had said very little while the rest argued, but now they all nodded and smiled and shook hands goodbye.

"Karen and I need to catch the ferry," Papa said nonchalantly as if it were something they did every day.

Once they were outside, he grabbed her arm and bounced off towards the harbor and the waiting 'dirty old stove' like a little boy going on an adventure. He continued to play gallant escort as he helped Karen to walk down the gangplank of the chugging *Nordby.* Soon the hawsers were cast off and the ferry started across to the mainland. They were both too excited to sit down on the benches clustered in the middle of the deck and instead hung over the railing, watching the water curl in front of the bow. The wind was from the south and the waves only slight, sheltered as they were between the island and the mainland; but it was strange to be going sideways to the wind without the deck heeling to leeward. The noise from the engine and the vibrating deck beneath their feet was not like the silent plowing of a sailing ship through the water.

Papa was as restless as if he were Lil-Anne's age. Undeterred by the 'No Admittance' sign, he opened the door down to the engine room. After carefully watching the giant pistons through the hissing steam, he explained to Karen, shouting over the engine noise, "It's the same principle as the windmill. The wind moves the wings around, rotating the horizontal shaft that, through the gears, rotates the vertical shaft, which turns the upper millstone. The wind starts out as motion in one direction, which then gets changed to circular motion. Similarly, the steam drives a piston back and forth and the gears change that into the circular motion of the screw."

Papa certainly was excited today—Karen had never heard him talk so much. She was still puzzling over the event of dinner and asked, "How did you get everyone to agree with you like that? You didn't even say anything."

Papa laughed. "People like to hear themselves talk, you just have to let'em and soon they'll figure out the logical thing to do and they'll think it was their idea all along."

By this time, they could see the people waiting for the ferry on the Esbjerg dock. Papa pointed at the empty wharves on their left, "There are no ships there now, but just wait until the wheat harvest is in, then plenty of them will be lined up to load grain for England. There on the right is the *Family Hope* out of Sønderho and beyond her you can see where they're building another warehouse. That's the one we're investing in."

On the bridge above them, the captain pulled a rope and a loud whistle signaled that they were about to land. Karen jumped a foot into the air—this ferry certainly was a noisy place. There was a whooshing sound from the stern as the skipper reversed the engine to slow the forward momentum. The helmsman spun the wheel just in time to turn the starboard side of the ferry alongside the dock. With a slight bump, they arrived. Arm-thick hawsers were cast onto the dock and a waiting hand quickly wound them around the bollards several times to make the ship come to a complete stop.

Karen was the first one off; as soon as the gangplank was put in place she ran up to the dock without waiting for Papa. They strolled towards the warehouse, he pointing out every new building. All along the narrow beach, wharves and docks were being built. Cubes of granite cobblestones were being pounded into the roadway on both sides of the shiny railroad tracks that were to transport grain to waiting ships. The new rails twinkled in the sun as if to say, "the train's coming any minute now" although it would be a year before the spur into town would be finished.

"It would be fun to ride the train," Karen said with longing and Papa's eyes sparkled in agreement.

On the other side of the street, new and half-constructed warehouses and storefront offices lined up like an honor guard. Flocks of sparrows clustered around two empty farm wagons to glean their share of spilled grain from the first harvest. On the hill in back of the waterfront, residential houses were springing up like mushrooms after a rain. In some of the front yards, climbing roses had been planted, but they were still small and scraggly. It was a busy place of dust and noise but with little grace and none of the mature dignity of Sønderho or even Nordby.

"It may be a grubby little place now, but just wait 'til the railroad comes, then you'll see," Papa said with enthusiasm. "This is the future."

"You sound like Pastor Engel. He says England's the future."

"It's all part of the same thing. They want our grain; we need their coal. That's what trade is all about. Sailing the North Sea may not be as lucrative as going to the Warm, but the money is much steadier. Steam ships will make it all so much more efficient. We just have to convince the shipping association."

Papa really is a landlubber—to him the tall ships are just money, Karen thought, but would never have hurt his feelings by saying so out loud.

They inspected the half-built warehouse and Papa seemed satisfied that it would be a sound investment. Karen was amazed that the shipping business was not just about sailing but much more complicated. It would be good experience for her to learn something about the land-based part and certainly more interesting than doing laundry or watering sheep!

Errands accomplished, Anders and Karen caught the ferry back to Nordby and retrieved the horse and carriage from the stable at the inn. They were both silent on the way home. Papa seemed to have used up his conversation for the day and Karen was thinking about how to describe to Peter all that she had seen.

Not until they glimpsed the mill on the horizon did Papa finally speak, "Be patient with Mam. She has a lot on her mind these days, with Christian running away to sea and Kirsten."

"She's much too worried about him—he's just a normal boy! But is there something wrong with Kirsten and the baby?"

"No-no, Kirsten is just fine. It's just Mama's way to worry, so try not to add to her troubles."

"But why? It doesn't make sense to be so crabby all the time about a perfectly natural thing like a new baby."

Nine

Great-Washday Tempers

At supper after the trip to Nordby, Lil-Anne wanted to hear every detail of their visit. Karen excitedly told about the wonderful day, not just in Nordby but Esbjerg as well. She would have left out their visit to Peter's mam but Papa casually mentioned that they had dropped in on Bodil Larsen. Karen started to explain how nice she had been and what interesting things she had from around the world. Mam got that disapproving look on her face that Karen recognized from anytime Peter was mentioned. To change the subject, she was about to say how she was looking forward to learning more about the shipping association when she noticed Papa shaking his head slightly.

"Let me handle this," he whispered while Mam was in the kitchen to fetch more butter. She had thought it was all settled and that Mam had already agreed, but apparently not yet. Karen wondered if Papa thought he could make Mam think it was all her plan—that would be more of a miracle than persuading seamen to invest in a warehouse!

It all came to a head the next day. It was great-washday again and Mam was being more demanding than ever. Karen was grouchy and complained, "Why can't we have flowers in the garden?" and "We never talk about anything interesting." Then when Mam asked her to fetch more water from the well, she said rudely, “Let Ellen do it. That’s her job.”

Lars-Anne, exhausted from hanging wet sheets, lost her temper, “Don’t you act all high-and-mighty. Just because you’ve been to visit fancy Bodil Larsen and had dinner at the fancy Nordy Inn doesn’t mean you’re too good to do the laundry.”

Karen was stunned. It was as if Mam were jealous. She might be bossy and critical but, except for her outburst when Christian ran away, she never lost her temper. “I don’t think I’m too good. I just need to do something more interesting,” she stammered, almost adding that Papa had said she didn’t have to help Mam anymore.

“Nevertheless, I’m sick of your being fresh. When would I have time to dilly-dally with a flower garden?”

Karen realized she had spoken too freely but she was too ashamed to apologize, sulking through her chores for the rest of the day. Even during supper she was unusually quiet, not able to say she was sorry nor to pretend that nothing had happened. Fortunately, Lil-Anne filled the gap with her excited chatter.

Later that evening, when her little sister was asleep and Erik had gone to his new room in the barn loft, Karen was getting ready for bed. When she returned from the ‘stinky place,’ she overheard her parents talking, this time about her.

“I’ve had it with her criticism,” Mam was saying. “I can’t ask her to do anything without her being sullen or answering back.”

“Just let her be. She’s having a hard time coming to terms with growing up and deciding what to do with herself,” Papa soothed.

“What’s to decide? She’ll go to some farm the next few summers, meet some nice young man, and settle down like the rest of us and our mothers before us.”

“I don’t think that’s quite how Karen sees her future. That’s part of her trouble. Besides I remember you telling me that at that age you couldn’t wait to get away from Sønderho and especially Big-Anne.”

“That was different.”

"Not so different, from her point of view."

"You may be right. Girl-Ellen's mam said the other day that she hopes I'm satisfied with her daughter's work; she's so sullen at home. I told her that Ellen's just as quick and eager as her sister and that the best girls are impossible at home but much more willing workers the minute they get a little distance from their mothers." Then she reminded him, "I came back to Sønderho—if Karen leaves, I don't think she'll ever return."

"You certainly did come home again—and brought me along to God's Island."

"What are we going to do with her?" Mam said. "I don't want to lose my temper again."

Karen was shamelessly listening at the closed kitchen door and thinking that Papa was at it again. By waiting and then saying just a few right words, he had made Mam figure it all out by herself. She debated whether she should sneak around to her room the back way, but felt she had a right to join in the discussion. She went back to *æ frankel* and made the floorboard creak as if she were just coming into the kitchen. Opening the door with a smile, she pretended to have heard nothing and that she was only coming to say goodnight. Mam looked embarrassed but Papa included her in the conversation by admitting they had been talking about her.

"Sit down; we want to talk to you. We were just discussing your doing the ledgers and the correspondence for the shipping association and the mill."

"I can get along with just Girl-Ellen," Mam agreed.

"What about the sheep?" Karen asked, trying not to show how eager she was.

"Erik can bring them to the meadow in the morning when he takes the cows," Papa said. "They'll get fatter grazing there anyway."

Mam didn't look pleased at this last change in the routine, but it was settled. Karen would start the next day by organizing Papa's office. Mam went back to her knitting and Papa unfolded the paper with a satisfied smile on his face. He really had done it. Mam thought it was all her idea—except for the stupid sheep.

Anders changed the subject by pointing to a picture in the paper. "Here's one of those new automatic harvesting machines that my brother bought; they certainly look handy," he said. "Maybe when our ship comes in we can persuade Jensen to share in buying one. And maybe we should get one of those horse-driven threshers. If we're really lucky, we can afford both."

"What do you mean, 'when *our* ship comes in'?" Karen said.

"Uncle Paul's *Marianne*; you know we...," Miller started to explain.

Mam interrupted with a warning look, "Just an expression, dear," and then, "Time for bed."

Karen crawled into the tightbed next to Lil-Anne but couldn't sleep. She sensed another mystery. *If they'd just tell me what's going on. I have a right to know.*

She heard Papa's calm voice, "We should explain about the *Marianne* and the mortgage on the mill. When she starts doing the books, she'll figure it out anyway."

"I don't want her to worry. Rounding the Horn is so dangerous and what if...?"

"It's better if she knows. We're well insured so even if something should happen to the *Marianne* it won't be like it was when you were a child."

"Don't even say such a thing!"

"You really should tell her about Karen and Peter."

Karen strained to hear Mam's soft reply, "I don't want to talk about it. She must know about them anyway, everyone does."

"Then why does she keep asking questions?"

Karen was puzzled. What Karen were they talking about? Was there really another Karen as Pastor suggested? *If everyone knows, then why don't I?* Then she was asleep.

The next morning she started her new job. Ordinarily, no matter how much Mam fussed and fumed about cleaning it, no one was allowed to touch anything in the small office that was squeezed between the master bedroom and the southroom. They could sweep the floor and dust what was within reach but only if none of the papers or books were moved. Papa had his own system and could find whatever he needed, but now Karen was to be in charge and was allowed to reorganize. There was too much to do in one day so she confined her efforts to the table that served as desk. She collected the ledgers lying there, reading the labels in Papa's scrawly hand: 'Farm,' 'Mill,' and 'Shipping.' There was only room to stack them on the floor and she decided to ask Papa to make some shelves for her along the back wall; otherwise the place would soon look like Pastor Engel's study.

At night, when she studied the books she borrowed from Pastor, she sat at the dining room table under the big lamp that hung down from the beam. That was also where she wrote letters, including the thank you letter to Bodil Larsen that Mam had insisted on. Karen had protested that they had only been there for morning coffee and Papa needed to visit her anyway on business. Mam had said, "Nevertheless...."

Now Karen was writing for serious business, so she prepared Papa's desk in front of the window by laying out a new steel nib for the penholder, a bottle of black ink, and stationery on a big fresh piece of blotting paper. To get her started, Papa dictated the first letter and a long list of people who were to receive copies. The letter was all about the dinner meeting in Nordby and the investment opportunity in Esbjerg. The next time the bank notified them of a money transfer from Uncle Paul or from one of their other ships, the association would have enough to buy shares in the new warehouse. Karen didn't know half the words Papa used but was ashamed to ask. Papa corrected her spelling and she wrote out another draft, hoping that eventually she would figure out this new language.

He also showed her how to keep the mill ledgers up to date. Stressing the importance of keeping accurate records, he gave her notes that he had scrawled on scraps of paper about bags of grain brought to the mill or flour ground and delivered to customers. She was to enter them neatly in the ledgers.

"When I was an apprentice, Master's mill burned down," he explained. "If we hadn't kept careful books we never would have been able to collect the full insurance. Also, farmers sometimes forget how much grain they brought and get upset if they think they aren't getting enough flour back.

Having good records helps our reputation for fair dealing." Then he explained about insurance.

By the next day she was ready to start working. It seemed odd to be writing in the middle of the day and all by herself in the small room. At first she was distracted by sounds of Mam calling Girl-Ellen, Papa and Erik talking by the well, or the mill wings creaking. Soon, however, the outside world receded and Karen dipped her pen, remembering to wipe the nib against the side of the inkwell so no shameful blots would drop onto the paper. She made clean copies from the draft, concentrating on her penmanship so hard that her tongue made a bulge in her left cheek. Soon a small satisfying pile of finished letters sat on the desk for Papa to sign. She would take the bundle to the post office after dinner.

Soon a routine was established and she spent most mornings in the little room writing letters or recording in the books. It took her longer than she expected to get the backlog of paperwork under control but she did find time to add installments to her letter to Peter. She still felt funny writing him about family matters like money and she hated to complain too much about Mam, but it was good to have him to talk to again.

July 26, 1874

I have a new job! I am helping Papa to write letters to shareholders in the shipping association and to keep the business books—no more laundry! If there are bills to be paid or checks for deposit, I also take care of them after entering the amount and what they are for in big ledgers. I have learned so much including that the family owns shares in several ships in addition to the "Marianne" and now we are about to buy into a warehouse in Esbjerg. Papa calls it "diversified risk." The business of the merchant marine is so much more complex and interesting than I could have imagined.

I went with Papa to Nordby for a stockholders meeting and on the way we stopped at your Mam's house so I could show her the photograph of the crew that Uncle Frederik sent. She was very nice and very proud of you. We also rode to Esbjerg on the new steam-ferry. Sønderho is a much prettier town and I prefer sailing on a proper ship.

Not only is my job interesting, but there are other advantages. Since I see all the bills of lading and checks that Uncle Paul sends home, I feel part of what you do and know more about where you are—even if I have to run to the atlas to find some of the places. The other nice part is that I have a much better place to write you. It is very quiet in Papa's little office and Mam doesn't ever come here, so I can write you in peace without worrying what she thinks about it. I will try to write you every day and mail a letter to St. Thomas once a week, until you tell me your next address—will that be South America?

Mam is worse than ever, though she did agree to have me work here and it helps not to have her boss me around all day. For some reason she is very worried about Kirsten-Mos, even though everyone says she is just fine. I am getting very tired of no one talking about the baby—maybe they expect to say, "Surprise! The stork brought a present last night!" I suppose I should not be saying things like that to a man like you, either. Are you shocked? As for Christian, it is as if it is bad luck to even mention him. There was another telegram from Captain Nielsen. They are stuck in Rotterdam waiting for wind. At this rate, by the time Christian does come home, Latin School will already have started. You can imagine how Mam feels about that!

Ten

A Stormy Arrival

After church the Sunday following the excursion to Nordby, Kirsten and Granmam came to dinner, as usual. Kirsten was becoming very large and it was hard for her to walk all the way to the mill, but Big-Anne said it was good for her. Karen and Lil-Anne went to their room to change out of their best clothes and when they came back, Granmam was at the stove frying *bakskuld*, an island delicacy of small dried flounders. Frying them was supposed to be Karen's job, but Granmam liked to be in charge. The door to the pantry was open and Mam was down at the bottom retrieving butter and clotted cream. The house had no basement, only a large pantry, partly below ground. It kept food cold during the summer and frost-free during the winter.

Papa was already sitting in his chair at the far end of the table reading yesterday's newspaper. Erik Innkeeper often gave him old copies and he liked to read them cover-to-cover. Kirsten-Mos was also at the table on a chair next to the kitchen. This was really Mam's seat but she couldn't fit on the bench anymore and needed to sit near the window so she could see to knit. Although the clouds were gathering for a coming storm, in the summer midday the lamp was not needed.

Lil-Anne was supposed to set the table, but Karen helped

so she wouldn't get scolded for forgetting something. The child took the runner off the table and the two girls spread out a checkered cloth. Karen reached for the plates on the rack along the inner wall, while Lil-Anne neatly placed a napkin by each chair and four in front of the bench where the young people sat. They all had their own distinctive cow's horn napkin rings, even Granmam and Kirsten, on which Christian had scratched their names. Then she crawled along the bench on her knees to arrange the cutlery. Karen had to remind her that it was Sunday and that Girl-Ellen was back home with her own family.

As in all Sønderho houses, the northern inside wall was covered in ceramic tiles all the way from Christian's room to the kitchen door; so was the southern wall in the southroom and in Miller's office. Although they were very decorative they were also functional, especially in winter when the damp sea air that condensed on the tiles could simply be wiped off. The section between the windows in the northroom had been replaced just last fall from Dutch tiles that Uncle Paul's ship had carried on his last trip home from Holland. Over the years, boxes and boxes of inexpensive odd lots had been bought and used as ballast on the final leg of Fanø voyages. Most of the tiles had a flower in blue or maroon paint, but a few had a human figure or sailing ship. On the wall just behind Lil-Anne's place on the bench was a blue outline of a man. She had made up a series of adventure stories with her "funny man" as the hero and she never failed to pat him and say hello whenever she crawled by.

Finally all was ready and everyone was benched just as a low rumble of thunder announced the approach of the storm. Mam sat at the end of the table nearest the kitchen and Papa at the other end. Big-Anne and Kirsten were on chairs along the outside, while Lil-Anne, Apprentice-Erik, and Karen were strung along the bench. During the week, Girl-Ellen sat on a chair next to Lars-Anne, from where she could quickly dash out to the kitchen, while the bench seat next to Papa, usually Christian's, had been usurped by Lil-Anne.

While they were eating, Karen told about her exciting new job. Papa added what a great help she was and claimed that she was so efficient that he barely had work enough for her to fill mornings. Before Mam could invent some new chore for Karen, Granmam fortunately asked if she had time to come to the Southhouse in the afternoons. "Now that Kirsten can't assist me with birthings, I would like your help," she said. "Most of the time I just need you to keep the other children out of my way, but eventually we'll see what develops and if you like the work."

She would have said more except suddenly Kirsten gasped and clutched her stomach. She explained that her pains had been coming for a while but she hadn't wanted to spoil dinner. The midwife took charge and hustled her to the bedroom, catching Lars-Anne's eye as she went by. Soon they both returned, Big-Anne announcing that they might as well do the dishes as they would have a while to wait.

Mam had turned white in the face and said to Apprentice-Erik, "Run and tell Doctor Munck, it's time."

Papa added calmly, "Since Big-Anne says it'll be a while yet, assure him he need not come until after the storm."

"Time for what?" said the boy, puzzled.

"The baby! " Karen yelled. "It's time for the baby, you nitwit!"

Everyone started talked at once. Lil-Anne wanted to know what baby, Mam reprimanded Karen for talking about it in front of the child, and Granmam told them to calm down, they didn't need the doctor at all since she had delivered more children than he. She, too, gave Erik instructions. "Go tell Mrs. Jensen next door that we'll need her in a while."

"Lil-Anne'll find out soon enough," Karen protested. "What's the big secret? She's seen plenty of kittens and calves born."

"Is that why Kirsten-Mos is so fat?" Lil-Anne marveled. "Why didn't anyone tell me?"

"Why indeed?" Karen mumbled.

"Wear your oilskins," Mam said to Erik. "It's going to rain soon."

"I'd rather get wet, I can't run in them things," the boy said and dashed out the front door in his bare feet.

Papa lit the oil lamp hanging over the table against the sudden dark and went back to reading his paper. Kirsten-Mos was knitting again. "How can you knit?" Karen asked. "I'd be too excited."

"She says it's going to be hours yet and I need to do something. Can't you open a window? It's so hot in here."

Karen knelt on the bench along the wall to open one of the windows. She knew it would be closed as soon as Granmam came in, but at least they would get some fresh air first.

After they had washed and dried the dishes, Karen resumed her own knitting; even Lil-Anne was struggling with a grubby square that was to be her washcloth. Karen was glad that Kirsten was having the baby at Millfarm; that way there was some chance that she might be allowed to watch. Otherwise, they might have told her nothing, just announcing the addition to the family the next morning as if he had been dumped down the Southhouse chimney.

Everyone was quiet. Karen, in an attempt to fill the gaps in the conversation, suggested brightly, "Lil-Anne, show Granmam how well you can read." She reached up over her head to the top of the beam and retrieved a well-worn copy of Hans Christian Andersen sitting next to the Bible. She turned to the *Princess and the Pea* and Lil-Anne haltingly read the familiar story, carefully enunciating each word. Karen had picked that story because it was nice and short but had second thoughts when the little girl finally came to:

> *"One evening there was a terrible storm. There was lightening and thunder, the rain poured down—it was something dreadful! All at once there was a knock at the city gate, and the old King went out to open up. There stood a princess. . . ."*

Just as Erik returned from his errands and was removing his drenched clothes in *æ frankel*, there was a bright flash outside and everyone jumped at the loud crash that came almost simultaneously. Miller peered out the window to make sure the mill had not been hit and Kirsten-Mos gave a little gasp. Lars-Anne's face went white but, through clenched teeth, she said, "Go on child, you're doing fine."

All over Sønderho, people would be huddled in their houses, afraid that lightning would strike. Fires were a terrible hazard; once a thatched roof was ablaze, even the frantic efforts of the brigade could not save the house.

Papa always reassured his children that Millfarm was the safest house in town because it was protected by the mill on its tall dune next door and the mill was protected with lightening rods. Yet everyone was jittery, especially Mam who was always especially tense during storms.

Bravely Lil-Anne tried to continue her reading, but Kirsten-Mos interrupted quietly, "Karen, I think you should take her to your room."

"But I haven't finished yet," Lil-Anne protested. "I wanna read the best part, where they decide she's a real princess after all!"

"You can read it to me," Karen said quickly, picked up the book and grabbed a candle; with her elbow she pushed her protesting sister towards their room with the encouraging words, "You're doing so well, you'll be all ready for school in the fall." At the door Karen looked over her shoulder straight at Granmam and said firmly, "I'm coming back. I'm a woman now and I'm not going to miss it."

Lars-Anne opened her mouth to say, "Certainly not," but stopped when Granmam said, "Let her stay, she might as well learn what it's all about—especially if…."

Miller grabbed the apprentice by the neck and shoved him the other way, towards the kitchen. "Let's go check on the animals," he said to the sputtering boy and led him through *æ frankel* towards the scullery and the door into the stable.

Big-Anne calmly helped her youngest daughter through the southroom and the office into the big bedroom. Lars-Anne ran by to make up the bed, grabbing the newspaper on the way to protect her precious horsehair mattress. She was very proud of her four-poster bed, the one Anders had insisted on buying when they married. With unusual firmness, he had said that he was much too big to sleep in a tightbed and that he didn't care what the custom was. Then she returned to the northroom to clean up the puddle under Kirsten's chair.

When they had finished the story, Karen left the big-eyed Lil-Anne in the northroom with Papa and Erik. She walked through the back hall to her parents' bedroom and found her aunt sitting in the tall bed propped up by pillows. She looked very young in the white nightdress, her hair in a neat braid over one shoulder. Granmam was returning from the kitchen stove with a basin of hot water and a stack of clean towels. Mam was bringing in chairs.

"Go get a chair for yourself and get my knitting," Granmam said to Karen. "It's going to be long night. You're to do exactly what you're told and keep out of our way."

Several hours of quiet industry passed. Big-Anne knew her business, as always. Karen knit away on her sock, trying to concentrate on the tricky part of turning the heel. Between the flashes of light and loud rumbles from outside, she heard groans from the bed. All this didn't seem very different from helping with the sheep or the calving last spring except that Kirsten-Mos was a lot louder. *Being a midwife is certainly more interesting than keeping house or farming*, she thought. Of course she'd have to wait a few years and then go to the mainland to study for the licensing exam. Karen wondered how long that would take and how one would go about it. Well, Granmam would know. Granmam had obviously thought about it too—was Karen perhaps being tested? Everyone had an idea of what she should do. First Mam and learning housekeeping, then Papa and running a business, now Granmam. Even Papa Angel had ideas for her future. Even if she couldn't become a pastor, he seemed to think she could become a scholar. Maybe her future wouldn't as boring as she feared; maybe her possibilities were not so limited. This year could turn out to be interesting.

Periodically Granmam sent her to the kitchen to refill the basin with hot water from the pot on the stove. Granmam was fanatical about keeping everything clean and washed her hands every time she examined Kirsten. It wasn't that Big-Anne subscribed to the controversial germ theories of Dr. Lister from Scotland, who had preached washing before surgery, rather that she was convinced that dirt and sin were bedfellows. Neither was acceptable at God's miracle of birth.

Each time Karen walked through the northroom to the kitchen, Papa and Lil-Anne looked at her expectantly. "Not yet," she repeated.

Erik had milked the cows, for there was a pitcher of milk on the table and even Lil-Anne had managed to find some food in the pantry for supper. Anxious to be seen as able to take initiative and be useful, Karen put some cheese and bread on a platter and brought it into the labor room; if nobody else was hungry, she definitely was. Later in the evening, she put a protesting Lil-Anne to bed without being asked.

Else Jensen arrived from next door, the rain dripping from the old oilskin jacket that she had thrown over her head. She hung it and her soaking outer skirt on a hook in *æ frankel* and replaced her sloshing clogs with carpet slippers. She went into the bedroom with her knitting and sat down, quietly waiting for further developments.

As the storm faded outside, it got noisier inside. "Here we go," Big-Anne finally announced and got very busy. "Karen, light the second lamp and bring it over here. Stand at the end of the bed and hold it up over my shoulders so I can see. Lars-Anne, put more pillows behind Kirsten so she can sit up. Else and Lars-Anne, help her push."

The two women moved to either side of the laboring woman, supporting her thighs with one hand and grasping her hands in the other. "Push," they urged periodically. Karen couldn't see much from behind Big-Anne and barely hear her calm instructions, but she could certainly hear her aunt's increasingly loud grunts which culminated in a screeched, "No-o-o-o."

Karen kept silent. *This is much worse than a calving,* she thought. She wasn't sure she ever wanted to go through this herself, much less take Big-Anne's place.

"Come on child, once more. You're doing fine," Granmam said. Kirsten yelled angrily at her mother and then screamed again.

"It's a boy!" Grandma exclaimed and held up a red, squalling baby by the ankles, as if in triumph. Kirsten must have said something for she added, "Of course he's healthy, listen to those lungs."

She turned to Karen. "Go tell Miller his nephew has arrived; he can come in in a few minutes. Then bring me the flannel blanket from the rack in the kitchen."

When Karen returned from the northroom, Lars-Anne had washed the baby. Swaddling him in the warm blanket, one tiny hand sticking out next to his cheek, she handed him to Karen. "Isn't he perfect?" she asked.

Karen couldn't believe how beautiful he was. His face was all puffed up and red, but when she reached out to touch his cheek, his tiny fingers grasped hers and his little mouth opened like a bird's looking for food. Only when Kirsten-Mos asked for her son, could she tear herself away long enough to carry him over to the bed.

Doctor Munck walked in followed by Papa. There were now so many people clustered around the bed that Doctor could barely get at his two patients. He finally chased out everyone but Granmam, saying, "Let them sleep now."

Before he was allowed to check his patient, Granmam pointed to the basin that she had refilled with clean water. "Oh yes, I know, cleanliness is next to godliness," Dr. Munck chuckled. "You and Lister are in cahoots."

Karen, the last to leave the room, paused at the door. "What's his name?" she asked.

"Frederik," mumbled the sleepy mother as her eyes closed, the baby lying next to her and making contented suckling noises.

"For Paul's father," Granmam explained. "They decided before the *Marianne* sailed. But remember, it's a secret until the baptism."

Everyone was called after someone else, Christian for Papa's father, and now Frederik, for his grandfather. To make matters worse, the King's name was Christian and the Crown Prince was called Frederik. *Everyone has an important name. Except me*, Karen grumbled as she softly closed the door.

Eleven

The Mysterious Painting

The morning after the baby's birth, everyone slept late. Big-Anne had gone home and Karen had crawled into her tightbed next to Lil-Anne. Lars-Anne had taken over Christian's room while Anders bunked with Erik, leaving Kirsten and the baby to luxuriate in the big four-poster. When Girl-Ellen arrived at her usual time to milk the cows and set the breakfast table, all were asleep except for Lil-Anne, who was the first one up and had already fed her pesky chickens.

"And then they chased me to bed and wouldn't tell me anything. But Karen said that when I woke up I'd have a new cousin. Where d'you suppose she is?" she asked Girl-Ellen, handing her the basket of warm eggs that she had just collected. Ellen, who had four younger siblings, quickly figured out what was what and warned Lil-Anne to be very quiet.

Erik was the next to appear, surprised to have woken up with a roommate. He reported that Master was still in his day clothes and dead to the world. Ellen having already learned the routine of the household and sounding a bit like her absent mistress, instructed Erik to take the cows to the meadow and then tend to the sheep. One by one the rest straggled in; Mam was embarrassed at having overslept but was quickly reassured that all was in order, even if slightly behind schedule.

Lars-Anne was soon in command. "Kirsten will stay here until after the baptism. Big-Anne said the baby is well enough to hold it next Saturday, if Pastor agrees. We have a ton of work to do."

Apparently Mam had persuaded Granmam that the party after the baptism was to be held at Millfarm and soon she was giving everyone their orders. Anders and Erik were to go to the post office to send telegrams while Karen and Lil-Anne walked into town to announce the birth, leaving Lars-Anne and Ellen to clean the house from top to bottom. Lars-Anne had a long list of additional errands for Karen. "Go to the Jensen farm first and ask Else to send her two older girls over here Wednesday so Lil-Anne won't have to recite the *barselfest* invitations alone." The word *'barsel'* meant 'birth', and the party that followed a baptism was called the *barselfest*. Young children in the family delivered the invitations verbally. "Ask Pastor Engel about having the baptism on Saturday and then go to Southhouse. Tell Granmam that you'll bring back whatever Kirsten needs and to give you the list of who is to receive invitations. Take Lil-Anne with you, so she won't be underfoot."

Before leaving, Karen brought Kirsten her breakfast and Lil-Anne came in to see her new cousin. He was still called 'the baby' since Pastor was supposed to pick, or at least approve of, his name and it would not be made public until he said, "name this child" during the baptismal ceremony.

"Aw, it's a boy. I wanted a girl," Lil-Anne complained. She was soon reconciled when he opened his eyes and studied her very seriously while clutching her proffered finger. In fact she was entranced and ran off to tell Girl-Ellen how beautiful he was.

"Granmam left orders to give you plenty of milk," Karen said handing her aunt a mug of still warm, foaming milk. "She said it'll help yours come in."

"I know, I know. She always says that what is to come out must first go in."

"I also came to see what you need from the house. Mam says that the bonnet and the christening bag are still here from when Lil-Anne was named, but I'm to fetch other stuff. Lil-Anne and I will make sure everyone in town hears the news; she and the Jensen girls will deliver the invitations on Wednesday." Then as an afterthought she asked whether Kirsten minded everyone having made all the decisions for her and whether it was all right with her to have the *barselfest* at Millfarm.

"No, it's fine. They know best and I'm kind of tired." Then, slipping into the habit they all had of calling Granmam 'she' in her absence, Kirsten-Mos added, her eyes twinkled, "Having the *barselfest* here solves one problem; she'll have to allow us to serve punch!" Karen was very surprised. She had always assumed that Kirsten-Mos agreed with Granmam about everything, including the sinfulness of alcohol.

"What were you going to call the baby if it was a girl?" she asked.

"Marianne."

"You were going to name the baby after Uncle Paul's ship?"

"Of course not; after Paul's mother. She was a great lady, always kind to everyone, one of Jesus's blessed peacemakers. The *Marianne* was named after her."

It made Karen nervous when people talked about Jesus like that, as if they actually knew him. Granmam and Kirsten-Mos went to prayer meetings on Wednesday nights as well as regular church on Sunday. They talked about spreading the good news and salvation of the inner-person. That part was all right, but why did salvation have to be so dreary? Why did they disapprove of most of the fun things in life, like dancing and beer? Karen much preferred the glories of the sand and sea of her island to depressing theology. Fortunately, Pastor Engel followed the modern teachings of his idol, Bishop Grundtvig.

Karen understood just enough of the readings that Pastor gave her to know that this charismatic preacher, writer, scholar, and poet had advocated extensive religious and educational reforms that angered the conservative establishment. His followers would later be called the "Happy Danes" in contrast to the members of a contemporary movement of "Pious Danes" that preached a somber outlook on life. Papa had chuckled when she mentioned what a great man he was and explained that the King had made him a bishop only because the Queen was one of his disciples.

Karen much preferred when Pastor had them sing one of Grundtvig's many beautiful hymns that praised nature and creation, rather than the old-fashioned ones about sin and misery. Mam, who usually had little to say about religion, said evangelism was for poor people who needed good news about the next life but she herself was too busy. Karen thought Mam was in serious need of cheer in this life. Granmam said the prayer group had been there when she needed them, which was more than you could say for some people, but she wouldn't elaborate. Papa agreed with Pastor about Grundtvig and said he saw no sin in a beer after a hard day's work and a lively dance on a long winter evening.

Karen reluctantly tore herself away from her aunt's pleasant company and went to find Lil-Anne to make the announcement rounds. On the way to the Jensen farm next door, they rehearsed saying together, "Kirsten Larsdatter Fredriksen delivered of a baby boy at four o'clock this morning at Millfarm."

The Jensen and Andersen families were good friends as well as related by the mysteries of Sønderho kinships, their houses often referred to as the 'twin farms' because they lay so close and looked almost identical. The size of a Danish farm was measured, not in cattle or acreage, but in the number of wings on the house. On the mainland, the biggest farmhouses were 'four-wingers' with main house, stable, and barns connected and built in a square around a cobbled courtyard. Millfarm and its Jensen twin, on the other hand, were known as 'double' farms because their barns lay parallel rather than being attached to the main house. Anders, whose family owned a four-winger on the mainland, had been surprised to see the smallness of his future home when he first came to Fanø, and even more surprised to learn that Millfarm and the Jensens' were among the largest in Sønderho.

Else Jensen greeted Karen and Lil-Anne cheerfully at the kitchen door, her two daughters peeking out behind her skirts. She listened with a smile when they chorused the formal announcement, even though, having been there for the event, the birth was not news. Then Karen asked if the Jensen girls could help Lil-Anne with the *barselfest* invitations on Wednesday.

Else readily agreed and then suggested, "I'll bring the punch on Saturday. That way your mam won't have to argue about it with Big-Anne. I have a really beautiful bowl and silver ladle that Lars-Anne borrowed for the other baptisms. Who's going to carry the baby?"

"Aunt Marie, Uncle Paul's sister, I guess," Karen said, thus revealing the secret that the baby was to be named after his paternal grandfather and therefore his daughter Marie would have the honor of bringing the baby forward to the font.

Karen and Lil-Anne, chewing on cookies from Else's bountiful kitchen, walked on to the parsonage where Pastor Engel approved of the plans for the coming Saturday. He suggested that Karen stop by sometime next week as he had something to tell her. Then they walked down the broad main street, stopping at almost every house to spread the good news. At the southern end of town, they found Papa and Erik in front of Granmam's house, loading the wooden cradle into the wagon.

"Big-Anne is messing around in the attic; she needs your help carrying stuff down," Papa informed Karen. "We'll leave the wagon for you."

"Please bring Lil-Anne home with you, and I'll stay and help Granmam," Karen said. She ducked her head under the lintel to step into *æ frankel* and climbed the stairs to the loft.

Granmam was rummaging in a big chest, sorting through clothes. *Æ pjegger* bobbed up and down on top of her head as the tiny woman alternately straightened and bent over to place the garments in the wicker basket at her feet, as if she were a hen, pecking at grains. The loft, as at Millhouse, ran the full length of the house. It was dark, the only light coming from windows at the end gables and a small window in the dormer over the front door. The loft was stifling hot and Karen went over to open the shutters for some fresh air, bending her head so she wouldn't bump into the underside of the thatched roof.

She wandered around looking at all the old chests and furniture piled against the rafters, wondering at treasures brought home from foreign lands and now discarded here among piles of ceramic wall tiles, broken chairs and cobwebs. She sat down on a three-legged milking stool so she could admire a porcelain elephant that she thought was Chinese. Next to it was a Negro head carved out of black wood and a small Greek statue of marble. A wooden toy sailboat with tattered sails and a broken mast lay abandoned on an old chair with a missing cane seat. Thinking that the boat could someday be fixed for Frederik, she picked it up and then saw a painting with its front to the wall over in the corner. Curious, she had barely turned it around when Granmam said crossly, "Get away from there. You'll get all dirty."

"What ship is that?" Karen asked but Granmam didn't seem to hear and thrust the basket of clothes towards her, impatiently gesturing that she should take the other end and follow her down the stairs.

Together they carried the basket of musty clothes into the scullery. In summer, the stove in here was only fired on laundry or on bath day, but today a kettle filled with diapers was bubbling over a lively flame. For the next hour they lugged water from the well for scrubbing and rinsing baby clothes and old diapers. They were both quiet, Granmam brooding and Karen deep in thought about the painting. She had looked at it just long enough to be able to recall a white-hulled bark, carrying all her sails and heeling in the wind, white foam at her bow. Why was the painting hidden away with its face to the wall as if being punished? Granmam obviously would not talk about it. If Karen owned a beautiful painting like that, she'd hang it in an important place. Maybe, if she didn't want it, Karen could have it...but no, that would never be allowed.

Karen wrung out a little nightgown as if her hands could squeeze out the answers to her questions. "Hey, you're twisting the life out of it," Granmam protested. "Be gentle, it's very old."

When they finished with the wash, the two women loaded the basket of wet clothes on the waiting wagon next to the cradle, and Karen drove home to the mill. Stringing the laundry line in the courtyard, she hung the clean clothes where they could dry quickly in the sun. Soon a small cry signaled that mother and son were awake and Karen went into the bedroom with an armful of clean diapers, offering to change the baby so Kirsten-Mos wouldn't have to get up.

"Look at the big boy," she crooned. "Don't cry, I'll bring you to Mam as soon as you're clean." She raised his bottom by grabbing his ankles with one hand and slipped the folded triangle of a fresh diaper underneath. She fumbled at first; it had been a long time since Lil-Anne had needed diapers. Frederik would have sprayed her apron if she had not quickly covered him up, laughing at her inexperience with boys. She pulled the top of the triangle between his legs and joined the three ends just below the band over his bellybutton, slipping two fingers next to the baby's skin and fastening a safety-pin through all the layers, managing not to prick him or herself. When she pulled a pair of knitted wool soakers over his padded bottom, Frederik stared at the top of her head where the tails of her headscarf were draped, his deep blue eyes large and round. His eyebrows arched and his mouth curled as if in surprise.

"Is that a smile for me?" Karen said wiggling her fingers in front of his face. "She tells me you're too little, but I don't believe it, I think you're laughing at me."

She had a hard time re-swaddling him, his firm his little legs kicking against the restraining blanket. "I think he's training already for the King's cavalry," she said as she laid him in his mother's waiting arms.

"His papa wouldn't like him to be a landlubber," Kirsten-Mos protested with a smile as she unbuttoned her borrowed nightgown and guided his searching mouth. Karen sat down in the chair that had been placed next to the bed, thinking that maybe Frederik was worth the fuss and bother after all. It was good to finally relax for a few minutes. She had seldom been alone with Kirsten-Mos but when the rest of the family was not there to dominate the conversation, her aunt was pleasant to talk with. She didn't say much but was the only person, except Papa, who didn't have secrets and was willing to answer Karen's questions.

Kirsten put Frederik over her shoulder and rubbed his back until he gave a loud burp that made them both smile. Karen asked why no one had talked about him before he was born. "Papa didn't even carry the cradle down from the loft until today and the old baby clothes weren't washed until this morning."

"But I've been knitting and sewing for months," Kirsten pointed out. "The old clothes and the cradle weren't needed until now, so why fuss?"

That was so like Kirsten-Mos, who never fussed about anything. It was so restful here with her. Maybe she was one of God's peacemakers; like Paul's mother.

"She always says it's bad luck to talk about a baby beforehand," Kirsten said as if she had thought more about Karen's question. "She's helped with so many births and says so many babies die so soon that it's better if you don't get too attached. But I think that was more the case in the old days when she was young." She looked down at the rosy baby sleeping in her arms and added proudly, "Frederik is very healthy."

Karen started to get up to fold diapers, but saw her chance to ask her next question, "Why was Mam so worried about you?"

"She wouldn't worry—she knew Big-Anne would take care of me; she's a very good midwife."

"But she was, couldn't you tell?" Karen insisted.

Kirsten said she hadn't noticed and no one had said anything. That was Kirsten-Mos too, she had no curiosity and seemed to notice very little. She was as docile as an old cow. But that wasn't fair, she was too nice to call her that.

Then Karen asked about the painting in the loft. "It's a white-hulled bark just like the *Marie* that hangs by the pulpit in the church nave."

Kirsten recognized the *Marie* but didn't remember ever having seen a painting. She never went up there; it was too dark and spooky. Then she had an idea, "Maybe it's my papa's ship," she said. "Before I was born, he went down with the *White Karen* on the way home from Lagos. She must have put the painting away after that; she never talks about it."

Karen opened her mouth to ask more when Mam appeared carrying a tray of chamomile tea and buttered bread for the new mother. She shooed Karen back to her chores. Recognizing that she would now learn nothing else, Karen went to work, so full of new questions she could hardly concentrate.

Twelve

The Baptism of the Crown Prince

The whirlwind of preparations for the baptism continued throughout the week. Karen wanted to run over to the rectory to find out what Pastor Engel had to show her and tell him about the mysterious painting of her grandfather's ship, but Mam kept her so busy running errands that she barely had time to keep up with the paperwork. On Wednesday morning, the two Jensen daughters, only slightly older than Lil-Anne, reported for duty right after early breakfast and drilling the three fell to Karen. She remembered what the girls needed to do from when Lil-Anne was born and the job of reciting the *barselfest* invitations had been hers.

"Don't forget to tell everyone it's at Millfarm not Southhouse," Mam said.

"I won't, but they'll all know by now," Karen reassured her.

Soon she was satisfied that the girls were letter-perfect and herded her flock into the bedroom for a dress rehearsal in front of Kirsten-Mos. The three recited in chorus, nervously but without flaw, "Greetings from Kirsten Larsdatter Fredriksen and the family. This Saturday, you are invited to walk to church at half after nine and to *barselfest* at Millfarm after the baptism."

Kirsten-Mos applauded enthusiastically and the children were dispatched with a long guest list of kith and kin, starting with the Jensens next door. At each house their performance would be rewarded with handfuls of sweets and by the end of the morning their stomachs would be so full that they would have no room for lunch.

That afternoon, Karen went to get Kirsten-Mos's empty lunch tray, opening the door very quietly so as not to wake anyone who might be sleeping. To her surprise she found Else Jensen and Mam sitting on either side of the bed and the three women gossiping and giggling as if they were young girls. The noise seemed not to disturb the baby, who was peacefully asleep next to his mother, safely nestled between pillows so he couldn't roll off the bed. Lars-Anne was looking more relaxed than anyone had seen her for months and as entranced as the rest of the family by the new baby.

As Karen came into the room, Kirsten-Mos was joking, "This open bed feels so strange. I am positively afraid of falling out."

"Anders and I fell out one night!" Lars-Anne admitted, not realizing that Karen had come in. "I was black and blue for a week and we laughed so hard that I felt sure we would wake everyone."

Else laughed but Kirsten-Mos blushed and playfully poked at her sister, "Oh you're terrible to tell us that." Then she saw Karen in the doorway and, clapping her hand over her mouth as if to stuff the suggestive words down her throat, blushed an even darker red.

Mam and Else merely laughed again. Mam certainly had been in a good mood ever since the baby came. But how could her parents both fall out of bed at the same time? Then Karen figured it out and it was her turn to blush. Could it be?...Her parents wouldn't...Surely?...!

"There you are," Mam said, as if Karen could not have understood. "Else came over to say that Lil-Anne is picking heather at her house on Friday, and to invite us all over to supper that night. I'll stay here and keep Kirsten company but everybody else can go over there as soon as you've all had your baths."

The four women then discussed the *barselfest*. Most of the baking and the rest of the preparations would be done on Friday. Because the weather was so fair and half the town was expected, they would set everything up in the courtyard and the menfolk would carry over an extra table from Else's. On Saturday, Lars-Anne would get up at dawn to fire the oven for the final baking. Anders had already been asked to be godfather and sister-in-law Marie was to be godmother in addition to carrying the baby.

"Else, Paul and I would like you to be the second godmother," Kirsten said. It was church canon for a boy to have two godmothers and one godfather, the reverse for girls, to ensure a proper Christian upbringing and to become guardians if the parents died.

"I'd be honored to stand up for little Frederik," Else answered, revealing that she had guessed the baby's name.

Naming the baby reminded Karen of her burning question about the beautiful ship in the painting. Since Mam was in such a good mood, she dared to ask, "Am I called for Granpapa's ship?"

"Certainly not! Ships are named to honor people, not the other way around," she replied brusquely.

Just then there was a knock on the door and Marie came in to admire her new charge. The opportunity was lost to find out more, but Karen still felt sure that she and the old ship were connected by some mystery other sharing a name. *Who was the first Karen? The one for whom we were named?*

On Friday, Anders volunteered to take care of the animals so everyone would be free to bake. He reminded them to call him when it was time to rake the hot coals out of the oven. "This is a job for the man of the house," he said every baking day. "I don't care that other women rake their own ovens. It's too dangerous."

The baking oven was a brick-lined cavity in the chimney, closed by a heavy iron door. It was heated by filling it with dry heather and peat that burned until only glowing coals remained and the bricks were heated through. Then the coals were raked into a heavy iron scuttle and the loaves of bread pushed into the oven with a long wooden paddle that had been soaked in water so it would not burst into flames. Women's voluminous skirts were ill suited to this highly dangerous operation, but the island housewives had learned to rely on themselves in the absence of their men. Anders often told a tragic story from when he was a boy; a kitchen maid had been badly burned when her apron and skirt had caught fire, just because she wouldn't wait for one of the men to help remove the coals. He insisted that this was his job at Millfarm. Lars-Anne let him; he interfered so little in the management of the house that she let him have his way on the few things about which he really cared.

Usually bread dough was put up early in the morning since it needed to rise for several hours. This time, however, Lars-Anne wanted the breads and rolls as fresh as possible for the Saturday guests, so she made the quicker batters for cakes on Friday. The yeast dough would be put up in the evening so that it could rise slowly in a big wooden trough during the cool night and be ready for baking very early Saturday morning.

The kitchen was humming with activity. The three women choreographed their movements to avoid tripping over each other, slipping in and out of the room and up and down the pantry steps as if in a well-rehearsed dance. Girl-Ellen was set to churning extra butter for the big day and Karen went to retrieve sheep cheese from the loft where it was aging in a nest of hay. It was covered in a crust of mold that Karen had to scrape off before it could be served to company. Lars-Anne placed several heavy irons on the stove to be heated; she trusted no one else to press the snowy white linen tablecloth for fear that it would be scorched. Between the heating oven and the constantly fired stove, the small space soon became so stifling that Lars-Anne removed her long stockings and both scarves so that only her small under-kerchief remained to keep her hair out of eyes and food. The other two women gratefully followed her example.

Before long, Big-Anne appeared. She wanted to make sure that Lars-Anne would not make the pastry and challenge her reputation for making the town's flakiest. Rolling the dough out on a floured wooden table, she spread the top with fresh butter, folded the dough, rolled it again, and repeated the process until there was a stack of paper-thin layers separated by sheets of butter. Soon several long strips of pastries stood ready on the table, some decorated with dollops of egg custard, others with chunky stewed apples, and the rest with the blueberries that she and Lil-Anne had picked the day before. Anders was called in to rake the oven and the sheets of pastry were pushed into the hot interior. Every few minutes they were rotated to ensure even baking, until finally she declared them done.

At the same time Granmam was keeping an eye on Karen as she stirred batter for a large 'sister-cake.' Soon the house was filled with a delicious aroma that brought Erik and Lil-Anne swooping like scavenging gulls and begging for bowls to lick or over-done cookie scraps to nibble.

"Back to your weeding," they were commanded and they slunk away to their odious assignment of cleaning the courtyard. They were to scrub the cobblestones, encrusted with layers of barnyard droppings, and weed the spaces between, packed with blackened sand and stubborn dune grass. On the morrow not a single one of the visiting ladies would pick up a speck of dirt on the hem of her best long skirt—not from Lars-Anne's courtyard!

"We'll be lucky if we even get dinner," grumbled Lil-Anne.

Soon both were thoroughly soaked from carrying water buckets from the well on the other side of the house, around the stable end, and into the courtyard. Then they got into a friendly water fight, splashing each other as well as the cobbles at their feet. Eventually, they did get dinner, but it consisted of cold leftovers on plates passed through the open kitchen window and balanced on the windowsill. "Clean off those grimy hands first," Girl-Ellen reminded them; she was fast learning to give orders just like her mistress. For dessert, they had slivers of over-browned pastry-ends dunked in buttermilk.

Saturday morning dawned fine and events went according to plan—with both Big-Anne and Lars-Anne in charge, they would not have dared otherwise. The women invited "to walk to church" arrived exactly at half-past nine, and as soon as they were benched, refreshments were served. Else's bowl, filled with a mixture of rum, mead, beer, and syrup, was placed on the table and punch poured into coffee cups with the beautiful silver ladle.

"Fine way to go to the Lord's house, drunk as common sailors," grumbled Big-Anne. No one paid the slightest attention.

Then Kirsten appeared dressed in her finery with a white linen scarf over her forehead peeking out from under a black bonnet. Her nightshirt and matching pleated apron were made of silk. Marie, carrying the baby, stood on one side of her so that all could admire him. Then he was placed in the traditional white silk christening bunting trimmed with silver and gold ribbons.

Anders pulled up the wagon, which Lil-Anne and the Jensen girls had decorated with purple garlands of blooming heather. Kirsten was lifted on board and handed her precious bundle. The wagon set off for the short ride to the church, moving slowly enough so the rest of the family and the women guests walking behind in a long train could keep up. Kirsten had wanted to walk so she wouldn't be a bother but Big-Anne, although she did not believe in coddling her mothers, had said it was too soon and the rest of the day would be tiring enough.

The parade was greeted outside the church by the rest of the town, whether invited guests or no. The baby was exclaimed over and everyone's party finery critically examined. Kirsten, Marie, and Else were escorted inside to the special chairs reserved for the mother-to-be-churched and her attendants. The remaining women filed into their pews to the left of the altar and the men went to their smaller section on the right.

Pastor Engel was always at his best with babies and today was no exception. Little Frederik, who seemed to have inherited his mother's placid nature, slept peacefully through the ceremony. He did waken with a small start when the cold water hit his head, but his brief cry was more *pro forma* than a protest. He fastened his large blue eyes on the pastor's face and his delicate eyebrows rose in twin arches of surprise. Pastor Engel beamed at the small bundle in his arms and raised his own bushy brows in subconscious mimicry as he returned God's new soul to the waiting Marie.

He hiked his cassock to climb up the winding stairs to the pulpit. Every head turned and even the smallest member of the congregation watched his progress in respectful silence. He carefully balanced his hymnal on the railing of the pulpit, smoothed the white pleated ruff around his neck, ran a large hand through his bushy hair, cleared his throat, and plowed into his sermon. He knew that the minds of his congregation were on the important festivities to come rather than his modest efforts, so he tried to keep his sermon short. Soon, however, he became absorbed in his own rambles on the joys of babies, the importance of family, the support of the town, and the place of tradition. He was better than he knew and was always surprised at the rapt attention he received. The sincerity of his words had long since captured the hearts of the adults and the youngest children were enraptured by the spectacle of the string-bean wagging his bushy brows, flapping his arms, and beaming benevolently down at them. Those slightly older were counting the minutes until, invariably, he knocked his hymnal off the railing. When this happened, pennies furtively changed hands and a wave of suppressed giggles traveled through the ranks of the boys. Today, the preacher managed at the last minute to catch the flying book, to the winner's delight since the take was double if the book was retrieved before it could hit the floor. The good pastor was so absorbed in his delivery of 'the living word' that he noticed nothing, thanks in no small measure to the watchful eyes of the elders in the congregation who ensured that the children did not stray too far beyond the limits of churchly behavior.

Karen tried to concentrate on her beloved mentor's message but was distracted by the ship model that hung from the rafters close to Papa Angel's head. The name *Marie* covered the stern in large gold letters but the gleaming white hull was so distinctive that she had no trouble recognizing this as the brig in the painting that Kirsten-Mos thought was Granpapa Lars's *White Karen*.

She was brought back to her senses by the announcement of the final hymn. Lars-Anne slipped out of her pew during the first verse to rush home to put the final touches on *æ barselfest* before the hungry guests could descend on Millfarm. Granmam rose also and gestured with her head for Karen to come and help. The congregation filed out of the church to smile and nod their congratulations as they passed by the newest member. Once everyone was outside, Kirsten took off in the wagon while those that had been invited to the feast lined up behind the godmother and baby Frederik. Led by Marie and followed by the other godparents, the festive parade set out for Millfarm, walking at a brisk pace so the child would learn to be swift in life's duties.

As the guests arrived, they were seated at the tables set out in the courtyard. Anders and Erik had put out enough chairs and benches for thirty-five people and soon they were filled. Cherry wine, coffee, cake and pastry were passed. Then young Frederik was handed to Anders at the head of the table.

"In the days of the Vikings," he intoned seriously, his booming voice carrying without difficulty even to the children's table across the courtyard, "Young men went a-viking on daring voyages, crossing the seas in their long-ships. When a baby was born in the home of an absent father, it was customary for the head of the household, if he wished to acknowledge the child as a member of the family, to set him on his knee. It is therefore fitting, since Paul too is on the high seas, that I as godfather, 'knee-set' this child and recognize Kirsten Larsdatter's boy as Frederik Paulsen."

With these words Anders set the baby firmly on his right knee, supporting the wobbly head in his large callused hands. Kirsten beamed and the assembled company raised their glasses with a loud 'hurrah' and the baby was handed to the next guest for another blessing.

Thus Frederik was passed from lap to lap, each man or woman saying a few words about the child. Big-Anne chose, as expected, to praise the baby's health and good looks, while others merely jiggled the child or mumbled a few words of welcome. Tollmaster Rasmussen, who had retired as Captain twenty years earlier, predicted that this sturdy child would someday follow his illustrious grandfathers Frederik and Lars, as well as his father Paul, to stand on the bridge of a family ship. This prediction inspired Karen, who had been wondering what to say, so when it was her turn, she raised her glass and proposed a toast, "To Crownprince Frederik!" to which everyone responded with a triple "hurrah!"

Mette sat on her other side but was too shy to do anything but plant an enthusiastic kiss on the baby's forehead. Pastor Engel said that one priestly blessing was enough for one day and by this time Frederik's patience was at an end, so Kirsten brought him into the house. The absence of the guest of honor was hardly noticed as the toasts and gossip continued.

When all had had their fill of refreshments if not of gossip, Lars Jensen brought out his fiddle and played a lively tune. Although dancing was usually reserved for the winter when there were more men to go around, Anders grabbed Anne's hand and pulled her up over her laughing protest that she couldn't possibly dance on cobblestones and she must look a mess by now. When Lars took the hint and switched to a dance melody, the two began the promenade that started the intricate dance called *Sønderhoning*. Several other couples joined them, each woman slightly ahead of her partner and on the outside as they circled around on the courtyard 'floor.' Gliding over the clean cobblestones, each pair represented a ship at sea running before a following wind. After a few measures, Anne let go of her husband's hand and he took a step backwards to let her pass in front of him, as when a ship comes about and momentarily the sheets are loosened. Then Anders stepped forward again, twirled Anne to face him, and clasped both her hands in his, behind her back. They bobbed and turned, again a ship at sea but this time sailing into the wind and riding up and down the billowing waves. After a few turns, Anne's skirt picked up the rhythm and stood out behind her, a wake of heavy pleats.

Karen watched her parents with envy, admiring the grace with which they perfectly interwove their feet, their steps in 3/4 time in contrast to the 2/4 rhythm of the music, neither tripping over the other nor on the uneven cobbles. As they came near her table, Papa bent down to whisper in Mam's ear just loudly enough for Karen to overhear, "Remember the first time you showed me how to do this? When I saw you standing in the big barn at home, you looked so lost. But you wore that strange turban with pride, as if saying to the world, 'I don't belong here, I was made for something better.'"

Anne laughed up at him. "You were so kind but such a clumsy oaf. Now you aren't half-bad at *Sønderhoning*—for a foreigner."

Karen had taught Peter *Sønderhoning*. Being from Nordby, he hadn't learned the steps, at least not properly. He was very graceful on the dance-floor, never a clumsy oaf, so he had quickly learned well enough to almost rival Papa. Karen remembered the feel of his body against hers, the warmth of his hands enfolding hers. That was how she wanted to spend her life, running before the wind in Peter's arms.

The music changed to a Danish folk melody, and Karen jumped up. She grabbed Apprentice-Erik's hand and said, "Come on Nitwit, let's dance too." Erik reluctantly obeyed and tried to follow his master's graceful example. Even though he knew the steps from home, he found it hard to dance with Karen. She was a good deal taller than he and tended to lead, tripping him up.

At the beginning of the next tune, Miller took pity on Erik and relieved him of his duty. "Go dance with Lil-Anne," he said, pointing to the child, jumping up and down in her eagerness to join in.

Karen was thrilled to dance with her father. The music became faster and faster as if to test their dance skill and they had to stop talking just to keep up. At the end of the dance, Anders gave Karen's hand the traditional slap to thank her for being his partner.

Finally, Lars Jensen struck up the tune to 'The Cockscombed Hen,' a Danish folkdance for one man and two women, always a favorite in Sønderho because there were seldom enough men to go around. Else Jensen had been sitting on a bench, enviously eyeing Miller and his family. Since her husband was playing she had to sit on the sidelines. Now she saw her chance as she and Anne each grabbed one of Anders's hands.

Karen found herself sitting next to Mette and across the table from Pastor Engel. She leaned over and said, just loudly enough for her voice to carry over the music, "I found a painting in Granmam's loft. It looks just like the *Marie* in the church nave."

Papa Angel exclaimed, "That was one of the things I wanted to tell you. I've been going over the old records and discovered that the *Marie* is really a model of your grandfather Lars's ship, the *White Karen* that sank off the African coast."

"What a beautiful name for a beautiful ship," Mette said, overhearing the conversation. "Why was the model called the *Marie* instead of its true name?"

"Perhaps because the model wasn't finished until after the brig sank, and it would have been considered bad luck to keep the name," Pastor speculated. "That reminds me of my other discovery. Karen, go look at your grandfather's gravestone and read all the names and dates on the stones around there. I think you'll find the answers to many of your questions."

“But Granpapa isn’t buried in Sønderho, he stayed out there,” Karen protested.

“There’s a memorial to him in the northwest corner of the church yard. When you’ve been there, stop by my study and we can talk.”

“Then come and tell me all about it too,” Mette said.

Thirteen

Flowers for Karen

Karen had decided that she would get up early Sunday and explore the cemetery before breakfast. How long could it take to look at a couple of old gravestones? She knew where Granpapa's was, but had never paid much attention. It was just after dawn when she got out of bed and stumbled into the northroom so she wouldn't wake Lil-Anne when she dressed. She was nibbling on some leftover pastry when Papa came in rubbing his eyes.

"Oh. It's you," he said. "What are you doing up at this hour—don't you know it's Sunday?"

"I have to go somewhere to see something," Karen said vaguely hoping to avoid questions, but she was so engaged in unraveling what she thought of as 'her mystery' that she couldn't resist asking where her name came from. "Pastor Engel says to look at Granpapa's tombstone."

"Do what he says and read the inscriptions."

"Why can't you just tell me?" Karen said. "It would be so much easier."

"It's not my family, not my story. You need to figure it out for yourself," he replied.

On the way to the cemetery she picked some flowers and strode the path towards church, her face glowing with excitement. She lifted the latch of the gate on the west entrance to the cemetery that surrounded the old building, and made her way between the moldy gravestones. They leaned towards each other as if exchanging town gossip and some were so old that they were lying down to rest, covered with soft blankets of moss.

As she crossed to the northwest corner, Karen saw the swish of a pleated skirt and the anonymous back of a scarf-covered head leaving through the gate on the opposite side. She wondered who else was about this early on Sunday morning but was glad that the woman had left and she was now alone. Suddenly feeling nervous about what she would find, she shifted the little bouquet of flowers from one hand to the other. She stared at the memorial to her grandfather in front of her. The granite surface glared back, Captain Lars eternally in command. Although the sun was up, the stone was in the shadow of the thorn hedge on the other side of the fence but it was not hard to read the imposing letters that announced the long ago tragedy. Granpapa's name was level with her eyes, the letters of his title as large as those of his name, as if they had all been conferred together at baptism:

In Remembrance

SHIP OWNER AND CAPTAIN LARS KROMANN

b. 15 Sept. 1811

d. off Lagos in Africa Jan. 1851

Beloved Husband and Father

Resting in the Deep

For the first time it became real to her that Granpapa Lars was Granmam's husband and Mam's father and that they must have loved him as much as she loved Papa. Mam was born in 1839, so she was only twelve when she lost her father. How terrible that must be, to lose your papa. They didn't even know what day he died.

Below the big letters was a smaller inscription that she could barely read in the shadows:

Cabinboy Peter Larsen
b. 3 Oct. 1837 d. Jan. 1851
Beloved Son and Brother

The little bouquet of flowers dropped from her hand as she realized what she was seeing. This Peter who died the same month as the Captain, must also have gone down with the *White Karen.* If he was named 'son of Lars,' in the old manner, he was Mam's brother! She stood in shock for several minutes, her thoughts racing. This uncle that she had never heard of had the same name as her own Peter Larsen. But Peter was alive and well. Wasn't he? She had had a letter from him just a few days ago.

She knelt to gather the scattered flowers into a more respectful bouquet and noticed that there was another bunch of flowers next to hers. Granmam's she realized. That must have been Granmam whom she had seen leaving the churchyard. She had a vision of the tiny figure, still wearing black and coming here every Sunday, as if she had lost husband and son months instead of years ago.

Her eyes strayed to a smaller neighboring stone that she vaguely recalled belonged to her great-grandparents. Her mind was still full of the family tragedy, as she absently read their names. She barely remembered old Captain Niels Kromann who had died when she was little, but received another shock when she read: 'Karen Jensdatter Kromann 1799–1854, beloved wife,' above his name.

"Great-granmam was called Karen! It's true then; I'm not named for a ship. That's what Papa Angel meant for me to understand!" she said aloud.

Pleased that she had decoded his message, she noticed another bouquet of flowers at the foot of a stone on the other side with the inscription: 'Karen Larsdatter Hansen, 8.22.1831–12.17.1850 and infant daughter b. 12.17 d.12.20.1850.' Another Karen, she realized with surprise. She noticed yet another inscription at the base of the stone that looked like it had been added. She pushed aside the tall strands of grass covering the name:

FIRST MATE JENS HANSEN
b.10.9.1825 d. Jan.1851 off Africa
May they rest together in peace

Who was this tragic family that had died in such a short time? Then she noticed the date of the first mate's death; he must also have gone down with the *White Karen* off the African coast. Also, if his wife, Karen Larsdatter, had been named for her father, according to the old custom, then this Karen was the Captain's daughter, dead in childbirth, and that made her Mam's elder sister. *I was named after my aunt, not my great-granmam*!

Suddenly, it was too much. Karen sank to the ground and wept for her long-dead family, her self-confidence shattered. Although she had never known them, not even of them, she was overcome by a feeling of loss. All these young lives, not much older than herself, they had never had a chance to become anything and here she was preoccupied with who she was and what she wanted to be. It finally dawned on her that there was no secret. The mystery that she had been trying to find out about all summer was not about her at all but about other people. She felt guilty at having bothered Mam and Granmam with her selfish curiosity. No wonder Mam didn't want to talk about this, no wonder no one dared mention the baby before he was born, in case...It was too horrible to think about what could have happened to sweet Kirsten-Mos and darling Frederik. And what if Uncle Paul never came home? Or her own Peter?

Yet, they were my family too. It would have been so much easier if someone had just told me. Long ago!

The sun, now over the trees, shone in Karen's eyes and she realized that she was about to miss breakfast. Not wanting to be late and have to answer a lot of questions, she dried her eyes on a corner of her apron and quickly split her little bouquet into three, one for each stone. Then she stood up, squared her shoulders and whispered, "Karen-Mos, I'll make you proud. I'll be somebody for us both."

After church, Karen drove the wagon to settle Kirsten-Mos and Frederik back at Southhouse. On the way home, she stopped by the parsonage to visit with Pastor, who confirmed what Karen had figured out from the parish records. He had very little to add and Karen was in a hurry to get back so she could write Peter. She poured out her heart to this her best friend, ending,

I had no reason to be so worried all summer that I did not belong here in Sønderho—yes, I really did wonder sometimes since no one would tell me about the past. It is so common for men to be lost at sea and women to die in childbirth, but that makes it no easier when it happens in your own family. I guess no one wants to talk about tragedies because it would be too sad. Hearing what can happen so quickly makes me think, though. Pastor and Grundtvig are right, we have to look for joy or life would be dreadful. I am going to try not to be so selfish and not to think that the world revolves around me. Other people have feelings—Mam too, even if she does not share them with anyone.

I am so glad that I have you to confide in to help me sort all this out. I will write more next week and send this to Sao Paulo, Brazil, as you said in your last letter. I am so glad you came safely through the hurricane—I try not to worry about you. I know you are not the Peter Larsen who was my uncle, even if Mam seems to confuse the two of you.

The following week she was to start helping Big-Anne with deliveries. They had agreed that she would do her paperwork at Millfarm in the mornings and then come to Southhouse after dinner. Preparations for the baptism had kept her so busy that she had a backlog of bills and receipts to enter into the ledgers. If Granmam didn't need her, she would take care of Frederik so Kirsten-Mos could rest. Although Big-Anne had little for her to do as yet, she discovered that taking care of a new baby meant doing a lot of extra laundry. It was therefore a week before she had time to visit Mette.

Finally Sunday came—the day of rest. When the last Amen sounded in and the women led the men out of church, Karen whispered to Mette, "Do I have a lot to tell you. I found out about my name, and lots more stuff about my family."

"Come to my house this afternoon and we can talk," Mette whispered back. I'm sure it'll be all right with Mam if you stay for supper." Then

Karen had to run to catch up with her mother who was calling to hurry up and come home for dinner.

As soon as the dinner dishes were done, Karen went to Mette's. Everyone there was taking a nap, so the two friends went in back of the house to talk where they wouldn't disturb anyone. Sitting on a grassy hummock between the inland meadows and the town, Karen poured out her long tale of detective work and the sad family story. Mette knew, of course, about the sinking of Lars Kromann's ship. Shipwrecks happened every year and both of them had thought of it as a long-ago event that didn't concern them.

"I don't know why I never read the names on his stone before," Karen said. "I remember seeing it at funerals, but I didn't pay much attention. Who would have thought a bunch of old names on moldy tombstones could be so tragic and yet so interesting?"

"Big-Anne must've wondered this morning who left those flowers last week," Mette said.

"She probably guessed, she always knows everything," Karen replied. "She's worse than Mam that way."

"It's so sad for your mam, losing first her sister, then her papa and older brother all at once," Mette said. "That must be why she never wants to talk about it."

"It's almost as if she's angry, but that doesn't make sense." Then Karen had a flash of insight, "Maybe this is why she's so desperate to keep Christian away from the sea and for me to marry a landlubber! And why she always says seamen can't be trusted. After all, her father and brother left her and never came back."

At supper that night, Karen discovered that Mette's mother was another source of information. It all started when Mette asked, "Mam, did you know that Karen had an aunt who was called Karen and who died?"

"Of course, dear. Karen Larsdatter and I were in school together. We were best friends."

Karen stared at Emma with open mouth. It had never occurred to her that her mysterious aunt would have grown up in town, gone to school, had friends, and that everyone did know what had happened. Except of course, it was a long time ago and since no one ever talked about the past, Karen and Mette wouldn't have heard.

After finishing the dishes, they went out into the garden to enjoy the fine evening and Karen asked again about her aunt. Emma settled into her chair, folded her hands in her lap and focused her eyes on the far-away past. Then she began her story, speaking slowly and distinctly,

> "In the spring of 1850 Karen Larsdatter and Jens Hansen had been married only a few months when he sailed away with Captain Lars Kromann. A month before Christmas, Karen went into labor, but she and the baby died soon after. Four months later, the news came that the *White Karen* was missing off the coast of Africa and was probably lost with all hands. Lars-Anne came running over here in hysterics. She had come home from school and found Big-Anne already dressed in widow's weeds making supper as if it were nothing at all. Kirsten was born only two weeks later."

Emma paused but Karen urged her to go on.

> "Everyone admired Big-Anne. She worked very hard without ever complaining, doing whatever she could to earn a little money, but they were very poor. The family had invested everything they had to buy and outfit the *Karen* for the trip to the Warm. She was supposed to sail around Africa and bring home a cargo from the east to make everyone rich. There had not been enough money for insurance, so when the ship was lost, Big-Anne was left with a broken father-in-law, two children, and no money. Of course, her parents at Millfarm wanted to help, but she didn't want to be dependent. She found a few odd jobs, but often all they had to eat were the fish she exchanged for worms she dug at the beach. She held her head high, but it was hard to go from being ship-owner and captain's wife to digging worms."

"What did Mam do? How did she feel?" Karen prompted. Emma barely seemed to hear though she continued,

"Life was hard for Lars-Anne too. The next winter, Big-Anne took baby Kirsten to the mainland so she could get her midwife's license and Anne moved to the mill to live with her grandparents. Even when Big-Anne returned, Lars-Anne stayed at Millfarm—she and Big-Anne didn't get along well after everyone died. She had another year of school but as soon as she was confirmed, she went to the hiring-fair in Ribe to help support the family. The first couple of summers were terrible for her, though she never complained. Finally she was lucky. Christian Andersen recognized a hard-working girl, hired her on the spot, and brought her home to his farm. They liked her so much she worked for them for several years, even staying during the winter. Anders was the youngest son...."

Emma smiled at Karen, "...And you know the rest."

Karen began to understand Mam's behavior this strange summer. It finally made sense: her hysterics when Christian ran away to sea, her worry about money, and her happiness that Kirsten and Frederik were healthy. "Mam should be proud, not ashamed of how hard she worked," Karen said. "But why won't she talk about it? I need to hear from her what it was like. So I can understand."

Emma patted her hand and tried to explain, "Lars-Anne has never been one to dwell on the past and doesn't want you to worry or feel sorry for her. She's not ashamed, she just wants a better life for her children."

"It's like a fairy tale with trials and tribulations and a tall prince who rescues the beautiful maiden from a life of drudgery," Mette said. "It even ends: 'And they all lived happily ever after.'"

Except that Mam's not happy, Karen thought.

Fourteen

Bringing in the Sheaves

Christian and Karl had not yet come home on the *Fortuna*. There had been another terse telegram from Captain Nielsen:

In Bremerhaven for repairs STOP *Home in two weeks* STOP *Boys fine.*

"That storm, the night Frederik was born, hit all down along the coast," Papa explained, showing them the headlines in the newspaper about flooding in Holland and Germany. "We were lucky that Sønderho didn't flood—I keep telling the town council we need a dike."

Mam stared at the headlines and, focusing on the word 'repairs', became nearly hysterical. "I told you the sea is dangerous. There's something Nielsen isn't telling us. The *Fortuna* was wrecked in that storm. I feel it."

"But he just said 'repairs'—that could be as simple as the loss of a spar. And the boys are fine!" Papa protested. "They're going to be a little late, that's all. I'll write to Ribe Cathedral School and explain, it's not a big problem."

"But he isn't ready. He hasn't studied enough," Mam protested.

"I've talked to his tutors; Teacher, Doctor, and Pastor all say he'll be fine."

Looking at her mother's closed face and tight lips, as if she refused to say or hear more,

Karen thought, *There's something Mam isn't telling us. The boys are fine, but she doesn't believe it.*

That night, Karen finished her letter to Peter, so she could mail it the next morning.

> *I wish I could complete the puzzle about what happened to Mam when she was a child. I think that, sad as it must be to lose most of your family within months of each other, there must be more to her story. It was so long ago, yet every time a ship is lost at sea or we have a storm, she closes up and looks like a storm herself. She never talks about it and absolutely refuses to tell me anything about when she was young. I just do not understand and do not know how to make her explain it to me. Other people just babble away with the least encouragement, but whenever I broach the subject of my name or the "White Karen," Granpapa Lars, or Uncle Peter, she just clams up. It does not make sense to brood about something so long—she should just let it be. So she didn't get along with her mother—who does? Is that enough to make one leave home for good, not just the summer?*
>
> *Always your friend,*
> *Karen*

The harvest season in Sønderho started with the cutting of the grass in June and ended with the digging of the last potatoes, carrots and cabbages in October. The peak of the season came in mid-August when they harvested oats, barley, and a little wheat. Soon the mill would be filled with sacks of kernels waiting to be ground into flour and delivered around town to his customers. None of the crops grew well in the sandy soil and dampness of the island, so they also had to import grain, especially wheat, from the mainland. In the fall, Miller would make several trips with his own boat to get extra grain or order shipments to be brought on one of the *everts.*

Even so, there were enough fields to keep those with farms busy with the scythe and rake. Many of the families in town were not farmers and even those who had stalls with a cow or a couple of sheep had either no fields to harvest or very small ones. Yet people turned out to help a neighbor in exchange for a little money or a few sacks of flour to feed them through the winter. In homes where the men were at sea and the girls on the mainland for the summer, harvesting was left to women and small children. Everyone had to share in the race to harvest the crops in the short time between the end of the growing season and the beginning of fall rains. It took a farmer's practiced eye to decide whether to let the grain mature yet a few more days and risk having it rot if the weather turned wet.

During the next couple of weeks, the weather was perfect for ripening grain and, finally, Miller judged that the grain was ready to harvest. All other work stopped and everyone hiked out to the fields north of the mill carrying rakes over their shoulders, white bundles containing food for lunch tied to the tops. The women were dressed for the occasion in white aprons, face-masks, and gloves. Girding bands were tied around their red skirts to keep them out of the way. Miller pushed a wheelbarrow with scythes and milk cans filled with drinking water. Harvesting was hard and thirsty work.

Miller hefted his scythe and started off, taking long strides down along the left side of the wheat field. He swung in rhythmic strokes, leaving a neat swath of cut stalks, followed by Karen who gathered piles into her arms and deftly tied them into a sheaf with a handful of straw. Lars-Anne cut the next row, walking along the cleared path left by Karen. Unlike most Sønderho women, who used a small hand-sickle to cut grain on their smaller fields, she was proud to swing a full-sized scythe, but although she was strong and practiced, she couldn't keep up the pace set by her husband. Smaller Erik, who followed her, therefore had plenty of time to tie his sheaves. Even Lil-Anne had a job, raking strays into little piles for later bundling. At the end of each row, Miller turned at right angles to start the next swath, and so on until he returned to the beginning. There he stopped and surveyed the progress. Filling the ladle with water, he took a long swallow and poured the rest over his head. He sharpened the scythe with long strokes and started the next swath. When he caught up with Lars-Anne, they traded paths, neither breaking stride, in a well-practiced harmony as intricate as when they were on the dance floor.

When they finished cutting the wheat field, they stacked the sheaves, leaning them upright against each other to form shocks. These would be left for several days to dry in the warm sun before the grain was brought back to the barn. Then they went to the next field to cut rye.

The evening after the last field was harvested, Anders leaned back in his chair and puffed contentedly on his pipe. This year the harvest was good and the proud rows of shocks a satisfying sight. His happiness would be complete if the rain held off yet a few days so the sheaves could dry and be brought safely to the mill. "Christian managed to get out of work, again!" he quipped.

Lars-Anne ignored his mention of the forbidden topic, but, though tired, she too looked satisfied. She was always grateful for her strong landlubber Anders but not least during the month of August. She felt sorry for the other women whose husbands were still away, leaving them to manage both house and fields.

The grain was finally dry enough to bring home and the Andersen and Jensen families shared the work, horses and wagons. The women and the eldest Jensen boy carried sheaves to the two men who pitched them into the first wagon. Lil-Anne and the Jensen girls ran excitedly back and forth trying to help but getting in everyone's way while Karen and Erik stood atop the growing pile in the wagon to distribute the sheaves. As soon as the first load was ready, the two horses were hitched to the wagon. Miller drove home, Erik perched on top of the load to keep everything from falling off. Meanwhile, the rest of the workers started on the next wagon.

Late Friday afternoon, they reached the last field and were ready to bring home the final load. Else Jensen held the reins and Lars climbed up next to her on the seat and struck up a merry tune on his fiddle. Miller tossed the squealing smaller children to the top of the pile as if they were mere bundles of grain, and the wagon set off for the Jensen farm followed by the rest of them on foot, singing and laughing. On the road they met a wagonload of celebrants from another farm and they could hear singing in the distance. It seemed that most of the town had agreed that this was the day to bring home the sheaves.

Big-Anne, Kirsten and baby Frederik greeted them in the Jensen courtyard between the house and barn. Lil-Anne slid down from the top of the wagon, landing on the ground before anyone could catch her. She ran up to her aunt, "Did you see me, Kirsten-Mos? Did you see me way up there?"

Once the grain was piled into the barn, Else dashed into the house, pursued by everyone laughing and threatening her with scythes and rakes.

She barely had time to slam the door in their faces when they banged on it, threatening to overturn all the crocks in her kitchen if she didn't bring food and drink immediately. She shooed them away and, tradition satisfied, they peacefully sat down at the trestle tables in the yard. From her Bridge in the kitchen, Big-Anne commanded the women to bring out platters piled high with fish, sausages, cheeses, and breads. Karen poured elderberry drink for everyone and sent the Jensen boy to the well to fetch cold beer for the men.

Lars played some more melodies on his violin but everyone was too tired to dance or even sing. The children begged Anders to tell them about the harvest party on his Papa's big four-winger farm.

"But you know that story as well as I. You make me tell it every year," he teased. "We brought in the grain and then had a big party in the barn. *Basta*—finished."

"No, no you have to tell us everything: about all the horses and the wagons and the band in the first wagon leading them in," Lil-Anne protested. A grinning Papa relented and told them everything, prompted by a chorus of children if he left anything out. He finished with the best part, the harvest dance in the big barn when he and Lars-Anne had first met.

"There stood your mam up against the wall in the barn. She had been working on Papa's farm all summer and they had asked her to stay for the winter too because she was so proficient, not only at farm work, but also in the house."

Lil-Anne wanted to know what 'proficient' meant, but everyone shushed her. "Listen and you will learn," Papa said and continued, "I had never met Anne because I was apprenticed to a miller in the next town and only came home for the harvest fest. I asked her to dance because she was so beautiful and exotic standing there with her strange turban. She looked so lost but then I was the one who was lost—forever."

Lil-Anne clapped her hands and exclaimed, "And whenever anyone wanted to dance with Mam, the Prince said, 'She's dancing with me,' just like in *Cinderella*."

Sunday morning was cloudy and it began to rain, not a big storm as on the night Frederik was born, just little showers alternating with patches of blue sky. In church that morning you could tell who had finished bringing in their grain by their triumphant grins. The more it rained, the happier Anders looked. Those who still had shocks sitting in the fields looked worried and only relaxed when the sun peeked between the clouds and shone through the windows.

Pastor stepped up to the pulpit and just then the sun broke through the clouds and lit his face as if he were an angel bringing good tidings of more great weather. He managed to weave together thanking God for the harvest; exhorting the children to work hard at school, due to start next week; and blessing the absent sailors on the sea. He mentioned the parable of the prodigal son as if to remind Lars-Anne to prepare a welcome for her errant son. He quoted the parable of the sower, Peter's attempt to walk on water, and the bountiful nets of fish from the Sea of Galilee. The congregation smiled and nodded in approval, as if it all fit together and made perfect sense.

Lars-Anne, as usual, left during the last hymn. Karen thought she looked tired, with black shadows under her eyes, as if she hadn't slept for worrying about Christian. It seemed nothing could convince her that he was fine and would be returning soon. The rest of the family was walking back to the Millfarm for dinner when Ole Svensen came running up behind them. "The *Fortuna*...," he shouted breathlessly. "She's coming 'round the Hen."

Everyone started to talk at once. Karen was carrying baby Frederik and Lil-Anne jumped up and down so hard she nearly knocked them over. Ole finally caught his breath but could only tell them that Old Captain Rasmussen had sighted the ship through his spyglass. She was under full sail and heading for the Hen. He estimated that it would be at least an hour before landfall.

"We'll go home and eat dinner before we all go to the harbor," Anders said, relief plain on his face.

When they told Lars-Anne the news, Lars-Anne did not look relieved, but paled as if she feared the news would not all be good. She said it was unseemly to go running to the harbor, she would greet her son in the privacy of her home, as tradition held. Only Kirsten-Mos and Frederik could be persuaded to stay behind with her and, after a hurried dinner, the rest of the family departed in the wagon.

Most of the town was on the harbor beach. The *Fortuna* was making slow headway down the sailing channel under just enough canvas to keep moving. The crew was in the rigging, furling the last of the mainsails. The ship was now close enough so that they could make out Karl and Christian waving down from where they stood balanced on the main topsail crosstree.

"I'm glad Mam can't see this," Karen said, wondering if the boys were deliberately showing off that they now belonged on this lofty perch and could not be reproached. Task completed, they nonchalantly slid down the ratlines as the ship dropped anchor and came to a gradual halt. They were the first off as soon as the gangplank had been slid out, Karl rushing into the arms of Marlene Nielsen. As soon as Christian's feet touched sand, Lil-Anne flung herself at him, clinging to his leg so he could barely walk. "Hello squirt," he acknowledged as he managed to extricate himself and turned to face his father. As if unsure of his welcome, his head was bowed but he was grinning from ear to ear, his freckles merged into one brown band across his nose. His naked torso was as brown as the mahogany railing, his long hair bleached almost white, and his bare legs spread as if to balance his lanky body on a heaving deck.

"Welcome home, son," said the father softly, shaking hands as if they were strangers. "You've grown."

Fighting the tears in his eyes, the boy puffed out his chest and bragged, "I hadda buy new shirts in Rotterdam, the ol'one split right down th'back and I hadda wear Cook's to church on Sunday."

"Let me see your hands. Now those are what I call a worker's."

"I even have calluses on my feet from the rigg'n." Big-Anne and Karen were required to inspect hands and feet and squeeze his biceps. Karen even managed a quick peck on his cheek, which he brushed away, blushing.

By this time Captain Nielsen had come down the gangplank and, after greeting his wife, came over to Anders. He sent the two boys to fetch their gear. "They'll stay here but tomorrow the *Fortuna*'ll sail on to Esbjerg," Nielsen said.

Anders pulled the Captain aside and Karen caught snatches of the conversation. Papa had noticed the flag at half-mast and asked about the storm. "We were reefing sails when the main top-mast was hit by lightning and went down, carrying Seaman Abelsen from Bergen with it," Captain Nielsen explained. "We were only a half-day out of Bremerhaven, so we limped back for repairs."

Papa mumbled relief that the bad news was no worse, despite Lars-Anne's intuition, and went on to apologize for his son stowing away. Nielsen's shrugged with a casual, "Boys'll be boys." In a louder voice, he went on to tell how useful Christian had been when the cook had reeled on board in Liverpool and passed out drunk in his bunk for two days. "Got rid of him in Rotterdam, I don't put up with that. But Christian did fine instead and we found a new cook for the trip home."

"You mean Christian was your cook for two days?" exclaimed Papa, roaring with laughter. "Heaven help you!"

Meanwhile the boys had retrieved their gear from the cabin before the mast and stowed Christian's in the wagon, including a heavy wooden crate. The boys said their farewells to the rest of the crew and the Andersens drove home.

"Just wait 'til Mam gets you," Karen whispered to her brother.

"Was she mad?"

"I thought she was going to fly into flint shards, like a troll in a fairy tale," Karen said, but didn't elaborate because Lil-Anne was all ears.

"Are we to drop the box off at Nielsen's house, or is it yours?" Anders asked his son, to change the topic.

"It's not mine, it's for Kirsten-Mos," Christian said but didn't elaborate.

Karen poked her brother in the ribs and pointed to the red Danish flag waving on the pole in the back garden. "I guess she's decided to welcome you home after all," she whispered.

Lars-Anne was standing in the door. Wiping her hands on her apron, she waited on the step in barely contained dignity.

Christian climbed off the wagon and walked slowly towards his mother, as if to postpone the dreaded moment. "I'm sorry," he mumbled contritely, looking down at the hem of her apron.

"As long as you're safe," Lars-Anne said. Finally, her arms enfolded her son.

Fifteen

Christian's Adventures

Lars-Anne quickly became the busy housewife again and true to form said, "Karen, help Lil-Anne with her bonnet and then set the table. Your scarf needs fixing too. Boys, go wash up, supper's ready. Christian, go say hello to Kirsten-Mos and your new cousin in the northroom. They stayed to welcome you home."

"But I have things to show everyone, and presents," Christian protested, but was firmly told to wait until after supper. Obediently the boys, including Anders, went to the well to wash.

Christian was unusually talkative at the table, anxious to tell of all his adventures. Before he could be stopped, he launched into the drama of their recent storm at sea, the loss of their topmast and the tragic death of the Norwegian sailor.

Mam was horrified. "See what could have happened to you? I knew there was a dreadful accident, I always know."

"Karl and me were never allowed that high aloft," Christian stammered, surprised at his mother's vehemence. "Besides, Abelsen wasn't from here," he finished lamely, as if that made his death all right.

Attempting to divert attention, Papa pointed out that they had forgotten to put salt on the table. He succeeded better than he hoped for Christian automatically jumped up from his seat and was halfway to the kitchen before Karen could even stir. Mam looked up in surprise. Then Papa roared with laughter and explained that they now had a cook in the family. He told the whole story while the boy slunk back to his seat, blushing. Granmam frowned in disapproval when she heard that her grandson's mentor had been a drunken sailor. Mam rolled her eyes in disbelief at her son's newfound skill and expressed wonder that the crew survived his cooking.

"Aw, it was only for two days that me and Karl hadda do it. The rest of the time, I just fetched and carried whenever Cook said jump," Christian protested.

"Will wonders never cease," Papa murmured.

"Granmam and me picked blueberries yesterday," Lil-Anne announced as a big bowl of fruit and clotted cream was carried in, the dessert that had been postponed from dinner. Afterwards, when everyone had thanked Mam for the meal, Christian again automatically jumped up to clear the table. He caught himself in time and pretended he was just getting up to fetch his duffel, but not before everyone had had another good chuckle. Christian unloaded his possessions in front of everyone, including his boots, very smelly socks, one crumpled spare shirt, a damp sweater, and stiff oilskins. "Get those filthy things off my table," Mam commanded in horror, but Christian protested that there were presents wrapped inside.

"For you," he said proudly and handed his mother a small bag of bulbs from the middle of his shirt. "They're tulips from Holland and if you plant them on the south side of the house, they'll be beautiful next spring. I wanted to get you some porcelain poodles in Liverpool, but they were too expensive." He was too busy unwrapping more treasures to see Mam rolling her eyes once again while she mouthed a silent, "Thank heaven!" and Papa winked at Karen.

Unaware, Christian babbled on, "'sides Skipper was an old mother hen and wouldn't let Karl'n me ashore 'cept to go to the seamen's mission on Sunday."

"I should think not," mumbled Granmam. "The stories I've heard of Liverpool...."

"And tobacco for you," Christian said to Papa, who had already lifted his pipe off its hook on the wall to ready his evening smoke. Smiling his thanks, Papa ceremoniously stuffed and lit the bowl, without mentioning the wet wool and smelly feet with which the good Dutch Indies tobacco was strongly flavored. He leaned back in his chair and, putting the black stem in his mouth, he puffed his appreciation. The pipe was so long that the stem hid behind the fullness of his beard and the bowl rested in his lap.

"English licorice for you and chocolate for Karen," Christian continued as he doled out two bags of treats to his sisters. Lil-Anne puzzled over the peculiar black chunks in a little paper cone. Candy was a rare treat but this stuff looked very strange. She wasn't sure she'd like it. "And here's a picture postcard from Bremerhaven for you and Kirsten-Mos. There wasn't time to mail it," he added, handing Granmam a creased card that had been rolled in his boot for safekeeping.

"Looks like Captain let you on shore sometimes," Big-Anne said.

"Skipper was strict in Holland too, but he made Bo's'n take me'n Karl to the market so's we could buy new shirts. Aren't they great?" he proudly pointed to the spare cotton shirt on the table. It was an even more garish green than the one he was wearing. Mam shuddered.

After everyone had admired the presents and Christian had been ordered to remove his smelly belongings, Anders announced, "There's a surprise for you too, Kirsten; out in the wagon. We better look at it there; it's heavy and we'll bring it to Southhouse tomorrow."

Everyone trooped out to *æ frænkel*, exchanged their house slippers for clogs and clustered around the wagon, still waiting in the yard. The dog had been contentedly chewing on his bone but now ambled to the end of his chain to see what the commotion was. Anders chased away a couple of hens that had settled on top of the wooden chest in back of the wagon and pried off the lid.

"I know what it is," exclaimed Kirsten clapping her hands and hopping on one leg, as if she were Lil-Anne and not a dignified matron. "It's my Marianne. Paul promised he'd order a set when he was in Rotterdam."

Sure enough, when the lid and a pile of straw were removed from the box, there lay stacks of Dutch tiles, safely nestled in a thick bed of sawdust. An artist had faithfully rendered a portrait of the *Marianne* on fifty ceramic tiles. They were to be fit together like a mosaic on the wall of Kirsten's southroom, where a space between the windows had been left for them when the room was re-tiled last year. Why did Mam shudder again, Karen wondered? Ship portraits in tile were beautiful and the *Marianne* was so graceful, surely Mam couldn't dislike it as she did ugly poodles or a cheap shirt. Karen remembered the painting in the attic and realized that Kirsten-Mos had found a way to make sure that her ship could never be hidden away.

It started to rain again and Anders hurriedly closed up the precious box and made the boys help him push the wagon into the barn.

Back at the table, Erik and Christian were getting acquainted. "Didn't you get seasick?" Erik asked, recalling his misery when Miller first brought him to Fanø.

"Nah, you get used to it after the first day; but you should try climbing the rigging to reef sails in a storm!" Christian bragged to his admiring landlubber friend. "The first time I hadda scrub the deck, the water bucket fell over every time the ship changed tack. It almost rolled overboard, and me too when I tried to catch it. Bo's'n whacked me good for being careless. How's I supposed to know to keep it tethered like a wandering sheep? But I sure learned quick."

Fortunately, Mam hadn't heard. When she returned from the kitchen with the coffeepot, she said to Christian, "Too bad you were delayed; you'll have to leave tomorrow for Ribe. You've already missed a week of school."

"But I just got home," the boy protested.

"Let him stay the week and I'll sail him over on Sunday with the morning tide," Papa declared. "I'll get him settled at his boarding house and spend the night with Ingrid. It's been ages since I've seen her."

A family argument ensued about Christian missing another week of school and sailing on the Sabbath. Big-Anne disapproved; Kirsten silently sided with her mother, merely nodding as Big-Anne spoke. Lars-Anne argued that he could go by himself on the *Lene* in the morning. Christian said he didn't really care whether he went Sunday or Monday or maybe not at all. Karen, for once, kept out of the discussion.

Anders finally settled the question by saying, quietly but firmly, "It's my boat and my son. We sail with the tide next Sunday."

Karen was jealous, thinking that while Christian was going places to learn exciting new things, she would be stuck in boring Sønderho. She had an idea. "Papa, can't I go to Ribe with you and Christian? I'd like to visit Ingrid-Fas also."

Papa was about to say she could come when Mam objected, "Papa can't just show up with an extra person like that, even if she is his sister."

"Nonsense, she'd love to get to know Karen better and there's plenty of room at the house." But Papa didn't insist, as if he didn't want to argue anymore.

"Don't look so sad, we'll visit Christian in the fall when we go to the fair," Mam said.

Karen perked up; she had only been allowed to go to the big fair the last few years. Then Lil-Anne whined that she wanted to go too.

"Certainly not," said Mam. "You'll stay with Granmam and Kirsten-Mos, as usual."

To stop the child's whining, Papa asked Karen to read a story. "Yes please," Lil-Anne said, diverted from a losing battle. "The one about the smart Papa."

She has that one right, Karen thought, taking down Hans Christian Andersen's *Fairy Tales* and turning to 'Father knows best'. *It's a good thing that someone in the family knows what she feels and isn't afraid to say so.*

All week, Mam gave Christian a stream of advice about how to behave in the city. Not content with just getting the budding scholar's clothes ready, she told him to write at least once a week and study hard. "Mind your manners, especially if you go to Aunt Ingrid's house. When people don't know you, all they have to judge you by is your behavior. It reflects on your family too."

"But Ingrid-Fas knows me. We went there for tea last year, don't you remember?"

"Nevertheless, don't speak unless spoken to."

Karen wished Mam would stop making Christian nervous. He wanted Papa to be proud of him and not be treated like a mama's-boy.

Sunday morning, it seemed like the whole town turned out to see Christian off. Even the guests from the Inn walked down to the harbor, curious about the commotion. A battered wooden chest filled with the boy's clothes and books was sitting at the dock next to two baskets, one with overnight things for Papa, and the bigger one filled with lunch for the trip. Karen helped Papa load the boat, leaving Christian to say his good-byes. He tried to act the big man embarking on a great adventure as he dutifully shook hands with his tutors and thanked them for all they had done for him. He gravely made the rounds of the crowd receiving good wishes from each, stopping at last in front of Karen.

She handed him a little bundle. "Here Nitwit; for you. I finally finished those stupid socks. They're to keep your feet warm in the drafty halls of learning. The squiggle up the side is called a 'clock'—to help you be on time." Then she couldn't resist giving him a final hug.

Christian started to return her embrace when he realized that his friends were hooting and whistling. "Thanks," he mumbled, his voice cracking. Recovering, he yelled to his audience, "My stupid sister always slobbers all over me."

At the end of the circle, he did hug Lil-Anne and Mam. Then he made the rounds again, and hugged Mam and his little sister once more. Lil-Anne clung to his legs alternately begging him not to go, then to bring her along. He finally disentangled himself and bravely jumped on board with his back to the crowd so they couldn't see him wipe his eyes. Having been away from home, he knew what it meant to be homesick. This time he was not going to sea but to the unfamiliar life of a serious scholar. And this time, it was not altogether by his own choice.

Papa cast off and let Christian steer while he pulled up the sails. As the wind and incoming tide caught the boat, loud cheers and much waving of handkerchiefs started from the shore. As soon as the little boat was on a steady course, they could see Christian open the lunch basket with his free hand.

Papa sailed back the next day and Karen made him tell all. He explained that they had been able to sail all the way up to Ribe. "We only had to tow the boat at the bend in the river, then where it turns south we ran before the following breeze right to Shipsbridge Street. We tied up at the dock just below the cathedral."

Just when they had wondered if they would have to lug the chest all the way to Christian's lodgings, a short bow-legged man with a pushcart appeared, doffed his cap and offered his services. "He looked a bit scruffy but it turned out he was a fellow veteran from the battle of Kolding. I could hear from his accent that he was from south of the new border." Papa explained. He went on, quoting Svend and his colorful South-Jylland dialect: "Yeah, A's from Flensborg-way. In '64, A'd just been drafted and was in boot camp up north. They shot m'friend but the rest of us gave'm better'n we got. After the war, A sure weren't goin' back to have no German be boss of me, so A came here to Riwe."

"Never mind all that, how was Christian's lodging? Did the Lehnfelts seem all right?" Mam interrupted impatiently.

"Master Lehnfelt and his wife board twelve students, including Christian. He's a small thin scholarly looking man with a *pince nez* on his nose and a limp handshake. He'll be Christian's Latin teacher at the school. Mrs. Lehnfelt's a motherly woman who looks able to care for a whole brood of adopted chicks. Before I left, Christian was surrounded by the other boys and making friends already." Papa chuckled, "When we said good-bye, he made sure there was enough distance between us so a hug was out of the question. I reminded him that if he ever needed anything to send a note to Ingrid-Fas. And to write home."

"Did you see any storks?" Karen wanted to know. "Ribe is called the 'City of Storks'," she explained to Lil-Anne.

"I know that," the child said impatiently. "Shh, I want to hear."

"There's a whole stork family across the street from the Lehnfelts. Someone had tied a wagon wheel by the chimney for them and they won't migrate south until October. A youngster, his beak and legs not yet turned red, was walking along the ridge of the roof towards his nest. He raised one leg at a time, like he were picking his way through swampy reeds." Papa demonstrated.

"That's the way Peter walks!" Lil-Anne exclaimed.

"Peter does have stork-legs," Karen laughed.

Papa continued his drama, first describing the landing of the Papa bird on the chimney with a wiggling frog in a flag-red beak, then mimicking the young stork eagerly grabbing his afternoon snack, throwing his head forward, and sliding the still-struggling frog down his gullet. "No one else was looking," he said, as if disappointed.

Karen exclaimed, "Don't people know how wonderful they are? The parents fly all the way from Egypt just so their young can be born right here!"

"I guess people are used to seeing them," Papa said. "There are so many in Ribe."

"I think they should look, I'd never get tired," Lil-Anne sighed.

"How are your sister and her family?" Lars-Anne prompted.

"They all send greetings. Cousin Margrethe and Cousin Jens want to know when they will get to see you," Papa added to Karen and Lil-Anne. Before Lil-Anne could beg to go to the fair again, he went on with a frown, "I'm worried about Ingrid, she looked pale. She said it's only that she's *enceinte*— you know how she likes to use French words. They're thrilled, but after what happened before...."

Karen puzzled over the French word but finally figured out that her aunt was expecting a baby. Why couldn't people just say so? They had no difficulty describing calving, lambing and the birth of piglets. Papa had told her that with people, things like that could only be talked about in 'euphemisms'. Even Granmam talked about 'helping' her women and being 'called in' but seldom talked straight out about her midwifery. She had heard that Ingrid-Mos had had 'problems' with Jens so that's probably what Papa was referring to. Karen wanted to ask when the baby was due and what the problems were, but knew she shouldn't in front of Lil-Anne. Her little sister was pretending to be a stork, mincing up and down the room, lifting her legs; she seemed to have no clue what the conversation was about.

Sixteen

Summer's End

After the harvest was safely stowed in the barns and lofts, Sønderho settled into the usual routine of summer's end. Threshing would continue during spare moments all winter, but the first separation of the kernels of grain from the dry chaff had special significance, marking as it did the end of the summer harvest and the beginning of the fall season. It was therefore with deliberate care that Miller placed an armful of grain in the middle of the clean-swept floor of the barn and untied the band of straw that held it together. He and his apprentice faced each other across the sheaf. The tall, muscular Miller swung his flail a few times to set the rhythm, but soon his slender partner picked up the timing and the two swung their whip-like tools with steady alternating thunks. Erik attacked the tiring chore with his usual earnestness, but could not keep the pace set by the experienced miller for more than a short time.

"We'll soon put some muscles on that skinny frame of yours," Miller consoled. "That's enough for today; we'll let the seed corn wait until the kernels have hardened. There's a nice breeze, so let's winnow what we've done."

The animals, including the sheep and Lil-Anne's hens and chickens, were now let loose on the unfenced fields, to root the remaining stubble and glean the fallen seeds. Lil-Anne's job now became to hunt down eggs and chase her flock back to the house at the end of each day. The dog was brought along to help out, and he excitedly barked at the hens and playfully nipped at the gander's tail. The bird hissed and fumed but at least he was too distracted to bother his little mistress. They made quite a parade coming back to Millfarm, Lil-Anne leading, eggs carefully cradled in her apron, followed by squawking hens, flapping geese, and the excited dog running back and forth to pick up stragglers.

Tante-Black became the talk of the town. She had let her sheep loose too early and they had helped themselves to still-growing oats in the nearest field that belonged to Little Jess. When chased away by the irate owner, they had run off to the 'Fuzzy Mountains' and started to eat the grass. A hundred years ago, these sandy hills between the Hen and the North Sea had been the first to be planted with spiky dune grass to protect the town from blowing sand. With typical Sønderhoning humor they had been named the 'Fuzzy Mountains.' Little Jesse was the beach bailiff, and he had charged Tante-Black a stiff fine for damage to the grass. That he had been the one to chase the sheep from his field onto the forbidden lands made no difference; duty was duty and it was his job to fine careless sheep owners.

Tante-Black's neighbors and family were called in to help round up the errant sheep and they chased them up and down the dunes for the better part of an hour. When they were all safely back in the fold, all the workers gathered back at her house for the obligatory thank-you coffee served by her flustered twin sisters, Tante-Brown and Tante-Blue. Hans Thatcher, returning from outlying meadows at the end of the afternoon, found the town in an uproar and full of wild stories. He rushed to his aunt's house, full of apology that he not been able to help in the family emergency. Finding everyone laughing though exhausted, Hans exclaimed, "A trowed you was dead. But here you is, just drinking coffee!"

They all laughed as they drained the last from their cups and ate the final crumbs of Tante-Black's 'chamberboys'. All next week, whenever Hans met a new victim, he retold his tale with dramatic embellishments, chuckling as much at his own expense as that of his careless aunt. He finally stopped when a new listener beat him to his punch line by saying, "A trowed you was dead," before he could get the words out.

The following Sunday, Pastor Engel preached about the responsibilities of being a good neighbor, using as his texts the parable of the lost sheep and the Sermon on the Mount. The congregation nodded solemnly, but Karen was not sure whether he was scolding Tante-Black for being thoughtless, reprimanding the bailiff for being overzealous, or Hans for not looking out for his relatives.

Hans Thatcher would have come to his aunts' aid sooner but he had been at the meadow north of town to gather his annual supply of thatch. After the storm the night Frederik was born, Miller had found puddles of water in the loft and Lars-Anne recalled watching Hans' father working on her Granpapa's house when she was a little girl. That must have been twenty or twenty-five years ago, so it was about time for a new roof. Hans was therefore engaged to replace the roofs on both Millfarm and Southhouse.

Lil-Anne and the cat faithfully showed up every morning to supervise. First Hans and his apprentice removed the old thatch from one side of the house and hauled it away, covering the exposed roof boards with old sails, in case of rain.

When the roof was bare, Hans lifted Lil-Anne up and set her on the edge of the wooden boards. "Is it all right, so far?" he teased. When she nodded solemnly from her high perch, he added, "Tomorrow we start putting on the new thatch. Will you be here to see that we do the job right?"

The next day, not only Lil-Anne but also the two Jensen girls sat in an attentive row atop the berm that protected the garden against the west wind. Lil-Anne had unchained the dog and brought him from the other side of the house so he could see that everything was all right. The day before, he had been disturbed to have strange men walking on his roof and wouldn't stop barking. Hans spread a bundle of thatch along the edge of the roof while his helper climbed the stairs to the loft and squatted inside, ready to receive the long needle that Hans poked through the reeds. Back and forth they sewed to tie the bundles in place, stopping periodically to lay a new batch. When they had completed that first important row they stopped for a stretch and a cold drink.

"Do we pass inspection?" Hans asked the audience.

"It looks too thin and very scraggly," Lil-Anne said. "The thatch is way down over the windows and it's all uneven, like Pastor Engel's eyebrows."

"We'll add more layers and trim the edge nice and neat later," Hans explained. "The roof needs to stick out over the windows far enough to protect the house against the summer sun, but not so far that the slanting rays can't warm your southroom in winter. When we're all done, it'll look nice. Then maybe we can lend Pastor our shears so he can trim his eyebrows."

At the end of the day, Anders and Lars-Anne came by to see the progress and expressed the hope that Thatcher could work on Big-Anne's house next. "Assuming your little helpers are faithful in their attendance," Papa teased.

"We can't, next week we start school," Lil-Anne said importantly. "I'm seven and I can read."

"Don't brag," Mam warned. "Stine Thatcher will know that soon enough."

Lil-Anne blushed. In her excitement she had forgotten that Hans' wife was the teacher.

"Well, come by after school and tell me if Stine is as good a teacher as your mam," Hans laughed. "We'll make you inspector of schools as well as of roofs."

The women had their own end-of-summer chores. Aside from the usual housework, there were cranberry preserves to be made, and rose hips to be picked from the wild bushes that grew in abandon along the inland meadow. Black clusters of elderberries sagged on their branches, waiting to be made into juice and poured into bottles for winter fruit soup. The loft was filled with drying herbs, everlasting flowers, and heather hanging from the rafters in fragrant upside-down bouquets. The parsley and other herbs would enliven their monotonous winter diet, the chamomile made into teas to soothe sore throats and fevers, and the flowers made into festive wreaths to decorate weddings and holidays. Hops and barley would be brewed in large copper kettles for beer and mead.

There were fish to be dried, smoked and salted. Mornings at low tide, women were at the western beach digging worms for bait. These were threaded on hooks fastened every few inches along fishing lines that were neatly set in wooden boxes to be used by the fishermen the next day. Ole Fisher's Jacob picked them up mid-afternoon when he delivered each day's catch. The cleaned fish, mostly small flatfish about the size of a man's hand, were tied in pairs by their tails and hung out to dry one on each side of the line, waving in the wind like wet socks. Later they were smoked over a slow fire of peat covered in wet seaweed, and finally salted and stored in big barrels. Some of the fish, called *bakskuld,* would be saved for the men to take on board when they left in the spring, but most were kept for winter dinners. They were delicious when fried in butter and served with boiled potatoes and parsley sauce, though by the end of February, everyone longed for more variety.

Karen went to Southhouse every afternoon now to help Granmam or Kirsten-Mos. The house was one of the oldest in Sønderho, having been built in the middle of the eighteenth century. The northroom was larger than at the mill, but there were no bedrooms at the far west end like those at Millfarm where Karen, Lil-Anne and Christian slept. One could still see marks in the ceiling where a bank of tightbeds had originally been.

The southroom had been divided into a smaller sitting room and the main bedroom. The south sitting room was heated in the winter by the weak sun slanting through the windows below the steeply overhanging roof, but mostly by a cast iron stove.

When the Captain and Kirsten had been married they had taken over the house and the main bedroom where the baby now also slept in the old family cradle. Big-Anne had moved to the east end of the house. This room, once upon a time the stable, was the weaving room where Lars-Anne and Kirsten had slept when they were little. Big-Anne still had her loom and spinning wheel there and even a treasured sewing machine bought for her by the Captain. A tightbed was built into the wall shared with the scullery, where laundry was done and the family took their Saturday baths. Here a stove heated water in big washtubs for clothes and people and, in the winter, also warmed Big-Anne's tightbed on the other side of the wall.

Late summer chores were slightly different at Southhouse from those at Millfarm. Like Mam, Granmam picked herbs for cooking, but even more for medicines. Every time she returned from the heath she added mysterious bunches to those already hanging in the loft. Karen liked being with her grandmother because although she was very bossy, she loved to tell stories about when Mam or Kirsten-Mos were little, or even from her own childhood, long ago. She kept up a constant monologue as they worked, interrupting her own story to explain what they were doing. "Put the sheets in the sun so they will bleach," or "Brush hard under the seam of that skirt so you'll get rid of the moth eggs," she would say. However, she would ignore some of Karen's tentative questions as if she did not hear, especially if she asked about Granpapa or about when Mam was Karen's age. She did not dare mention her newly discovered uncle nor her namesake aunt.

Granmam extracted digitalis to treat heart disease and heal wounds from foxglove, and from broom a diuretic, all the while explaining their uses to Karen. "These are powerful medicines to be used sparingly and wisely," she warned. "Blueberry leaves are for diarrhea, and blackthorn berries are for constipation. Broom is picked in the spring when the flowers are out, but they are rare here on the island," and so on.

When Frederik woke from his nap, Karen would change him and bring him out into the garden to lie on a blanket. Granmam's suspicion of night air did not extend to summer sunshine and the three women and the baby enjoyed the good weather while it lasted. He seemed to bring forth a torrent of memories from Granmam and she gave endless advice about childcare and told about her experiences as midwife to most of the town's babies. Despite Karen's lingering discomfort about the pain and blood of Frederik's birth, she listened avidly. She imagined herself assisting Granmam and they continued to discuss the possibility.

They made juice from rose hips and elderberries as Granmam mumbled about female troubles and childbed fevers. She told about difficult pregnancies and complicated deliveries, recalling breech-births and babies born with the cord wrapped around their necks. Karen noticed that when Big-Anne talked about being a midwife, she didn't mince words. At the same time, she never mentioned names and never gossiped about her patients. Karen appreciated being treated as an adult and her respect for her grandmother's knowledge grew. One day, she asked why so many people used euphemisms to discuss pregnancy and illnesses, but had to explain what the word meant.

"Eufism, smu-fism, you can't treat something if you can't talk about it," Granmam explained. "If you're going to be any help to me you need to learn to call a spade a spade. But never forget that most women are not comfortable talking about themselves and you have to respect their sensibilities. The trick is to listen hard and help them tell you what is really wrong."

Although June through November were the busiest months of the year for Big-Anne and her services were called on several times each week, there had yet been no need for Karen's help. Most of the women had at least a mother, sister, or best friend who came for the birth and took charge of the household while the midwife attended the woman in labor. Indeed, it was common for a newly married woman whose man was at sea to live in her mother's house at least through the birth of the first child. When Frederik was born, Karen had seen that a lying-in was a social event that called for many women, as well as an expert midwife like Granmam. Karen despaired of ever being allowed to help, but Big-Anne assured her that the day would come. Meanwhile she had plenty to learn.

There was a constant stream of women of all ages, pregnant or not, to Big-Anne's bedroom, which she used for consultation. Although she was licensed to deliver most babies on her own, she was conscientious about referring any serious problems to the doctor. For minor medical problems, outside her profession, she was willing to give what she carefully called 'neighborly advice.' The doctor himself was not above consulting her about this or that or referring patients with a prescription for an infusion or one of her famous elixirs. Boys of all ages came to her door for help with their skinned knees or fish-hooked fingers. They seemed more willing to confess their clumsiness to her than to the 'foreign' doctor and they stoically submitted to her thorough cleaning, stinging ministrations, and sharp tongue.

Karen understood the boys' confidence in her skill. When her monthly flow had started a few years ago, she had run in panic to Granmam rather than Mam. Big-Anne answered her questions in a straightforward manner and told her what she needed to know.

Then Granmam had added, "It may seem unpleasant and a big nuisance to become a woman. But don't let anyone tell you it is the curse of Eve, for having children is God's blessing. Nothing worthwhile is ever won without a price." Karen would never forget what she had said. Now, seeing Kirsten-Mos's glowing face whenever she looked at Frederik, she could only agree that babies were indeed a blessing.

School started and Lil-Anne began first grade. On the first day, she waited outside for Mam and Karen to walk with her, new slate proudly tucked under one arm. The slate, Karen had told Lil-Anne, was for practicing her letters and numbers.

"I don't know my numbers so good, are you sure I'll be all right?" Lil-Anne asked.

"You aren't expected to know everything the first day, " Karen told her, giving her hand a comforting squeeze. Usually Lil-Anne had warm soft hands, but today they were stiff and cold. "That's why we go to school, to learn new stuff. You're a smart girl, so don't let anyone tell you there's something you can't do."

The school buildings were located at the south side of town, at the edge of the Fuzzy Mountains. The main building for the older children looked like most of the other houses in town, a long box of red brick running from west to east. It was a relatively new building with 1866 proudly written across the western end. The long north side had two green double doors through which the children marched into *æ frankel* leading to their classrooms. Above each door there was a small gable with a squat window into the storage loft under the thick thatch roof. Twelve white-trimmed windows on this side matched by fourteen on the sunny south side brightly lit the classrooms. In front of the building, the sand had been leveled for a playground and planted with wizened grass. Across the playground from the main building was a smaller version housing the primary school that Lil-Anne was to attend.

Stine Thatcher stood in the door to welcome her pupils with a big smile and shake hands with each one. As they went by, the girls bobbed slightly at the knees and the boys nodded their heads. She called them by name, knowing them all, new as well as returning children. Karen was glad that at least Lil-Anne would start here and not have to be stifled by Teacher Madsen for several more years. Karen vowed that no one would be allowed to squash her little sister's free spirit and wonderful imagination. There had to be a way to convince girls that they were just as smart as boys and could be more than just future mothers. Perhaps Karen should become a teacher. *Nah. Then I'll be stuck here forever and never get to see the world.*

Lil-Anne clung a little at the last minute, but she really had no reason to be afraid. She had hung around the playground with Karen, the teacher was Mam's friend, and she had known the other children her whole life. One shy foreign girl was noticeable because she wore no Fanø bonnet. Her papa was the new smith in town and the family had moved to Sønderho at the beginning of the summer. Lil-Anne had met Sidsel a couple of times, so now she squared her shoulders, adjusted her slate, and went over to the little girl.

Lil-Anne took Sidsel by the hand and said, "You can come with me. Our teacher is Stine Thatcher and she's really nice. You can do this. Don't forget to curtsey and shake hands. That's how it's done."

They shook hands with Teacher and were swallowed by first grade. Karen and Mam stood there, amazed by this new Lil-Anne. There was nothing for them to do but go back home, missing their little ray of sunshine already.

At the end of the day, Lil-Anne walked back to Millfarm with the Jensen girls; they were older and knew the way. "Teacher had me read out loud and said I did fine," she announced as soon as she was in the door. "We all counted numbers together; I can do that." Then she proudly showed them her slate where she had printed 'ANNE' three times. The letters had been half erased by her elbow, when she had carried the slate under her arm. They were so crooked that the last 'E' was missing because there wasn't enough room. But she was proud.

Karen was going to walk her the next morning but Lil-Anne told her, "You don't have to go with me. I'm in first grade now and I can do that."

Papa laughed, "'I can do that' is going to be her favorite saying."

Seventeen

Storyteller

As September slipped into October, the weather turned colder and indoor activities shifted from the northrooms to the brighter and warmer southrooms. Though the stoves here would only rarely be fired for several more months, shawls were brought out and the oil lamp lit in the afternoon. The spinning of wool and the knitting of socks and mittens began in earnest to ready hands and feet for the coming winter.

The outdoor chores also shifted. First came the slaughtering of animals, all falling to the knife, except the sheep and those that would bear young in the spring. Larger pieces of meat were smoked or preserved in spices and brine; the rest was chopped and stuffed into cleaned animal intestines. These sausages were salted in big crocks, hung in the loft to dry, or smoked in the scullery chimneys. Suet and beef blood were mixed into blood-sausage, pigs feet were gelled, hides were scraped and larger pieces sent on the *everts* to be sold in Ribe. Nothing was wasted. Eggs were washed, wrapped in paper, and placed in big crocks in cellar pantries; while sheep fat was rendered for soap and melted tallow was poured into molds for everyday candles.

Else Jensen was the town beekeeper. All summer, the bees had been busily gathering pollen from the purple heather that covered the central part of the island. Now it was time to extract honey and wax from the hives. Sønderhonings were slightly suspicious of Else's magical power over the swarming bees, but Karen had hung around these fall chores since she was little and had no more fear of being stung than the bee-mistress. This year, when as usual, Mam sent Karen over to help in exchange for a share of the golden harvest, she protested, "I'm busy in the office. You should have asked me first." Mam said, "Nevertheless."

Fortunately, Karen was all caught up with the flurry of mill receipts brought by the grain harvest, and she enjoyed working with Else. For several mornings, they took trays of combs dripping with honey out of the hives, being careful to leave food enough to feed the bees over the winter. They drained the honey and poured it into jars, then cleaned the wax and put it aside before replacing the empty trays. At the end of next month Else would pack straw around the hives to insulate them against the winter cold, but that was a job quickly done without needing Karen's help. The wax would be saved and later made into special candles. Else took special pride in her skill in dipping the braided wicks into the melted wax to produce the beautiful creamy tapers that would decorate church and farms for Christmas and Easter. This year, she promised that Karen would be allowed to make a few candles of her own, instead of being banned from the scullery lest she overturn the kettle of hot wax and burn herself.

Finally they were done and Else filled a basket with honey jars for Karen to bring home. As Karen returned to Millfarm, she ran into the postman and he handed her two envelopes, with the wink that signaled a letter from Peter.

"I just have to put the honey jars in the pantry, then I'll be right there," Karen replied cheerfully to Mam's call to come to dinner. "There's a letter from Christian."

"You certainly are in a good mood today," Lars-Anne said.

After dinner, Karen politely listened to the reading of her brother's letter. Although he dutifully wrote the required page once a week, it was hard to tell from his few sentences how he liked school. This time, he sent greetings from Ingrid-Fas and the two cousins since he had been invited to their house for Sunday dinner. He reported that she was now feeling well and enjoyed being able to go for short walks. "She says it would not be fitting for her to leave the garden but she seems fit enough to me," he wrote. The rest of his letter contained the usual complaints about the food and perennial requests for more money. Karen barely contained her impatience to be off to Southhouse where she could read Peter's letter without irritating Mam.

Her aunt was sitting in front of the window, her lace-making pillow in her lap. Her chair was between her two prize possessions, her son asleep in his cradle and the tile picture of the *Marianne* on the wall. "Don't wake Frederik," she whispered. "Did you hear from Peter? Mine came this morning, it's from Dutch Guyana."

"Mine too. I guess they've started the trip south on their way to round the Horn."

Big-Anne came into the room carrying a pot of coffee. It was another blustery day and too wet to work outdoors. The baby's diapers and clothes hung in the loft but would take hours more to dry, so she poured a cup of coffee for herself and Kirsten and settled in her chair with her knitting. Kirsten pointed with a lace-bobbin at Karen, who was sitting in a corner reading her letter. Big-Anne nodded and smiled, remaining silent because of the sleeping baby.

Ever since his sad letter about the burial at sea, Peter's letters were wonderful. He wrote delightful and funny descriptions of everything that he was experiencing, but he also added personal notes about his feelings and plans. His loneliness and longing for home shone through his delight in telling stories of strange places and wonderful people. This letter was no exception. After a colorful description of the Dutch colony of Guyana he went on, "This trip will make me rich enough to do whatever I want." He was a little vague about exactly what that was. Perhaps like Karen, he didn't yet know; perhaps his promise to Papa still lingered between them. Meanwhile the great adventure of rounding the Horn was ahead. He wrote, "I've been reading Richard Dana's 'Two Years before the Mast' in order to prepare. Perhaps you can find a Danish translation."

Won't he be surprised by how much English I've already learned, she thought. *Maybe Pastor will let me study Dana next.*

After Frederik woke up and was fed, he settled on Karen's lap, content and apparently absorbed in the women's chatter. Kirsten-Mos needed little urging to read aloud the letter from Paul. It was interesting to hear Uncle's version of the Caribbean islands and the South American continent, but Karen didn't feel he had Peter's talent for storytelling. A little self-consciously, she opened her letter from Peter again. Putting Frederik on Granmam's lap, she read aloud:

> *In the seventeenth century, the Dutch traded colonies with the British. In exchange for 'Niew Amsterdam' in North America, they settled in Guyana and transferred the name to the capitol. The English renamed their northern colony 'New York' and everyone knows that they got the better part of the bargain.*
>
> *The estuary of the Surinam River is incredibly beautiful and nothing like I have ever seen before. Wild animals come down to the shore to graze. Green parrots and a smaller variety in all colors, parakeets I think, fill the air with raucous cries. Large black cormorants swim along the islands to fish in the river. They are ugly birds compared to Danish storks. You cannot swim here—the water is filled with hungry crocodiles and poisonous snakes.*

Karen read on. She was in the midst of his amusing description of a Creole flower girl who, in sing-song fractured Dutch, had a hand-waving argument with a Jewish merchant and his East-Indian factor, when Tante-Black dropped in with a plate of warm cardamom bread.

"Read it again," Kirsten-Mos pleaded and, handing their guest a cup, added, "You have to hear this, it's very funny."

Karen hesitated but there was no way out. Kirsten-Mos was so naive, little realizing that Peter's letter would quickly become juicy town gossip. Tante-Black would go home and tell her sisters, then Tante-Brown and Tante-Blue would tell everyone else, and Mam would be furious. The town would be ready and waiting for the Yes-party the minute Peter stepped off the *Marianne*.

The story *was* funny and Karen enjoyed reading aloud, so maybe it wasn't all bad. At the end of the impromptu party, she promised to bring another letter the next day. Peter had written a great story about the mighty Mississippi River and a Negro riverboat captain, black as the ace of spades....

From that day, on cold afternoons, the neighbors would drop in to hear Karen read aloud from Peter's letter. Sometimes she did some quick editing to leave out parts she didn't think he would want to share with everybody. On occasion, she retold the story in her own words when she felt it could be funnier or more dramatic and soon developed skill at drawing in her listeners. Her audience grew to fill Kirsten-Mos' southroom and they never seemed to tire when she had to retell anecdotes again and again because her treasury of letters was still quite small. Sometimes someone would bring a letter from a husband or son at sea to share with the group. Neither these writers nor readers had the talents of the Peter-Karen combination, and soon Karen was asked to pick out the kernels of drama from the chaff of reports on the comings and goings of ships in foreign ports, and weave them together into an entertaining story.

Mam, of course, came to Southhouse out one day on an errand and was indeed furious. At supper, she looked about to say 'certainly not' and Karen was readying a stubborn 'nevertheless' when Papa intervened with a suggestion that she also entertain the family at Millfarm with her tales.

Karen embellished Christian's summer adventures into a story of 'The boy who ran away to sea and learned to cook.' Although everyone recognized the source and was therefore doubly amused, Karen left out the embarrassing private family parts and created a tale acceptable even to Mam. Peter's sad tale of the young man who died of yellow fever was a favorite, however. This too had to be edited but even the bare facts spoke for themselves—a story to which all could relate since most of the town had lost a friend or relative to the diseases of the tropics. Tante-Brown and Tante-Blue nodded wisely when the dangers of the night-miasma were mentioned, perhaps confusing tropical diseases with Danish legends of fairies luring the lonely night traveler to deadly revels.

One night, Papa read aloud from the *Fanø Weekly*. The paper had started a column entitled 'Letters to Home' and encouraged readers to submit letters from the far-flung community. This week's contribution was about the evils of the African slave market. Although the story itself was interesting, the writing was so self-righteous and moralistic that Lil-Anne fell asleep during the first boring paragraph.

"Why don't you send in one of Peter Larsen's stories?" Papa said.

"I couldn't do that without asking him, and it would take months before he could reply," Karen protested.

Mam, for once accepting the situation, had practical advice. "Would a newspaper column be any worse than telling his stories all over Sønderho? Why don't you write one of them up and send it to Bodil Larsen? Ask her what she thinks."

Lil-Anne had apparently been listening after all and had the last word. "Tell Peter's mam my favorite about the flower lady fighting with the skinny Indian with the turban. I never heard of a man wearing a Fanø scarf. That's so funny."

The next morning, she sent Mrs. Larsen in Nordby Lil-Anne's favorite story and asked her opinion of submitting it to the paper. Two weeks later she had her answer when Peter's story appeared. The mailman was grinning from ear to ear when he delivered the paper and showed everyone the byline: 'Peter Larsen as retold by Karen Andersen.' "The whole town is talking about the two of you," he reported gleefully and poked Karen familiarly in the ribs.

This wasn't quite how Karen had intended it to happen but it was too late now. The whole situation was out of control. What good was Papa's confidence that oceanic distance would keep Peter and her out of trouble when Providence contrived his own disasters? There was no way out. She would have to confess the whole mess to Peter in her next installment. Maybe he would never write again.

She stared at the words: 'as retold by Karen Andersen,' thrilled to see her name in print. *Next time, I'll tell them my name is Karen Andersdatter,* she decided.

Eighteen

Sightings

The last of the big fall chores came in the middle of October with the digging of the late vegetables: carrots, onions, cabbages and finally the potatoes. The few horses in town were put to hard use plowing and loosening the long rows of hilled plants, while those with smaller fields had to dig by hand. Then began the backbreaking labor of collecting the tubers into baskets. The Sønderho girls who had left last May for summer work were still on the mainland, so every hand remaining on the island was needed for this final harvest. It was cold and miserable work, especially on wet blustery days when blue hands, more chilled than warmed by sodden, fingerless gloves, had to search through the even colder soil to rescue the precious tubers on which winter meals depended.

The best part of the potato harvest was that its end signaled the return of the young girls. They arrived in noisy, laughing boatloads from their summer jobs, each carrying a small sack of wages innermost in her little bundle of belongings. Each moved back to her childhood home to await the return from the sea of sweetheart or last spring's new husband, the hard-earned money carefully placed at the bottom of her chest.

Gerda was one of the first girls to return from the mainland. She came to Millfarm to help her sister, Girl-Ellen, but Karen thought her more interested in hanging around Mam. Karen was irritated though she should have been used to what happened every fall. Past generations of Mam's household helpers dropped by to ask advice about how to do this or that, or to chat about their latest young man—all on the pretext of 'helping out.' Karen didn't get it. What would make anyone volunteer to work in someone else's house? What was the great attraction? What made Mam such a queen-bee to the young girls in town? Talk of bossy!

Gerda was no exception, telling stories about the farm on Sylt where she had been a milkmaid, how big it was, how stingy the food, and how bossy the mistress. Mam came in from the scullery carrying the oil lamp she had been cleaning. She hung it over the table by the window and started to fuss over the potted geraniums in the windowsill—the only non-functional decorations in her otherwise spare living room. Gerda and Ellen were scraping rust off the iron stove with wire brushes to ready it for a coating of stove-black and Gerda was going on and on about how Lars-Anne was so much more organized than her summer-mistress. Her vigorous scraping punctuated her words as if she were ridding herself of bad memories with the flakes of rust gathering on the newspaper on the floor.

Karen was sitting in the study struggling to find an arithmetic error in her latest ledger entries while listening to the conversation between the two sisters through the open door to the southroom. She waited to hear if Gerda would talk about her Klaus, who had not yet returned from the sea, but his name was never mentioned. Was it all over between them? Or was there to be a Yes-party as soon as he returned? Perhaps Gerda didn't know either. She certainly seemed edgy enough whenever a ship was sighted. She probably hadn't heard from Klaus all summer, he wasn't much of a scholar. Not like Peter. No one could write like him.

Karen's pen, poised above the ledger to correct the error that she was searching for, took fate into its own hand and dripped a splotch of ink onto the page. Karen tore off a corner of blotting paper with an irritated sigh and sponged up the little pool. As soon as it was dry, she slammed the ledger shut in disgust.

"I'm going to Granmam's," she announced to the startled workers as she marched through the southroom on her way to *æ frankel*. She had been so quiet they were unaware that she had been in the next room, overhearing every uninteresting word.

"Wait for me," Gerda called after her, jumping up and throwing the wire brush to the floor. "A needs to go to town too."

They stopped at the well to wash the ink and soot from their hands. Karen was tempted to start pumping Gerda about Klaus, but she waited until they were on the Westerlands path to town. Having learned something from Papa about how to make people talk, she restrained herself and merely said, "You must be glad to be home. Did you have had a rough time this summer?"

"Nah, it was all right. I didn't have it bad like one of the milkmaids on the next farm. From Nordby she was. The farmer's son nearly took advantage of her, but then she sort of led him on. She took off her Fanø scarf for the harvest dance and walked out with him after he had too much beer. Lars-Anne warned me not to do that. She said if I wore my Fanø scarf, the men would respect me. But this girl wanted to be popular like the Holsteiner girls. It was only when she screamed for help that he took her seriously and let her go. Nothing like that happened to me, but then A let'em all know that A had an understanding with Klaus back home."

What do you know, Papa's way works, Karen thought triumphantly. She could barely contain her curiosity to learn more, but aloud she just said, "That helped?"

"Oh yes, not that Klaus and me really have an understanding; just sort of, you know. But the men left me alone after that. It didn't keep me from having fun after quitting time and at the dance, though. You should go to Sylt, it's a great island. Like here, just bigger."

Yeah, like here but stolen from Denmark by the Germans, Karen protested silently. "Didn't it bother you that they make you speak German?"

"Nah, Master was Danish and likes to hire Danish girls for the summer; just his nasty wife was German. But she wasn't really that bad, just not as good a mistress as Lars-Anne. Well, A'm turning off here to go to the Inn. A want to hear if Old Captain Rasmussen has heard anything from his son. Klaus is on their ship. Will you be at the dance this Sunday?"

Without waiting for an answer Gerda disappeared down a path winding between two houses, leaving Karen to savor her newfound ability to find out what she wanted to know without saying much; just like Papa. Maybe, she thought, someday she could even get Mam to talk to her.

As she often did in odd moments, Karen wrote an imaginary letter to Peter. She would tell him about Gerda and her Klaus to see if he would take the hint. She wondered if she should go to the first fall dance this Sunday. Well if Gerda could have fun even though she had a 'sort of understanding' with Klaus, then why shouldn't Karen? Maybe she wouldn't write that part to Peter.

October was also the month when, one by one, the masts of the returning Sønderho fleet rose over the horizon. Old Captain Rasmussen was Customs Inspector and usually was the first to sight an arriving ship from his perch in the dormer of his second-floor window and call down the news to the first passer-by on the path below. As if carried by the west wind, word spread almost instantly around town and a crowd gathered below on the dirt street, until Rasmussen called out the name of a long-awaited bark or brig. The crowd then split: the children and young girls running out to the Hen to be the first to greet returning father, sweetheart, or friend. Meanwhile, wives and mothers hurried home to raise the welcome-home flags, put the last polish on spotless homes, and light the fires for homecoming dinners. The crowd at the Hen could have a long or a short wait depending on the vagaries of the wind, but eventually a welcome sight would round the point and make its way from the 'Hard-Deep,' and sail up the channel towards Sønderho harbor. The ship's railing would be lined with cheering seamen and the shore with those waiting to welcome them home. However long it took until the gangplank could be lowered, whether the ship had to tack or she were racing before a brisk following wind, whether she were the first to arrive, or the last to return before the bad weather, all cheered until every throat was hoarse. Final greetings on the beach often had to be completed in whispers.

One day, when Rasmussen lingered over his morning coffee at the Inn, an eager youngster ran into the dining room. Only at the last minute did he remember to kick off his clogs at the door, arriving at the Captain's table barefoot and breathless, barely able to deliver his message, "A seen a big'un crossing the Hard-deep."

The Captain grabbed his coat, made his way to his house next door and ran up the stairs to his airy loft, the eager boy at his side. One look through his spyglass confirmed that a ship was indeed on its way, but the identity was a disappointment. "It's just a fishing tub, loaded with cod," he called down to the upturned faces on the street below. The crowd quickly dispersed until the next sighting and the over-anxious boy slunk off to school.

That afternoon, Karen had no sooner stepped into Kirsten-Mos's south-room than her unusually agitated aunt greeted her with, "I'm glad you're here. Smith's little Sidsel came for Big-Anne, her mam needs her but she's with Stine Madsen. Sidsel didn't know where Stine lives, so please go after her and show her the way. Take Frederik with you and I'll go to Smith's house and see what I can do until she comes."

Kirsten had barely blurted out her confused message and handed Karen the surprised Frederik, when she was gone. Karen kicked off her slippers, re-donned her clogs, and went out the door, her cousin riding on her hip. She found little Sidsel halfway to Stine's house, sitting in the middle of the dirt path and sobbing, lost in the confusion of the winding pathways between nearly identical houses.

"A can't find it," she hiccupped, rubbing her eyes with grubby hands. "Mam needs her, and A can't find it."

Karen sat down next to Sidsel with Frederik between her legs. She pulled a handkerchief from her sleeve and wiped the little girl's face. "It'll be fine, you'll see. I'm Lil-Anne's sister, Karen, and I'll make sure Big-Anne gets the message. You just go home and tell your mam that we'll be there soon. Your house is down the end of that path and to the left. It'll be all right." The little girl sniffed once more, but scampered off in the right direction.

Karen and Frederik found the Madsen house in an uproar. Captain Madsen had returned the week before to find his wife twice as big as when he sailed in February and his five children running wild from lack of a father's firm hand. "Shut up," he roared at them as if he were still on his quarterdeck, pounding the table in the northroom so hard the coffee cup jumped on its saucer. Just then his mother came from the kitchen carrying a pitcher full of hot water and tripped over the youngest boy. The soaking boy sat down hard on the floor surrounded by broken pitcher and yelled like a stuck pig. The other four siblings joined hands and danced around their dripping brother, chanting a nursery rhyme.

Karen quickly closed the door on the chaos and comforted the startled baby Frederik, who in his short life had never seen so much confusion. They beat a hasty retreat through *æ frankel* and into the southroom beyond. Here, under Big-Anne's firm rein, peace reigned. Stine's sister was quietly sponging off a baby girl, whose protesting cries were almost drowned out by the noise from the next room. Big-Anne blocked Karen's view of Stine in the tightbed built into the end wall, but her soothing, quiet murmurs assured that all was well.

"Ah, Karen," Big-Anne said without turning around, as if she had eyes in the back of her head. "Go do something with those children. Get them out of the house so we can have some peace."

Karen quickly explained her errand and Big-Anne changed her orders. "We're almost done here. You," she added pointing with the peak of her scarf-covered head towards Stine's sister, "Give the baby to Stine to suck and tell the Captain that he can come in and see his new daughter." Then pointing to Karen she added, "Bring the children to Smith's house and tell Lone that I'll be there as soon as I can. Then take the children and Lone's Sidsel out somewhere. I don't care where, just get them all out of our way."

Karen was about to protest that she couldn't possibly manage six children plus Frederik, but Big-Anne must have read her mind for she said, "You can figure it out."

And it came about as Big-Anne commanded. Karen shifted the wide-eyed Frederik higher on her hip, took the now-dry youngest Madsen child with her other hand, and lured the remaining four away from admiring their new baby sister. She promised to tell them exciting adventures, as she made sure they were all bundled against the October winds. On her way out the door she saw the proud father unlock the corner cupboard and take out a bottle of port and two cigars, one for himself and one for his mother.

They crossed the street in front of Brinch's store on the way to Lone's house and ran into an excited Gerda. "Klaus is coming, Klaus is coming. A's going to the Hen," she called out as she dashed by.

"Hey, wait," Karen yelled. When Gerda stopped until they caught up with her, she added more quietly "Do me a favor and take these children with you. It's going to be hours yet before the ship comes in, and I have to go to the smithy to pick up Sidsel. Then I'll join you."

Gerda took over the gaggle of excited children as if they were her own younger siblings and herded them firmly towards the Hen.

Smith was by his forge, puttering distractedly with his tools. The fire was lit, and Sidsel was pumping half-heartedly at the bellows. There were no iron rods in the fire, so Karen suspected Sidsel had been given the job to keep her occupied.

Karen lifted the latch on the front door and stooped under the lintel to the house. There was no emergency here; Kirsten and Lone were calmly knitting by the window in the southroom. Frederik broke into a big smile when he saw his mam and wriggled all over with joy. He settled contentedly in Kirsten-Mos's lap, sneaking a comforting thumb into his mouth, and immediately fell asleep having had enough adventure for one day.

"This is Karen from Millfarm," Kirsten explained.

Lone Smith smiled and offered her hand. Her blond hair was in a neat bun at the back of her head, the lack of scarves proclaiming her a foreigner from the mainland. Karen, on those rare occasions when she needed to be introduced to a stranger, was usually pointed out as 'Miller's daughter' so she almost turned around to see whom Kirsten meant. "I'm Lil-Anne's sister," she said for the second time in one day and shook the proffered hand. Then she explained that Big-Anne would be there shortly and that she was taking Sidsel to the Hen. Old Captain Rasmussen's ship had just been sighted.

"At least you have a nice day for being outside," Lone smiled and, pointing to some old cotton quilts in the corner, added, "You'd better take some of those blankets along in case there's a breeze on the point." Then she caught her breath as another contraction came on.

Outside by the forge, Karen found Lil-Anne playing with Sidsel and the three of them walked to the Hen where they found Gerda and the children settled on top of a dune.

"There she is; the for'ner," the eldest of Stine's children taunted, pulling one of Sidsel's long braids, whereupon his siblings joined hands and chanted until their new victim started to cry.

"No she isn't. She's my friend. You leave her be," Lil-Anne staunchly defended her friend. She would have launched herself at the teasers, except that Karen quickly grabbed her sister's arm.

"This is going to be a long day," Karen thought and looked around desperately for something with which to distract everyone. Gerda came to her rescue. "A hear you tell great stories," she said.

"Yes, tell us'n a story," the children begged and changed their chant to, "Sto-ry, sto-ry, sto-ry...."

Karen made them all sit down and Gerda arranged them in a circle at the storyteller's feet. Glancing at the expectant faces, including Gerda's, Karen had an idea.

"This is a true story of two men, both called Klaus, who lived in the same village," she began with a grin.

"Is this on Gerda's Klaus? Is this from Peter's letter?" the children asked in chorus.

"No, be quiet," Lil-Anne commanded, "this is one of Uncle Hans's stories. The one about rich Big Klaus and Lil-Klaus. Lil-Klaus is poor but smart and fools the other one by...."

"Who's telling this story?" Karen asked with mock severity. "And you know perfectly well that Hans Christian Andersen isn't our uncle."

"Well, I want him to be," Lil-Anne mumbled. "I can pretend, can't I?"

Karen noticed that a crowd of adults and children that were waiting for the ship had gathered at the foot of the dune. She paused while everyone settled and then went on, raising her voice so all could hear, "Big Klaus had four horses and Little Klaus only one. All week Little Klaus had to plough for Big Klaus...."

The returning ship was indeed that of Captain Rassmussen and his son. Gerda's Klaus was on board and gave Gerda a resounding smack on the cheek, lifting her high off the ground in a big bear hug. He did the same to all the girls and would have included Karen, if she'd let him. Then he went home to greet his mother and was not seen again until Sunday, leaving the gossips to draw their own conclusions about him and Gerda.

In Sønderho, the cycle of life was reflected in the church services, with baptisms throughout the summer and funerals in winter, but October and November were filled with celebrations for the return of the men. Except for the exuberant public reception at the harbor, a homecoming was private. Not until the following Sunday would the newly restored family groups emerge from their houses and promenade to church. They would wend their way down narrow paths to converge along the main street into a dignified procession. Each returned father was dressed in his best clothes, his proud wife clinging to his arm. Seamen sons followed, trailed by excited daughters and children. The women were dressed in silk finery, scarf ends bristling on the tops of their head. Their faces shone with happiness, but they carefully walked without a hint of 'swishing,' mindful of friends whose husbands would return no more.

The rest of the congregation came early, the men standing outside to greet friends they had not seen for six months with hearty slaps on the back. The boys clustered around the captains hoping their heroes would say a kind word or tell a salty tale. The wives pushed their daughters before them out of earshot and entered the vestibule to have their finery inspected and critiqued by the town gossips. Only then could everyone proceed into the church and the service begin.

Pastor Engel fluttered up the aisle of the nave, joyfully greeting his flock now being restored to full strength. He hardly knew which family to greet or which baby to bless first. His fall sermons usually rambled on about children and families sprinkled with a few prodigal sons. Everyone followed his words with rapt attention. Despite tragedies and tensions of still awaited ships, all was well in Sønderho and the love of the shepherd for his flock was unstintingly returned.

Mam was always aloof during this time of year, as if she could not decide between pride that her husband was at her side every week, or envy that she had no special chance to show off her handsome man. Karen usually looked forward to these fall celebrations, but this year she was irritated by the triumphant smiles of wives and sweethearts. She watched Gerda and Little-Klaus closely at services the first Sunday after his return, but both circumspectly avoided any eye contact lest the town jump to conclusions. He came with his family, she with hers, and there was no hint of any agreement.

Karen's sympathy was with the anxious-looking women whose men had not yet come back or those in new widow's weeds whose husbands would never return. She thought of Peter, who by was by now somewhere off the tip of South America. Rounding the Horn was dangerous. His last letter had come from the Falklands weeks ago. They had been waiting for a good wind, but she was not yet expecting even a telegram announcing the safe arrival of the *Marianne* in the Pacific Ocean. First they would have to sail up the west coast of South America to a port with a telegraph office, or to meet a ship coming in the other direction that would take a message to the Falklands.

Not many Fanø ships ventured to the Pacific. They preferred the relative safety of the waters off the African or North American continents to the more lucrative but chancier distant shores on the other side of the world. She turned her eyes onto the *Marie* hanging by the pulpit, as if keeping the image in her heart would keep Peter safe.

The dance on the Sunday evening after Klaus's return kept the town gossips busy all week. Karen went out of curiosity, and had a constant round of eager partners, most of whom stepped on her feet. They were all very boring. Of more interest was Mette's new circle of admirers. Her sixteenth nameday had been last month and the unmarried men swarmed around her. Soon the darknin' evenings would see lanterns approaching the front door of the Cockeyed house and one shy sailor after another would knock to seek 'advice' from Mette's parents, suddenly recognizing their superior wisdom.

Although Klaus and Gerda came and left the dance separately, they were constant companions throughout the evening, dancing with luminous intimacy or sitting on the sidelines holding hands and gazing raptly into each other's eyes. No one else tried to dance with Gerda, but Karen fully expected that if someone had, Klaus would have dismissed his competitor with a tone rivaling that of Cinderella's Prince. She bet that within only a few Sundays, Klaus would walk to church with Gerda's family. They would have the first Yes-party of the year, then Klaus would move to Gerda's house, the bands would be read, and a wedding would follow as soon after Christmas as they could get a Royal letter. It was all just as expected and Karen found it very boring.

Nineteen

November Market

It was a good thing that Lil-Anne was not allowed to come to the November Market in Ribe; the family would have had to spend the whole time worrying about where she was. Since starting school she had become very independent and was seldom where she was supposed to be. When Mam complained that Lil-Anne was becoming irresponsible like Christian, Papa pointed out that she was just growing up.

"But she's a girl," Mam said, as if that explained anything.

When they sailed away in the *Lene,* tearful Lil-Anne stood on the beach, clutching Granmam's hand. In Ribe, Christian met them at the dock, school having been dismissed in honor of the fair, and the four of them wandered around the colorful market along the banks of the river. The baker's boy, weaving in and out among the booths, carried a tray of warm rolls with which to tempt customers. Hawkers called out prices for everything from kettles to leather belts. Well-dressed burghers mingled with stolid farmers in wooden shoes and their wives in folk costumes from different parts of the region. The women from Fanø stood out with their kerchiefs.

Papa was, as usual, excited about the history. "Just imagine, there's been a market here beside the Nipsaa since the Stone Age—eons before the Vikings," he exclaimed. "The first settlers probably came down here to trade flint axes and arrowheads—and willow baskets just like that one." He pointed down in front of his feet where a woman sat surrounded by baskets, rug beaters, and coat hangers.

"This is made of bamboo, not willow," Mam pointed out, slicing the air with a rug beater, as if she were testing a sword for balance. "I'll take it," she said, giving it to Anders.

"You get the idea," Papa laughed, handing the women some coins, while Mam went next door to examine a bowl at the potter's booth.

After a lunch of sausage and cheese, which they ate at a small table in front of one of the busy restaurants, they walked up and down the narrow streets, admiring the old houses. "They look just like the houses in Rotterdam," Christian explained. "The narrow gable-side faces the street, except in Ribe they're much wider."

Papa started to explain that Ribe wasn't as crowded as the cities in Holland so street-front property was not at a premium, but Karen and Lars-Anne took his arms on either side and pulled him away—they were here for shopping, not history lessons.

After a few more purchases, they walked up the hill towards the Cathedral in the central square to have tea with Papa's sister Ingrid and her family. Uncle Thomas was an importer and lived with Ingrid-Fas and their two children in a three-storied, half-timbered house that was both business and home. The imposing corner building had wide gables facing onto one of the medieval streets that radiated from the center of town. The first story was the smaller, the second and third stories jutting out over the street, the whole structure supported by age-blackened oak beams as thick as Papa's whole body. Smaller beams crisscrossed the stucco walls and the roof crowned the building with cheerful red tiles. Karen was even more impressed with the ancient horse chestnuts towering over the large walled garden in back—she had never seen trees so majestic.

Papa explained, as he always did, that the house was about 350 years old, probably predating the disastrous town fire of 1580. "It's been in your

Uncle Thomas's family for 150 years and he's very proud of it. His office and store are on the first floor; the family lives in back and on the floors above."

A serving girl, new since Papa had been there last, answered the bell and bobbed when Anders introduced himself.

"Mr. Andersen, *Madame* is resting but will meet you and Master Christian in the sitting room for tea. I'm to show you up." She stopped uncertainly when she caught sight of Lars-Anne and Karen behind the Miller's broad back, and forgetting her mistress' tutoring said in a broad rural accent, "She didn't say naught about the ladies."

Fortunately, just then the children came clattering down the stair, the elder girl shushing her younger brother since Mama was resting. They greeted everyone, especially Karen and Christian whom they vaguely remembered from last year. Cousin Margrethe was eleven and a very serious young lady with a pale thin face and long delicate hands that she kept demurely clasped in front of her white pinafore. The hem of her dress was far enough above the top of her high-top shoes to allow the lacy trim of her pantaloons to show. She gave a small bob to her aunt and uncle, making the long corkscrew curls bounce on her neck. Papa bent down and let her kiss his whiskery cheek.

Cousin Jens was an exuberant eight, his white sailor suit askew and wrinkled. He shook hands politely enough, bowing a little at the waist and bringing his heels together with the faintest suggestion of a click. He squinted up at Karen and said, "I'm Jens; I'm eight. My real name is Johannes, but my mother thinks that sounds too German, so I'm a good old Danish 'Jens' for every day."

Karen smiled at the freckled eager face. "Our pastor's name is Johannes too, Pastor Johannes Engel. I like him very much and call him 'Papa Angel.' Only don't tell him I said so. He might not think it was funny."

The children dragged their cousins out to the garden to inspect the last roses of summer. Then they tiptoed to the top floor nursery to admire Margrethe's porcelain doll from Paris and Jens's rocking horse with a real horsehair mane. Margrethe showed Karen to a little room where a pitcher of water and clean towels were ready, in case she wanted to wash her hands and straighten her clothing before tea. The younger girl curiously watched her cousin take off and retie her headscarf so that none of her hair showed.

"Why do you and Aunt Anne wear those things?" she asked.

"Because of the wind. All the women in Sønderho wear them. Its traditional and reminds us who we are and to stand tall," Karen said, realizing she sounded just like Mam. Her younger cousin seemed more satisfied with the explanation than she herself had ever been.

"How can you do all that without a mirror?"

"At home, the mirror is in my mother's room so I learned to tie by feel. Looking in the mirror just makes it harder because everything is backwards."

Ingrid-Fas was waiting in the second-floor sitting room and greeted her niece and nephew warmly. Karen remembered her as a tall friendly woman, a more delicate and feminine version of her brother, with Papa's ready smile and affectionate nature. She was much more talkative, though. She was not as beautiful as Mam but looked very fashionable with her pale indoor complexion and a flowing white linen dress covered with lacy flounces. It was a comfortable looking 'tea gown,' designed for home-wear and meant to disguise her rounding figure.

Inspecting her niece, she exclaimed over how tall Karen had become. Although Karen usually disliked the habit grown-ups had of discussing her as if she were not there, her aunt now won her heart by proclaiming to her sister-in-law, "She looks so like you when we first knew you, such a lovely face. It's a good thing that she only takes after her papa in height—he's much too square for a girl. I recognize Anders's eyes and dimples, though. You two do make beautiful children." Barely pausing for breath she asked, "How are you all? When do I get to meet the famous Little-Anne? Do let her come next time you're in town."

Papa quietly brought her up-to-date in a few sentences, then said with a worried frown, "But you look so pale. Are you still feeling ill? We heard you were resting."

"One has felt rotten, but one is better now," Ingrid-Fas replied. "The Doctor tells me I must rest and rest. It's a great nuisance, interferes dreadfully with one's social life, but then I can't appear in public anymore, anyway. We're thrilled and hope that this time...."

At this point, Uncle Thomas came in to join them. They chatted about other things for a while, the subject finally turning to books. "I do love to read," Ingrid-Fas enthused. "And now with all my resting, I am just going through everything I can lay my hands on."

"Karen is the one with the books," Lars-Anne said with a pride that surprised Karen. "I don't have time and Anders hardly reads other than the newspaper."

Ingrid-Fas turned to Karen, "Tell me, what have you read that's interesting?" She seemed impressed when Karen mentioned Bishop Grundtvig. "Of course, our Pastor doesn't approve of all his reforms. Rector at the Latin School thinks there is not enough drill in Grundtvigian educational philosophy. He says, 'Children are naturally lazy. If we do not make them memorize, they learn nothing.' Of course, Rector only talks about educating boys; girls interest him not at all. But we aren't all lazy, are we Anders? Some of us like to learn; we don't need someone to tell us what books to study in order to be educated."

At this point, Uncle Thomas, who had been otherwise silent, objected that he had graduated from the Latin School and it was the best thing that had ever happened to him. "After all, they have been educating boys for close to seven hundred years so they know what they are doing. No upstart reformer, even a bishop and barely a real one at that, should blather about educating the masses. And as for women, learning just makes them restless and they don't have the capacity."

"You'll have to admit Grundtvig wrote nice hymns and beautiful poetry," Ingrid-Fas countered.

"Well, I don't go much for poetry," Uncle grumbled.

And so it went all afternoon. There was more to Ingrid-Fas than idle chitchat. She had a genuine curiosity about the world and the people around her. Karen could see how her father had learned to be so quiet. As a child he had probably let his sister do all the talking.

All too soon, it was time to go. The family just had time to take Christian to his lodging before they had to catch the *Lene* for the return trip. Christian dutifully introduced Mam to Teacher Lehnfelt and his wife and then disappeared to be with his friends. Teacher looked exactly like Papa had described. He removed his *pince nez* with one hand while extending the other limply towards Lars-Anne. Motherly Mrs. Lehnfelt looked as if she had no trouble caring for all her adopted children.

Papa pulled Karen forward and said with a straight face, "This is our daughter Karen, another scholar for Latin School." He paused just long enough before smiling to savor the teacher's confusion.

Karen didn't know whether to grin or blush at Papa's foolishness. *Am I really this transparent?* she wondered.

The schoolmaster finally gave a dry little cough to acknowledge that he understood the joke. His wife had a better-developed sense of humor and laughing heartily. She offered tea but Mam declined, explaining that they had to catch the *evert* for home. Christian came to say good-bye, but kept his distance so there would be no embarrassing kisses in front of his friends.

The following week, Lars-Anne was preparing for St. Martin's Feast. She looked for Lil-Anne, late in coming home from school, again. "I'm used to it with you and Christian," Mam complained to Karen. "You two are always wandering off, but Lil-Anne has always been such a biddable child."

"She isn't any more biddable than I. She just hangs around the mill to be near Papa," Karen said. "She's probably at Sidsel's, like last time."

"She should come home from school first, so I know where she is. Nevertheless, I'm glad she isn't here because I wanted her out of the way while I kill the gander. She gets so upset when we slaughter any of her animals."

"She won't mind your killing this one; she hates him so much. She calls him 'Martin Goose' and looks forward to seeing him served up with plenty of gravy. Then she wants a new pillow from his feathers."

"Good, then she can do the plucking, it'll help her develop patience." With that, Mam instructed Karen to find Lil-Anne and bring her to Southhouse. "Keep her away until later in the afternoon."

Saint Martin's Day was the eleventh of November and a goose dinner with all the trimmings was traditionally served the evening before. Karen had always thought the feast was named for Martin Luther, but was surprised to learn in confirmation class that it had nothing to do with the German reformer. The holiday was from the Catholic Middle Ages and celebrated the saint-hood of the Bishop Martin of Tours in France. Papa always said, "It would take more than the Reformation to keep Danes from having a feast—even of a saint."

Karen smiled to herself as she walked towards the forge in search of her missing sister. She liked this holiday. Maybe this year she'd be allowed to make the *æbleskiver*—appleslices, those delicious fried puff balls that had nothing to do with apples and weren't even slices. By this time, she had wandered through the town and could see the smithy at the end of the path. Two little foreign girls were playing on the stoop to the house. She recognized little Sidsel's long braids, but the other child with the tussled blond curls must be visiting from the mainland. Then as she came closer, she realized with a start that the other child was Lil-Anne, without her bonnet.

"What are you thinking, looking like that?" she scolded as soon as she was close enough to be heard.

"Sidsel is always getting teased about being a for'ner," Lil-Anne answered. "I thought she could borrow my bonnet, but we couldn't get it on right. So I'm not going to wear mine. They wouldn't dare tease me. I'll just tell 'em, Christian'll beat 'em up."

"Christian isn't even here, how can he beat them up?"

"Well then, you do it," Lil-Anne said, jutting out her chin and looking defiantly up at her sister.

While Karen retied her sister's underscarf, she told the two girls who would be the guest of honor at the upcoming Feast. "Goody, I knew it," Lil-Anne said triumphantly and then added to her friend, "I better go home now, my other geese'll be upset. Besides, I have to start training the next leader. I'm bigger now and I can do that, 'sides it's a she so she won't be so mean. She wouldn't dare."

Ducking out from under Karen's arms, she added, "It's time I wore a grownup headscarf. Sidsel, you keep this," and with that she tore the bonnet from Karen's hands and handed it to her surprised friend.

Karen had to bite her lip to keep from laughing. Mindful of Mam's instructions, she started to call after the little girl who was scampered up the road, a clog in either hand, blond curls bouncing. Then she decided it was useless and let the child go home. What would she think of next? 'Biddable' was hardly the right word. *I should be more like that,* she thought. *Make up my own mind and just do it.*

Karen continued to Granmam's by way of Brinch's store, thinking about the ships that had not yet returned. Most of the seventy ships and men that had left Sønderho in the spring were now safely back for the winter, but not all of them would be coming home. Every year, some Sønderhonings settled in the fabled frontiers of the Americas or were seduced by a warmer climate. Then there were the dreaded telegrams of disasters at sea that came periodically. Too many men washed overboard, died from tropical diseases, or plunged from tall masts onto heaving decks below.

After Captain Rasmussen's son and their ship had arrived in late October, there had been no sightings for more than a week. Then several ships had straggled in with broken spars and tattered sails, reporting a bad storm in the English Channel. Two ships had been so damaged that they had to be left in the dry docks of Liverpool and their crews had taken the steamer *Esbjerg* home. Mette's uncle had returned from Africa with consumption and was not expected to survive the winter. Tante-Black's son Little Hans was sailmaker on the *Else-Marie* out of Nordby. Neither he nor his ship had yet been heard from.

Papa said last night that everyone was worried about the *Else-Marie.* Usually Anders Miller was too busy to gossip with the Captains on the Exchange by the harbor, but yesterday he had joined them on the bench for a brief chat.

"They've left it too late," Captain Rasmussen had declared authoritatively and puffed on his pipe. "After St. Martin's is not a good time to be on the Deep-Blue." The man had retired from the sea a good twenty years ago, but everyone nodded respectfully.

Anders usually stayed out of the ship-talk. but could not resist contributing his enthusiasm for the latest technology. "We should switch to steam, then we wouldn't be at the mercy of the weather." His opinion was greeted with a hoot, and Anders used an urgent errand as an excuse to escape the good-natured scorn the seamen heaped on their friend, the technology-happy landlubber.

At supper when he related this exchange to the family, he finished with, "Nevertheless, they'll see. The days of sail are finished and steam will take over."

Karen was 10,000 miles away, worrying about Peter, when a gust of wind carried her right into the arms of an equally distracted Hans Thatcher coming out of the post office. The telegram in his hand and the distress on his face was a portend of bad news. He barely stopped and, muttering an apology, hurried down the street. When he turned onto the path towards Kirsten-Mos's house, Karen, still full of thoughts about Peter, had a moment of panic. Then she realized that Papa, not Hans Thatcher, would be chosen to tell dreadful news to Kirsten. Karen followed Hans through the Southhouse door and was just in time to hear him asking Granmam to come with him to Tante-Black's house.

"She's going to take this hard," he was saying. "She doted on that boy."

Granmam, as usual sensing Karen's presence before she had a chance to say hello, said, "Karen, run to Pastor Engel and tell him to come quickly. Little-Hans has drowned. The *Else-Marie* foundered in a storm off Biscay Bay. Three of the dead were from Nordby—and then there was Little-Hans."

Karen ran all the way to the parsonage where Pastor's Ellen greeted her with a friendly, "Just in time for tea."

Pastor said, "Now that we have finished Dickens, I think we should read some Mark Twain in honor of Peter's adventures in the New World." Karen finally caught her breath enough to interrupt him with the dreadful news. He grabbed his Bible and was out the door.

"Please stay anyway," Ellen said. "You look like you need a cup of tea."

When they had settled in the parlor, Karen and Ellen discussed Tante-Black's tragedy and how this widow of fifteen years would now only have two sisters left of her family. Then they talked of the other tragedies of the season.

They sat silent for a few minutes, thinking of Tante-Black's family: five generations of Sønderho seamen, now at an end. They worried that in her grief she would crawl into her tightbed, turn towards the wall, and give up.

"Like Inger two years ago when her husband died." Ellen said. "We have to do something to show her that life goes on."

Karen changed to a more cheerful topic, "Pastor mentioned we might start reading Mark Twain, but I wondered if he has heard of Richard Dana. Peter recommends his book, *Two Years before the Mast,* about sailing around the Horn and life in California."

"I'll certainly ask him," Pastor's Ellen replied. "I'm sure his friend in England, Sir Donald, will be glad to get it for us." Then she pointed to a newspaper on the table. "Pastor saved his *London Times* for your papa. It has an interesting article on Dutch windmill design."

The two women studied the diagram before them. The Sønderho mill was called a *stubmølle*—stumpmill, because the main body of the mill rested on a stump. When the wind shifted, the miller manually rotated the whole tower by means of a heavy wooden boom until the attached wings faced into the wind. However, the diagram before them showed an ingenious design from Holland that used the wind to head the wings in the right direction.

"Papa will really enjoy this and start planning a new mill," Karen enthused. "I have to show him right after supper. Besides, I'll need a distraction for Mam; she gets so moody when there's bad news from the sea. This way she can fuss at Papa for his modernization schemes. She doesn't really mean it, but it gives her something else to think about."

Karen rolled the newspaper into a sausage and tucked it under one arm so it wouldn't blow away. Outside, it was already dusk, although it was barely four-thirty. Thick clouds raced by, so low that it seemed they would sweep the whole town off to sea, and Karen had to lean into the wind to stay upright. She debated tacking back and forth across the road like a ship at sail, but settled on walking backwards to keep the sand from stinging her eyes.

Finally arriving at Millfarm, she had to tug hard at the front door to get it open and then push to close it again. Girl-Ellen was alone in the kitchen, struggling to light the stove that heated the southroom. A heavy downdraft from the chimney kept blowing out her match. The stove was a modern marvel that Uncle Paul had brought back from Norway for Southhouse. Lars-Anne had liked it so much that Miller ordered another for Millfarm. Its cast-iron body heated the southroom, but the back extended through the wall into the kitchen, from where it was filled with peat or coal without messing up the sitting room.

"Where is everyone?" Karen asked.

"Miller is still in the barn with Erik. Lil-Anne is out gathering up her chicks, and Mistress is in the southroom," the girl explained. "Mistress Jensen brought the bad news. She just left."

Karen exchanged her clogs for house slippers and hung her heavy outdoor shawl on a peg. She went to the southroom and found Mam perched on a bench, sitting in the dark. She had already changed into the purple scarves that were a sign of half-mourning. In short halting sentences Mam recited the latest news, "Tante-Black says her life is over. Else says she just sits there staring out the window. Sidsel and Ane-Marie are having hysterics."

Karen didn't know what to say but lit the lamp. "It's freezing in here. Let me see if I can help Girl-Ellen get the stove going." She disappeared into the kitchen and soon came back with cups of coffee and warm shawls. The roaring sound from the stove promised that soon the room would be warm.

Karen sat down next to her mother on the bench, wondering if she would be allowed to hold Mam's hand. She had a sudden insight and said softly, "Do accidents at sea remind you of Granpapa Lars and Uncle Peter?"

Mam nodded and haltingly told the long-buried story. Her voice was low, every word being hauled out one at a time from the bottom of a deep well. It was as if Mam had forgotten to whom she was speaking. Karen sat very still, straining to hear so she could remember the words. Later, she would fit them together, like the tiles on Kirsten-Mos's southroom wall. These were the missing pieces of her mother's past.

"The spring after Papa's ship went missing, Big-Anne left for the mainland to study for her midwifery exam. She took Kirsten with her but I was sent to Millfarm to live with Granmam and Granpapa while Mam was away. No one would tell me what really happened to Papa and Peter, saying it was better not to talk about it. I had nightmares almost every night, dreaming that they were calling for help and I couldn't move, did nothing to help. Sometimes it was Karen screaming that I heard in my dream. It had taken three days for the baby to be born. By that time Karen was so weak that she couldn't nurse. Nothing Big-Anne did helped, and they both died. No one would talk about that either. She left me."

Karen wasn't sure whether Mam was talking about Kirsten-Mos dying or Big-Anne leaving for the mainland. Then the pieces fell into place. "Is that why Big-Anne wanted to become a midwife? Because she didn't know how to help Karen?" she asked.

"That's what she said, but she just wanted to get away. I needed her but she didn't want me. I wasn't Karen."

But that isn't true! You know she had to leave, Karen wanted to protest but she realized that Mam had sounded like an angry twelve-year-old. She did know better, but all these years she had needed to say the words that no one wanted to hear.

Mother and daughter sat silently as darkness continued to fall. The wind had died with the setting sun and only the ticking of the clock could be heard. Lars-Anne sat with her worn hands limp in her lap, eyes glistening with tears that still would not come. Karen thought of that young girl. She imagined what it must have been like to lose a father, a brother, and a sister and then be left behind once again, this time by her mother and baby sister. Hearing the story in Mam's voice was very different from when Mette's mother told it.

But Mam wasn't done talking.

"November came. Like now. We were expecting news of the *Southern Breezes.* Then she was sighted, running before a heavy west wind. Before she could round the Hen, the wind suddenly shifted to the south and the ship was blown onto a sand bar. The men on land tried three times to get the lifeboat through the surf, but the waves were too strong. The captain and crew lashed themselves to the masts to keep from being swept overboard.

"They kept calling for help. We all stood there and watched while the ship was pounded to pieces. They kept calling for help and I watched them drown. At night I hear them still, only they're Papa and Peter, calling for help."

Lars-Anne came to herself. She picked up Karen's hands and for the first time looked her in the eye, "I don't want that for you. I don't want you to stand on the Hen waiting for a man who never comes home."

Twenty

Running Before the Wind

[The Pilgrim was] going along at a great rate, dead before the wind, with studding sails out on both sides, alow and aloft, on a dark night, just after midnight, and everything as still as the grave, except the washing of the water by the vessel's side; for being before the wind, with a smooth sea, the little brig, covered with canvas, was doing great business, with very little noise.

—*Two Years before the Mast* (1836)
Richard Henry Dana, Jr.
1815-1882

Pacific Ocean, December 1874

Peter was pacing the deck of the *Marianne* as she sailed up the California coast. After more than three months at sea, this last night-watch was passing but slowly and the first mate, like the rest of the crew, was longing for their arrival in San Diego, anticipated by the end of the coming day.

Their last chance for real shore leave had been in Dutch Guyana in the autumn. Little did Peter know that Sønderho and Nordby were by now enjoying the colorful description of the Surinam River that he had written to Karen. From Niew Amsterdam, they rode the current along the Brazilian coast, heading south by east as much as possible. Just before they crossed the equator, the color of the water became very dark; even far out to sea a powerful current carried silt and mud from the mighty Amazon River. They did not see land until they rounded the eastern-most point of

Brazil, where they turned south-southwest. They were hailed by a ship coming out of Pernambuco harbor, heading back the way they had come. Further south they paused briefly in Sao Paulo to unload a shipment of Barbados rum, pick up mail, and lay in fresh food and water.

From there, the wind had been contrary all the way down the Atlantic coast and the *Marianne* had tacked close-hauled. They stopped at the Falklands only long enough to hear a report of favorable winds for rounding the Horn, so they made a hasty departure. Still, "favorable" only meant that they eventually arrived in the Pacific Ocean after a passage filled with all the expected dangers; a dramatic tale to tell future children and grandchildren.

Peter had no opportunity to write to Karen, since much of the time all hands were needed on deck to clew the main sails up or down, depending on the vagaries of the wind. The rest of the time, he collapsed in his bunk, sleeping when he could. Only after rounding the Horn, when the *Marianne* had briefly caught a good wind to carry them north, Peter could finally sit in his cabin and add to his letter to Karen.

November 15

I would describe our passage around the Horn, but can do no better than quote from "Two Years before the Mast." We even hit the worst of the storms within a week of when Richard Dana crossed in early November of 1834—forty years ago! He wrote:

"We found a large black cloud rolling on towards us from the south-west, and blackening the heavens. 'Here comes Cape Horn!' said the chief mate; and we had hardly time to haul down and clew up, before it was upon us. In a few moments, a heavier sea was raised than I had ever seen before, and...the little brig...plunged into it, and all the forward part of her was under water... threatening to wash everything overboard."

That is pretty much what happened to us but we are now safely around and will soon pass the Chilean Island of Juan Fernadez. Please pardon my inadequate translation—I hope your mastery of English has progressed far enough so you can soon read the original for yourself, he writes so vividly of life at sea.

From Juan Fernandez they sailed due north to the primitive port of Lobos de Tierra in Peru, where they made a brief stop to replenish supplies and load a cargo of guano and nitrates for the farms of California. Captain Fredriksen had hoped to spend Christmas in San Francisco, but they were becalmed in the doldrums and by the time they caught the northern trade winds, it was December. After that, the long leg north to North America was tedious. The prevailing winds carried them well west of Southern California and from there they had to tack back east to San Diego.

By this night in mid-December, they had been sailing on a steady larboard tack for the better part of three days, the *Marianne* barely heading towards land as her prow plowed a curl of pale green foam. During the afternoon watch when all hands were on deck, the crew found every excuse to work near the larboard rail and search the eastern horizon for the sight of fog-shrouded hills at the entrance to the bay. They awaited the 'Land Ho!' from the lookout in the Fore Top, although all knew they were still too far west.

The night was quiet and the starboard watch was asleep in the forecastle when the wind died completely and the sails luffed ineffectually. Peter had just come on watch. With little to do but await a dawn breeze, he paced the deck, thinking of home and looking forward to the first mail call in months.

Peter awoke from his musings when the helm alerted him to a shift in the wind to the west. "All hands ahoy!" he called and heard the echo below deck. Captain Fredriksen must have already felt the change in the *Marianne* because he came on the bridge just in time to give the command to come about. He had reserved for himself navigating the last leg to the long awaited port, a privilege of rank he seldom asserted. "Helmsman, set the course due east," he called, his sea legs firmly braced on the bridge of the *Marianne*. "Bosun, square the sails, we have a following wind to carry us all the way to the harbor entrance."

Briefly consulting the sea-chart, he confirmed what Peter had already guessed. "We'll arrive there soon after sun-up, pick up our pilot, and be at anchor before the afternoon fog rolls in."

"Ready to come about," the Bosun called out, and the men ran up the rigging to adjust the jibs and forward staysails. The brig swung in a great arc through the heaving swells of the Pacific Ocean. Gradually she straightened as the timbers creaked and the sails snapped. The royals ballooned and the yardarms squared against the rails. As the *Marianne* came about, the Danish Flag flopped lazily against the stern pole and it seemed as if they slowed. Peter knew better, knew that at full-sail and with a following wind they were, as Dana had said, "doing great business, with very little noise."

Most of the starboard watch remained on deck rather than going to the forecastle to sleep, waiting for the next call for "all hands aloft" to reef royals and topgallants. They ignored that it was still before dawn, hardly caring how many hours it would take. All knew that they would need to slow their headlong run when they came among the smaller craft outside the entrance to the bay. Captain would wait as long as he could, anxious to fly as fast as possible towards port and show off his ship; nothing made a seaman's heart beat faster than the sight of a ship at full sail, running before the wind. Soon the point of land that guarded the magnificent, natural harbor appeared off the larboard bow, and the pilot climbed over the railing to navigate them safely to their anchorage in the bay.

As usual, the first man off the ship was Captain to check in with the harbormaster. Knowing how anxious the men would be to hear from home after 20,00 miles at sea, he quickly returned and handed a large bag of mail to the second mate. Hansen immediately held mail call for the waiting crew, calling "Skovby," and handing the old salt the first envelope. "Larsen" was next, followed by "Pedersen, " and another "Larsen." He then called out "Hansen" before he realized that it was for himself. When the next letter was for also for Peter, the crew started to laugh. Peter's arms were now so filled with envelopes that they threatened to fall to the deck. "I have a big family," he mumbled apologetically, not quite willing to admit that most of the letters were from Karen.

Hastily retreating to his cabin and sitting in the only chair by a small corner desk, he piled the letters on the floor to the left of his chair, in order of postmark. On top was the letter from Karen telling about her family's tragedy. Responding to his emotional letter after they had had Klaus Holgersen's burial at sea, it seemed as if a dam had burst, for Karen poured out all her worries about her mother. Peter had lost his own father a few years ago, so he could understand how hard it must have been for Lars-Anne. Yet his family was relatively well off because Peter was already at sea and between his earnings, insurance, and fortuitous investments in other ships, his mother had managed. To lose sister, father, brother, and brother-in-law, and then to have financial problems as well, must have been that much more difficult. Peter wished he could put his arm around Karen to comfort her. Yet, he was surprised at how upset she was about events that, after all, had happened long before she was born. He hoped that the relationship between Karen and her mother would improve; now the story was out in the open.

He added the envelope to the special pile of letters from Karen on his desk. Next was a thick envelope containing clippings from *The Fanø Weekly* and a very apologetic letter from Karen, confessing their new collaboration. The clippings contained several of Peter's stories as retold by Karen. Peter smiled and read the letter again, the words already memorized:

> *I hope you will forgive me, but I only sent the first story to your mam to see what she thought. Before I knew what had happened, she had sent it to the paper. Then the editor wanted more and now everyone is talking ~~about us~~. Mam is furious. ~~She thought I would be safe from gossip with you away~~. Your mam, however, is bragging about you all over Nordby, so proudly that we can hear the echo all the way to Sønderho."*

Although Karen crossed out some words, Peter could still make them out. He chuckled as he imagined Lars-Anne's reaction. He read the clippings and had to admit that he was thrilled to see his name in print. As far as he could see, the stories had not suffered from Karen's rewrite—on the contrary she wrote amazingly well. He couldn't decide whether he should tease Karen in his next letter about what she had done or praise her writing. On the whole he thought he would say something nice to reassure her. She seemed so worried that he would be angry with her.

The *Marianne* only stayed in San Diego long enough to lay in fresh fruit and water. The town had grown since Dana had described it as a small Mexican village, but fifty years later, the isolated American town still had little to offer. At the last minute, Peter stopped by the post office to buy stamps and mail his letters to home. He was assured that, although they would go by way of San Francisco, they would reach there before the *Marianne*, traveling by mail stage on the famous *el Camino Real*—the Royal Road. From there the letters would go by cross-continental railroad to New York.

Soon, the capstan creaked as they pulled up anchor and headed north again, officers as well as crew anxious to make way, even if it meant spending Christmas at sea. A well-earned landfall in San Francisco Bay and the fabled city that most of them had never seen, loomed large in their imaginations. Then they would embark on the biggest adventure of all, crossing the Pacific Ocean to the mysterious Orient.

Twenty

A Mysterious Bundle

Sønderho, December 1874

During December, Sønderho hunkered down in an onslaught of dreadful weather. Days of wind-driven rain alternated with longer periods of still dampness so pervasive that it seemed knitted shawls and wool skirts would never dry, fog and spirits never lift. Women ventured outside only when they had urgent errands at Brinch's and children dashed through the wet to get to school. The Inn remained strangely empty, while the men puttered half-heartedly at home, tackling chores that had been postponed during their summer away. Lamps remained lit all day, the clouds dimming the few hours of daylight between sunrise at nine and sunset at four in the afternoon. Big-Anne and Kirsten slowed their activities to a minimum, creeping through the days; even Frederik changed his usual cheerful gurgling to a fretful whine.

At Millfarm, Anders Miller muttered about rotting grain and unyielding cows. He even growled at Erik who dogged his footsteps and disconsolately went through the motions of his chores. Lil-Anne, who on the best of winter mornings fussed over having to get up in the dark, had to be pushed out the door to feed her chicks and trudge off to school. Only Lars-Anne seemed immune, having rebounded from her depression after her talk with Karen. In fact, she seemed uncommonly cheerful, as if she had finally exorcised her

childhood ghosts, sweeping them out of her house with the sand from the kitchen floor to be carried away with the swirling fog. She tried to stir up the rest of her family in a whirlwind of preparations for the Christmas season and Christian's return home, but no one else had her enthusiasm for cleaning every nook and cranny. As usual, she made enough cookies to supply the whole town, in case they came to call, but even the smells wafting from the oven failed to entice more than half-hearted begging for scraps and burnt pieces.

Karen, who usually enjoyed the fuss of Christmas preparations, couldn't get into the spirit of the season, unable erase the dreadful images of her mother's story. She became that lonely young girl, abandoned by her family and the cries of the drowning seamen rang in her ears. Hoping that writing would help, she settled in the study to add to Peter's letter.

> *I am such a selfish dolt. I should have learned last summer that other people's secrets are not my business. Sometimes they are better left buried and forgotten. I am used to the mam who orders everybody around, not to the one who talks of screaming seamen. The Peter who would have been my uncle and the Peter who is my love become one and I am so afraid for you. I want to run away from all this tragedy and go back to the blue skies and white clouds of summer. If only you were home safe....*

Just then a large tear dropped onto the middle of the sheet of paper. "Oh, drat," she exclaimed, barely restraining herself from using the expletive that Papa used the other day when he hit his thumb with a hammer. "Now I'll have to redo that whole page." *Perhaps I'll leave out the stuff about Peter. If only I could get off this dreadful island. If only it would stop raining. If only Peter would come home!*

There was a knock on the door and she hastily covered up her letter and wiped her eyes with her apron before answering.

"Un's got three fellas in oilskins asking for un," Girl-Ellen announced gleefully. "They're too wet to come in æ parlor, so A told 'em to wait in *æ frankel.*"

Karen was irritated and wondered why these foot-stomping louts were bothering her. She thought she'd made it perfectly plain to all her dance-partners that she was not available, but then curiosity and Mam's lessons on hospitality took over. "Well we can't let them stand out there dripping. Tell them to put their wet clothes in the scullery and show them into the southroom while I get the coffee."

Karen quickly smoothed her crumpled apron. Automatically her hands went up to check that her scarf was on straight and that no unruly locks had escaped their confines. She ducked into the kitchen and soon appeared with a tray of coffee and cups, fearing that the blush in her cheeks would reveal her excitement at having her very own callers. Three of the young men who had swarmed around her and Mette at the Sunday dances were indeed lined up barely inside the door. Her nervousness was soon overcome by a nearly irresistible urge to giggle at the red-faced figures before her. On her invitation to sit, they scrambled for the nearest bench which, although long enough to accommodate two Sønderho ladies and their voluminous skirts, had trouble with three strapping male bottoms. There they sat staring at their clogless feet, their big toes poking through the holes in their socks, and their callused paws threatening to crush Mam's best china coffee cups.

Finally the leader cleared his throat, blushed some more, and managed to stammer, "Terrible weather we're having."

Karen bit down the sarcasm on the tip of her tongue and resisted saying that she assumed they weren't dripping on Mam's floor because they had been swimming. No. She had learned how to put people at ease and get them to tell their story, so she just smiled encouragingly and waited as if she had nothing better to do.

The young man on the leader's right picked up the thread and continued, "We thought we should have a party. At Mette's house."

"We need you to help," added the third.

Gradually her callers' plan emerged. Bored with the droopy weather, several of the young people in Mette's and Karen's confirmation class had decided to give Mette a traditional *bindebrev*—a binding-letter—in honor of her sixteenth nameday. When it had been delivered they would capture her and 'bind' her to the stove until she promised to have a party.

"But her nameday was over a month ago," Karen couldn't resist protesting, half-jealous that her friend would have such an honor.

"We know that, but we weren't here then and her nameday is the closest. The next one isn't until way next year and yours was last spring. We need a party now."

"We want you to write the letter. You're so good at it," said the emboldened leader with a grin.

Soon the four young people were sitting in a circle on the floor with paper and inkwell in front of Karen. All self-consciousness evaporated and with much laughter and many crossed out lines, a poem emerged in praise of beautiful Mette and her incomparable virtues. Karen suppressed the mental image of her best friend's chubby face and robust figure—well, poetic hyperbole was part of a traditional *bindebrev.*

With stern instructions to her friends to keep the noise down, Karen brought the draft back into the study. A few minutes later she emerged with a clean copy in her best penmanship and on her best paper. The poem was neatly folded and they lit a candle with which to melt the sealing wax. Since Miller's signet ring with an imprint of the mill would prematurely reveal the identity of at least one of the senders, they hunted for a suitable blunt end with which to flatten the wax. With much hilarity they located a wooden spoon with a broken handle in the kitchen and the three young men fought over the honor of affixing the seal on their precious missive.

Mam had at first chaperoned the impromptu gathering by lurking in the northroom with the door slightly ajar, but she soon decided to go about more useful chores. She had banished Lil-Anne and Sidsel to the loft to play so Karen could entertain her callers in peace, but the girls were now called back down and their help enlisted in delivering the letter. The young men tripped over each other, explaining to the puzzled Sidsel what was going on, until Lil-Anne firmly told them to be quiet and she'd do it. "We're all going to Mette's house and, while I hide because she knows me, you'll give her the letter. Then everybody will come and tie her down and tickle her until she promises to give a party."

The two girls were bundled up against the rain and slogged down the road, followed by Karen and the three young men at a suitable distance. Before they could cross town to the Cockeyed House they were joined by the rest of the young people who had lain in wait to participate in the climax of the plot.

Sidsel timidly knocked on the door, coached by Lil-Anne from around the corner of the house where she hid out of sight with the rest of the gathering crowd. Emma Hansen answered, but Mette was not within. Finally she was located in the stable, forking hay to the bored cows chewing cud in their damp stalls. Puzzled she opened her letter, blushed, and, now knowing what was expected, dashed into the loft in an attempt to escape. She led her friends a merry chase until the most fleet-of-foot captured her, buried her in hay, and finally tied her, not to the stove, but the nearest beam in the loft. Finally, she breathlessly promised a party on the morrow, her final surrender witnessed by the laughing friends gathered below.

"But they didn't tickle her," protested Sidsel.

"Well, I would've," said Lil-Anne.

The party was a huge success. The energy of the young people finally succeeded in lifting everyone's spirits, helped by generous servings of coffee punch. The party was intended for Mette's young friends, but several women had shown up to inspect her debut as a hostess. They too seemed impressed, the departing guests heaping praise on the novice. Tante-Black even complimented Mette on her apple cake, an honor she bestowed on few.

Only Tante-Brown and Tante-Blue were critical and before they were out of earshot of the house they loudly complained, "The food was good, but," said one, "She didn't *urge* enough," finished her sister.

"Mette urged me at least twice to have a second piece of cake," Karen protested, irritated at the sour old gossips.

"It's only her first party," Kirsten-Mos added. "She'll soon learn that you have to urge at least three times."

Even the weather responded, as if it too had been cheered by the party. The wind changed, a gentle breeze blew the fog off to sea, and the next day dawned bright and dry. Lars-Anne fired up the scullery stove before sunup and soon had a kettle of linens boiling in soapy water. Well before midday dinner, the laundry was rinsed and hung out to dry. "This may be our last chance to do a great-wash for months," she needlessly explained.

The whole town followed suit and by noon every yard had white flags flapping in the breeze.

The *everts* were pushed off the sand and set sail for Ribe to bring back sorely needed supplies. Lars-Anne had worried that the weather would keep Christian on the mainland until after Christmas. Papa had reassured her that Sister Ingrid would make sure the boy had a proper holiday. Lil-Anne stated firmly that she wanted him home, so there. "He missed my birthday but he *can't* miss Christmas!"

On her last trip on December 22, the *Lene* brought a special passenger and by mid-afternoon Christian came striding towards Millfarm, a mysterious bundle on his back. No one noticed his arrival because they were all chasing a squealing pig around the courtyard. The pig, usually kept chained to one side of the stable door, had gotten loose when Papa untied it. The dog was straining on his chain and barking and the geese were lined up in the safety of the barn door. "This time it's your turn—serves you right," they hissed.

All were contributing to the deafening noise, all except Lil-Anne who had been sent over to the Jensen farm on an invented errand. The pig seemed to understand his intended fate as the guest of honor at Christmas dinner because he darted back and forth from Anders to Lars-Anne to Girl-Ellen. He was finally captured when he skittered across the cobblestones and ran smack into Karen's skirts. She sat down abruptly and was laughing so hard that she barely had the presence of mind to throw herself over the squealing pig and wrap her arms around his neck.

Papa and Erik were trussing the protesting sacrifice when Christian called out, grinning from ear to ear, "What kind of welcome is this?"

The laughter turned to delighted cries and everyone clustered around the boy. He threw his burden aside to prepare for hugs from his mother and elder sister, which he seemed not to mind at all. The cries of "you came" and "I knew you would" and "I didn't think I would make it" almost drowned out those of the excited animals.

Lil-Anne came out of nowhere and, catapulting herself over everyone, latched onto her brother's neck. Christian managed to loosen her stranglehold, and Mam finally had a chance to get a good look at him. "My, you've grown," she exclaimed. "I think you're going to be even taller than Papa."

Christian couldn't stop grinning, stuck out his chest some more, and even included Karen in his approving glance around home.

"I've grown too," chirped Lil-Anne. "I've learned to tie my scarf; all by myself."

"So you have, Squirt," he answered and, noticing a warning frown from his older sister, refrained from pointing out that the scarf was by now sadly in need of retying. "Look what I brought," he said pointing to the mysterious bundle of green branches on the ground. "A Christmas tree," he added lamely when everyone looked puzzled. "A Christmas tree like Papa's always talking about from when he was a boy."

Anders had finally finished tying the pig's legs securely and had a chance to greet his son properly. "A Christmas tree!" he exclaimed, as excited as the boy. "What a great idea!"

"I bought candles too. And holders. But I can't figure out how to put them on," Christian said, pleased that at least someone was enthusiastic.

"Well I don't know where we'll put it," Mam grumped. Then, remembering the wonderful Christmas she had spent at the Andersen farm before they were married, she regained her sunny mood and added, "Maybe we can dig up some colored paper at the store and make heart baskets. Granmam Andersen showed me how to weave them and I think I remember how. It's a good thing that we made all those cookies. We can hang some on the branches."

As soon as they were cleaned up from the slaughtering, the boys were dispatched to Brinch's to see what they could find in the way of decorating supplies. As they disappeared down the road in the growing dusk, Erik eagerly told Christian about their tree at home, and the cookies his mam used to make, and the cute thing his little sister had said last year, and....

Anders, a definite bounce in his step, returned to the stable door and the hanging pig to complete the messy work of draining the blood. The rest of the family went into the house, Mam last. She was humming softly.

Will wonders never cease, Karen marveled. *Mam never hums. She sings beautifully but she* never *hums.*

The next morning, Lars-Anne was up well before the sun to continue her preparations, but as soon as she could decently pretend that dawn had arrived, she raised the flag to show that Christian was safely home. The final stage of butchering the pig was to prepare and set aside every scrap for later use, although Anders's main purpose was to carve out the two loins for Christmas dinner. The carcass was flayed, the hide to be sold later, the fat below the skin was put aside to be rendered for lard, the intestines carefully taken out and cleaned to be stuffed for sausages, the shanks cut off the hams so they could be smoked, and the rest of meat carved into smaller cuts. Lars-Anne stood ready to receive the loins. She brought one into the kitchen for safe storage in the cellar and dispatched Christian with the other to the neighboring farm. His two-fold mission was to bring the Jensens their Christmas roast and also show them that he was indeed safely home for the holiday, in case they had missed the flag. Meanwhile, Erik brought each cut of pork to the kitchen where the women were kept busy boiling, salting, and stuffing. The two hams and shoulders were hung in the scullery chimney to be smoked. Lars-Anne smiled, satisfied they had a good supply of hams for wedding presents, in case of a busy winter.

By late afternoon everyone was grimy. After rinsing off the worst of the dirt by the well, they were grateful to take their turn at the tub of hot water in the scullery. That night, 'Little Christmas Eve,' all crept into their tightbeds exhausted but satisfied that they were ready for Christmas.

Twenty-Two

Christmas

The change in the weather brought cold during the night and by mid-morning of the day of Christmas Eve the rain of the past few weeks changed to sleet. No one minded, everyone was so busy with preparations for the holiday. Even Lil-Anne willingly rose before cockcrow and flew at her chores so she could finish the paper decorations she had started the day before. With tongue firmly entrenched in her cheek, she bent over paper strips and flour-and-water paste to fasten links in a colorful chain. Karen draped garlands of heather and dried flowers around the walls of the north-room, usually the only decorations used on this nearly treeless island. Mam and Girl-Ellen were busy in the kitchen stirring pots and firing up the oven. As soon as the animals were fed and watered, Miller and the two boys went to the barn where they hammered and sawed, putting together a stand for the tree. A cold lunch of cheese and sliced potatoes on slabs of buttered bread was hurriedly washed down with milk and beer and as quickly cleaned up to make room for dinner preparations.

Lars-Anne pulled the loin of pork from the pantry. She made deep slashes in the thick layer of fat all the way down to the meat and rubbed the scored skin with coarse salt so the strips would brown to a crisp in the oven. Potatoes were peeled and covered with salted water, bowls of sour red cabbage were brought up from the pantry, and a large pot of rice was set to simmer on the back of the stove for porridge. Finally by mid-afternoon the food was prepared: the roast was placed in the oven, potatoes and cabbage set to cook, and Girl-Ellen sent home to be with her own family.

Christian proudly carried his little fir tree into the southroom and Papa shooed Lil-Anne away, saying children were not allowed to see it until after dinner. "Only the men of the house decorate the tree."

"Christian isn't a man," Lil-Anne protested.

"But it's his tree," said Papa as he firmly closed all the doors.

"It's time to set the table anyway," said Mam. "Don't forget, we'll be eight, not counting Frederik."

The table was covered with the snowy white linen cloth that Mam had woven for her trousseau when she was Karen's age. Beeswax candles were placed on a runner down the middle and flanked by bunches of dried heather. Lil-Anne distributed plates, napkins, forks and knives to each seat. She brought out the special porridge spoons that Kirsten-Mos had carved from cow horn and replenished the salt dishes. Karen filled pots with butter, untied the oiled paper covers from bottles of fruit juice and poured their contents into ceramic pitchers. She filled other pitchers with dark beer, and placed all the food in *æ frankel* to keep them cold.

When all the preparations were finished, the kitchen was again cleaned, the floors swept, and the water bucket filled at the well. The steam from all the cooking had condensed on the tiled walls in the kitchen and northroom so Karen wiped them down with an old linen towel until their paint sparkled with holiday spirit. Lil-Anne was sent outside to bring scraps of meat to the dog so he too would know that it was Christmas, and Anders mounted a sheaf of wheat on a pole to feed the birds. Finally Lars-Anne surveyed her domain. "We're ready," she declared. "Everyone get dressed."

"Can I take the bowl of porridge to the Nisser?" Lil-Anne pleaded as she did every year.

"No, that's my job. You can do it the rest of the year, but if the Christmas porridge doesn't come from the woman of the house, Nissefar doesn't count it. We want him to take good care of the animals tonight, don't we?"

Lil-Anne nodded solemnly. Papa had explained that the reason Millfarm was so lucky was that they took good care of their Nisse family. Whenever there was leftover porridge, she was allowed to bring it up to the loft. Although these gnomes were supposedly invisible, she was convinced that she saw Nissefar's red hat behind a bale of hay and heard him say 'thank you'. Everyone knows that if Nisser aren't given their porridge, at least at Christmas, they play mean tricks on humans. On Christmas Eve, Nisser take special care of the animals. Only they are allowed to witness when, at midnight, the cows, sheep, and horses kneel in their stalls to honor the Christ child.

"Don't forget a big pat of butter on top," Lil-Anne reminded Mam.

"I won't forget," Mam said.

Karen smiled to herself at this familiar discussion. Last night Lil-Anne had made her tell the old story of the Nisse who had been so angry at not getting butter on his porridge that he had climbed down from his loft and killed the farmer's prize calf. Then he ate the porridge anyway and was ashamed to find the melted butter had seeped to the bottom of the bowl. To make up for his terrible mistake he gave the farmer a big bag of gold.

But at Millfarm, Lil-Anne took good care of the Nisser, and at Christmas even Mam believed. Or maybe she just believed that following tradition and that doing everything the right way would keep the family safe. *Maybe it's really all the same,* Karen mused. Tradition kept the family together, connecting them to the land and the past. That way, they knew they could survive whatever came. When Mam was a child, she had had to do things right to survive. Papa had once said something like that, but Karen hadn't really understood what he meant, until now.

While everyone was getting dressed, Granmam and Kirsten-Mos arrived with a well-bundled Frederik. Granmam took over the kitchen and supervised the placing of roast and vegetables on the serving platters. Meanwhile Mam lit the candles on the table and then closed her eyes briefly to allow the spirit of Christmas to settle over the room. She rang the gong that Papa-Lars had brought home from China long ago and smiled as her family, including Apprentice-Erik, filed in and were benched. Then she and Granmam carried in two big bowls of rice porridge and set them at either end of the table. Thick pats of butter melted on top of mounds, surrounded by a moat of dark beer.

Lil-Anne remembered just in time that Christian was to sit in his usual place next to Papa on the end of the bench, so she scooted into her old place in the middle. "Merry Christmas, Funny Man," she whispered, turning and patting the painted man on the wall tile behind her seat.

They ate the porridge in the old way, sharing a common bowl. They took turns dipping a horn spoon into the bowl, tipping in a little of the melted butter and some beer. Mam had hidden a single almond in one of the bowls; the finder would have good fortune during the coming year. Kirsten-Mos was embarrassed to be the lucky recipient and tried at first to sneak it back into the porridge nearest Lil-Anne. Lil-Anne was tempted to claim it, but decided she would get caught.

"Kirsten-Mos always gets it," she sulked. "It's not fair. I never win."

"You don't need luck," Papa grinned. "You make your own."

"A got the almond last year, at home," Erik piped up. "That's why A's so lucky and Master chose me as his apprentice." Then realizing his boldness he blushed and, lowering his eyes, concentrated on licking his spoon very clean. Usually quiet, he had been even more subdued at dinner during this, his first Christmas away from home.

No one paid any attention to him as they were in the middle of a heated discussion about who had won the almond last year. And the year before, and before that....

After the dinner dishes were cleared away and washed, Papa directed the family to wait in the dark northroom with the door closed while Christian lit the candles. Soon he opened the door to a chorus of 'Ahs.' Only Lil-Anne stood mute with awe, the light from the candles on the tree, reflecting in her eyes. Anders and Christian had placed the little tree on the table between the southroom windows, but to the child it seemed as tall as the mill.

Christmas presents were not usual in Sønderho, but Anders had, as was his wont, selected one special gift for each of his children, this year placing them under the tree.

Christian quickly figured out that the grand pocketknife was for him and that the other one must be for Erik. The apprentice smiled gratefully at Anders through a suspicion of tears. He cheered even more when

Lars-Anne handed him a large package tied with string and bearing many stamps. His family had not forgotten their absent son.

Karen received a smaller package, wrapped in brown paper. It was a book of Hans Christian Andersen's *Fairy Tales*, beautifully bound in brown leather. She read the inscription on the flyleaf: "To the new storyteller from Uncle Hans, Christmas 1874."

"I thought you needed a copy of your own," Papa said. "Mam's is falling apart."

Lil-Anne would have been jealous except that she was absorbed in opening a small box covered in black velvet. Inside she found an amber heart on a silver chain. She ran to Papa and threw her arms around him, "You didn't forget, you didn't forget. Thank you, thank you."

"How could I forget? You kept reminding me," he chuckled.

In the fall, Karen had taken Lil-Anne amber hunting on the west beach and she had found a large piece. Soon after, Papa had taken the brown lump to the amber grinder in Nordby, but had teased her after each trip by claiming that he'd again forgotten to bring it home. Karen fastened the chain at the back of her little sister's neck, and Lil-Anne immediately tucked the heart under her nightshirt for safe keeping, patting it every few minutes to make sure it was still there.

Mam pointed out that no one would see it. "I don't care," the little girl insisted cocking her head to one side. "I know it's there just the same."

Even little Frederik was remembered with a little whalebone ring that showed hard wear from his cousins' teething.

Lars-Anne started to sing a carol. She reached for Anders's hand who grabbed that of his eldest daughter and so on down in a chain that wound its way into every room in the house. Kirsten-Mos was at the end, carrying a chortling Frederik on her free arm. Only Big-Anne remained behind saying she was getting too old to go jumping around on a full stomach. Kirsten gave her a brief look of concern, but was waved away. After completing the rounds to the reverberations of several traditional carols, they returned to the southroom.

Anne moved to the middle of the room, the rest of the family forming a circle around her and listening with rapt attention to her clear voice.

Softly, she sang the first line: "Fair is the earth, fairer still God's heaven. Beautiful the soul's pilgrim way!" Gradually, her voice rose to a crescendo as she finished the first verse, "Through the lovely lands of earth, we go to Paradise in song!" Then her voice faded away again as she sang of the passing of time and of generations, finishing, "Mankind, rejoice, today is born our savior."

When the last notes faded away, Anders wrapped his arms around his wife and whispered, "Thank you my dearest. Thank you for reminding us once again what this night is about."

"I thought it was a New Year's hymn, because of all that stuff about time passing," Erik whispered to Christian.

"It's Papa's favorite so Mam sings it for him at Christmas. Sometimes I get the feeling they forget we're here."

But Anders had heard and explained, "Even though *'Jul'* now-a-days is our name for Christ's birthday, it used to be a Nordic solstice festival. *'Jul'* is the word for 'wheel,' the symbol of the sun and therefore of creation and time. It is fitting to sing Ingemann's beautiful hymn to honor the birth of the fairest of all."

Kirsten went to tuck Frederik into his cousin's tightbed and Christian was sent to bring Papa's pipe from its hook on the wall. Erik said, "Goodnight and thank you for the great knife." He tucked his unopened package from home under his arm and went across the courtyard to his room over the barn. Papa smiled down at Lil-Anne who had curled up in his lap and added, "Karen, bring me the Good Book; it's time we heard from St. Luke. Some people are ready for bed."

Christmas Day dawned crisp and fair. The sun rose barely in time for church, but by the time the family set out, it was just far enough over the horizon to make the ice that covered everything glisten and sparkle as if Sønderho were decorated for the great day, outside as well as in.

After the service, Lil-Anne made sure the whole congregation knew that not only had Christian come home just in time—but that he had brought a real Christmas tree to Millfarm. The family barely had enough time to eat leftover pork roast and red cabbage before the callers came to inspect the foreign curiosity from the mainland. Platters of cookies and pots of coffee punch were brought to the southroom. It was fortunate that the supplies were plentiful because there was a steady stream of curious visitors all afternoon and well past sunset and, by custom, no one was allowed to leave empty-handed lest they carry away the spirit of the season.

"I never saw such a thing," said Tante-Brown in a doubtful tone, reserving further judgment until she could hear other opinions of the tree.

"Cousin Vilhelm told us about one once," Tante-Blue reminded her and then turned to the rest of the room to explain. "You know, our cousin from Nordby who was an apprentice shoemaker some place up north by Viborg until he went to America and died of cholera." This gloomy story reminded her to report that Tante-Black was feeling poorly and was sorry she couldn't come calling.

Others were more enthusiastic. Carpenter Hansen reported seeing whole forests of fir trees in his travels, so tall they were used to make ship masts. Else showed Lil-Anne how to make a star out of tinfoil for the top of the tree—she had read somewhere that that was the way it was done. Everyone applauded the addition. The men and some of the women withdrew to the northroom for cigars and Jamaica rum.

Even Lil-Anne tired of showing off "my tree," as she called it. She seated herself strategically under its table and started to leaf through Karen's new book. "Here's a story called *The Fir Tree*," she suddenly exclaimed, interrupting Mette telling Karen about what her latest beau had said the last time he came to call.

"Don't be so rude when your elders are talking," Karen corrected.

"But this is important. It's about a Christmas tree. You have to read it. Right now."

And there was no help for it. Everyone wanted to hear what Hans Christian Andersen had to say about Christmas trees. If the great man approved, they must be all right.

Karen settled in a chair by the lamp. She waited patiently for the rest of the room to settle, the women filling the chairs and the benches while the young people had to be content with the floor. Even the buzz of conversation in the northroom stilled and the door was pushed open a little further. "The Little Fir Tree, by Hans Christian Andersen," Karen read:

> *A little fir tree stood in the forest, such a pretty little fir tree. It grew in a good place, had all the air and sunshine it wanted, and was surrounded by a number of bigger companions, both firs and pines. But the little fir tree was in such a passionate hurry to grow that it paid heed neither to the warmth of the sun nor the sweetness of the air.*

And Karen read about the little tree and its longing to know where the tallest of the big trees went when they were felled and stripped of all their branches. She read about the stork that reported having seen them on his way home from Egypt, new ships with proud tall masts. "They asked to be remembered to you," the stork said to the little tree.

The audience nodded. They knew about tall masts, even if few of them had seen trees growing in a forest. When the tree wondered about the destination of the smaller trees that been cut but had kept all their branches, Lil-Anne clapped her hands and exclaimed, "I know where they went!" Karen read on,

> *"We know, we know!" twittered the sparrows. "We've been peeping in the windows in town; we know where they go. All the glory and splendor you can imagine awaits them. We looked through the windowpanes and saw how the trees were planted in the middle of a cozy room and decorated with the loveliest of gilded apples, honey cakes, toys, and hundreds of candles.*

"I told you, I told you this was a good story," Lil-Anne said triumphantly.

"If you keep interrupting, we'll never finish," said Karen. She described the wonderful experiences of the little tree, how it was brought to town to be loaded with candies and brightly lit candles, and was surrounded by admiring children and adults. Lil-Anne sighed with satisfaction; this was as it should be.

But then the story went on to tell of the sad fate of the sparkling tree. After Christmas, it was thrown into a dark attic with only mice and rats for admirers, where it repeated the only fairy tale it knew until even the mice tired of it. Then the tree was heaved into the yard, lost all its fine needles, and was chopped up for firewood.

The tears streamed down Lil-Anne's crumpled face, "I'll love you even when all your needles are gone," she sobbed. She would have embraced the tree except a few of the candles were still smoldering. "I'll never let them chop you up for firewood. I don't want to hear that awful story again. I never want another Christmas tree."

The few remaining guests departed shaking their heads. They always knew there was something wrong with those for'ners on the mainland. They had such strange customs. To chop down a tree for a few days of glory when it could have grown into a very fine mast! A good mast could last a long time. Even Hans Christian Andersen didn't approve, so that was that.

No one at Millfarm had any appetite for supper, although, if truth be told, Christian and Erik remained oblivious to the downfall of the tree's reputation and had raided the pantry when no one was looking. It took a while for Lil-Anne to stop sobbing, but then she remembered her precious amber heart.

Papa too said it was a wonderful present that had brought back some happy memories. He comforted Lil-Anne by saying that after Epiphany, they would move the tree out into the yard so that it could keep its fine needles and provide shelter for the birds until spring. Mam was secretly relieved that she would soon be rid of the clutter and it seemed unlikely that anyone would want a tree in the future. Erik yawned contentedly, murmured goodnight, thanked everyone for a lovely day, and went off to his room over the barn. Kirsten and Big-Anne bundled up Frederik and to a chorus of 'Merry Christmas' they too walked home. Before going to bed, Lil-Anne was even thoughtful enough to hug her brother goodnight and mumble, "It *is* a beautiful tree. You didn't know."

Twenty-Three

A Difficult Choice

Karen tucked Lil-Anne into bed and Erik went to his loft, with a soft 'Merry Christmas,' to everyone, clutching his new knife in his pocket. Papa had started to blow out the few remaining candles on the tree, when Christian came back from his room with an envelope, saying apologetically, "I completely forgot to give you this. It's from Ingrid-Fas."

"I wondered why I hadn't received her usual Christmas greeting," Papa said, moving closer to the lamp so he could see to read. "It looks like she's making up for it being later than usual by writing a nice long one." He broke the seal and skimmed the first page. "She sends greetings to everyone and also from Thomas and the children. According to Mrs. Lehman, Christian has behaved himself and is doing well at school."

He read on, looking increasingly serious.

"Is everyone in Ribe all right? Is she ill again?" Lars-Anne asked.

"No, so far she feels well, but the doctor wants is taking precautions. There is a message here for you, Karen.

"First I should tell you that the doctor is worried about Ingrid's confinement. She was very sick after Jens and has lost several babies since then. The doctor wants her to stay in bed for the next few months. She's like Lil-Anne and has trouble sitting still for very long, so this will be very hard for her and she is worried about the children. Here is her message for Karen, but it's really a question for all of us.

Dear Karen,
As your Papa will have told you, I am going to have to stay in bed for the next several months. Instead of "enceinte" I really think they ought to call it "imprisoned."

"It's so like her to joke even about something serious, like this," Papa interrupted himself, explaining that *enceinte* is French for 'encircled' and also for 'expecting.'

"I don't get it," Christian grumbled.

"Never mind," said Mam. "Some ladies think it's refined to speak French. Danish is good enough for me."

"I think she does it to be amusing, not to sound refined," Karen said impatiently. "Do go on, Papa."

I hope you will take pity on me and come to my rescue—in short, I would like you to be my companion during this time of waiting. The children too need someone to help pass the time and take them places now that I can not. Dear Sister Anne, please lend me your sweet daughter for a time. I promise that she will see the sights of the town and will be properly escorted to suitable concerts and plays. We will read uplifting books and she will further her cultural education.

Everyone sat in stunned silence until Lars-Anne mumbled, "Certainly not, she's too young."

The discussion went back and forth, pros and cons were trotted out. Mam was against having her daughter be a lady's maid and children's nurse. Papa countered that being companion to her aunt and cousins was very respectable. Christian reported that Ribe was a great place but hastily added that he hadn't had much chance to see the sights because the Lehfelts were very strict about everyone studying very hard.

"Nevertheless, she can get all the good books and culture she needs by staying here and studying with Pastor Engel," Mam said as if nothing else were needed.

Karen was annoyed that nobody asked her what she wanted, even Papa, but she just said, "I can't think now. I'll decide tomorrow."

"Yes, let's sleep on it," said Papa.

Papa's advice was easier said than done. Karen felt exhausted but couldn't settle down. She tossed and turned until Lil-Anne, who never woke during the night, mumbled, "stop kicking," and she forced herself to lie still. She could hear soft voices from the other side of the wall. Mam and Papa were probably talking about her but Mam seemed to be doing most of the speaking. Maybe Papa was, as usual, letting her persuade herself that he was right. *Is he? Should I go?*

She thought she heard Papa say, "You don't make much sense—you don't want her marrying a seaman but you won't let her go where she'll meet anyone else."

She could only hear part of Mam's reply, "Nevertheless, I'm afraid for her; I don't want her to...."

Karen was tempted to get out of bed and listen at the door, but the bed was warm and the floor cold. Finally she was overcome by the excitement of the day and her eyes closed.

When she opened her eyes again it was still dark out, but in the faint light from the moon, she could see a stork sitting by her bed and prodding her shoulder with his beak.

"I have a message from Peter. I flew over his ship on my way home from Egypt," the stork whispered. "He says to wait for him on the dune by the mill so he knows where you are."

"Peter isn't in Egypt and it's the middle of winter," Karen mumbled. "You're not supposed to be here until spring. I would only go to Ribe for a few months and be back again long before Peter comes home. I want to travel and see the world, I promised Karen-Mos."

But it wasn't a stork that was prodding her, it was Lil-Anne. "You're talking in your sleep. You told me to wake you early to light the fire in the kitchen, so we can give Mam and Papa breakfast in bed."

The girls were too late. Mam was already up and had porridge and coffee heating on the stove. "Lil-Anne, feed your chicks and find us some fresh eggs," she directed.

It was getting cold and looked like it might snow. Papa and Christian went to the stable to feed the animals and give them fresh bedding. They came back to *æ frankel* stomping their boots and playfully picking straw from each other's tousled hair.

All during breakfast, the discussion of Ingrid's invitation continued, though it seemed as if Mam had switched from 'whether' to 'when.' Still no one asked Karen what she wanted. Since she hadn't yet decided, she didn't want to waste arguing until she knew which side to fight for. Lil-Anne looked from one to the other trying to figure out what everyone was talking about. When it was finally explained to her she wailed, "Karen can't go. I can't sleep *all* by myself."

As soon as chores were done, Karen announced that she was going to town. "Wait until after dinner and we'll all go together," said Mam. "We need to call on everyone who came yesterday, but morning is not the right time. Besides, if we aren't here this afternoon, no one can come here—I've done all the entertaining that I want for a while."

"No. I'm going alone," Karen said firmly. "I want to ask Pastor Engel's advice about Ribe and I have some other people to see."

Surprisingly Mam said neither "certainly not" nor "nevertheless." Stunned by this grown-up independent Karen, she said nothing at all. When Karen emerged from her room wearing two extra skirts and another layer of socks, Lars-Anne handed her two baskets.

"You can't go calling empty-handed," she mumbled then gathered momentum. "Here's some red cabbage for Pastor's Ellen, and you'll want to talk to Big-Anne as well, so bring them their milk. Also, here are some fresh eggs and chicken soup for Tante-Black since she's poorly. Lil-Anne wants to visit Sidsel; please make sure she delivers a plate of cookies to Lone without nibbling."

Karen was so pleased to get away that she didn't bother to argue that she hadn't intended to run errands all over town. Lil-Anne was already bundled against the cold, equally anxious to leave. The two sisters walked down the Westerlands path into town.

"Are you really going to leave me?" Lil-Anne asked plaintively.

"I don't know yet. I have to think about it. You'd be fine, you'd have Papa all to yourself."

"But you're my sister. You can't just go. Who'll keep the bed warm?"

Their first stop was at Tante-Black, who was more than 'poorly.' "Doctor says she has influenza and maybe pneumonia," Tante-Blue said mournfully.

"We're supposed to give her soup," said her twin sister, taking the basket without so much as a thank you. "How we're to do that when she won't turn from the wall, I'm sure I don't know. We'll probably catch it too. Then who'll feed *us* soup?"

Karen and Lil-Anne left as quickly as they could without being rude, using Lil-Anne's visit to Sidsel as the excuse for not lingering. They would not be offered Christmas chamberboys here today, but then there was no danger that they would carry the Christmas spirit out of the house either; the only spirits here were gloomy ones.

Smith's forge was cold for the holidays and the cobblestones slippery with ice, but the two girls negotiated their way to the front door without spills. Lil-Anne and the cookies were safely delivered with an enthusiastic exchange of 'Merry Christmas.' Lone seemed ready to have a chat over morning coffee, but Karen pointed to the pitcher of milk and explained that Kirsten-Mos was waiting.

Kirsten-Mos met her at the door with her finger over her lips, saying that Big-Anne was also feeling 'poorly' and resting.

"She says it's just a touch of rheumatism from the damp weather this month, but I'm sure she's running a fever, and rheumatism doesn't give you a fever," Kirsten-Mos said with a worried frown. "I made her go to bed. She was in the scullery before dawn, boiling up the wash kettle for diapers and looking really awful. I don't remember the last time she was sick."

"I'll help you hang the wash," Karen volunteered. "I hope she doesn't have Tante-Black's 'flu." She went on to tell Kirsten about the letter from Ribe. "You know about difficult pregnancies, maybe you can tell me…."

Kirsten had learned much about midwifery from being Big-Anne's assistant over the years. Although she was usually reticent to speak about anything personal, she explained what she knew of Ingrid's past pregnancies, almost as if they were fellow professionals. "Jens was born several weeks early and nearly died. Even now, I understand he's a little slow. Then Ingrid caught childbed fever and was bedridden for a long time. After that she had three miscarriages, but the danger of that is past now, it usually happens early on. Her doctor probably wants her in bed to keep this baby from being born early. Big-Anne wouldn't agree. She says that staying in bed just weakens the body. She and Dr. Munck argue about this all the time but she says doctors are too ready to act instead of leaving everything in God's hands."

"Is that why Uncle Thomas wants Ingrid-Fas to have another child? Because he thinks Jens is slow?" Karen asked. "Why do you suppose she keeps having babies if it's so dangerous for her? You'd think she would stop."

Suddenly Kirsten-Mos clammed up saying, "This isn't a fit subject for a young maid."

"Granmam says for me to ask about anything, and I need to know what to expect before I can decide," Karen protested, but the discussion was clearly over.

"At least tell me, should I go to Ribe?" Karen called after Kirsten-Mos, who had left the room to pick up Frederik from his morning nap. The only answer was a "drip, drip" from the wet diaper in her hand.

"I do hope Granmam isn't sick for long," she muttered as she went out the door. "She'll tell me what to do."

Karen's conversation with the Engels was more circumspect. She didn't want to mention her aunt's pregnancies right out, so they talked about this and that. Papa Angel was concerned to hear about Tante-Black and he promised to call on her in the afternoon.

"I won't disturb Big-Anne," he said. "She'll just want to sleep until she has recovered. God is always with her. She doesn't need my poor help."

Then Ellen asked for the details of the Christmas tree events of yesterday. She had already heard three different versions but felt Karen was a more reliable source. In retelling the story, Karen emphasized the humor and added her own embellishments ending with Lil-Anne's dramatic reaction. Then she turned to the Pastor and asked, "Why do you suppose H. C. Andersen would tell such a sad Christmas story?"

"Many of his stories are not for children at all. This one is really an allegory of his life as an artist. Andersen is the small tree in the forest, surrounded by the giant literary figures of our time. He has never felt appreciated, thinks he was pushed away by society to tell fairy tales to children, the mice in his story. He doesn't understand that he really *is* recognized as one of Denmark's giants, at home as well as abroad. He has a very suspicious and depressed nature. Not at all like Grundtvig, more like Kierkegaard," Pastor finished mournfully.

The three of them sat in silence for a few minutes. Pastor bent his long frame in half, resting his chin in his hands so he could look directly into his young guest's eyes, and said with a smile, "Well, you didn't come to visit two old people to talk about gloom and doom. I think you have something else on your mind. Tell us what is troubling you."

Thus encouraged, Karen related the request from her aunt and all Papa's pros and Mam's cons.

"Do you want to go?"

"I can't decide. On the one hand, I hate to leave my friends, yet winter is such a dreary time here even with all the parties. Mette keeps talking about going to a farm on Sylt next summer, but I would like to do something more interesting. Maybe a stay in the city would help me decide about the future."

The Pastor leaned back in his chair and made a steeple with his index fingers. "Ribe isn't exactly the big city, but there will be plays and concerts for you to attend. Ludvig Schrøder, the Rector of Askov Folkschool, usually gives lectures during the winter about their grand experiment in bringing Grundtvigian idea of education to rural young people; you must hear him.

And of course, they have many more books for you to study than my modest library can provide."

"Do you think I'm too young to be on my own?"

"Nonsense," said the Pastor, lifting his eyebrows for emphasis. He dismissed all doubt with a sweep of his arms.

"You won't be on your own; your aunt will look after you," Ellen added patting Karen's hand. "When will you leave?"

"After New Year's Day, when Christian goes back to school," Karen said and then realized that she had decided.

During the next week it seemed as if half the town came down with influenza. Tante-Black continued to turn her face to the wall and refused to respond, even to Pastor Engel's entreaties. Finally her wish was granted and her small wasted body was laid out to the continual keening of Tante-Blue and Tante-Brown. It was left to Lars-Anne to comb out her few wisps of gray hair and cover her head in the black-striped bonnet that she had last worn at her confirmation over fifty years earlier.

Mette's uncle, lungs already weakened by tuberculosis, was carried off by pneumonia. Then several small children succumbed. There was hardly a family in town that was not in mourning for a relative. Every day Pastor Engel had to say the funeral service in a church that was nearly empty because of fear of contagion. The weather had turned cold and the ground was so hard that the men stacked the coffins on the north side of the church, waiting for thaw.

The house by the mill was untouched by disease and in the rest of the family only Granmam was ill. She stayed in her tightbed, growling at Kirsten-Mos or Karen to just leave her alone, she would be fine, just needed to sleep it off. Then after a week, she got dressed and went back to keeping her house, with only a pale face and an unwonted slowness in her step to show for her illness.

Karen was still vacillating about going to Ribe. She half hoped that she still had to persuade Mam, as if arguing with her would clarify her own mind. However, Mam's only question was about whether to send a telegram or write a letter. Papa finally splurged on a telegram stating that Karen and

Christian would travel together and come after New Year as soon as the weather allowed.

Mam then began fussing over what clothes Karen should take, giving endless advice on how to behave. "Stand tall, remember who you are and where you're from. Wear your scarf and you'll be treated with the respect owed a Sønderhoning," she said with a frown.

Karen recalled half-overhearing that Mam was worried about her going and, with sudden insight, connected that to the story Mette's mother had told. "The first couple of summers were terrible for her," Else had said. As if this were a common topic of conversation between them, Karen now said, "There's no reason I should have as bad a time on the mainland as your first time." She held her breath to see if Mam would answer.

"Just don't let anyone take advantage of you—kick hard and scream for help."

Karen looked at Mam in shock. "Is that what happened to you?" she whispered.

Mam looked at her hands and whispered back, "The second summer, Master cornered me in the barn and would have had his way with me except I kicked him hard in his, eh… shins and screamed at the top of my lungs. When Mistress came running, he pretended that he had found me with one of the hands and my yelling was because he slapped me—the lying …."

"What happened then?" Karen hardly dared ask. Mam seemed to have forgotten to whom she was talking. Even if she didn't say the forbidden words, it was clear what she meant.

"Mistress knew perfectly well what had taken place—I could tell by her eyes. But I was sent away in disgrace with a bad character in my hiring book. I almost couldn't get another job. If it hadn't been for Christian Andersen…."

"That's not fair!" Karen protested.

"That's the way it is for girls on their own."

Suddenly Karen's fears from the beginning of the summer about not really belonging on Fanø came flooding back, and she blurted, "You didn't get pregnant did you—that terrible man wasn't my father, was he?"

It dawned on Mam how the story had sounded to Karen, "Certainly not," she exclaimed in horror. "How could you think that? You were born a year after Papa and I married."

For the first time, since Karen was a very little girl, Mam hugged her and they wept in each other's arms. "Dearest, don't be afraid. You'll be fine. Just be careful," she murmured, stroking Karen's cheek.

"I'll stand tall and make you proud," Karen sobbed.

Mam dried her tears and, pretending that nothing momentous had happened, went on with her advice on what to pack. However, her frown was gone and she smiled at her daughter.

Karen felt as if a burden had been lifted from her shoulders. Another piece of her mother's past had fallen into place. How proud she was of Mam, never again would she resent her advice and criticism. *Mam does love me. She does want the best for me,* she told herself. Finally, she felt free to leave Sønderho.

New Year's day it snowed and snowed until Millfarm was buried in white mounds, twice as thick as the thatch roof. Every morning they woke to the sound of Papa and Erik shoveling snow and chipping ice from the cobblestones; snow even had to be cleared from the windows so they could see inside the darkened rooms. Erik moved to the main house and shared Christian's tightbed, lest he be stranded in the barn and be unable to dig his way out. The sheep were found buried in snow, huddled against the stable door. Although accustomed to roaming the heath in the winter, they had just enough sense to know that in bad weather they needed to come home where they would be fed.

Lil-Anne was in seventh heaven. She climbed into the loft and jumped out the dormer doors into the soft pile of snow. Then she shrieked half in delight and half in fear when she found herself inside a white well, unable to stand because her hands and legs just sunk in deeper when she tried to push herself up. After the men dug her out, she persuaded Christian to help her stomp down a sledding path to the mill and drag the toboggan to the top of the hill. When Christian was Lil-Anne's age, Papa had made it out of old barrel boards, but there was seldom enough snow to use it. The two children piled on the toboggan and, laughing so hard they forgot to steer, they slid into a snow bank. Up they went and then down, over and over; sometimes they sat upright, Lil-Anne between Christian's legs; sometimes they lay, one on top of the other.

"You have to come too, Karen," Lil-Anne yelled.

"Certainly not," said Mam. "She has to help get her clothes ready."

But Erik and even Papa had turns. "We haven't seen this much snow for as long as I can remember," Miller marveled. "Even the winter of '49, when I was a boy and the snow was above my head, it wasn't this deep. And it hardly snows on Fanø; not this much, not while I've lived here."

"Yeah, we never get to use the toboggan," Christian complained, his cheeks glowing.

Two days into the new year, when Karen and Christian were supposed to leave, it became very cold; so cold that the water between Fanø and the mainland froze during the night-time low tide and was broken into a thousand shards by the waves of high-tide during the day. Sailing was impossible. Ice flowers formed on the windows even though the stove was stoked all day and Papa got up in the middle of the night to add peat to the fire. Everyone wore their day clothes to bed and mitts during the day, even in the house. Lil-Anne borrowed a coin from Papa's purse, warmed it on the top of the stove and held it against the window. She pressed her eye to the little hole in the ice flowers. "I see her, I see the Snow Queen riding by in her sleigh," she exclaimed. "Just like Uncle Hans said."

On Twelfth-night, they lit three candles to celebrate the arrival of the Three Wise Men at the Christ child's manger. Huddled in the southroom right by the warm stove, they each picked a candle, betting walnuts on whose would burn the longest. Karen's was the last to go out. "That was the one I really meant to pick," Lil-Anne claimed but was hooted down by her brother and sister with cries of, "You always say that. You can't change your mind, just so you can win."

The cold and snow continued. At first Christian was delighted with the extra holiday, then he began to miss his friends at school and became bored with the lack of activity. Karen realized that hard as Mam had pushed to get him to school and much as Christian might complain about all the studying he had to do, he was not an altogether unwilling scholar.

Now that she had made up her mind, she was anxious to leave. She dreamt that Karen-Mos came to her and reminded her of her promise. "Karen-Mos, I'll make you and Mam proud. I'll be somebody for us all," she repeated over and over as she packed and repacked her small trunk. Why going to Ribe would make her somebody, she wasn't sure, but it would be a start. She had placed the small bundle of letters from Peter on the bottom of the trunk when Mam wasn't watching. Then she pulled them out again to tie them securely with a scrap of embroidered ribbon she had rescued from an old nightshirt. She had to repack everything once more to add the pin from Peter and the beautiful shawl from Uncle Paul that Mam didn't want her to wear. No one in Ribe would know to disapprove if she wore them.

"I'm tired of being trapped indoors day after day," she complained at supper one night. "I'm all ready to go, but this weather's impossible."

"The weather won't be any better in Ribe," Mam said.

"Well at least it'll be different," Karen sighed. "Something new, and not all this gloom and doom and caskets stacked in the church yard."

Papa finally said, "We'll get you off tomorrow, somehow. Christian needs to get back to school before half the winter is gone."

The next morning, he found some old runners in the barn with which to replace the wheels on the wagon and transform it into a sleigh. "Once we get to Nordby, you'll be fine. They'll break the ice to keep the ferry running and from Esbjerg you can take the stage to Ribe."

Finally the horse was hitched to the sleigh and their trunks loaded. Christian and Karen climbed up beside Papa and huddled under a heavy wool blanket. Mam, Erik, and Girl-Ellen, bundled in shawls, stood by the stoop to wave, but Lil-Anne broke into tears and refused to say good-bye. Finally, Papa flicked the reins and they glided down the snow-packed road. As they rounded the corner and turned north towards Nordby, they could see the little figure of Lil-Anne, standing on the hill next to the mill. Her cries of "don't leave me" echoed through the dunes.

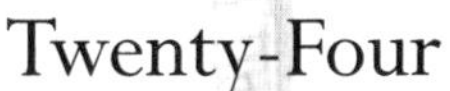

Twenty-Four

Winter in Ribe

Ribe, January 1875

For a minute Karen didn't know where she was. It was already daylight and she could see the sullen gray sky through the snow-covered branches on the tree outside the window. Next to her, the bed was empty; Lil-Anne must long since have gone to feed her chickens. Still groggy, Karen swung her legs over the side and, clutching her pounding head, tried to figure out why there was a tree outside the window and why she was lying in Mam's big bed rather than her tightbed. From the sound of voices drifting through the door, everyone must already be up and wondering why she was still here in the middle of the morning.

Then she remembered that she was in Ribe, having arrived at night after a miserable trip. She vaguely recalled that Christian had found a hansom cab at the station and told the driver where to go. At the house he had banged on the door until finally a grumpy Uncle Thomas in nightshirt and cap had let them in. Karen had been bundled off to bed with a fever, so exhausted she had no memory of being undressed and tucked under the covers.

Finally realizing that the pounding was not just in her head but someone at the door, she croaked, "Come." A wave of nausea hit and she quickly burrowed back under the down quilt, shaking with chills.

"Good morning, Miss Andersen," said the maid, bobbing without disturbing the full tray in her hands. "Cook sent me with breakfast. *Madame* wishes me to inquire how you are feeling and please to stay in bed until you are entirely rested."

She stood there waiting for Karen to sit up so she could place the tray of hot chocolate, rolls, curls of butter, and jars of honey and marmalade, on her lap. "Will Miss Andersen require anything else, perhaps a nice soft-boiled egg?"

Karen took one look at the food and mumbled, "No, please. I couldn't. Nothing." She made weak dismissing motions with her hands. "Maybe some chamomile tea. I think I have a fever." Recalling her manners, she tried to sound friendlier, "You may call me Karen. I hardly know who you're talking to."

"Oh no Miss, that wouldn't be fitting. *Madame*'s very strict. She's learning me to be a proper lady's maid." Then recognizing a fellow farm girl, she grinned and lapsed into a more comfortable dialect, "It be full hard sometime to remember all dem do's and don'ts. But Mistress says A has to if'n A wants to work in Copenhagen someday. Un just sleep in and un'll be right as rain quick like." With that she tucked the covers in tightly around Karen and, realizing she was being too familiar, blushed, bobbed again, and vanished out the door carrying the unwanted breakfast.

Karen gratefully closed her eyes. She realized that she must have come down with the 'flu like Granmam. She drifted off to sleep, thinking, *I hope no one else is sick.* She dreamt that it was Granmam, not Tante-Black who turned her face to the wall and was carried out in a coffin. Then Karen became that cold body lying in one of the coffins stacked on the north side of the church, waiting for the ground to thaw. The keening of Tante-Black's maiden sisters turned into Lil-Anne's crying, "Don't leave me Karen. Please don't go."

Then she wasn't in a coffin, but lying on big white bed with a black tree leaning over her, the dark branches clutching at her covers and brushing against her head. The branches turned into the tall legs of a stork sitting on her bed and pulling up her covers with his beak.

"I have a message from Peter. I flew over his ship on the way home to Denmark from Egypt," the stork was saying. "He says to wait for him on the dune by the mill so he can find you."

"That's what you said before I left home. But Peter isn't in Egypt; he's in the Pacific. Just because he has long legs like a stork, it's no good pretending he sent you, so go away. Even in Ribe, the storks go away for the winter, so you're only a dream. Anyway, I'll be home way before Peter," Karen mumbled.

"Yes, you're safe now," said a distant, soothing voice. "Poor child, she's burning up with fever and shivering at the same time. Put that warm brick by her feet and help me apply this poultice."

Karen felt her nightgown being pulled up and the poultice spreading warmth across her chest. "Christian. I have to get him to school," she mumbled.

"He went before sun-up. The errand-boy helped him carry his basket of clothes," said the voice again. Karen opened her eyes just long enough to recognize Cook and the maid, who was hovering in the background. "Lise, help her sit up so I can give her the infusion Doctor ordered. It's willow bark; Doctor says it's better than chamomile for fever," she explained, supporting her patient's head and making her drink a liquid so hot it burned her tongue.

"No willows or Christmas trees on Fanø," Karen mumbled and went back to sleep.

In her dream she was trying to persuade her mother to let her come to Ribe. "Certainly not," Mam said. "It isn't safe unless you keep your scarf on."

"I can't wear my scarf. I'm sick in bed," Karen mumbled.

"Nevertheless...," Mam said.

"Ingrid-Fas needs me but I can't get there, the weather is too cold. Papa, don't put more peat on the fire; it's too hot in here," Karen murmured.

Karen awoke bathed in sweat, the willow bark tea having broken her fever. She threw off the covers and fell asleep again. Now she was on the bridge of the *Marianne* with Peter. Flying fish jumped over the railing onto the deck, just as Peter had described in one of his letters. The tropical sun beat down on them, but there was a cooling breeze that dried the sweat off her bare head. Peter was calling out a new heading to the steersman. Karen said, "I'm so glad you're safe; I was so worried about you."

Don't worry, Peter; I'll wait for you, Karen murmured. *I just want to have adventures too.* Then she awoke, pulled up the covers and fell asleep again, this time without dreams.

Later in the afternoon she felt almost normal, but as soon as the willow-bark tea wore off, her head started to hurt. For the next several days Lise plied her with more infusions, hot possets, and soup. Finally she graduated to milk toast. The maid said that *Madame* insisted Miss Andersen was not to leave her room until she was entirely well. None but Lise was allowed to visit for fear that Ingrid would catch the fever.

The doctor came declaring that Karen could start to sit up. She had slept through his previous visits, but now he thumped her on the chest and listened carefully to her lungs. "Clear as a bell," he announced. "It's a miracle that you didn't get pneumonia after that long trip. Nothing like farm living to strengthen the body."

Ingrid-Fas wrote her a sweet note of encouragement, tucked into a leather-bound volume of poetry. "*La grippe* is a misery," she wrote. "The children and I had it two years ago, so we probably will not get it again, though one cannot be too careful. Everyone insists on fussing over me. I fear that you must be as bored as I." Karen deduced that *la grippe* was French for influenza.

Karen asked for letter paper and ink. She wrote Peter about the trip,

...There I was, the brave heroine escorting my younger brother to school, when I got sick. I threw up over the railing of the ferry. I, the future seafarer, the daughter of a sailing house, embarking on a quest to rescue my aunt in Ribe and getting seasick on a stupid little ferry. But it turned out I was not just seasick, I was plain old sick. Christian had to buy the tickets for the stage and practically lift me up the steps.

"Oh no, she is not really ill, the water was just choppy coming over from Fanø," he explained when they would not let me board the stage for fear of contagion.

Then we rode and rode for what seemed like days. I do not know what was worse, freezing in the lumbering coach as it struggled through the snow or

having to stumble into the stuffy crowded inns at the rest stops. We should just have spent the night in one of the inns, but I did not have the wits to suggest it and Christian did not know that Papa had given us money in case we needed to stay on the road. Some heroine!

She explored her room on shaky legs. Aside from the luxurious four-poster bed there was a little desk for writing and a comfortable reading chair. Her clothes had been unpacked and barely filled one drawer in the chest and one side of the large wardrobe. In the corner stood a little stand with a large bowl for washing; Lise brought a pitcher of hot water before every meal and emptied the slop bucket that was tucked underneath on a shelf. Compared to her tiny room at home, this was luxury, but Karen was beginning feel restless. She looked out the window at the winter-bare branches of the magnificent chestnut tree and studied the fashionably dressed people milling up and down the sidewalk. How busy with important errands the women looked, bundled in their wool cloaks and fancy hats. There wasn't a Fanø scarf to be seen.

At lunch Lise brought another note from Ingrid-Fas, this time, tucked into a novel,

As soon as your fever is entirely gone, Doctor says you may visit me. We will have such fun. My friends are empty-headed gossips and it will be a relief to have a serious conversation with someone. I wish I could show you the town but you must go shopping and model all your new clothes for me. We shall read Ingemann aloud; his story about King Valdemar when Ribe was the capital of Denmark is very entertaining but also teaches Danish history. The book with this note is not serious at all, but the latest romance that is making the rounds. Do not tell your mother, as she would be horrified. Your papa would think it utter drivel and that I have no taste! But a fever is not the time for education.

So Karen read until her headache returned, blushing at the steamy words about a lady pining for the return of her lover, the lord of the manor. This too was an education. The poems in Ingrid-Fas's first book were written in more eloquent and elegant words, but the romantic longings of star-crossed lovers were no less stirring. She puzzled over why one book was considered trash and the other literature.

She added to her long letter to Peter. She had to cross out long passages when overly romantic words from the novel sneaked from her fevered brain to her hand and flowed onto the paper before she could stop them. This was the last that would go to San Francisco, as she didn't know how long they planned to stay in California. Next week she would mail her letters to Australia.

What would she do when she recovered? What clothes could she possibly need to buy? She had brought two sets of aprons and matching tops, nearly new. Her three green flannel skirts should see her through the rest of the winter since it was getting warmer and even on the coldest days at home she never wore more than three at a time. It *would* be nice to have a set of silk scarves to wear to church. She wondered if the family ever went to the Cathedral. Sønderho ladies always came to Ribe to buy their head and neck-scarves from the Jewish Weaver. Maybe Ingrid-Fas would know where she could find his shop, even if she never wore Fanø scarves.

Karen wrote notes to Ingrid-Fas, her fellow prisoner across the hall, and letters to Mam and Papa telling them that Christian and she were safe but leaving out the worst of the trip and the severity of her illness. She received letters from them in return, saying that Papa had also had the 'flu, but not badly. There was even a short message from Lil-Anne, printed in big block letters: "I MISS YOU. COME HOME SOON. BED IS COLD WITHOUT YOU. LOVE, ANNE."

Finally Karen was pronounced fever-free and no longer contagious. She was ready to start her new life as companion to aunt and children.

Twenty-Five

Life in the City

If Karen had thought that her new life in Ribe would be one of leisure with nothing to do all day but read novels and poetry, she soon discovered otherwise. As quickly as her returning strength allowed she was sent on errands all over town, just like at home, only this town was much larger and here she was a stranger, constantly getting lost in its winding streets. Within a few days a routine was established which, although very different from that of Millfarm, was as filled with activities.

Mornings she was to see that Margrethe and Jens were dressed for school in time for breakfast with their father. Uncle Thomas, however, was short on company and long on frowns if the children made too much noise while he was reading his newspaper. Soon he would refold the paper and rise from the table. With a curt nod, he walked across the foyer and into his office at the front of the house, throwing the paper in the wastebasket on the way. Uncle Thomas was an importer of fancy fabrics, perfumes, and toiletries, mostly from France and Italy but even from as far away as the Orient. The business, including a retail shop, shared the first floor of the four hundred-year-old house with the foyer, the family dining room, and a small sitting room for receiving guests. Uncle made sure to tell Karen that *Bang and Son* had been in the family for over two hundred years and that the original "son" had been his grandfather.

After breakfast, Karen was to escort the children to school. The first day Jeppe, the errand boy, went with them to help her find her way home. The house was right around the corner from the central square and the school only a few streets away, but Karen soon discovered that it was easy to get lost. Although the cathedral tower was taller than any building, the medieval streets in the center of town were so narrow that the tall square tower hid behind the overhanging roofs of three-storied buildings.

She was not sure why the children needed her company to walk the short distance since they knew the way much better than she and were expected to return home by themselves. It soon became clear that eight-year-old Jens was a dreamer, easily distracted and reluctant to go to school. He needed a much firmer hand than eleven-year-old Margrethe could provide. Even after school he was more likely to stop to watch workmen putting up a new house or pause to listen to street singers on the square than to walk straight home.

Cousin Margrethe was the exact opposite of her brother: quiet and obedient where he was noisy and irresponsible. She did precisely as she was told, usually sitting quietly in a corner unless spoken to. Where Jens went out almost everyday to play with his friends, coming home with dirty knees and a filthy shirt, Margrethe never went anywhere and her white pinafore was always immaculate. Karen wondered if she had any friends. Sometimes she was tempted to knock their heads together to transfer a little of one personality to the other; one was too good to be true, the other constantly in trouble.

On her return to the house, Karen would retrieve the newspaper from the wastebasket in the foyer where Uncle had thrown it. It never occurred to him that the women in the house might read it as thoroughly as he. New mail lay on a little table by the door and Karen collected letters for herself and her aunt before going up the stairs to Ingrid-Fas's room.

This was Karen's favorite part of the day. Ingrid-Fas had usually completed her *toilette* and was "dressed," meaning that she had changed from her linen nightdress to a silk gown and *peignoir,* as Karen learned to call the flowing robe that a lady wore to entertain in her *boudoir.* She greeted Karen cheerfully from a funny chair that looked like a very narrow pillow-filled bed and was called a *chaise longue*. Pouring a cup of coffee for her niece, the two settled in to read the mail before discussing the news of the day. During the first few weeks, Karen received only one letter; it was from Papa but nothing came from Peter.

Setting her correspondence aside to be answered later, Ingrid-Fas said, "Well let's see what the politicians in Copenhagen are up to." She scanned the headlines and read the choicest articles aloud before passing the paper on to Karen. Although Karen seldom read the newspaper at home, Papa usually summarized the day's events at supper and she now had no trouble keeping up the latest developments.

"Papa likes to read the news too," Karen said. "He says that now we have the vote, it is the duty of every Dane to know what is happening."

"The *men* have the vote," Ingrid-Fas amended. "After twenty-five years, its about time they gave it to women too!"

Ingrid-Fas sounds just like Papa, Karen thought. However, she soon discovered that her aunt was also like Mam in making sure that Karen knew how to keep house. When Cook-Dorte reported the first day for her daily conference about the menu and other household questions, Karen tried to leave the room. "Please stay," Ingrid-Fas had said. "Running a city household is very different from living on a farm. I had an awful time when I was first married. You can learn by helping Dorte with the marketing."

Karen would never have believed how different housekeeping was here. At Millfarm, they used what was at hand or they did without. Mam had taught her so well that all the myriad details of baking bread, churning butter, making cheese, storing vegetables, preserving fruits, extracting honey, dipping candles, smoking ham, salting meats, and drying fish were just daily chores without mystery. Meals were plain and varied little except for special feasts, which consisted of predictable, traditional dishes. Now Karen had to learn to think in 'menus' and help make lists of everything they needed to buy. Then she and Dorte would make the rounds of the market and grocery stores and change everything around when they found what they had planned wasn't available. It was very confusing. In Sønderho, most food was homegrown and the only store was Brinch's, which sold coffee, tea and spices. The only other places to buy anything were at the factory, which made and shipped paints and dyes all over the country, and the smith who could make or fix any needed tool. The rest was either ordered from the mainland, came home with the ships, or was bartered with a neighbor. In the city, by contrast, everything had to be purchased from a separate store or market stall. At home, they used the oldest and most likely to spoil first; here only the newest and freshest would do.

After returning from marketing, Karen carried a tray with lunch for the two of them up to her aunt's room. Uncle Thomas ate in the dining room in lonely splendor before going back to his office. Privately, Karen thought that he should be the one to keep Ingrid-Fas company. After lunch her aunt rested, complaining that the doctor was an old fuddy-duddy; why did she need to rest since she wasn't doing anything?

This was Karen's own time in which to write letters or explore the town. Ingrid-Fas insisted on giving her pocket money, more money than she had ever had. At first she couldn't think of anything to spend it on, but occasionally she found a trinket or a bakery treat for herself. She began to enjoy her solitary explorations of the town, relishing her new freedom. At home, she could not walk anywhere without being spoken to and she could count on her behavior, good as well as bad, to make the rounds of town and be reported to Mam and Granmam. Here where she knew no one, she felt anonymous. She could roam the old cobbled streets and explore to her heart's content without speaking a word to anyone. It was true that many of the shopkeepers now knew her by name and often called out a greeting as she went by, but they seemed unlikely to talk about her. She discovered that her distinctive headscarf branded her as 'Importer Bang's niece' but if she raised the hood of the voluminous woolen cloak that Ingrid-Fas had lent her, she could blend into the crowds.

She loved to wander down to the market street and watch all the people coming and going. Hawkers called out from their stalls the virtues of their wares, and women walked around carrying overflowing baskets with which to tempt the passers-by. Street urchins ran everywhere, some begging while others snatched apples from a stand behind the owner's back.

One day, Karen bought a pastry fresh from the oven at the bakery. While munching on her treat, she saw a skinny little child lifting a wallet from a man's pocket. Since the boy looked like he needed the money more than the corpulent burgher, she said nothing. As the boy ran by, he winked at her, trusting that his secret was safe. She was glad that she had followed Cook's advice and kept her money securely in a bag under her apron. On the other side of the square sat a clogmaker on a bench, a pile of wooden shoes of all sizes displayed at his feet. Next to him stood a fishwife beside a large tub of live fish. In her hand was a large knife with which she had just cut off the head of a still wriggling cod. A cat came out of nowhere, grabbed the fish head and ran off before the woman could do anything but brandish her knife with a string of swear words, the likes of which Karen had never heard.

She recalled her plan to buy silk scarves, a plan that was to precipitate a cascade of events that no one could have anticipated. It all started innocently enough. She thought the weaver's shop was down an alley from the vegetable stand where Cook bought potatoes and onions. Hesitating at a corner in momentary confusion, she lowered the hood on the cloak so she could look in all directions.

To her surprise, a man's voice called out, "Hey Miss, is un lost?" She should have turned away, but forgot that in the city young ladies should not respond to strange men, especially one as scruffy looking as the bandy-legged gnome before her.

"Un's looking much better than last, if Miss'll pardon me saying so," he said with a friendly grin. When Karen looked puzzled he exclaimed, "Ah! Un don't remember. A met the stage that night un came to Riwe. Brother Christian hailed my cab. Sicker'n a dog un were. He were one worried boy, but right quick. That Latin School has sure learned him right."

She wondered if this was the loquacious carter who had carried Papa's luggage last fall when he came to bring Christian to the Latin School. "You're Svend Schultz, aren't you?" Reassured by his nod that this was no stranger, she explained her errand.

"Jew-Taylor's shop be just down the alley behind the Inn. A's going right by to deliver some goods to the Jewish butcher two houses on. Us can walk together. A don't know why our meat isn't good enough for 'em and they have to have their own butcher, but dem's just their ways. They's good people."

Svend indicated that Karen should walk on the narrow sidewalk while he pushed his handcart in the gutter. Pointing out the various sights, he entertained her with a steady stream of gossip about the history of Ribe, his dialect so thick as to be almost a foreign language. His view of history was as telescoped as looking through the wrong end of Uncle Paul's spyglass, the scandalous behavior of medieval monks mixed in with stories about the Dutch-style merchant houses of the sixteen-hundreds. All were told as if they were yesterday's gossip. Her self-appointed guide explained that the few Jewish families in town all lived together down one alley and that they had come to 'Riwe' to escape the turbulence of Bismarck's wars that were to bring about German unification.

"Here we are," he finally said. Not content with merely dropping Karen off, he introduced her to the weaver and his wife while patting each of the flock of children on their heads and calling them by name. "Mr. Schneider, A's brung un a very pretty customer," he said. "Un take good care of the Miss here, she be special and Importer Bang's niece besides." With a wave of his hand, he went on his way.

So much for anonymity. Smiling at Karen's headscarf, the weaver said that women from Sønderho were among his best customers. He had a beard like Papa except it was longer and untrimmed. Even the front locks of his hair reached to his shoulders and were curled like corkscrews. Karen tried not to stare while trying to figure out why he would wear his hair like Margrethe's.

Pointing to her head, she explained, "I'd like to buy a scarf like this, only in silk. My mother recommended your shop." That wasn't quite true, but she knew that everyone in Sønderho bought from the Jew-weaver.

Mr. Schneider readjusted the little black cap that threatened to fall off the back of his head and said something to his wife. It sounded like a dialect of German, but Karen could not understand. The woman, whose hair was covered with a white kerchief, brought out a stack of scarves. A girl, about Margrethe's age, came up and shyly suggested that she could translate for her mother if there were any questions. The girl's head was also covered but long brown braids fell to well below her shoulders.

Karen debated for a long time. The silk material glowed in brilliant hues of green, blue, and purple. A solid-blue scarf to match her eyes looked lovely but that was the traditional color for mourning. She finally picked one with festive red and blue stripes on a darker blue background. Giggling as she draped it on top of her every-day cotton scarf, she bent down to look at herself in a mirror on the counter. Her mind was made up so she declined politely when Mrs. Schneider suggested, in heavily accented Danish blended with German, that she might like to go behind a curtain and try it on.

A young man stepped out of the back room to take her money while Mrs. Schneider wrapped her package in brown paper. Judging by the family resemblance, the youth was her son, perhaps a year or so older than Christian. He had the slight, stooped build of his father, with the same pale face, long side-curls, and black cap that perpetually threatened to slide off his head, but his beard was much shorter. He told her the price in excellent Danish with only a slight accent and Karen almost panicked; never had she bought anything so expensive. But she had the money and Ingrid-Fas was always urging her to buy something for herself.

The young man seemed very shy and did not look at her when he gave her change, but when he held out the package for her to take, he glanced up and their eyes met briefly. She was struck by his luminous eyes, so dark they were almost black, like the bottom of a well at night when all you can see is a reflection of the stars overhead.

His sister, still at Karen's elbow, blurted out, "I know your cousin Margrethe. We're in the same class at school. She's always very nice to me and helps me with my Danish spelling."

Karen was pleased that Margrethe apparently had at least one friend. "You're Hanna, aren't you?" she asked, recalling Svend's introduction. She would have tried to find out the name of her brother, but the cathedral bell announced two o'clock. She hurriedly picked up her purchase and rushed home. Mentally drafting her next letter to Peter, she wrote, *Svend tells wild stories with history and legends all blended together.* When she described the weaver's family, she thought that it might be better not to mention the interesting young man.

Uncle Thomas required the children to report at the store before the two-fifteen chimes of the cathedral clock. Since school let out at two, that was barely time enough for Jens to dawdle. Usually Uncle Thomas was out of the house by this time, but his assistant, Mr. Lauritzen, wrote down the exact time by the wall clock when they checked in.

After that, Jens was free to go outside and play with his friends as long as he said hello to his mother, changed from his school knickers, and was back at dusk. Margrethe, who did not have to change her clothes since she never went out, went upstairs to chat with her mother. Although usually quiet and subdued, with Ingrid-Fas she was a different child, vivacious and full of questions. *She's like the tropical lizards that Peter told me about; the ones that change color to blend with their surroundings*, Karen thought.

Late afternoon was social hour when Ingrid-Fas's friends came to tea. At first Karen was a curiosity and they questioned her about everything from her exotic turban, as the ladies called her headscarf, to life on Fanø. She offered to demonstrate how her scarf was tied, but that was not required. Soon these "flighty Twitterers" as her aunt privately called them, tired of the novelty and returned to their accustomed gossip about Ribe. The chatter seemed much as at home and no more consequential. Usually they reported the town's latest social event or gossiped about whoever was not present that day. Karen discovered that by bending industriously over her knitting she could appear to be shyly but politely listening to the gossip while her mind wandered to Peter on the other side of the world. Margrethe was excused as soon as she had curtseyed to each guest, but in a few minutes, she would quietly walk back in and hide in a corner, appearing so engrossed in playing with her Parisian doll that no one realized she was listening. The rest of the time, the doll sat neglected and Karen suspected that her cousin was disguising active eyes and ears with behavior more childish than her years.

Supper was a stilted formal affair in the dining room on the main floor. Ingrid-Fas, of course, was served dinner on a tray, but punctual attendance was required of everyone else. Uncle Thomas presided over the table, his pocket watch next to his plate. He discouraged conversation, though he usually asked Jens what he had learned in school that day. He didn't deem it necessary to ask the same of his daughter.

"When can I start piano lessons?" Jens asked one day.

"Piano lessons are not for boys," his father said. "You are too much of a dreamer, music would just encourage you to drift off somewhere. It's bad enough that your mother insists you take dancing lessons, but I suppose you do need to learn some social graces."

Jens made a face. "Karl Poulsen takes violin, what about that?" and he moved his arms as if he were playing a fiddle.

"Johannes!" his father thundered so loudly that Karen jumped. "Behave yourself. One does not wave one's arms about at the table like a savage. Eat your cabbage. You too, Margrethe."

"Mama doesn't make us," Jens muttered and Margrethe cringed. Their father glared until they complied.

Karen couldn't decide whether it was worse for the children to be thundered at or to be ignored. She decided to suggest to Ingrid-Fas that cabbage be omitted from the menu until she could come down to dinner again and keep peace.

After dinner, Uncle usually went out, not returning until after the children were in bed. Karen and the children went upstairs to the parlor where Margrethe did her homework and practiced the piano. Karen was enthralled by this instrument, which she had never seen, Sønderho being too damp.

"If you can play songs or hymns, I'll sing and we can have duets," Karen suggested.

"My teacher just gives me Kulau sonatinas," Margrethe demurred.

"Surely no one can object to your learning to play hymns. I'll ask your mama."

Jens went across the hall to do his homework in Ingrid-Fas's room. This was his special time with her and Karen could hear them telling each other stories and laughing. He drew fanciful pictures of knights on horses fighting dragons in a large artist sketchbook that he kept in the bottom of his dresser drawer. It was the only one of his possessions which was never misplaced and whose pages magically never tore.

"He has such a wonderful imagination," Ingrid-Fas explained, showing Karen the drawings one evening. "Papa doesn't like him to draw, but he has trouble with reading and writing; pictures seem to help." Then, turning to her son, she urged, "Tell us about the knight, is he rescuing a damsel in distress?"

Karen was worried that she still had not heard from Peter. Early in December, Kirsten-Mos had received a telegram from the Falkands, relaying a message from the *Marianne* that they had safely rounded the Horn. Since then, nothing.

Finally, one snowy day, a letter with American stamps arrived and Karen ran to her room to read it. Peter had mailed it from San Diego in mid-December, sending it to Sønderho from where it had been forwarded to Ribe. It had probably been delayed by the bad weather on the Atlantic Ocean. At lunch, Karen couldn't resist sharing Peter's description of rounding the Horn with Ingrid-Fas. Afterwards back in her room, she read it for a third time.

The children arrived home from school, soaked to the skin and had to change into dry clothes. It was too miserable for Jens to go outside, and no one came to visit Ingrid-Fas for tea. "I'm bored," Jens declared. Even Margrethe was restless.

"Karen had a letter from Peter," Ingrid-Fas said brightly. "Do you mind reading it to us?"

Karen blushingly complied by extracting the precious envelope from the front of her nightshirt. While she read aloud, Jens drew a picture of a sailing ship. "I can't get the sails right," he complained. "You're supp'sed to know about stuff like that, tell me what to draw. How many sails on each mast? What are all those ropes called?"

Karen was delighted to explain. There was little about ships at sea that a Sønderhoning, even a girl, did not master at a young age. She was amazed at what close attention the boy paid and how quickly he, whom everyone treated as if he were slow-witted, learned the intricacies of rigging. Then he explained it all to his mother and together they wove a tale about a ship traveling about the world. Even Margrethe joined in the conversation, seeking Karen's advice about cargo and ports of call.

She brought the big globe from the sitting room and soon they were deep into a geography lesson. Karen explained about longitude and latitude, the vagaries of winds and ocean currents, and intricacies of navigating by the stars, south of the equator. They traced the route of the *Marianne* and discussed the countries and territories where she had stopped.

"They were really lucky to round the Horn so quickly," Karen said. "Sometimes they have to wait months and months for the right wind."

Ingrid-Fas leaned back on her pillow with a triumphant smile. "I knew it!" she muttered. "I knew Karen would be good for them."

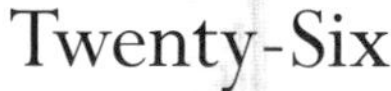

Twenty-Six

San Francisco

California, January 1875

The *Marianne* lay gently bobbing a few miles out from the Golden Gate, all but a few staysails reefed. Finally, a small boat came alongside and the pilot climbed on board to guide the bark through the Narrows and into San Francisco Bay. Setting only enough sail to make steady progress, they wove between the many craft crisscrossing from one shore to the other. Nearing Yerba Buena Cove, they shifted to a starboard tack and luffed into the wind as the men swarmed up the ratlines to reef the sails one by one in a well-choreographed dance of the sea. Captain was as particular about his crew's performance as if he were the master of a navy frigate and Mate Peter was prepared to see that the final sails would be reefed exactly at the moment they dropped anchor. This was no mean feat for a ship of *Marianne's* size, but a maneuver they had repeated many times over the past ten months. Only in her final leg tomorrow to unload her cargo at the *Embarcadero,* would the proud *Marianne* suffer the indignity of being pulled by a soot-spewing, noisy tug.

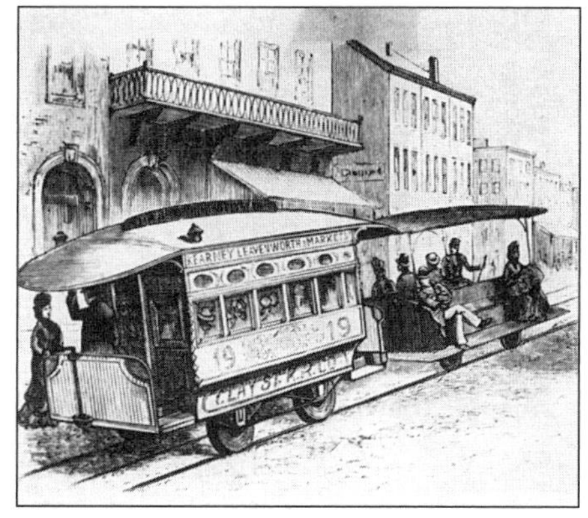

A day later, cargo holds empty and riding high, she was back at her mooring in the cove, only a few hundred feet from where her two principal officers were enjoying a beer. Tomorrow she would be towed to dry dock for badly needed repairs, but today her Captain and First Mate had met at the raucous dockside establishment after doing the town. Helped by mugs of beer and the shared news from home, they relaxed the formal distance between captain and mate that they usually maintained on board ship.

"Look what your niece's done now," Peter said showing off his latest mail.

"The Boy who Ran Away to Sea and Learned to Cook," Captain read aloud from the *The Fanø Weekly*. He laughed uproariously when he realized this was the story of Nephew Christian when he had stowed away on the *Fortuna*. Both Paul and Peter had, of course, already been regaled with the story by various members of the family, but here it was in print, bold as brass for the world to see and everyone to have a good laugh.

"I bet Lars-Anne was furious, having the story made public like that," Paul said, enjoying the image of his sister-in-law fuming. "Well, everyone knows about it already and what's the harm in having a little fun? But you know how she gets." He read the story again, chuckled some more and added, "Karen certainly knows how to tell a tale. Did you notice that her byline is 'Karen Andersdatter'?"

The two men went on to share the events of their day. Peter was very taken with the city and its babble of languages and cultures. Seamen coming and going from the orient, sodbusters down from the hills, and elegant ladies and gentlemen all rubbed elbows with laborers of many colors.

"Did you ever think about settling in America?" Peter asked the older man.

"No. Never. When we get back to Sønderho, I'm going to stick close to home harbor, dangle my son on my knee, and have as many more as Kirsten will allow. Maybe I'll make a few trips to England with hogs and to Norway to buy timber, but I'm done with traipsing around. From now on I'll see the wonders of the world through a stereopticon."

"But America seems so open, so free, so full of life and opportunity. Imagine over 70,000 people live in San Francisco alone." Peter stared into the last inch of beer in his glass as if it held an image of his future. Karen would never want to live this far from her beloved island, but he agreed with Captain that this roaming around the world was no way to live. A good way to earn a fortune, but a lonely way of life, even if one survived the next storm, the next tropical fever, the next time becalmed without freshwater.

"Have you ever thought to bring Kirsten on board?"

Paul laughed. "Kirsten is a lousy sailor, as we found out on *Marianne's* maiden voyage to Norway. No, you'll have to be the one to make her a 'Lady Ship.' Oh, don't look at me like that. You know Karen would make a great captain's wife."

"But Karen's only sixteen and I'm not even a captain yet!" Peter stammered.

"Well someday," Paul said airily. "And don't deny that you've thought of it!"

Peter blushed, for once at a loss for words. Captain was acting as if Karen and he were engaged, but he had promised her father not to even think about it until she was older. Much older. And as far as her mother was concerned, later was much too soon for Anne Andersen's daughter to marry a seaman.

He shook off his sudden melancholia and changed the subject. "Did you ride the new cable cars yet? Aren't they fantastic? I went to the steam plant that drives the system and they showed me all around. What a technological marvel."

Paul laughed and agreed that riding the cable cars up Clay Street to the top of the hill was a great experience. And such a view!

"Speaking of the view, what d'you think of these? The famous photographer Carleton Watkins has a shop on Montgomery Street." Peter proudly held up a card with a double photograph against the light. "This is of the new cable cars and here's a view of San Francisco from Russian Hill. This one you have to see in the stereopticon to get the full effect. It's from a place east of here called Yosemite. That rock in front jumps right out at you. It's called Agassiz. And here's a huge waterfall coming off the Sierra Nevada Mountains. You're not going to see anything like that sitting on the bench in Sønderho harbor." The two men squinted at the tiny pictures before them trying to imagine what they would look like in stereo.

Soon they fell to discussing the work that needed to be done on the *Marianne*. "There may be a leak in the bow," Peter reported. "The men are complaining that the forecastle has standing water and the pumps can barely keep up."

"They'll fix that in dry-dock," Captain Paul reassured him, then changed the topic to their next trip. "This morning I signed a contract to bring grain to Seattle. We'll haul lumber on the return trip, back here. That should keep us busy until the Trade Winds start in March and we can set sail for the Sandwich Islands."

Tomorrow, the two men agreed, they would have to find land quarters for the men and sign on replacements for those of the crew seduced into remaining behind in California. The crew too needed an overhaul on solid land; they were all home- and land-sick.

Suddenly Paul said, "I forgot to tell you, we've been invited to dinner by Shipbuilder Bendixen. Some soprano is going to sing afterwards. Shall I respond for you too?"

Peter readily agreed. "It'll be a long time before we'll hear a woman singing again!" He rose from the table and hailed the launch; suddenly he was in a hurry to return to the ship and write Karen about the wonders of San Francisco. "I'll relieve Mr. Hansen so he can go on shore," he said.

The next day, Peter took his package of stereo photographs and letters to the post office by way of the harbormaster. There was another letter from Karen, describing her Christmas. Her envelopes were usually thick with many sheets of cream paper covered in her neat blue ink, written over days or weeks as she waited to find out *Marianne's* next port of call. Knowing that they would be spending time in San Francisco, this letter was shorter, having been posted as soon as it was written. This time there was no *Fanø Weekly,* just an amusing story about Christian's arrival home from school on vacation and Lil-Anne's reaction to the Christmas tree that he had brought from the mainland. It concluded with the news that Karen too was to travel, albeit only to visit her aunt in Ribe. She and Christian were to sail as soon as possible after New Year.

By now, Peter had arrived at the post office. Before mailing his package, he crossed out the address on the front and changed it to: 'Frøken Karen Andersen, c/o Importer Bang, Ribe, Denmark.' He imagined the trip his letter would take: first by train, chugging over the Sierra Nevada mountains, speeding across the salt flats, struggling over the Rockies to Denver, steaming across the Great Plains to Chicago, and finally arriving in New York. It seemed a miracle that the trip by sea that had taken him months, could be accomplished in just ten days by going straight across the continent. After New York, his letter would go by packet to England and then by ferry to Esbjerg and finally arrive at Ribe after only three or four weeks of travel. He imagined Karen's surprise at opening his letter with the pictures and the look in her blue eyes when she saw the wonders revealed by the stereopticon.

He was tempted to put a stamp on his forehead, tie a string around his arms, fling himself across the counter, and say to the postal clerk, "Send me home." He laughed aloud as he imagined the shock on the man's face. Turning to leave, he almost bumped into a fashionably dressed lady standing behind him in line. His thoughts were so filled with Karen that, for a minute he thought it was she standing before him in a lace-trimmed hat and lavender velvet dress. Quickly realizing his mistake, he apologized with a winning smile and a courtly bow. To hide his fluster he exclaimed, "What a fetching bonnet. Wherever did you buy it? I must get one for my fiancée." Without waiting for a reply, he bowed again and ran out the door.

The surprised lady looked speculatively after the handsome man. He sounded English, but his slight accent made her realize that he must be from the Danish bark, and his uniform indicated he was her First Officer. *What an interesting young man*, she thought. *I imagine he'll be at Bendixen's party. I must persuade Aunt Elisabeth to make me his dinner partner.*

As Peter rushed headlong down the hill towards his boarding house, he wondered how he could have mistaken the sophisticated lady for Karen. After all, he had never seen her in anything but a traditional green skirt, apron and overblouse. This lady had beautiful, long blond curls, but he only knew Karen had blond hair because her scarf often came undone and she had to retie it. *It must have been the dress*, he thought. *It's exactly the color of Karen's eyes.* Then he realized what had popped out of his mouth. "Fiancée!" he exclaimed aloud, much to the surprise of some pedestrians passing by. *I like the sound of that. Wouldn't her mother be furious?*

Little did he know that a vision of Karen, dressed in a lavender dress, would haunt his dreams for several months. Perhaps it was just as well that he had no time to write her that they should become engaged now and not wait for his return to Denmark. Karen might balk at being told instead of asked, and Peter would regret his impulse when over the next few days, thoughts of home and family evaporated in a whirlwind of social activities.

Captain Fredriksen and Peter, dressed in their finest striped trousers and frock coats, struggled up Russian Hill. Near the top, the stiff January breeze threatened their tall silk hats and they hastily removed them lest they fly away. Paul consulted a slip of paper he had pulled from his vest pocket and stopped before a three-story mansion heeling into the angle of the street. "She looks to be carrying too much canvas for this gale," he quipped pointing to the scallop-edged roof far above their heads.

Peter was still laughing when their host, Villum Bendixen, opened the door. Greeting them warmly in Danish, he pulled them through the vestibule and into the parlor. He introduced them, this time in heavily accented English, to his wife and a jumble of people around the room.

William Bendixen had retired from the sea ten years earlier and settled in San Francisco with his New England-born wife, Elisabeth. His thriving shipbuilding business was across the Bay in Mendecino where the *Marianne* was to be towed on the morrow for repairs, but tonight he wanted to show off his impressive home and influential friends to her Master and First Mate from the 'Old Country.' Villum, known to his wife by the anglicized 'William,' was a huge Viking of a man with a booming voice and generous heart. He was well aware that he owed much of his social and business success to the beauty of his home and the reputation of his wife as a gracious hostess, and he spared no expense to show both off to their best advantage.

Elisabeth barely reached his shoulder and would have been eclipsed by her giant husband except that no one could resist her captivating smile and lively black eyes. Her dark blue silk dress, which would have been austere on most women, accentuated her slim figure and called attention to a serene face framed by glossy black hair. Without apparent effort, she brought peace and harmony to any gathering, a gift that kept her husband's natural boisterousness within bounds and contributed to her popularity as a hostess.

Next in the receiving line stood her niece, who was visiting from Virginia. Isabel Kensington was stunningly beautiful. In marked contrast to her aunt, she was tall and willowy and had blond ringlets that cascaded down the back of her swan-like neck. When introduced to Paul, she said, demurely enough but with an exaggerated Southern accent, "Ah am so pleased to meet the legendary Captain of the beautiful *Marianne*."

She held Paul's hand only as long as courtesy dictated, then turned to Peter with mischief in her blue eyes and exclaimed, "Ah do believe, Ah've already had the pleasure of meet'n her handsome first mate."

Peter recognized the lady whom he had addressed so impulsively only hours before and bowed deeply over her proffered hand to hide his embarrassment. He noticed that her evening dress was even more attractive than the one he had admired at their chance post office encounter. It was of watered silk rather than velvet and of a deeper and bluer color than the lavender of the morning, a color designed to complement her eyes. The plunging neckline and the curve of the lace edging along her white bosom suggested much to someone who had been long at sea, perhaps more than was prudent.

All through dinner, Isabel hung on his every word. She clapped her hands in delight, sighed sympathetically, or widened her eyes in amazement, as the story warranted. Flaunting convention, she ignored all attempts by the gentleman on her right to engage her in conversation and, in turn, would not permit Peter to address the lady on his left. Elisabeth tried in vain to catch her niece's eye and to include the young people in the general discussion. She finally left them to their own devices but rushed the ladies to leave the gentlemen to their cigars as soon as the last dessert spoon had been lowered to its plate. Isabel appeared inclined to stay at the table, but Elisabeth's stern look in her direction brooked no argument.

A singing recital followed and Elisabeth kept her niece firmly by her side in the front row and hissed at her to behave. Afterwards, however, she could not prevent Isabel from pulling the young man out on the terrace to admire the view over the Bay. Isabel wasted no time in getting to the point. "Tell me more about this lucky fiancée of yours."

"Uh, yes, but," Peter stammered. "Well…we aren't exactly engaged…I haven't exactly asked her. Yet. Her mother wouldn't allow. We'll have to wait until I return to Denmark."

"Ah, tragic star-crossed lovers kept apart by the oceans of the world," Isabel whispered conspiratorially. "How romantic! Do tell me more."

She barely listened to Peter's rambles about the beauties of Fanø and his wonderful Karen. "Perfect," she mumbled, followed by a louder, "We must find some amusements to divert you from this heartache—if there are any in this gloomy provincial town."

During the next few weeks, as much as Peter's duties allowed, he escorted Isabel to the various notable sights around town, all thoughts of Karen dismissed. It was perhaps fortunate that Elisabeth would not permit Isabel and Peter to go off on their own but arranged for them to be with a company of San Franciscans. Elisabeth had earlier tried in vain to persuade Isabel to make suitable friends while she was visiting, but the bored young lady had proclaimed them dull and provincial. Peter was more interesting and a challenge to her social skills. There was little danger of a serious entanglement since he would soon be departing for the Orient. It therefore suited both Elisabeth and Isabel to have Peter be her escort and have the rest of the young people serve as chaperones.

January was usually the California rainy season but the weather cooperated with the wily young lady. They climbed Telegraph Hill to see the view and explore the ruins of the semaphore station. The whole group of young people rented carriages and drove out to the point of the Golden Gate to picnic and admire the tall ships from around the world gliding by under sail. The theatre season was in full swing and Peter enjoyed the several performances they attended, although they hardly satisfied Isabel's standards. The steam-ferry took them across the Bay where they hired horses from a livery stable. Even Isabel's criticism was silenced by the magnificence of the nearby forest of giant sequoia trees made famous by the naturalist John Muir.

Poor Peter hardly knew what had hit him. This well-traveled young man was not inexperienced in the ways of the world, but he was now in the hands of an expert flirt looking for diversion. Karen was far away and his fascination with Isabel soon became entangled with his admiration for the New World and the other enticements of San Francisco. It was therefore with some reluctance that he departed for Seattle when the *Marianne* was finally ready to sail.

The fair Isabel stood on the dock when Peter climbed into the launch that was to take him out to the anchorage. She was dressed in the same lavender frock and bonnet that had captured his attention two weeks earlier. She alternately waved a dainty handkerchief and daubed at nonexistent tears. She had chosen her costume with care to keep her in his memory. Little did she anticipate that, as she turned away to climb into her carriage, the peaked bonnet above her slim figure would instead remind Peter of the silhouette of a Fanniker woman—a particular Fanniker.

This was the image that would haunt Peter in the long night watches to come, but for the present, only the immediate past and future were on his mind. It was a troubled young man who paced the bridge during night watches while they cruised up and then down the west coast of North America. He tried to envision a future with the fascinating Isabel but could not reconcile this sophisticated lady with his ambitions at sea. This was not a woman to wait patiently on shore while her man roamed the world, nor would she tolerate the rigors and discomforts of shipboard life—the very idea was inconceivable. Yet he could not get Isabel out of his mind and his hopes were high that something would work out. San Francisco was full of opportunities and Bendixen an excellent contact.

Not until they were nearly in Seattle did Peter look for time to write Karen. Needless to say, his letter extolling the beauties of San Francisco and Puget Sound confined itself to the natural world and included neither dinner parties nor attractive young ladies. Nor did he mention the subject of an engagement.

Twenty-Seven

Sewing and other Lessons

Curly locks, Curly locks, wilt thou be mine?
Thou shalt not wash dishes nor yet feed the swine,
But sit on a cushion and sew a fine seam,
And feed upon strawberries, sugar and cream.
—English Nursery Rhyme

Ribe, February 1875

Karen was increasingly bothered that Margrethe never went out except for piano and dancing lessons and never to play with a friend. On the other hand, the dreary February weather was not very inviting and perhaps in school her cousin took on yet another role and became the perfect student who made friends with all the nicest girls. Margrethe was overly solicitous about her mother's health, to the point of anxiety if she detected the slightest paleness. Yet she never mentioned the coming baby. Was she blind to her mother's bulging shape or simply ignorant? Karen decided to spend more time with her and get to know her better.

Her chance to talk to Margrethe alone came, by accident, one afternoon when she had wandered into the store after lunch. She was curious about the import business and thought she could learn something about bookkeeping from Uncle Thomas.

"Mr. Bang is not here this afternoon," Mr. Lauritzen said. "But I would be pleased to show Miss Andersen around." The pale-faced assistant had long greasy hair and sweaty hands. When Karen first came to Ribe, he had treated her with the same superior disdain with which he spoke to Lise and Jeppe. Discovering that she was not a servant girl but his master's niece, he had suddenly become eagerly attentive and anxious to please.

However, his idea of pleasing was not quite what Karen had in mind. His answers to her questions about the operation of the business were too simplistic, as if he could not believe she had the capacity to understand complex explanations. He ignored her questions about how the accounts were kept and stared at her incredulously. When she showed an interest in the medicinal effects of various jars of imported herbs, he answered her with irrelevant talk of perfumes. Handing her some little pillows of lavender, he suggested with a sugary leer that Miss might wish to place some under her pillow. His clammy fingers lingered unnecessarily on her hand. Fortunately, the little bell on the outer door jingled and the assistant's attention and smile immediately switched to the greener pastures of a woman customer.

Soon after, the children came home from school. While Jens bounded up the stairs to change his clothes, Karen and Margrethe followed at a more sedate pace.

To her surprise, Margrethe giggled. "You should see your face—you couldn't wait to get away from Mr. Lauritzen!" she sputtered.

"I was only trying to find out how Uncle keeps the books. I do that for my Papa at home," Karen laughed. "He doesn't even remember showing Christian and me around the store when we visited a couple of years ago."

"You were too young then," Margrethe pointed out. "He pays no attention to little girls, but turns on his charm whenever a pretty lady walks in. He never really explains anything to women and especially not to little girls. Papa's like that too, he thinks we're too stupid to understand, but he lectures Jens all the time. He doesn't believe that I'm really interested and that Jens just doesn't care. The best way to find out anything around here is just to watch and listen. If you're very quiet, then everyone forgets you're in the room."

Karen looked at the child in surprise and decided there might be more to those watching eyes than she had supposed. This seemed a good time to talk to her cousin about her mother. Delicately she asked whether she wanted a baby brother or sister. Margrethe looked at her, shock on her face, but said nothing.

"Don't you know why your mother has to stay in bed?"

"I'd have to be pretty stupid not to know. It's just that nobody ever talks about it, even Mama's friends, even when they don't know I'm listening. Mama only mentioned it once before you came. I thought it was something one wasn't allowed to talk about."

"Well it's all right to talk to me, you just ask. My granmam is a midwife and she tells me anything I want to know."

Margrethe looked as if she couldn't think of where to begin. Karen wondered if she shook her cousin hard, would questions come tumbling out?

She did talk a few days later. "I've been thinking about whether I want a brother or sister. I don't know what would be best. If we have another girl, Papa will be so disappointed. He thinks Jens isn't smart enough to take over the business, but it's been in the family forever. When Grandpapa was alive, the 'and Son' on the sign was for Papa. He keeps it there, waiting for Jens. But if Jens has to take over, he'll never be allowed to do what he wants. On the other hand, if we have a boy, then Papa will never pay any attention to either Jens or me and he'll never notice that I could help him when I grow up."

This child doesn't miss a thing, Karen thought. "My brother doesn't want to be a miller like Papa and it's fine with everyone," she said. "But Mam wants me to marry one and then she can have me at home for ever."

Margrethe giggled. "I think Mr. Lauritzen is just waiting for me to grow up and marry him so he can have the store. Can you imagine having to look at that greasy smile every day at breakfast?"

Karen started to laugh. "Mam was so disappointed when Papa's new apprentice turned out to be a skinny little boy and much too short to be my husband. Even she saw that would not do. Lil-Anne, now there's a different story. She would love to have the mill, but the man she marries will have to be very special to be good enough for her."

"Is she so fussy? Would she be like Hans Christian Andersen's princess and say, 'You won't do' each time someone asks for her hand?"

"Certainly not. She's not a spoiled princess," Karen explained. "But she's very independent. She should be allowed to follow her own spirit. A little like Jens. What do you think he wants to be when he grows up? He doesn't seem slow to me."

"Who knows? He doesn't sit still long enough for anyone to find out. Maybe he'll be a famous poet. If he can ever learn to spell!" Then looking more serious she finally blurted out, "Is Mama very sick? Is she going to die? She almost did after Jens. Is the baby going to be all right or is he going to die like the last one and make everyone sad?"

Poor child, Karen thought. *Such a burden to carry and no one will talk to her about it.* She tried her best to be reassuring, explaining that so far Mama and the baby were just fine. She just had to rest so he wouldn't be born before he was ready. "That was the problem last time, the baby was just too little to live. But this one is almost big enough now."

"I wish it were over and done with. Papa used to be so much fun, but now he just yells at everyone and then leaves the house to get away."

I definitely have to do something, Karen thought. *I must tell Ingrid-Fas to be more open with Margrethe.*

The next morning, Karen admired Ingrid's intricate embroidery. "Would you like to monogram some pillowcases for your *trousseau?*" her aunt responded. "Or napkins—a bride can't have too many. Do you know how to hemstitch? Or I can teach you *Hedebo* embroidery for *têtière*. That way if Peter...."

At home Mam and Granmam's needlework lessons had been more practical, consisting mostly of spinning, weaving, and endless knitting. Kirsten-Mos, however, was an accomplished lace maker and had been instructing Karen in this fine art. She smiled thinking about *têtière*—the white embroidered doilies that graced the backs of the plush chairs in the drawing room. Mam would never let Karen bring such clutter home. Neither did she like settees with red plush upholstery, tassels, and fringes. "Certainly not," she would say.

Politely declining sewing lessons, Karen tried to turn the conversation to her worries about Margrethe, and said, "Would it be possible for me to take Margrethe out while you entertain your Twitterers? Does she have any school friends that we could visit?"

"I agree it's not healthy for her to stay indoors so much," Ingrid-Fas said thoughtfully. Then suddenly she burst out, "She drives me to distraction. She's so quick to learn, but never seems to have a thought of her own, never goes anywhere without me suggesting it. That's why I wanted you to visit us. We're kindred spirits, you and I. I hope you can teach her some independence."

"I think she's worried about you and the baby," Karen ventured.

"Oh, I don't think she knows about the baby. She's not a farm girl like you and I. She doesn't know about things like that. She may be worried about my health, but I've not told why I have to stay in bed. I don't want her to associate having babies with illness; I don't want her to be afraid when her time comes."

"You would be surprised what she knows. She thinks she isn't supposed mention the baby. What did you tell her about your last confinement?"

"We don't talk about that. It was such a sad time and she has never asked. She was too young and it isn't a fit topic of conversation for a girl her age. Let her just think the stork will bring the baby, that way if anything happens...."

Won't the children ask how the stork can come in the middle of winter? Karen thought but didn't quite dare say. Ingrid-Fas, nice as she was, was not as open on these matters as Granmam. Karen delicately asked a few more questions about her aunt's last pregnancy, apparently an early miscarriage. Afterwards, Ingrid-Fas had gotten her strength back very slowly and felt unable to get out of bed for weeks. Granmam had told her about cases like that, women who appeared to be just fine but couldn't seem to take an interest in their family or home, sometimes for months.

If Karen couldn't get Ingrid-Fas to talk more openly with Margrethe, she would have to try again to calm the child's fears. Just think if something did happen; it wouldn't do to blame it on the stork! Remembering what she had learned about Mam's childhood, Karen knew what damage could be done if children weren't allowed to talk about their fears. How different might Mam not be if her nightmares hadn't been buried?

Again the next morning, Ingrid-Mos was sewing and Karen knitting. She asked her aunt, "Why do you use so many French words?"

"Since the war, no one wants to speak German so now French is all the rage. My friend Charlotte Holm and I have been taking lessons. You'll like her. She'll be home soon from her winter trip to Italy."

They fell silent while Ingrid started a new thread and Karen retrieved a dropped stitch. Then Karen said, "Pastor Engel thinks we should all learn English. He says that the future of Denmark lies to the west, not the south."

"Didn't you tell me that you were studying English with him? Perhaps you could teach Margrethe."

"I'm just a beginner and I'm finding it very hard. Pastor has been reading aloud from some very difficult books. He says one should learn a language by listening to great literature; he calls it the 'natural' way, the way a child learns to speak. The trouble is, I don't remember the words very well."

"Maybe we can find a teacher for both of you. I'll ask my friends. One of the Twitterers will know of someone."

Sure enough, that very afternoon, Michel Mogens, an impoverished nephew of the Bishop's wife, was identified. He had studied in England and now gave lessons, hoping to save enough to move to Copenhagen and have his poetry published. Ingrid-Fas wrote him a note, asking him to come for an interview the next morning. Jeppe was sent to deliver it to Mr. Mogens's room and wait for a reply. The invitation was accepted.

That evening when Uncle Thomas heard about the plan, he disapproved. "Why waste good money on girls learning a foreign language?" Karen overheard him complaining to his wife. She would have felt embarrassed listening to their private conversation but Uncle had left the door open and was positively shouting.

"You've talked me into piano and dance lessons," he continued. "And Mama says they're appropriate for a young girl; but English? Furthermore, what good will a foreign language do Karen on that God-forsaken island? Why your brother wants to bury himself out in the sticks like that, I'll never understand. The farm where you grew up was isolated enough, but at least it's on land."

Ingrid-Fas pointed out that Jens too might benefit from learning a foreign language. "That's ridiculous!" Uncle roared. "You can't really think he would be able to do anything more than parrot a few words. Let him concentrate on his schoolwork and staying out of trouble. That so-called poet would not be a good influence on him. No doubt, he lives in some mouse-infested garret, and would fill his heads with fantasies."

"Fiddlesticks," Karen thought Ingrid-Fas replied. "He's Bishop Balslev's nephew and perfectly respectable; you can't expect everyone to be a businessman. Besides Karen is not the country bumpkin you think her, you should talk to her sometime. As for Margrethe, she needs something to keep her busy, she's so anxious these days."

"She's seems happy enough to me, but have it your way. You always do," Uncle Thomas muttered and stalked out of the room.

Karen was no longer embarrassed but furious. How could he say such nasty things about Papa, who always said he had exactly the life he wanted? He had chosen to marry Mam and move to the island to take over the mill. He gloried in his work on Fanø, calling it God's Island. Buried in the sticks? Not her Papa, who knew more about the world than all of Ribe combined! He adored his wife, and loved his children. Uncle Thomas, on the other hand, was always grumpy and like that silly man in the English nursery rhyme probably expected his wife and daughter to spend their lives sitting on cushions, sewing fine seams and eating strawberries and cream. Well Karen would not live like that! It would not do for Margrethe either. Karen resolved to help her cousin and if Ingrid-Fas thought English lessons would help, then Karen was delighted to help; besides, then she could continue her own studies.

At ten o'clock the next morning, while the cathedral bells were still ringing, there was a knock on the front door. Lise showed Mr. Mogens up the stairs and into Ingrid-Fas's room. He was a thin, scholarly looking man.

Blinking nearsightedly around the room, his eyes fell only briefly on Karen before focusing his attention on Ingrid-Fas, when he heard the friendly greeting from her *chaise longue*.

"Michel Mogens, *à votre service*," he said with a charming smile that suddenly made him look much younger. When he bowed over her hand, a lock of hair fell over his forehead, completing the picture of the romantic poet. "*Madame* wishes to take English lessons?" he asked in Danish. He spoke as if he had been born in a Copenhagen drawing room and only the slightest trace of dialect revealed his Ribe origin.

"*Mais, non,*" Ingrid-Fas replied. Indicating Karen, she went on to explain that the lessons were for her daughter, Margrethe and niece, Miss Andersen, who was already an English student.

Mr. Mogens immediately turned his attention to Karen. If he was surprised that a country hick from Fanø, a young girl at that, would know any language other than Danish, he was too urbane to let on. He addressed her in a torrent of English.

Karen stopped him with, she hoped, a sophisticated little laugh. "I only begin," she confessed, searching for the words. "Pastor Johannes Engel be my teacher. Home in Sønderho."

Switching to Danish, Mr. Mogens asked her a few questions about what she had been studying. He smiled when Karen explained Pastor's unorthodox theories of language acquisition. "Perhaps, if you are to learn like a child, we should start with some children's stories. Though of less literary merit than Dickens or the romantic poets, they are considerably easier for a beginner. As for Miss Margrethe, we will begin with simple sentences and songs—singing is excellent for learning proper pronunciation."

Ingrid-Fas was charmed with the young man and requested that Michel come to the house once a week for an hour of lessons. Accordingly, each Wednesday afternoon punctually at three, he rang the bell and was shown to the upstairs living room. Though Karen and Margrethe were disparate in age and knowledge of the language, he found a suitable textbook for each of them. He discovered that Karen had absorbed more from Pastor Engel's unorthodox method of teaching than she had realized. The three of them practiced basic conversation about objects around them and everyday happenings. To everyone's surprise, Jens soon joined the little group and showed a remarkable talent for remembering and pronouncing new words. As long as he could hear them spoken and not have to depend on reading or have it labeled 'required for school,' he soaked up the new knowledge.

For her part, Karen felt very sophisticated taking private lessons from a poet. That Michel Mogens was a charming and handsome young man did not hurt. He was always respectful and his manners so proper that Karen did not hesitate to report this new development in her next letter to Peter. However, without intending to mislead, she never mentioned that Michel was twenty-six, and Peter would picture her new teacher as another Pastor Engel, just without the clerical ruff.

Twenty-Eight

Skating Outside the Walls

RIBE, FEBRUARY 1875

Karen was pleased that the English lessons were going so well. Michel, as he insisted they call him, turned out to be a gifted teacher with a wonderful sense of humor. He recited nursery rhymes, all the while acting them out to help them understand the words and made funny faces to alert them to nonsense syllables so they would not get confused. It was a pleasure to hear Margrethe relax and laugh at his clowning. Jens too responded to the teacher's novel methods of instruction. Still, Karen wanted to get Margrethe outdoors more and asked Ingrid-Fas for advice.

"Perhaps you can go skating down at the meadows," she suggested. "Jens too. You can borrow my skates, Lise will know where they're kept."

Karen had an idea. "I met a classmate of Margrethe's the other day. They seem to be friends. Maybe Hanna would like to come too."

"Excellent, by all means invite her. You need to go soon, before the ice melts. If you go this Saturday, when the children are home early from school, you will have all afternoon."

Margrethe and Jens were delighted at the suggestion and

Hanna was thrilled to be invited. She had no skates, but Margrethe told her that didn't matter since they could slide on the ice. Hanna's parents reluctantly allowed her to go even though it was the Sabbath, but insisted that Jesse come along.

Saturday was bitterly cold and snowy and no one felt like being outdoors, but a week later, the weather was beautiful and sunny, yet cold enough to keep the ice from melting. Right after lunch, Karen and the children were at the frozen meadows on the other side of the river from town. While Jens went dashing off to play with his friends, Margrethe helped Karen buckle her skates onto her ankle-high shoes and urged her out on the ice. Karen had a hard time staying upright, her feet each going its own way. She fell backwards, getting snow all over the back of her skirt. Margrethe helped her up and, skating backwards, showed her how to glide, first on one foot then the other. At first Karen was embarrassed at her clumsiness, but then she noticed that Margrethe was getting a kick out of being able to teach her older cousin.

The cathedral clock had barely chimed one-fifteen when Hanna, cheeks glowing and braids flying, came running across the bridge, dragging Jesse behind her. At first, Karen didn't see them, because she had to keep her eyes on her feet. She was a quick learner but by the time Hanna and Jesse arrived, her ankles were sore. Pleading for a rest, she dove for the security of the bench where Jesse was already seated.

"This is my brother Jesse. He's here to protect me," Hanna said, smiling as if it were a joke. Jesse jumped up and politely shook hands, though he would not meet Karen's eyes.

The girls went dashing off, arm in arm, Hanna trying to glide in her shoes. Karen invited Jesse to sit back down on the bench. "Unless you are planning to skate," she said when he seemed to hesitate. "I won't bite," she added with a twinkle in her eyes when Jesse perched on the far end as if too shy to get any closer. As before, he was very quiet, so to start the conversation Karen commented that Hanna seemed so happy to be here. He told how his sister had pleaded and pleaded to come and explained that on Saturdays, the Jewish Sabbath, they usually stayed home after services. Ordinarily they were not allowed to go outside the city walls.

"But Ribe hasn't been fortified for ages; you can barely see where the walls used to be." Karen protested. "Besides, you're just as safe here on the meadows as in the middle of town."

"It's not a matter of being safe," he explained. "The *Torah*—our Bible forbids us to work or travel on the Sabbath, so staying inside the walls is symbolic of not traveling."

"Your father sounds like my Grandmother. She didn't want Papa to go sailing on a Sunday, but Papa says that sailing isn't work for him and that he'll keep the Sabbath holy in his own way."

"Watch me," Jens interrupted. They were so engrossed in talking that they hadn't noticed him come up to the bench. He shouted, "See how fast I am," and was off again.

"Where do you have services?" Karen asked curiously. "I didn't see a Jewish church near the store."

"We're too small community to have a synagogue, so we just meet at someone's house. We barely have a *minyan,* the minimum of ten needed to have a service."

"It seemed to me I saw enough people at your house last week to make ten any time," Karen laughed.

"Well they have to be adult men, so my mother and the children don't count. Since I had my *Bar Mitzva* four years ago, we're eleven. Before that, if one of the men was sick we had a problem." He paused looking out at the children playing on the ice. On the other side of the meadows, the children had made a glide path and a laughing Hannah had joined the queue, waiting to slide.

"I sound like an ancient Rebbe," Jesse stammered. "I'm just a stiff old bore. I don't know how to speak to a pretty girl—usually I'm not allowed."

Karen blushed. It had been a while since a young man had paid her a compliment. "With us, we can have a service if we have two or three people, as long as we meet in God's name," she said, remembering a confirmation lesson and wondering what a 'bamitsva' was.

Now it was Margrethe's turn to interrupt. "Karen, if you're not going to skate anymore, can Hanna use yours?"

Nodding, Karen bent down to unfasten her skates from her boots, but had trouble with one of the straps.

"Here, let me," Jesse said, kneeling down on the ice. Now it was his turn to blush. Hastily, he handed Hanna the skate and rose back to the bench, looking at his hands as if they had acted without his permission.

To change the subject, Karen blurted the first thing that came to mind. "Are you going to be a weaver too?"

"Papa wants me to become a rabbi. In the spring I'm leaving to go to school in Lithuania."

"Why do you have to go all the way to Lithuania? Is that a Jewish university?"

"There's a famous yeshiva there. That's what a school for Jewish studies is called."

"What about Hanna, does she like to study? Is she going to the yeshiva too?"

"Girls aren't allowed. She'll finish secular school and then stay home until she marries and has children. She has plenty to learn before she can be as good a housewife as our mother."

"Me too," Karen sighed and then exclaimed resentfully, "I don't know who decides what girls can and can't do. Back home, the men go to sea in the summer and women run everything. But then when the men come home, there's trouble if a couple can't agree who's captain in the house. But everybody still pretends that women don't need to know anything but housekeeping."

"I suppose it's all according to tradition. Men and women have different roles to play in life. Many Jews forget that in the Middle Ages there were famous woman scholars and Deborah was a judge in ancient Israel."

"Pastor Engel, from home, told me that Bishop Grundtvig preached that girls should be educated just like boys. He had three wives, so he knew what women can do!"

The two young people continued to talk about their differing lives. That is, Karen talked and Jesse mostly listened. She thought, *Jews don't seem that different to me, everybody says they're strange, but Jesse's really nice—a little reserved, but not very different.* Aloud, she said, "Christian and Jew, Ribe burgher or Fanø seaman, each has his own walls. But walls are there to protect, not to imprison. The trick is to find the gate."

Jesse seemed surprised. "I never realized that girls, especially a *shiksa* would chafe under the yoke of tradition." When Karen looked puzzled, he explained that *shiksa* means a non-Jewish girl. Then, as if afraid to seem too personal, he asked hesitantly, "What about your kerchief? Is wearing it a commandment on Fanø?"

"To hear my mother talk, you'd think it was," Karen laughed, "but it's just a custom, though St. Paul said to keep our hair covered in church. Papa says the real reason for the scarf is because of the wind and the sand getting in women's hair, but my mother thinks I'll lose my virtue if my hair isn't covered."

"I'm sorry to babble on," she apologized. "But it's so good to have a real conversation with someone my own age. I guess I've missed that being away from home. You must be older than you look, though. I'm sixteen. My friend Peter—he's first mate on my uncle's ship—he's twenty-four. I like to write to him, but it's better to talk in person. He's on the other side of the world and it takes weeks for him to answer my letters!"

"Are you and Peter engaged?" Jesse asked, but without waiting for an answer blurted awkwardly, "I'm going to marry the Rebbe's daughter in Lithuania."

Karen had no chance to find out more because Margrethe skidded to a stop in front of the bench, spraying ice chips all over them and saying, "Hanna fell and she's crying that her ankle hurts."

Propriety forgotten, the two chaperones looked at each other in dismay. Some protectors they were, not even paying attention! They ran across the ice to the fallen girl, nearly falling themselves. Jesse lifted his sister and carried her back to the bench, his slight frame struggling under the burden.

Karen unlaced the boot and gently felt the injured foot. She didn't think anything was broken but said, "She can't walk on that ankle, we'll have to carry her. Margrethe, go find Jens and tell him we have to go." With that, she helped Hanna to stand on her good leg and put her hands out towards Jesse, saying they should make a seat to carry the girl. Jesse hesitated momentarily as if he feared her skin would burn, and then resolutely clasped her hands.

"Now Memme will never let me go anywhere, ever again," Hanna wailed.

Slowly and awkwardly the two young people made their way across the snow with their sobbing burden and trailing charges. They were preparing to climb the bridge across the river into town when Karen heard Svend's familiar voice, "Does un need help? A's got my cart here if Hanna needs a ride."

Making better progress, the little group soon arrived at the weaver's shop, closed for the Sabbath. They were greeted by a flock of children and Mrs. Schneider, who came hurrying down the stairs, wringing her hands.

Karen explained that it wasn't serious. "When my little sister fell and twisted her ankle, Granmam just wrapped it in a bandage and told her to stay off it for a few days. She's a midwife and takes care of everybody's scrapes and bruises."

"Jesse, vere was you? Who hit her? Vas a fight?" the mother accused.

"It was just an accident," Jesse reassured her. "No one pushed her, this is Denmark. Here people are nice."

A heated discussion followed in rapid Yiddish. Karen thought she and the children should leave. Quickly she said goodbye, claiming they needed to get home in time for tea, and hustled her charges away.

"Why is Mrs. Schneider so worried about Hanna?" Margrethe asked as they walked through the unlit store. "The big boys are rough but they aren't mean."

"I guess because they're Jewish," Karen replied softly. "Papa says that in some countries Jews are hated. That's why the Schneiders came to Denmark. They've only been here for a few years, so Hanna's mother doesn't trust that here they'll be safe."

"Who would hit Hanna? She's a girl," Jens pronounced, slamming the door behind him.

When Karen and her cousins walked through the door they saw a frantic looking Uncle Thomas coming down the stairs. As always, sensitive to her father's feelings, Margrethe turned pale. "That's Dr. Nygaard's carriage outside. What's wrong with Mama?"

"Mama!" Jens wailed. Both children were about to run up the stairs when Karen grabbed one of their arms in each hand and said firmly, "We need to wait here."

Although her stomach was doing flip-flops, she turned to Uncle Thomas and asked calmly, "Is it time? Should I take the children to their grandmother's?"

Uncle Thomas looked surprised, as if he hadn't noticed them standing in the foyer, and stared blankly at his niece. Karen was about to repeat her question and ask whether perhaps Uncle Thomas would prefer to take the children himself. She would be glad to stay if she could help. Then they heard the soothing boom of Dr. Nygaard's voice at the top of the stairs, "You just rest now. Everything will be fine."

He closed the door to Ingrid-Fas's room, came down the stairs, and explained that it was a false alarm. "This sort of thing happens often. It only means we're getting closer. I've given her a sedative so she should sleep for a bit. The important thing is to stay calm and for Ingrid to rest."

"What sort of thing? Closer to what?" Jens asked. "I want to see Mama," he cried, struggling to free himself from Karen's grasp.

"Hush," Karen warned. "Your mama's all right. She just needs to rest." *Doesn't anyone ever explain anything to these children?*" she wondered and turned to Uncle Thomas. "Why don't we take the children somewhere so Ingrid-Fas can have peace?"

"Do what you think best. Take them to Weis's for tea or something," he answered vaguely. "I'm going out."

What? Now? Karen thought. *He's always going out. Where does he go?*

Margrethe must have heard her thoughts because she mumbled, "He'll probably go to Grandmama's. He goes there all the time, to get away from us." Then louder she added, "I'm still cold. Can we go to *Weis's Stue* for hot cocoa?"

"Yes, please, please," Jens begged. "Papa took us once. It's great; with paintings all over the walls, and pastries, and everything."

Just then an elegantly dressed lady emerged from the small downstairs parlor. She stretched out her hand and said, "You must be Karen. I've heard so much about you. I'm Charlotte Holm and Ingrid's my dearest friend. Banker Holm and I have just returned from traveling and I rushed over as soon as I could to entertain our favorite prisoner. Doctor Nygaard had already been sent for, so I waited down here to make sure all was well."

Judging by the delighted grin on Margrethe's usually reserved face and Jens's enthusiastic greeting, this must indeed be a favorite visitor. Karen shook the proffered hand and curtseyed, "How do you do, Mrs. Holm. Have you seen Aunt Ingrid? Is she all right?"

"Yes-yes. And please call me Charlotte. I had some unpleasant episodes like this with my last darling. It's nothing. I told Thomas that, but he panicked, as usual. Men! They don't understand these things! I don't know what he could be thinking, running home to Mother like that and telling you to take the children to Weis's. You can hardly go there unescorted. However, I'll be glad to take you. One result of having a reputation as an eccentric matron is that I can do as I please and no one is surprised. The Ribe burghers have long since ceased being shocked. By all means, let's go for cocoa." With that she let Lise help her into a fur-trimmed cloak and swept out the door, without checking whether anyone followed.

"Mrs. Holm's full of fun. She tells great stories about her travels," Margrethe whispered as she ran by Karen who was still rooted in the foyer. "She went to the World Exposition in Vienna last summer and this winter they went to Italy."

When they had been seated in a discreet corner of Weis's, Karen looked around curiously. From the way Charlotte had talked about it, Karen half expected to see drunken one-eyed pirates staggering between the tables. However if possible, the place was even more respectable and dignified than the inn in Sønderho. The age-smudged beams were decorated with carvings and scrollwork and the walls covered from floor to ceiling with wooden panels painted with fanciful scenes of ships and landscapes.

A large pot of hot cocoa and little cakes were placed before them. Pouring a cup for each, the astonishing lady asked the children, "So what have you been doing with your poor *Maman* confined to her room? You must tell me all your adventures." Charlotte hardly paid attention to the answers, being more talkative than Ingrid-Fas and her speech as colored with foreign words. She needed little urging to entrance her companions with tales of waltzing through the night in Vienna in the fabled *Rotonda* pavillion. "Johann Strauss, Jr. composed the most marvelous pieces especially for the exposition," Charlotte said. "But that was last summer. On this trip, first we went boating on Lake Como, but it was really too cold. Then we went south to see the Blue Grotto by the enchanted island of Capri in the Bay of Naples. See Naples and die," she added, spreading her arms dramatically. She had a curious way of speaking even to the children, never explaining anything but seeming to assume that they knew all these fabulous places as well as she and that she was merely updating them on what they were like *this* year. Her enthusiasm was so infectious that all three of them listened with rapt attention.

"I met an artist once who had painted Lake Como," Karen said. "But he didn't believe I knew where it was."

"Silly man. Now Darlings tell me what you have been doing with yourselves in the dark and damp North." And so the children eagerly interrupted each other to tell their mother's friend all about skating and drawing and English lessons and their romantic poet in his garret. Jens restlessly got up from the table and circled the room looking at the pictures on the walls. Much to the amusement of the other patrons, he demonstrated his newly acquired knowledge of ships by naming each type of vessel and explaining the fine points of their rigging. Karen, flustered at the ill manners of her charge, said, "Jens, do sit down and behave."

"Oh let him be," Charlotte told her. "He can go into the other room and look at the paintings there while we talk. Now, you tell me what you've been doing since you came to Ribe."

"Well, Ingrid-Fas and I have been reading some wonderful Ingemann stories and Grundtvig poetry—I thought he only wrote hymns and sermons, but his poems are marvelous. And last week we went to the cathedral to hear Bishop Balslev preach, but he was too learned for me."

"How dreadfully dull. What about balls? Are there any good plays or concerts in town? One forgets how provincial poor Ribe is. That's why Banker Holm and I go to Italy and Paris for the opera season."

"Just being here is adventure enough for me. It's much livelier than Fanø, but I do miss the weekly dances we have at home. Your children, do they travel with you?"

"Oh no, my dear. My precious moppet died of diphtheria in '69 and our son is a student at the University. He's studying to be a doctor, but I think he'll never make it. He pays more attention to the lovely ladies of Copenhagen than to anatomy. He certainly doesn't want to travel with his *parents ternes.*"

"My brother may become a doctor, at least if my mother has her wish. He's a student at the Latin School and I get to visit him on Sundays."

"I did hear you have a scholar in the family. I'm not surprised that Ingrid's wonderful brother should have a brilliant son. Now what about you? I understand you're famous and write for a newspaper."

"Well I've had a couple of stories published but only in the *Fanø Weekly;* nothing famous. The stories are not really mine; I just write up what other people tell me."

"You're too, too modest. I'm impressed. I've never met a Danish authoress before. We'll have to see if we can't find some young people and some more stimulating entertainment for you. When Ingrid wrote me that she was *aliteé,* she urged me to hurry home to introduce you to Ribe *société.* You can be my companion. Mr. Holm will not be dragged away from his bank when we're at home. That's why I make him travel. In Ribe he's very dull, but in *Paris—oh la la!*"

Karen was thoroughly captivated. Here was someone who had traveled and knew the world.

All too soon, Jens came back from his tour of the rooms and Margrethe pointed out, much to Karen's surprise, that the cathedral clock had begun to play the six o'clock chimes. Flustered she rose and excused their hasty departure. "We have to run. Uncle Thomas is very particular about us being punctual for dinner."

"I forget how *bourgeois* everyone is here. How barbaric to eat before ten."

"At home we're usually in bed by ten and up with the chickens!" Karen laughed.

"Au revoir, à bientôt."

"I think that means 'good-bye'," Margrethe whispered to Karen on their way out.

Mail was delivered morning and late afternoon, and ordinarily Karen checked the table at the foot of the stairs the minute she walked into the house to see if there were any letters for her. But today she didn't check until after dinner. Earlier there had been the confusion when they returned from skating, and now they were late. It was therefore not until evening that Karen finally read Peter's letter about their miserable Christmas at sea and his first impressions of San Francisco. It had been addressed directly to Ribe, so he must have received her own Christmas letter first. It was confusing to have such a long delay; Peter responded to her stale news of months ago, and she learned what he was doing long after he had sailed to somewhere else.

The next day was Sunday and it was evening before she could add the next installment to her letter, the last she would mail to California. After that, he had said to send letters to Australia. Their next port would be the Sandwich Islands, but their arrival date was uncertain and their stay would be short.

Sunday, February 9, 1875

Where to begin? This week I finally had some adventures. It all started with our outing to go skating with Margrethe's friend, Hanna. As I told you, Hanna's family is Jewish. Her older brother, Jesse, came too. He is very interesting. There is no reason to be jealous, he would not even look at me because I am what they call a "shiksa" *and he is engaged to be married to a girl in Lithuania. She is the daughter of a famous rabbi, a sort of pastor although the word means* teacher. *Jesse is supposed to go study there come spring—imagine, they have never even met! I suppose Mam would just love to pick my fiancé for me, but I'll decide that for myself, thank you!*

Karen paused for a moment, wondering if that was too frank. She wanted to tell him what happened this afternoon. The impromptu party at *Weis's Stue* had to wait for the next letter.

Today we went to services at Sankt Caterinæ Church (that is Ribe-Latin for Saint Catherine's, the æ *makes it possessive—is that not stuffy?). We usually go there instead of the cathedral since it is less overwhelming though impressive enough. I miss Papa Angel's sermons—at least I could usually figure out what he was talking about. But the music is wonderful. A huge choir sings on the balcony accompanied by an organ! I wanted to turn around to see where the beautiful sounds were coming from, but that's not considered polite. I will especially miss the organ when I go home again; it has a wonderful sound.*

After church we always have dinner with Uncle Thomas's mother, Agathe Berg—I secretly call her Queen Agathe. Every other week it is at her apartment (bigger than all of Southhouse), and we would have been there this Sunday except that Uncle Thomas was worried about Ingrid and the baby so we ate here with the Queen. I wished I could skip the whole thing and just have dinner with Christian at his lodging where I have a standing invitation. The Queen is a holy terror, criticizing everything from the menu to Margrethe's hair and Jens's squirming. That is why I always have to be there, so I can whisk the children off just as soon as dinner is over, by which time both of them are usually close to tears.

This week it was my turn to be raked over the coals. She started in on how I dress. She said it was not appropriate for her son's niece to look like some servant girl from the country and that my turban *makes me look like an* African barbarian.

I was very proud of myself, biting my tongue. Then she complained that the children and I had been seen in disreputable company, by which she meant Svend Schultz, the carter who gave Hanna a ride on his cart yesterday. She had no right to say that, he has never behaved improperly and he was a great help to us.

Jens, bless his heart, tried to intervene, and explained that we had been skating and Hanna had been hurt and we had to help her home. When the

Queen found out that this was Hanna Schneider you would have thought disaster had struck. I don't know if she was more shocked by Margrethe having a Jewish friend or being seen in the part of town where she lives!

She laid down the law about where I could take the children. I suppose that was her right, but when she tried to tell me how I should dress and where in town I could walk in my free time, I lost my temper. I'm ashamed to say that I told her, she was not my grandmother, I would dress as I was accustomed, and go where I pleased. Then I walked out.

Margrethe told me later that she then lit into Uncle Thomas about my behavior (which I admit was abominably rude), complained about my being seen at Weis's (at Uncle Thomas's suggestion and chaperoned by Mrs. Holm, about whom I will tell you later). She made some really nasty comments about his wife's family (that is, me) and then even Uncle Thomas had had enough.

He sent the children out of the room, but it did no good since he yelled so loudly that we could all hear, "You leave Ingrid out of this. My angel is suffering, all for the family. I will not have you criticizing her. If anything happens, I will never forgive you."

At that, the Queen grabbed the bell on the table to summon Lise, as if she were still the mistress of the house, and demanded her wraps. "I know when I am not welcome," she screamed and stormed out.

The children had run to their mother's room, leaving the door open for Ingrid-Fas to hear the dramatic finish. She who is supposed to have peace and quiet! However, she seems to have borne it all with her usual good spirits and is none the worse for wear.

Dearest Peter, I don't know how to help. Everyone is so on edge and all I seem to do is get in the middle of it all. I may have misjudged Uncle Thomas; he really does seem to love Ingrid-Fas but cannot cope with the tension. The poor man is so worried that when anything bad happens he rushes out of the house to escape. The Queen Mother is no help. Margrethe says she has always been strict; she and Ingrid-Fas do not get along very well, but now it is worse than ever. At least, in only a few more weeks the waiting will be over.

It is now time for bed, so I can get up to help the children off to school. Like Lil-Anne, I hate to get up in the winter, in the dark. Tomorrow we are to go to the station and see the trains. I wish I could board one and it would whisk *me to wherever you are, or at least to Sønderho and Millfarm. Sometimes home seems as far away as you.*

A bientôt, mon amour,

Karen looked at the ending, decided the last two words were too bold, and crossed them out.

Twenty-Nine

The Fair Isabel

I do not love thee Isabel, and yet thou art most fair!
I know the tempting of thy lips, the witchcraft of thy hair,
The winsome smile that might beguile the shy bird from his tree;
But from their spell I know so well, I shake my manhood free.

I might have loved thee, Isabel; I know I should if aught
Of all thy words and ways had told of one unselfish thought;
If through the cloud of fashion, the pictured veil of art,
One casual flash had broken warm, earnest from the heart.

But words are idle, Isabel, and if I praise or blame,
Or cheer or warn, it matters not; thy life will be the same;
Still free to use, and still abuse, unmindful of the harm,
The fatal gift of beauty, the power to choose and charm.

I do not love thee, Isabel; I would as soon put on
A crown of slender frost-work beneath the heated sun,
Or chase the winds of summer, or trust the sleeping sea,
Or lean upon a shadow as think of loving thee.

—John Greenleaf Whittier, 1807-1892

San Francisco, Late February 1875

The Marianne returned to San Francisco, and, as soon as Peter could, he rushed up the hill to call on Isabel. The maid conducted him to the conservatory where Mrs. Bendixen was having tea. Elisabeth invited the young man to sit next to her and gently explained that Miss Kensington had gone home to Virginia last week.

"Did she leave me a note?" Peter asked in shock.

Elisabeth took his large callused fingers between her own dainty hands and said, reverting to the plain speech of her Quaker heritage, "Isabel treated thee most inconsiderately. Her behavior was inexcusable and I'm sorry that I allowed thee to call on her." She went on to explain that Isabel had had a scandalous affair back in Virginia that had ruined her chances of a suitable marriage there. "My sister sent her here hoping she would find a new life, but Mr. Bendixen and I could do nothing with her. She was obviously as unhappy and restless here as at home. Finally, we sent her back with friends who were traveling east. She seemed as glad to go as we were to see her leave."

"She led me to believe…I thought…," Peter stammered.

Her dark eyes brimming with compassion, Elizabeth let the young man pour out his confusion and dismay. When he finally rose to take his leave, she assured him that he was welcome for tea anytime during the rest of his stay in San Francisco.

Over the next few days, before the *Marianne's* departure for the South Pacific, Peter called upon Elisabeth whenever he could. He poured his feelings into her sympathetic heart, telling her of Karen waiting for him in Denmark, of his mysterious first encounter with Isabel, and his confusion about his future.

"I realize now that a large part of Isabel's attraction was that, somehow, she reminded me of Karen. But to see Karen in that woman, whose only interest in me was as a plaything, a she-cat with a mouse; Karen, whose intelligence and goodness shines through every word she writes! How could I be so stupid?"

"Most young men thy age are impulsive and romantic. That's why we women love you," Elisabeth said sympathetically. "Thy actions were without fault and thee should not blame thyself."

The day before their last day in port, Peter called one final time. It was a Wednesday, the day Elisabeth usually received guests, and several ladies were already settled on the terrace with tea and cake.

"This young man is First Mate Peter Larsen off the *Marianne* out of Denmark," Elisabeth announced to her circle of friends. Peter made the rounds, bowing over the extended hand of each lady as she was introduced, clicking the heels of his boots. He kept his eyes strictly each lady in turn, and allowed his mouth only the expected platitudes, trying valiantly to ignore the murmurs around him of, "Isn't he handsome?" "So tall," "Such beautiful European manners," and as one lady succinctly sighed, "Oh, my!"

Finally, Peter was allowed to sit next to his hostess and balance a cup on one knee and a plate of cake on the other. The usual gossip having been interrupted, the ladies questioned the visitor about where he had been and he was urged to relate his adventures at sea. Wishing to impress his audience, Peter pulled out the latest *Fanø Weekly*, saying casually, "I just received a copy of an article that I wrote. If you will permit me…," and he read aloud his description of the Surinam River. He translated so smoothly that the ladies did not realize he was doing so.

The tea ladies were charmed with the handsome Danish seaman and impressed by his article. Then it was time for them to disband. There was much gathering up of belongings and many good-byes before departure was accomplished. As each lady left the terrace, Peter rose from his chair and bent over her gloved hand.

At last, alone with his friend and armed with another round of tea, Peter could turn the conversation to what was foremost on his mind: Karen. Peter confessed his impulse to propose to her and marry as soon as he returned to Denmark, but worried that her mother would never consent. Elisabeth shrugged off his concern as easily as Captain Fredricksen, saying, "William tells me that Danish women are as independent-minded as those of the Society of Friends. If Karen wants thee, she'll find a way."

"I feel like I'm on the Bay out there," he sighed. "Every time I think it's clear sailing, the fog comes in and obscures the way."

"The fog seldom comes up this high, so thou can get a better view from here," Elisabeth said sympathetically, reverting to her friendlier speech. Then, coming to the crux of the problem, she asked, "What bothers thee most: Karen's independence or her mother's obstinacy?"

"She's so restless and I worry about her leaving Fanø. It's so hard to keep her image before me when she isn't there by the mill."

"Surely thee is not worried about her constancy? She's the most devoted, faithful young lady I have ever heard of."

"Well yes, but she has a new idea in every letter. First she started writing stories, now she went traipsing off to Ribe—what will she do next?"

"Thee just wants her to stay home and listen to her mother?"

"I guess not. I guess she's better off away from her mother's influence. Lars-Anne is so stubborn that she'll never agree to our marrying and Karen is more than a year away from the age of consent."

"Suppose you could get married when you return, then what?"

"Captain Fredriksen has promised me command of the *Marianne* soon. I would so like to show Karen the world, to bring her here for tea, to Hawaii, and the silk market in Canton."

"On board Lady-ship *Marianne?*" Elisabeth's eyes sparkled with mischief. "What is to keep thee from doing just that?"

"When? I can't stand the thought of having to wait another year to get married."

"Cannot the Captain marry you at sea?"

At that moment William Bendixen returned home, unexpectedly because they had thought the fog would trap him at the boatyard across the Bay in Mendicino. The conversation turned to other matters until Peter feared he had overstayed his welcome and bid goodbye.

It was not until after he had left the house and jumped on a cable car to return to his boarding house that Peter understood what Elizabeth had meant. "Ding, ding," went the conductor's bell and Peter almost lost his grip on the strap to tumble down the hill. "It's so obvious," he suddenly realized. "That's how we do it! We can be married at sea!"

He looked at the fog swirling towards him. It no longer seemed ominous but beautiful and mysterious. Ahead, a woman came out of a doorway and disappeared into the mist. He barely stopped from calling out, "Hey, Karen, wait for me!"

The *Marianne* was to sail from San Francisco to Maui in the Sandwich Islands with a cargo of lumber from Seattle and wheat from California. It was her first mate's responsibility to prepare the ship and load the cargo securely. Grain can be dangerous, especially if the hull springs a leak in a storm; wet wheat swells and has been known to break a ship apart. Peter therefore followed Captain Fredriksen's orders and double-lined the hull of the *Marianne* with some of the lumber from the cargo.

Peter was also responsible for seeing that they had a full crew before they sailed. He needed to replace the two ordinary seamen and the second mate that had defected in San Francisco. The mate, or bosun, was homesick and wanted to sail on a European-bound ship, and the other two wanted to settle in California. He had signed on two replacements for the sailors, one being a young Native from Maui with whom he was very impressed. However, he despaired of finding a second mate to be in charge of the crew. On the last day they were loading the final cargo, when another sailor came on board seeking a berth. He was an appealing freckle-faced Norwegian with good papers but too young to be a bosun. Reasoning that without a bosun an extra sailor would help, Peter signed him on. As they shook hands, he said, "Welcome aboard. Stow your gear in the forecastle, then report to the cargo hold."

Peter looked over the rail of the bridge to where Kelolo, the Native, was maneuvering a stack of lumber down through the forward hatch. He had noticed how smoothly the cargo loading was going despite the lack of a second mate and attributed this to the natural leadership of Kelolo. That gave Peter an idea and he yelled down, "Hey Kelolo, secure that crane and come up here a minute." While waiting, he checked the log for another look at the Native's credentials and noted with satisfaction that he was indeed a seasoned seaman.

The Islander grabbed his shirt from the rail and slung it over his left shoulder then climbed to the bridge as effortlessly as if he were walking the beach. He was stocky and muscular, with long dark, wavy hair, neatly bound with a leather thong. The brown skin of his bare chest glistened with sweat and his legs were spread, bare feet gripping the deck as if he expected it to toss him about. Peter got straight to the point. "It occurs to me that you have considerable experience before the mast and it's time you were promoted. We need a second mate and the men seem to take well to you. What about it?"

Kelolo looked stunned. He squinted up at the first mate, a good head taller than he, then recovered enough to say with a deprecating grin, "Do you think they would listen to a little darky like me?"

Peter laughed. "You've already shown that you have their respect. On this ship we don't judge a man by his size or pay attention to the color of his skin. Call all hands on deck."

Kelolo donned and buttoned his faded blue shirt and, straightening his back even further, called the crew to stand below the rail. Captain Fredriksen had stood at the back of the bridge watching Peter's inimitable style of leadership that led by persuasion rather than command. First Mate looked like a Viking Chief, an equal among warriors, whom he was rallying to go on a raid.

"We now have a full crew," Peter called down to the men, hardly needing to raise his voice to be heard. "I present to you our newest members, Knud from Skagen, Olaf from Bergen, and Mr. Kelolo from Lahaina. Kelolo is our new Bosun. What say ye, are we ready to weigh anchor on the turning of the tide? Are we ready to depart for the Sandwich Islands?"

After a resounding affirmation from the crew, he turned the rail over to the Captain, who added a few words. Mr. Kelolo dismissed the men and ordered them to return to the loading of the last lumber and final battening down of the hatches.

"That was well done," Captain said to Peter as they bent over the chart of San Francisco Bay, plotting their course. "I like the cut of Kelolo's jib, he's a good man."

"Cargo all secure," Kelolo reported and relayed the orders to the crew to weigh anchors. The capstans creaked and water dripped from the hawsers as they were raised into place. All hands went aloft to set sail and soon the bark slipped between the other ships in the bay, caught the breeze and tacked towards the Golden Gate to the Pacific.

Only that evening did Peter have time to unwrap the package that Elisabeth had slipped under his arm as he said his final goodbye. Inside lay a slim book, *Selected Poems by John Greenleaf Whittier* written in gold leaf on the cover. A slip of paper marked a page. With growing amusement, Peter read about the not-so-fair Isabel.

When the second verse began, "I might have loved thee, Isabel; I know I should if aught/ Of all thy words and ways had told of one unselfish thought," his sense of humor was restored. By the end of the fourth and last verse, he was laughing aloud.

Yet the image of Isabel, as he had first seen her in the lavender dress, continued to haunt him in his dreams. To his confusion, it was frequently Karen's face that smiled at him around the brim of the bonnet. When Karen's next packet of letters caught up with him in Sydney, several months later, the mystery only deepened. She too had worn a lavender dress, linking Karen, the country girl, and the glamorous Isabel in a way he would never fully understand.

Thirty

Karen's Lavender Dress

Lavender's blue, diddle, diddle,
Lavender's green;
When I am king, diddle, diddle,
You shall be queen.
—English Nursery Rhyme

Ribe, March 1875

Karen's part in the mystery of the lavender dress started when she and the children returned home from an outing to the tower. All of Karen's life, the cathedral tower had beckoned to her from across the water. On a clear day it could barely be seen from Sønderho, floating on the horizon, but to her it was a symbol of life off the island. Now that she was living in its massive shadow, it had lost none of its magic. Every time she went around it in the square or listened to its booming bells, she stopped in wonder that she was really here.

She had timidly asked whether climbing to the top was allowed. Ingrid-Fas said, "of course" and the children enthusiastically chorused their desire to go.

"It's been absolutely ages. The grown-ups never want to take us," Jens said.

"Papa complains it's too far to climb, but I think he's afraid of heights," Margrethe explained.

Today, after school, they had climbed the granite steps that wound up through the smaller spire next to the massive square tower. Crossing over to the tower itself, they passed the huge mechanism of the cathedral clock, then up and up a series of wooden stairs. A waist-high parapet surrounded the open top, a reminder of when this was a watchtower for defending the town against marauders.

They looked down over the whole town and the tiny ant-people hurrying below on the square. The children had to count every tower and point out every landmark. A panoramic view of flat countryside extended for miles in all directions. Karen looked west across the meadows in the direction of the North Sea and Sønderho. She had hoped to see home from here but she was disappointed to see only a thin line in the horizon that might have been Fanø. "It's strange that on a clear day like today, from home I would be able to see the cathedral tower, but even from up here we can't see the mill," she said wistfully.

"Here go the bells," warned Jens. They laughingly held their ears as three loud gongs announced it was a quarter to three.

"I'm freezing, let's go home," Margrethe suggested. "Mama said Mrs. Holm is coming to tea."

They returned with sparkling eyes and red cheeks, piling their damp clothes into the waiting arms of the uncomplaining Lise.

"There's a letter for you on the tray, Miss," Lise announced. "It just came with the afternoon post."

The day before, a letter had arrived from Peter describing San Francisco and Puget Sound, so Karen knew it was too soon to hear from him again. Neither of her parents wrote very often, so only seldom did she hear from them. Her disappointment in not being able to see the mill from the tower had left her homesick so she was glad to see Mam's handwriting.

Carrying the letter, she brought the children upstairs for tea with their mother and Charlotte. Ingrid-Fas was her usual cheerful self although Karen knew that she still suffered from periodic pains. Doctor kept reassuring them that they were only preparation for the coming event.

Charlotte was modeling her latest dress of maroon and green silk that hugged her generous hips. Karen thought the outfit would have looked better on someone with a slimmer waist and a fashionable hourglass figure. *"C'est le dernier cri,"* Charlotte was explaining, as she slowly turned to reveal the exaggerated bustle. Jens wanted to know how she could sit on a chair with all that stuff under her. Ingrid-Fas suppressed a smile but reprimanded the boy for his rudeness.

Charlotte laughed and, not at all put out, demonstrated how the horse-hair stuffed bustle folded up against the back when she perched at the edge of a chair. "*Les couturiers parisien* don't think of the practical aspects of their creations," she chuckled. "However, this is an improvement over the crinolines they dictated a few years ago."

"But boys don't want to hear about fashion," she continued. "Tell me what you did today; judging by your rosy cheeks you must have been up to something exciting."

"We climbed the tower and saw Ribehus," Jens explained. "Where King Valdemar lived in the olden days."

"In the old-old days, during the early Middle Ages. When Valdemar the Victorious made Ribe the capital of Denmark," Karen corrected.

"And knights, and battles, and horses," Jens chanted. Ducking behind a chair, he pretended to pull his bow and shoot arrows down at an invading army on the street below.

"It was very windy and we could see for miles and miles," Margrethe said. "Karen wanted to see the mill on Fanø but it's too far. You should have seen her jump when the bells rang!"

Tuning out her cousins' chatter, Karen undid the seal on the envelope from home and devoured the latest news. A small piece of paper dropped into her lap. *I MISS YOU. COME HOME SOON. LOVE, ANNE*, it said. Seeing the block letters, bouncing across the page, brought back Karen's homesickness and she had to blink away tears.

"Sad news from home?" Ingrid-Fas asked.

"No, not at all. It's just that it's from my sister. I guess I miss her more than I realized. She's such a sunbeam on a dreary day." She held out the note for all to admire.

"The letter from my mother is about Gerda and Klaus whose first banns were read two Sundays ago," she explained. "They'll be married next week and if I were home, I'd be a bridesmaid," she added regretfully. "They've been waiting for the King's permission letter."

"Is he a prince? Is that why they need the King's permission to marry?" Jens asked, eyes growing large.

Karen laughed and explained that Klaus was just a seaman and Gerda used to be her mother's helper around the house, but Gerda was not yet eighteen so Pastor Engel had to write a letter for them to Copenhagen to get permission to perform the ceremony.

"You mean they got a letter from the King and she's just a maid?" exclaimed an impressed Margrethe.

"Well it's not signed by him personally, it's just called the King's letter because it's sent in his name," explained Ingrid-Fas.

The children pleaded with Karen to tell them what the wedding would be like. She put on her best storytelling expression and smiled down at her cousins sitting expectantly at her feet. "Last winter, Gerda and Klaus only danced with each other at the Sunday dances. 'She's dancing with me,' he would say every time someone else invited her to the floor."

"Like the prince in Cinderella!" Margrethe piped up.

"Precisely," Karen replied. "But the course of true love must be tried and they were too young. In the summer they were separated while Klaus sailed to Africa for fruit and spices and Gerda took a job on Sylt to learn farming and earn some money. When they returned in the fall, he said it again, 'She dances only with me.' Last month they had their Yes-party."

"What's a Yes-party?" asked Jens.

"If you are quiet and pay attention I will tell you," Karen said sternly. The children promised to be good and Karen described the engagement party. She did not tell them that after the Yes-party Klaus had moved home with Gerda and shared her tight-bed. Karen knew that off-islanders thought this Fanø custom shockingly un-Christian. Much as Pastor might rant and rave, this was the custom for as long as anyone could remember.

"A few days before the wedding the dividing walls in the house will be removed and the floor cleared to make room for the party after the wedding. Gerda's younger brothers and sisters will go to the houses of all their friends and family to issue the invitation to the church and party at the house. 'Bring soft shoes,' they'll say. That means there'll be dancing afterwards. For the wedding, Gerda will be dressed in a white linen apron and shawl. Her mother will braid her hair on top of her head and sew on a crown of dried flowers and lace. Her bridesmaids will also have braided hair and smaller crowns of flowers. After the ceremony at the church, everyone will process through the town to Gerda's house, where they'll eat and dance all night."

Jens was fascinated. "They *sew* the crown into her scalp? With a real needle and thread?"

Karen laughed. "The crown is only sewn to the braids, not her scalp!"

Margrethe sighed and asked if there would be lots of presents.

"Most people will bring practical presents, like a smoked ham or sheep cheese."

Jens said, "How do you know it'll be like that?"

"Because that's the way a wedding always is," Karen said.

Ingrid-Fas nodded. "At Uncle Anders and Aunt Anne's wedding, Karen's mamma was dressed exactly like that. And we danced all night. Not me, of course, because although they tried to show me the steps, dancing Sønderhoning is so complicated that only someone born there can learn. The next day, everybody slept in. In the evening, there was a second-day party and we danced again."

As if she had been there, Karen continued her story, "Papa and Mam danced the first dance. It starts with a march, except that each couple glides along to symbolize the ship of life running before the wind. Then the groom lets go of the bride's hand, as if releasing the sail when a ship is to come about. The couple face each other, the bride puts both her hands at her back, and the groom holds her hands in his and they circle around the floor, twirling and bobbing."

"It's spectacular. Why they don't trip or step on each other's feet, I don't understand," Ingrid said.

"The bobbing is to show the ship tacking into the wind, and sometimes they do step on each other's feet or even fall," Karen laughed.

"Like a marriage," Charlotte added, caught up in the symbolism. "Smooth in the beginning and then rough."

"It takes much practice," Karen said, thinking literally. "Mam likes to tease that her feet were pretty sore by the end of the wedding feast. Papa learned, though, and now they're the best dancers in town," she bragged.

"How about Peter? Is he a good dancer?" Margrethe wanted to know.

"He's a wonderful dancer and getting better at Sønderhoning. He's from Nordby and they don't dance quite the same way," Karen explained, and then added dreamily, "In fact, he's not bad at all."

Jens interrupted, "I'd rather hear about San Francisco. Karen, you promised to tell us what Peter wrote and show us the pictures."

While the children looked at the photographs through the stereoscope, Karen recounted Peter's lively description of San Francisco, its beautiful bay and the fantastic mingle of peoples from all continents of the world on its crowded streets. Jens was particularly thrilled with the cable cars and Margrethe shrieked with amazement when she saw the dizzying view down into the Yosemite Valley.

"Peter wrote that, across the bay from San Francisco, there's a beautiful forest with red trees," Karen continued. "They're so old that they're almost as tall as the Cathedral and as big around as the King Oak. I'd love to see that."

"…And the cable cars take you up higher than our tower," Jens interrupted. "Chinese coolies pull on these long ropes to get the cars up the hill."

"Well not quite. I don't understand either, but Peter said they are pulled partly by gravity and partly by steam with steel cables buried in the street. He drew a diagram; we can look at it later."

They all agreed that the cable cars should be called the Eighth Wonder of the World.

Jens was excused to play with a friend. He thumped down the stairs making clanking noises as if a great rattling chain pulled him along.

"I think it is time for a new letter to the *Fanø Weekly*," Ingrid-Fas suggested.

"Or maybe to the *Ribe Times*," Charlotte amended. "I know the editor. Write it up and we'll bring it to him. Then you'll also be a famous reporter here." She paused just long enough to catch her breath. "That reminds me. Ingrid and I were talking before you came home. The Bishopess is going to have a *soirée* Saturday next. Karen, please come *avec moi*."

"The Balslevs always have such interesting people," Ingrid-Fas assented. "The editor is bound to be there and your English teacher, so you'll at least know someone."

"Am I old enough to go to a *soirée?*" Karen's voice betrayed her longing.

"Fiddlesticks! No one will know who you are or question your age. Everyone will have seen you at the concert beforehand and they'll assume from the way you're dressed that you're a woman of the world."

"What concert? Dressed how?"

"Jenny Lind's, of course; didn't we tell you? The party's in her honor. Ingrid will lend you something delicious to wear, *très élégant*." At the funny look on Karen's face she added, "You didn't think to go in your everyday clothes? And we'll have to do something marvelous with your hair. You do have hair under that scarf?"

Karen admitted that she did indeed have hair, more than she could easily hide under her kerchief. She would have been offended at the implied criticism of the way she dressed, but Charlotte obviously only had the best intentions, and her enthusiasm was infectious. Besides, the legendary Jenny Lind!

Margrethe, entering into the spirit, urged Karen to show her wonderful hair. Blushing, Karen unwound her kerchief and undid her long braid so that her blond hair cascaded down her back. "No curls though," she said glancing at her cousin's ringlets with envy. "Not like Margrethe or Lil-Anne."

Charlotte tipped her head to one side and said, "No matter. We can use a curling iron. Ingrid, what about that lavender velvet gown of yours? It's sophisticated without being too *décolleté?* I hope her waist is small enough without cinching; it wouldn't be healthy at her age."

Soon the three women and the usually restrained Margrethe were giggling like schoolgirls. Karen stripped off her neck scarf, nightshirt, apron, and several wool skirts. Standing in her shift, she explained that she had worn all her skirts for their trip to the tower. Meanwhile, Charlotte had rummaged at the back of Ingrid's closet for the gown and now slipped it over her *protégé*'s head.

"Without all those skirts, your waist is tiny. It's a perfect fit," she approved. "It's a good thing you and Ingrid are the same height. On me, this gown would trail along the floor."

"Are you sure it's all right for me to borrow this?" Karen asked of her aunt.

"Why not? It certainly is of no use to me," Ingrid-Fas laughed, glancing at the bulge under her *negligée.* "That slightly old-fashioned look is perfect on you. Margrethe, in that chest over there, the top drawer, there are matching gloves. The bonnet is on the shelf in the closet."

They experimented with her hair in various outrageous arrangements. First they piled it on top of her head in a look made her appear shockingly seductive; then they tried a ridiculous looking pompadour, then a bun that made her into a bookish blue-stocking. None seemed to suit the lavish velvet dress. They finally decided on a hairdo not too different from Margrethe's except that Karen would have soft curls instead of the younger girl's cascade of sausages.

"We'll just make her hair curl as best we can and pin it up at the back of her head with a ribbon," Charlotte declared, narrowing her eyes to admire her creation. "You will wear the bonnet to the concert and then take it off once you're at the Bishop's."

Margrethe disappeared down the hall into her room and returned holding a black ribbon, an amber heart suspended from its middle. "If you like, you may borrow this," she said shyly and tied it around her cousin's throat.

"*Parfait*," Charlotte said clapping her hands together. "Demure, mysterious, but not too old for your lovely young face."

Karen marveled at the various transformations she saw in the mirror. She did not have to travel to the other side of the world for adventure; merely a change in appearance made her feel like a different person. *Peter, you should see me now!* she thought. Little did she know, he had already seen her dressed almost exactly like this, in a mysterious vision in a San Francisco post office.

Karen blushed again and mumbled, "But what on earth will Mam say?"

"We won't tell, if you don't," Charlotte said in a conspiratorial whisper.

"She'll know," Karen sighed.

"But you're not doing anything wicked," Ingrid-Fas protested. "It's just a party at the Bishop's and you'll be well chaperoned."

"It's not the party. It's this wonderful dress. I feel like Cinderella going to the ball."

"And Aunt Charlotte is your fairy godmother," exclaimed Margrethe clapping her hands.

But Prince Peter won't be there, Karen thought sadly.

That evening she wrote her Prince the letter he would eventually puzzle over in Australia.

Thursday, March 5, 1875

Dear Peter,

Your wonderful letter from San Francisco has been a great hit with the children, who wanted to hear all about the cable cars. I had to explain three times how they work, although I hardly understand myself, even with your marvelous illustration.

This installment is about the further unraveling of Uncle Thomas. He is more silent and withdrawn than ever now that Aunt Ingrid's time is approaching. He hardly speaks a word to anyone, least of all the children. Yet Margrethe tells me about the wonderful outings he used to take them on. I wish he would spend some time with them now when they really need him.

Last evening, I accidentally saw another side of him. I wanted to ask Ingrid-Fas something and thought she might be asleep, so I opened the door a crack to check. He was lying on top of the bed fully dressed but Ingrid-Fas was snuggled in his arm, her head on his chest. They were so absorbed in each other that they didn't even hear me. At first, I thought nothing of it since Mam and Papa are always hugging each other, but then I realized how unusual it was. I became so flustered I hardly knew what to do, but closed the door as quietly as I could, hoping they would never know I had intruded on their privacy. He was practically crying, telling Ingrid-Fas how worried he was and how foolish she had been talking him into having this baby, just because she thought it would make him happy. Then he said a peculiar thing. "I never wanted the business. Why should I force it on my son?" he said. Then, as best I could hear (I'm becoming quite shameless listening at doors), "Let Jens follow his heart's desire, as my parents would never let me!" I wonder what he wanted to be? It's hard to imagine him doing anything other than studying invoices and writing in his ledgers. I hope it will all be over soon and that I can go home before long.

Mrs. Holm is the most amazing lady. She is taking me to hear Jenny Lind next week and then to a reception in her honor at Bishop Balslev's house. Is that not fabulous? I will tell you all about it afterwards. You should see the dress that Ingrid-Fas is lending me to wear; the fashionable ladies of San Francisco would be green with envy. It is lavender velvet and Margrethe tells me the color matches my eyes. I feel very guilty not following Mother's advice to continue to wear traditional Fanø dress, but she just does not understand the modern world. I do not think that going to a party at the Bishop's will compromise me.

I wish you were here and we could go together.

The day of the concert, Karen was too excited to eat dinner and went to get ready as soon as she was excused from the table. Lise practiced being a lady's maid by curling her hair and arranging it with a big black velvet bow at the back of her head. She could hardly believe the sophisticated vision that appeared in the mirror. Everyone fussed over her until she thought she would die with fright, and when the front door bell rang, she almost fell down the stairs in her rush to not keep Banker and Mrs. Holm waiting.

"Don't forget your cloak, Miss," Lise said draping the heavy wool over her shoulders.

"Un looks right beautiful, Miss. If'n un don't mind me bein' so bold," a voice whispered in her ear. There was the faithful Svend, transformed to Cinderella's coachman in a tall hat and black coat, holding the door of the carriage for her. Grinning from ear to ear, he gave her a boost into the carriage.

Charlotte patted the seat beside her and said, "Sit here so Mr. Holm can see what a pretty girl you are. This is the lovely Karen; I didn't exaggerate, did I dear?" But Mr. Holm was too busy telling the coachman to hurry and gave her only a perfunctory nod. Karen had never seen so many carriages, horses, and people as were milling about the meeting hall. Their carriage waited in line until Svend could drop them at the front door. Then it was their turn to climb up the flight of stairs and walk between the Greek pillars into the magnificent lobby.

The concert itself surpassed Karen's wildest imaginings. Jenny Lind looked older than she expected and pale, but her voice soared to the top balcony. A nightingale, indeed. All too soon, she stopped singing and Karen thought the concert was over. Charlotte explained that it was only intermission and they would go out to the lobby. Karen would have preferred to remain in her seat and listen to the music again, in her mind, but Charlotte insisted.

"We need to go for a stretch, while Mr. Holm has his cigar," she ordered. "Don't be surprised if *tout le monde* stares at you; most of them are half-blind without their spectacles and are just trying to figure out if they know you. Ignore them and by evening's end, all will wonder who the mysterious stranger is and you'll be *la triomphe*."

Out in the lobby people were slowly walking in a great circle along the walls of the long narrow room. Occasionally a cluster of people would stop to talk, halting the procession. Charlotte became irritated and said loudly, "This is not the way. Everyone should keep moving." More softly she explained, "At the Opera House in Paris this promenade is called *la grande marche*. Done right, everyone can see and be seen—after all that's why we came."

“I thought we were here to listen to the music,” Karen said.

“Well that too. But look who is here, our young poet, Michel Mogens. Do you not recognize my companion?”

The young man looked puzzled, not quite able to place the face before him. His eyes traveled from her white throat down to the amber heart, blushing as he bowed.

Karen’s eyes twinkled and, as she extended her gloved hand, she said in English, “I do believe we have recited nursery rhymes together—isn’t there one that goes, ‘Lavender blue—dilly, dilly/ lavender green’?” *What has come over me*, she thought, feeling giddy.

Michel blushed even more when he recognized his pupil. “But you are quite beautiful,” he stammered and could hardly tear his eyes away. Then he recovered and completed the verse, “Will you be my queen?”

As they continued to promenade, Karen noticed a man standing in a shadowy corner. “Jesse, is that you? I didn’t think you’d be here.” As he approached, she noticed that he looked different; his long side curls were brushed behind his ears and the ritual fringes were tucked into his pants.

“I decided it would be a sin to miss Jenny Lind, even if it is the Sabbath,” Jesse confessed. Coming closer, he whispered conspiratorially, “I came in disguise; I just hope father doesn’t find out, but then no one from the Jewish community is likely to be here. I thought if I stood in back, I’d not be noticed.”

Karen chuckled, “I’m in disguise too. I hope no one tells Mam what I’m wearing.”

“Your dress is marvelous. I saw you when you first came in and thought you were a great lady from Copenhagen.”

“I see you have acquired a swarm of admirers already,” Charlotte interrupted.

Karen realized she had forgotten her manners and introduced Jesse to Charlotte and Michel. She kept forgetting that Ribe wasn’t like Fanø where everyone knew everybody. Charlotte looked Jesse up and down and frowned slightly. Karen was glad that Jesse’s coat was well tailored, but she had to admit that he looked vaguely foreign and that his slight accent branded him as not Danish. Charlotte pointedly stared at his hat, but he made no move to remove it, and Karen didn't want to explain. Fortunately, the gong announced the end of intermission and they hurried to regain their seats.

After the concert, Jesse watched Karen and Michel climb into the Holm's carriage for the short trip to the Bishop's house.

"It's bad enough that the concert was so early just to suit *Madame*," Mrs. Holm complained as she settled on her seat, "But now she's *trop fatiguée* and won't come to the reception in her honor! I suppose we provincials have to be satisfied with the crumbs."

"But she sang so beautifully!" Karen protested.

"Well past her prime, if you ask me. Not to be compared with her performance in Paris in '62—fifteen curtain calls, isn't that right Mr. Holm?" Banker Holm's grumbles were lost in the depth of the carriage.

Svend closed the door to the carriage and winked at Jesse as he turned to climb into his seat. He cracked his whip over the horse's back and the carriage started with a jerk that nearly knocked over the passengers. Too stimulated to go home and face questions about where he had been, Jesse decided to take a walk in the cold night.

He was still walking an hour later when he happened by the Bishop's residence just as Svend drove up from around the corner. "The Duchess wants to go home," he grinned at Jesse. "If I know his Lordship, he be drunk again—flirtin' with the woman and insultin' the men."

"But where's Cinderella?" Svend whispered when Karen did not appear.

"I'll stay and make sure she gets safely home," Jesse whispered back.

It was a long wait, but eventually Karen emerged on Michel's arm. The two young people were deep in animated conversation, their heads bent towards each other. Jesse suspected that each had had more than their share of wine. He was wrong, at least about Karen; the excitement of the evening alone accounted for her glowing cheeks.

Concerned for his friend, Jesse made sure to stand where they could not avoid seeing him. With false heartiness he exclaimed, "We meet again. Did you have a nice evening?"

"Oh Jesse, it was just marvelous. Mrs. Holm wasn't feeling well and had to leave early, but Michel was kind enough to offer to escort me home so that I could stay."

"I'll bet he did," Jesse muttered sourly. "May I walk with you?" he asked. "I was just heading home from a stroll around town. My head was so full of the music I didn't think I could sleep."

Karen hooked her other arm through Jesse's, ignoring that he tried to pull away. Michel glowered at him over her shoulder.

Karen bubbled on, "I met the most fascinating people. Mrs. Holm introduced me to the editor of *Ribe Tidende* and he wants to see an example of my work. And I danced and danced—Michel showed me how to waltz! But the best of all was meeting Mrs. Schrøder. Her husband is the *Rektor* of Askov Folkschool. Imagine, she's a *teacher* there too. He's giving a lecture Tuesday afternoon—do come, Jesse."

Jesse didn't trust Michel. He would have liked to see Karen all the way home, but when they passed his street, he could think of no excuse and said goodnight.

A slow-moving carriage was coming the other way. From his high seat, Svend touched the brim of his hat to Jesse. Turning the carriage, he slowly followed the couple around Cathedral Square, as if he and the horse were tiredly returning to the livery stable at the end of a long evening. Jesse decided that, with Svend on watch, Karen would be safe, no matter what the poet's intentions.

Thirty-One

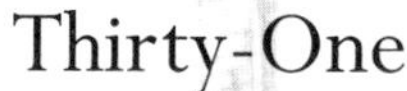

Mistress Moon

How beautiful the Queen of Night, on high
Her way pursuing among scattered clouds,
Where, ever and anon, her head she shrouds
Hidden from view in dense obscurity.
But look, and to the watchful eye
A brightening edge will indicate that soon
We shall behold the struggling Moon
Break forth,—again to walk the clear blue sky.

—William Wordsworth, 1850

Karen floated through the next day, giving her aunt a rather disconnected story of the evening. She managed to herd the children to church and look as if she were listening to the sermon. Michel, who was not usually to be seen on Sunday morning, sat two pews in back of her, his face romantically pale.

After the service, they shook hands with the Pastor at the door. While Uncle Thomas was saying that Ingrid was doing well, Michel furtively tucked a folded paper into Karen's muff and mumbled something in her ear. Back home, she only had time to glance at the crumpled piece of paper as Lise took her wraps; it appeared to be a poem.

Dinner was interminable, but for once Queen Agathe's critical comments flew harmlessly by Karen. When she and the children were excused, she hastily promised them that they would go to Christian's boardinghouse for tea and retreated to her room. A note was folded around the poem:

Dear Karen, I wanted to compose a poem especially for you, but had made no progress when I remembered Mistress Moon *by William Wordsworth. To me you will forever be "Karen who shrouds her head." I will watch for the "brightening edge to break forth, again to walk the clear blue sky." I could find no better words than these to describe the brightness of your hair and the blue of your eyes.*

The poem was in English and it took Karen a long time to understand what it said. She was reading it for the third time when Jens banged on her door to remind her of the promised walk. Queen Agathe would not permit Jens to play in the street on Sundays, but did allow the children to accompany Karen to visit Christian. Sundays were the only days the Lehman's allowed visitors and Karen often brought Jens as well as Margrethe, since the boy looked up to his older cousin.

"I am just writing a thank-you note for last night's party," Karen called, tucking her poem under the blotting paper on her desk. "We can drop it off at Bishop Balslev's on the way."

As they passed across the square, they saw Michel standing in front of the Cathedral. He greeted them in surprise and when he found out where they were headed, he exclaimed that he, too, was going to the Lehman's. "He was my teacher at Latin School. We didn't always get along, but Mrs. Lehman always makes me welcome for tea." He said it casually enough, but something in his voice made Karen suspect he had been lying in wait for them.

She thanked him for the flattering poem, keeping her voice low so the children wouldn't hear. She felt a little guilty at receiving a romantic note and fleetingly wished Peter would write her like that. But mostly she whispered because she thought the children might tease her. She didn't want Ingrid-Fas to find out, not because she was afraid of censure, but because she wanted to preserve this dream-like-experience of her first love-letter. If that's what it was. Michel was such a romantic and such a tease. She half suspected that he didn't really meant his extravagant language.

Soon the two young people were engrossed in conversation. The children trailed behind and giggled softly as they watched the two heads bending towards each other. "C'mon," Jens called loudly. "Mrs. Lehman will run out of cake by the time we get there."

"That'll be the day," Margrethe chuckled.

Sure enough, there was plenty of food on the table when they walked in. Mr. Lehman greeted Michel, removing his *pince nez* in his excitement at seeing his old pupil. Mrs. Lehman clucked over all four of them. Christian pulled Jens over to the older boys, while Margrethe accepted a cup of chocolate with a small curtsey and settled into the obscurity of a big chair.

Karen, who normally remembered her manners and did not speak until addressed, bubbled over with yesterday's concert and the party afterwards. She thought Mr. Lehman would be especially interested to hear about Dr. Schrøder's lecture but was shocked to discover that not everyone in the room was as fascinated as she with Bishop Grundtvig's concept of the folk school.

"Freethinking, liberal nonsense," Mr. Lehman mumbled.

"I understand that the girls actually use the gymnasium. In pantaloons!" Mrs. Lehman exclaimed.

"Yes but only during the summer program, when male students are not allowed on the school grounds," Michel explained. He changed to a less controversial topic. "Jenny Lind did a superb job last night. She ended with the Queen of the Night aria, from *The Magic Flute*, and her mature voice gave it just the right authority."

Karen, feeling as if she had stepped into a hornet's nest, decided to learn from Cousin Margrethe's example and just listen for the rest of the afternoon. The time dragged by while her mind seethed with unspoken protest and questions.

On the way home, she sought an explanation from her escort. "Isn't Dr. Schrøder a theologian? How can he be a freethinker?"

Michel was momentarily surprised. Although he was used to Karen's endless questions during their English lessons, theology was not his usual topic of conversation with lady friends. "Schrøder isn't a freethinker, but there's a state of war between the Latin and the Folk schools. Grundtvig went to Aarhus Latin School as a boy and hated it. He thought their educational philosophy stultifying and the school run like a prison. So he advocated reform, felt education should not be reserved for scholars but be available to the people, including women. He believed that all should have a chance to develop their spirituality and nurture their Danish consciousness. The rigid establishment theologians rejected Grundtvig as an upstart who was trying to turn their world upside down. When Schrøder started a school for the people according to Grundtvigian principles, the calcified thinkers in the Latin schools felt threatened by such revolutionary concepts."

"But Pastor Engel back home, he's a devoted Grundtvigian," Karen pointed out.

"There are some who say Engel had a promising career in the Church, but has been exiled to Fanø where his tainted ideas can do no damage."

Karen was silent the rest of the way home, pondering the expanding horizon of her world. How could she explain all this to Peter? Maybe it would not be a good idea to mention Michel.

Michel too retreated into his own dream world of moons and blue skies. As he left Karen and the children at the house, he asked whether he could escort her to Tuesday's lecture.

"You mean, you're not a calcified thinker?" she joked.

"I certainly hope not. The folk schools are doing incredible work and Schrøder is a charismatic, dynamic speaker. I expect he'll talk about his studies of ancient Scandinavian mythology, which are the foundation of much of his teaching at the school. The roots of Danish Christianity are fascinating."

At tea on Monday afternoon, it was with some trepidation that Karen mentioned to Ingrid-Fas that she would like to go to hear Dr. Schrøder's lecture the next afternoon.

"Why would you want to do that?" Charlotte asked. "If you really want to go, I suppose I could take you, but it sounds dreadfully dull and I do have another *rendezvous*."

"I don't mind going by myself. Besides Mr. Mogens is going to be there." Karen said, carefully not mentioning that Jesse was coming, as well.

Margrethe seemed about to give that away when Karen caught her eye and mouthed, "Don't even think it!" Margrethe ducked her head to hide a grin. Hanna had asked her in school that morning to tell Karen that Jesse would meet her at the lecture.

Ingrid-Fas seemed reassured that Michel would escort her, but Charlotte wasn't encouraging. "It was a mistake to let him take you home last night. If you're seen in his company again, there will be talk. You're too young to be going out with a gentleman friend, alone."

Everyone seemed determined to tell Karen what she could do. Karen was tired of Charlotte's bossiness. After all, she had been ready enough to have Michel escort her the night of the party. Why was it acceptable for Karen to go dressed to attract men's eyes, but not to talk to them? She was irritated to find that Charlotte, for all her world travels, was as provincial as the rest of them. She was a fashion dilettante but not really interested in serious ideas. Karen decided to let the two ladies argue it out, the way Papa always did. *I can just ignore what they say and go anyway.*

Finally a compromise was reached. Karen could go if she wore her everyday Fanø clothes, but instead of her distinctive scarf she should borrow a bonnet from Lise to hide her face. That way she would be recognized neither as Ingrid's niece from Fanø nor Charlotte's companion at the concert.

You see Mam, I can get in trouble whether or not I wear a scarf, Karen thought. *Just like at home, all anyone cares about is appearances and avoiding gossip.*

That evening, Karen dressed as instructed in her usual green flannel skirt and dark cotton overblouse with the blue print flowers, amber buttons, and matching apron. Her Persian silk shawl, fastened with Peter's scrimshaw pin, replaced her usual neckscarf and Lise's bonnet hid most of her hair.

Uncle Thomas opened the door when Michel rang the bell, and then took him into the small parlor off the foyer. Karen was curious but could hardly listen at the door; she assumed Uncle was telling him to bring her right home after the lecture. Michel was subdued and distant all the way to the foyer. He led her into an inconspicuous corner of the auditorium and, when Jesse joined them, acknowledged his presence with a glum, barely civil greeting.

The gentleman who introduced Dr. Schrøder dwelt only briefly on the history of Askov Folkschool since most of the audience had heard him lecture before. He told how it was impossible to continue the country's first school in Rødding after the Germans took over Schlesvig in 1864. Therefore, a year later, Dr. Ludvig Schrøder, Heinrich Nutzhorn and Rasmus Fenger, the principal and two teachers from Rødding, opened a new school in Askov.

Dr. Schrøder rose to the podium and soon the audience was spun in the magic net of his charisma. He spoke about his latest book, which was indeed about the relationship between Danish mythology and modern Christianity. He expounded on how important it was for the rural young to be educated in their religious and national heritage. Michel listened with rapt attention, but Karen had trouble following, since she didn't know enough about the subject. She noticed that Jesse's attention also flagged. During the question period, Michel asked about the comparison between the legend of King Skjold as told by Saxø *gramaticus*, and the version in the English poem *Beowulf*. Karen was impressed since she had never heard of Saxø nor of *Beowulf* and only dimly remembered the mythical King Skjold from school.

Jesse, unimpressed, whispered in her ear, "Who does he think he is?" Karen would have liked to ask about the Askov program for women. She had understood just enough to raise her curiosity, but was feeling too naive in the presence of all this learned talk.

Afterwards, people clustered around the famous man, and Michel insinuated himself through the crowd, ignoring his companions. Meanwhile Mrs. Schrøder, standing to one side just below the podium, recognized Karen from the Bishop's party and greeted her warmly. Karen pulled Jesse over and introduced him. "He's studying to be a rabbi," she explained, much to her friend's discomfort. Whether Mrs. Schrøder was merely being polite or was truly interested was hard to tell, but she questioned the young man for some time and even invited him to come and visit Askov. "We're always looking for interesting people to give an informal talk. We would love to have you visit." Jesse mumbled something about leaving for Lithuania soon.

Karen could contain herself no longer and blurted out, "Could I attend the girls' program at Askov? No one takes me seriously except Pastor Engel at home on Fanø. I want to learn more about history and literature and Grundtvig, and . . . and everything," she finished lamely, thoroughly embarrassed. *I can't believe I said that*, she thought. *I sounded like a complete idiot*.

But Mrs. Schrøder continued to be kind. "Of course you may come. The summer program is very much for girls like you who are enthusiastic and interested in learning. A recommendation from Johannes Engel is all you need to be accepted."

An excited Michel interrupted, grabbing her arm, "He wants to see my work and suggested I apply as a teacher! Isn't that fantastic?"

Karen asked, "Does that mean you would be my teacher if I went there this summer?"

"I'd only be there during the winter. The men's and girls' programs are quite separate and they don't allow bachelors to teach the girls." Then he stopped in shock. "You don't mean you want to be a student at Askov. Why would you want to do that?"

"Well, why shouldn't she?" Jesse protested.

"The girls are either stupid hicks right off the farm or rich merchant daughters, pretending to be Bohemian."

"It's because I'm an ignorant farm girl that I want to learn," Karen said huffily.

"Karen is neither a hick nor a Bohemian," Jesse protested. "She is as smart as any man."

Instead of apologizing, Michel glared at him. "You still here?"

"I do wish you two wouldn't argue," Karen said. "We should all be friends, we could have such fun together, such interesting discussions." Why did Michel always insult kind and thoughtful Jesse? Could it be because he was Jewish? Michel was usually so liberal, even if he didn't take women seriously, and being Jewish was what made Jesse so interesting. And Jesse, it was as if he didn't trust Michel, who was always a gentleman, even if he wrote poetry. Then it struck her—they were jealous! Of each other! *Because of me. Ordinary, plain old me*! She almost accused them to their faces, but instead grabbed an arm on either side of her and marched her two friends into the open air to cool off.

"I have an idea," she said. "We all need an outing. It's Christian's birthday a week from Sunday and my aunt has said we can rent a carriage for the day and go to the canal, or to an inn somewhere in the woods. Hanna could come too; and Michel, don't you have a sister? Oh please, let's do that. It's the only chance I'll have; I'll be going home soon."

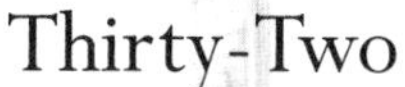

Thirty-Two

Aloha Oe

Thus sweet memories come back to me
Bringing fresh remembrance of the past
Dearest one, yes, thou art mine own
From thee, true love shall ne'er depart.

Farewell to thee, Farewell to thee (aloha oe)
Thou charming one who dwells in shaded bow'rs
One fond embrace 'ere I depart
Until we meet again.
—Liliuokalani, Queen of Hawaii, 1891-1893

Hawaii

The *Marianne* had smooth sailing all the way to Maui, riding before the constant Trade Winds that blew from the northeast nine months of the year. Peter was relieved that the Pacific lived up to its name, but he was still concerned about the wheat. He inspected the caulking of every seam daily but found no problems. He slept but fitfully however, dreaming of drifting in a lifeboat or being lured towards rocky shoals by a siren with Isabel Kensington's face.

It was also an easy passage because of the new Second Mate, on whom Peter came to depend more and more. He admired Kelolo, not just for his forthrightness and ability to lead, but also for his quick intelligence. During the long day watch when all were on deck, they found time to chat and became good friends.

Kelolo taught Peter that the islands were called Hawaii. "Only *haolis* call them the *Sandwich Islands* because that's the name Captain Cook gave us. We like *Hawai'i better*, though that's not why we killed him."

Peter laughed and then, looking sideways to make sure he was not offending, asked, "Is it all right to call your people *kananka*? Is it a slur the way *Chink* or *Jap* is?"

"Not really. *Kanaka* means 'man' and I'm proud to be called that—our women are *wahines*. But we're all proud to be *Hawai'i'ans*. Other words that you might like are: *aloha*—hello or goodbye and *meholo*—thank you."

"*Meholo*—In Danish it's *tak*. The name of my island is *Fanø,* but only Danes can pronounce that!"

"*Fano*," Kelolo tried.

"Close enough," Peter said.

Peter and his new friend also discussed women. When Peter confessed his problems with Isabel, Kelolo shrugged. "You had a good time, what else did you want?" he asked. He was more sympathetic when Peter described Karen, but pointed out that he could hardly expect her to wait for him for months, without any commitment on his part. "You had better ask her soon. She may make other plans, especially if she's as adventurous and independent as you say."

Yet, Peter was not quite ready. He still had an image of Karen as the eager child that had stood on the dune by the mill. That image had been blurred by her boldness as a writer and sudden departure for Ribe, but his body still longed for the sophistication of an Isabel and unfettered eroticism of a Janette.

After only a week of running before the northeastern trade winds, they heard the cry of "Land Ho" from the Crows Nest. At first Hawaii was only a mass of clouds on the horizon. As the *Marianne* came closer, the fog lifted to give them a glimpse of the rugged north coast of Maui, its cliffs rising steeply from the blue water and the lush green rain forest on the upper slopes shrouded in mist. Kelolo pointed out Mount Haleakala, rising 10,000 feet above the sea. An impressive backdrop to the cliffs, it was rimmed with cumulus clouds and silhouetted against the sky, as blue as the sea. Although Kelolo had been eloquent in describing his home, Peter was stunned by the beauty of the island.

"Mount Haleakala is the home of the sun god," Kelolo explained. "The volcano sleeps now, but if it wakes, most of the island will be destroyed by the ashes and hot lava. When I was a young man, I climbed all night to get to the top before dawn. We believe that the god will grant the sunrise worshipper a vision to guide his future."

Peter wanted to ask if Kelolo had had a vision, but didn't want to pry. Instead he said, "I thought you were a Christian."

"Of course, but the gods of Hawai'i take care of us and God takes care of the world."

Peter contrasted what he saw with his own island home. "Fanø is very flat. My girl and I used to go to the top of Kangaroo Mountain to watch the sunset, that is, she watched the sun and I watched her! We call it a mountain but it's just a puny sand hill. Our beach is beautiful, though. The pure white sand is a quarter mile wide and twelve miles long, running down the whole western coast of the island."

"Maui has a few nice beaches, but not like Waikiki on Oahu. Near Hana there's a beach of black lava sand, and one on the west coast has great surf. I'll take you there and teach you to ride the waves on a wooden board."

"I tried skiing in Norway with wooden boards strapped to my feet. We glided down a mountain for miles, but I never heard of riding the surf in anything but a boat."

"I never heard of this ski'ing. I saw snow once though. Moana Loa, the volcano on the Big Island, south of here, has snow on top. It's even taller than Haleakala. It's a long climb and I could hardly breathe at the top."

They rounded the eastern-most point of Maui, where they could see the village of Hana nestled between the green rain forest and a few fields. Slipping around to the southern coast, they finally came into a large open bay sheltered on the west by the nearby island of Lanai to form a roadstead—an open anchorage. The bustling town of Lahaina lay before them and many ships were at anchor, unloading and loading cargo.

"Most ships now go to Oahu," Kelolo explained. "But the Roads of Lahaina used to be filled with whaling ships unloading their catch of blubber for processing and storage on shore. They came here for our beautiful girls and wild parties. The missionaries ranted and raved, but it's hard to keep sailors from having a good time. Then they passed a law outlawing sailors in town at night and tried to keep the girls from going out to the ships."

Before they could drop anchor, outrigger canoes, filled with cheering natives, surrounded the *Marianne*. Peter later described their tumultuous welcome to Karen.

> *"Aloha" means both hello and goodbye in Hawaiian and we certainly were greeted with a big Aloha when we sailed into Lahaina Bay two weeks ago. Even before we had furled our sails and let go the anchor, outrigger canoes filled with cheering natives surrounded us. Mr. Kelolo told me to throw down a few coins and we watched the boys dive down through the clear water and retrieve them before they could sink to the bottom. Soon the natives swarmed over the railings like pirates, but instead of muskets they were armed with garlands of flowers, called leis, which they draped around our necks.*
>
> *Canoes greet every ship in this manner, but when word spread that Second Mate Kelolo was aboard a crowd also gathered on land. He must be related or friends to half the town, Hawaiian and Chinese alike, because they all showed up to greet the launch that brought us ashore, giving us so many leis we could hardly move.*

Peter chose his words carefully; he did not write that the natives that had greeted the *Marianne* were nearly naked, the men wearing merely a loincloth and the women not much more. Neither did he explain that the friendliest of all the natives was Kelolo's sister, Apikela, whose outrigger was among the first to reach the *Marianne*. She scampered on board to place a lei around the necks of first her brother, then Captain and Peter. Kelolo introduced his sister to his new friend. Peter was so startled when Apikela enthusiastically threw her arms around him that he nearly fell to the deck.

"Don't mind our friend," Kelolo explained. "He's lovesick."

"Me too, me too," Apikela laughed. "Cousin Kamekoa is finally going to marry his sweetheart. When we found out you would be coming on the

Marianne, we waited until we heard you were off Hanna; the wedding's tomorrow. The whole crew's invited."

The happy groom was introduced and exclaimed over. He also carried the mailbag that Apikela had lured out of the harbormaster's hands. "Most of it's for you," Apikela smiled as she handed Peter a thick bundle. She had separated his letters from the rest and wrapped them in large green leaves tied with maile vines. "Perhaps these'll cheer you up."

The wedding was a dream spectacle. The ceremony in the church was a marvelous blend of the familiar Christian service and Hawaiian color, but was followed by a traditional native celebration at the beach, drawn straight from tales of the South Sea Islands. The all-night luau did not end until the last guest had staggered home well into the morning. Apikela and her best friend made sure the first mate and Captain were well entertained and had more than their due from the keg of rum they had contributed to the festivities.

It was as pagan a celebration as Peter had ever witnessed. The slightly tamer description he wrote on the way to Sidney was sure to please the readers of the *Fanø Weekly*. The story's popularity would rival that of a legendary *Brullups Fest*—wedding feast, still told about in Fanniker South-rooms on long winter evenings.

> *The night after our arrival, Kelolo's large family held a wedding and a traditional "luau," an outdoor fest, to which they invited the whole crew. Aside from roast pig, baked all day in a pit in the sand, they served baked vegetables and fruit, the most wonderful of which were the pineapples. These were so luscious that the front of my shirt was all wet from the juice. The most peculiar food was "poi," a sticky paste made from mashed baked "kapu-kaiao"—taro root. These must be the friendliest people on earth and even the most memorable of Fanø feasts is nothing by comparison.*
>
> *After dinner, the women danced the traditional "hula" to a chant that tells the story of how their ancestors came to Hawaii from Bora Bora hundreds of years ago. We Danes are proud of how our Viking ancestors navigated by the stars across the Atlantic in their sturdy longboats, but at about the same time in history, Polynesians came twenty-four hundred miles in flimsy double-hulled*

canoes to settle the Hawaiian Islands. The chant tells the story, much as the Icelandic sagas tell the adventures of the Vikings. To doubters that his ancestors really came from Tahiti, Kelolo points to the name of the channel between Maui and Lanai, called "Kalai-kahiki' or the "Way-to-Tahiti."

Neither Captain nor First Mate had more than surreal memories of the last hours of the morning. Perhaps that was just as well or their Lutheran consciences might have kept them awake for the next few nights. Dawn's rosy fingers stretched across the horizon by the time they rounded up the crew and herded them back on board. During the day, a few unlucky strays had to be redeemed from jail with the payment of a stiff fine.

In his letter to Karen, Peter went on describe the mountains and the beaches, the frangipani or plumaria blossoms whose perfume pervaded the town, the exotic palm trees clustered along the beach, and the green foliage of the *kukui*—candlenut trees that lined the main street. He described the banyan tree in the town plaza, planted just last year to commemorate the fiftieth anniversary of the coming of Christianity to Lahaina. He told how this *Ficus beghalensis* from India would, within a century, become so large that it would fill the square with curtains of aerial roots. They in turn would grow into the ground until they looked like trunks of separate trees and the whole square would become a forest, all from that single tree. He did not mention that the *hula* was illegal and that the dancers wore little besides their grass skirts and flower leis. The pious missionaries had declared it indecent and passed a law against dancing. Even Peter had been taken aback by the gyrations of the dancers' hips, finding it nothing like the lively but staid *Sønderhoning* that Karen and he used to dance on Sunday evenings.

He said nothing to Karen about Apikela. He did not mention that she had been the one to show him how to eat *poi* by scooping it up with his fingers. The slim girl with the enchanting brown eyes and nut-brown skin captured Peter for the rest of their stay in Maui. In town she wore a mumu, that ugly ankle-length garment that had been imposed by the missionaries and transformed by the light-hearted natives into a colorful dress. At the beach she changed into a water nymph, wearing merely a strip of cloth over her narrow hips and flowers around her neck and in her hair. They raced into the foothills of Haleakela on scrawny horses and ate mangoes for lunch, the juice dripping from their chins. At sunset, she showed Peter how to catch the curl of a wave and balance on the long board for a thrilling ride on the surf. In the evening, they swam in Lahaina Bay. Apikela's mermaid hair trailed in the water and huge whales sounded so close to shore that they appeared to be in their midst. In the early dark of the tropical night, they built bonfires on the beach and ate and talked until dawn.

It was only with difficulty that Peter awoke each morning in time to supervise the unloading and subsequent loading of cargo. Later in the day, he met in town with Captain Fredriksen at The Master's Reading Room, which served as the Officer's Club, and they dealt with the volumes of paperwork and planned the rest of their voyage to the Orient. Peter was often the worse-for-wear but Kelolo, although he frequently had night watch on the *Marianne* after joining his sister and friend for an afternoon and evening of adventures, seemed not to suffer from the lack of rest. "I'll sleep at sea," he said.

All too soon, they weighed anchor for Sidney with a cargo of coffee, sugar cane, and whale oil. The capstan was secured, the sails unfurled, and the men slid down the ratlines and returned to their watch duties.

Peter checked their course and called to the steersman, "Steady as you go."

Only when he had time to look back on the receding shore, did he realize that he was still wearing the maile lei that Apikela had slipped over his brow before she said goodbye—*aloha*.

A little self-consciously, he removed the lei and sniffed the fragrant vine leaves. "Maile honors Laka, the goddess of the dance. Remember your Apikela and the hula," had been her last words.

"As if I could ever forget you, my goddess-of-the-dance," Peter whispered to the cloud-covered Haleakala, sinking into the horizon.

Kelolo appeared at his side by the rail. "Throw the lei overboard while it's still fresh," he advised. "Then you'll remember the sweet fragrance, not the withered leaves." He put his arm around his friend and added, "Apikala knows you had to leave for your own world and that you were hers for only a short while. Do not regret the time you had together."

"How can you leave Paradise?" Peter asked.

"When I'm at home, I get restless for the sea and bigger lands. When I am away too long, I long for Maui. I can leave because I know I will return."

"I feel the same about Fanø," Peter sighed.

That evening he wrote his letter to Karen, feeling guilty that he had not taken the time to do so while he could still have put it on the mail boat to the States. As it was, he not be able to post it for several more weeks, so it might be summer before she would receive it. He chose his words carefully, feeling that some of his experiences were too colorful even for Karen. It was better to let her think that Kelolo had been his only guide to the delights of the islands! He could not quite bring himself to propose marriage to Karen with the image of the nut-brown goddess hovering in the air and the intoxicating perfume of the plumaria blossoms clinging to his clothes.

During the night he dreamed of the hula, only the dancer had long blond hair and looked remarkably like Isabel Kensington. The melody changed from the beating of drums to the violin of Sønderhoning. He and Isabel were promenading side by side, Isabel wearing the lavender dress and bonnet from when they first met. The dance pattern changed and his arms were around Karen wearing the same lavender dress as they bobbed and swayed in the steps that symbolized a ship at sea. He awoke with the realization that the *Marianne* had tacked closer to the wind and that the bobbing was from the very real waves of the Pacific Ocean.

Thirty-Three

The First Stork of Spring

The day after Dr. Shrøder's lecture, Karen started to plan the outing to celebrate Christian's birthday. She suggested that her cousins should be the ones to obtain permission from Uncle Thomas and Ingrid-Fas, their enthusiastic begging being more effective than her timid request. Ingrid-Fas thought they should go to the Inn of the Old Eagle in the woods east of Ribe, as it was still too cold in mid-March to think of a drive to the coast. Uncle Thomas was dubious about the whole undertaking, being torn between an obligation to escort them and wanting to stay with Ingrid. They debated between taking the train, a plan endorsed by Jens, and renting a carriage, supported by Ingrid. On the one hand, an open carriage might be too cold on a bad day and the train could take them close to the inn; on the other, trains were such an unknown undertaking. Of course, Charlotte had to be consulted and, although she reassured them that the train would be fine, she suggested that a carriage be engaged with the dependable Svend as *cocher.* Finally a compromise was reached: if it were warm enough on Sunday in two weeks, the young people would go by carriage to the Inn of the Old Eagle.

Ingrid's term was rapidly approaching and the coming event was on everyone's mind. One day, Dr. Nygaard surprised everyone by declaring that the 'little mother' could now get out of bed.

"A little mild exercise will do you good," he said and suggested a short walk each morning and afternoon. "You can also join the family at meals. Just don't do the stairs more than twice a day."

"But won't that rush things?" Uncle Thomas protested.

"The sooner the better. All is now ready," Doctor said calmly. "Ingrid is weak from her long rest. We need to build up her strength and her appetite with hearty meals, plenty of nourishing soup, and fresh air."

Agathe was doubtful about the value of fresh air. "She is likely to catch a chill—Just remember, I warned you."

It was out of the question for Ingrid to be seen in town in her condition, but three turns around the garden at ten in the morning and at three in the afternoon were suitable. At first Thomas hovered each time she swung her feet out of bed, and insisted on walking before her when she went down the stairs and behind her when she returned to her room for a nap. Her 'episodes,' as Charlotte called her occasional cramps, continued, but otherwise little changed except that Ingrid seemed a little stronger each day. Privately, Karen felt there was much too much fuss, especially over whether or not Ingrid-Fas should be "seen."

The waiting continued but the atmosphere in the house changed. Meals became relaxed and Cook gloried in having 'her family' all together at the table. There were neither complaints from the children about the food nor admonitions from Papa about 'clean plates.' Having been granted this small taste of freedom, Ingrid was hungry for more. She longingly suggested that perhaps she too could join the great forest adventure. "Absolutely not," Uncle Thomas protested, horrified, and Doctor echoed his prohibition. "Not yet. In a month, you can go on all the outings you wish. Just in time to pick spring anemones."

Ingrid interviewed nursemaids but found all the applicants wanting. Shyly, Lise ventured that she was the eldest of ten children and had helped with several of her cousin's babies before coming to Ribe. Her promotion was agreed upon, a significant step towards fulfilling her ambition to qualify for a position in Copenhagen. The search continued, this time for Lise's replacement as maid-of-all work and eventually a satisfactory candidate was engaged to start the following week.

Soon after the baby was born, Karen's time in Ribe would come to an end. Ingrid generously suggested that she was welcome to stay and Margrethe pleaded with her not to leave, but Karen declined and tentatively set her departure for early April. Once the decision was made she felt relieved and realized just how homesick she was.

The great day of Christian's birthday party arrived and even the sky decked out in its best blue gown, dotted with a few fluffy clouds. Queen Agathe came for Sunday dinner and although she scowled at the eager chatter of the children at the table, she held her tongue now that the mistress of the house was presiding. No sooner had the Tower bell sounded its single gong to announce one o'clock than Svend knocked on the front door.

Hanna and Jesse were already seated in the carriage. It looked like a hay wagon that had been outfitted with two rows of seats on either side of an aisle that was piled high with blankets. When Cook came out to deposit a basket of provisions in the wagon, Hanna, suppressing a smile, hastily covered one that her mother had supplied. Jens bounded out the door, followed by a more sedate Margrethe, while Ingrid-Fas stood in the foyer enviously eyeing the preparations for departure.

At the last minute, Karen hesitated. "Are you sure you don't need me?" she said to her aunt. "You look tired today."

"Please go before I jump into the wagon myself and shock everyone," Ingrid-Fas laughed. "I didn't sleep well last night and just need a little nap. The best you can do for me is take the children and have a good time."

Michel came walking down the street with his sister Sofie on his arm. She was two or three years older than Karen and had a friendly but not particularly beautiful face, well buried in the hood of her cloak. She took one hand out of her furry muff to greet Karen and said with a smile, "Thank you so much for the invitation. We met briefly at Bishop Balslev's party, but I've heard so much about you from Michel that I feel I know you quite well."

Michel, noting that Karen was wearing her usual headscarf although she was bundled in Ingrid's heavy cloak, teased her, "I see that Mistress Moon is shrouding her head today."

Karen glanced at Jesse but was relieved that he grinned at the joke. She let Svend boost her up the small steps at the back of the wagon.

Distributing blankets to all his charges, Svend inquired, "Is *Mistress Moon* comfy? A have more blankets, un just ask." He mimicked the English words perfectly, having no idea what they meant, but liking the sound.

A loud 'rat-tat-tat' came from the house roof across the street. The first stork of spring had returned to Ribe. This voiceless bird was asserting his right to the nest on top of the chimney by pacing the roof and clicking his red beak, the only sound he could make. A loud cheer sounded from the wagon and Ingrid forgot herself enough to step out on the front path so she could better see the black and white bird with the cheerful red legs and beak. Soon pedestrians gathered on the sidewalk and craned their necks to admire the harbinger of spring. Without acknowledging his admiring subjects, the bird surveyed the other rooftops as if to look for the arrival of his mate. Some street urchins spied Ingrid's round shape and gleefully pointed first to her and then to the stork calling out, "Un better go see if a bundle has come fer un!" They started to chant, "*Stork, Stork Langeben*—Stork, Stork Longlegs," a popular children's song.

Agathe turned red and attempted to hustle her daughter-in-law out of the public eye, but Ingrid good-naturedly waved to the crowd before going in the door. The stork tipped his head to one side and gazed down at his audience with a haughty eye, a look that Karen felt was meant for her.

Peter Longlegs isn't here but I can have fun without him, Karen mentally called up to the figure silhouetted against the blue sky. *Next time you see him, you tell him that. And tell him to hurry home.*

The stork clicked his beak in answer, then stretched out his six-foot wings and majestically sailed towards the meadows to hunt for his Sunday dinner.

Svend cracked his whip above the backs of the two sturdy horses and the carriage jerked forward. They rumbled down the cobbled street to pick up Christian at the Lehman's. The birthday boy was eagerly waiting outside his boarding house with his roommate Jakob, who had also been invited. Several of their fellow students were enviously clustered at the windows behind them and Mrs. Lehman bustled out the door with a basket that she handed to Christian. With more cracks of the whip and cheers from the party, the wagon turned onto the street, across the bridge and down the country road.

"What are we to do with all this food?" Margrethe worried, staring at the three well-endowed baskets. "I thought we were going to have tea at the inn." The boys were already rummaging through the supplies and stuffing their mouths with cookies. Karen slammed the lid of the basket over the boys' fingers and laughed, "The only worries we have are stomach aches tonight!"

Michel began singing Ingemann's nursery song, "Stork, Stork Longlegs, where have you tarried so long?" Sofie came in on the second line in a pleasing soprano that contrasted nicely with Michel's tenor, soon joined by everyone else. Jesse was uncertain of the words, but Hanna leaned over and whispered each line into his ear. Even Svend rumbled in an off-key but enthusiastic bass, directing the chorus behind him with his whip. The horses showed their appreciation by speeding along the country road and the sun smiled her blessing.

They continued to sing and had almost exhausted their repertoire of familiar songs when they entered the forest. It was so ancient that the canopy of the giant oak and beech trees closed forty feet over their heads. Even the winter-bare branches were so dense that they blocked the sun and there was little undergrowth on the forest floor. On one side of the road was a field of fir and pine seedlings in the ragged lines of novice soldiers. Michel explained, "There is an agricultural school nearby and they are experimenting with different species of evergreens for the heath reclamation project up north. They found that plantings of firs serve as wind-breaks to control erosion and can be the first 'crop' after the plows break up the stubborn soil, matted with the roots of heather and broom."

"Teacher says we have to replace the land the Germans took in the war, by scientific cultivation of Danish farm lands wasted on the heath," Margarethe said, proud that she could contribute to the conversation.

Jens was more interested in whether there really was an eagle at the inn. Sofie answered, "There haven't been eagles in Denmark since well before the inn was built—it must be named for the folksong." Seeing Jens's disappointment she added, "But it's a grand place for a banquet."

They traveled the next mile through the forest without any more lessons in conservation. Hanna and Karen sat in awed silence. They had been told this was just a small wood, but these were the biggest trees that either of them had ever seen. Only a few treasured oaks grew in Sønderho though there had been talk of a fir plantation along the road to Nordby. Since her arrival in Denmark as a baby, Hanna had hardly set foot outside of Ribe and never to any place this magnificent.

They were getting cold and were grateful finally to see the sign pointing the way to the inn. The old timbered house huddled under an ancient beech tree with spreading branches shading the inn. Karen's heart leapt when the she saw the thatched roof; it reminded her of home.

The merry company was soon warming hands on cups of chocolate and tea, their feet propped in front of a glowing fire. A plaque hung over the mantle with the words to a folksong about an old eagle who invited all the animals and the birds of the forest to a banquet. Colorful animals and fantastic trees sported the surrounding walls. "A friend of mine painted the mural," Michel told them. Jens was fascinated and walked around the room studying each brush stroke. Then they had to sing the folksong, "In the forest, there was to be a banquet/at the home of the old eagle…."

The rotund innkeeper's wife brought a large platter stacked with flaky pastries and the conversation flowed effortlessly. Karen leaned back in her chair, pleased that her friends got along so well. The party was a definite success.

The return trip would have been unremarkable except for its dramatic finish. As they approached town, Michel began to recite the twelfth century ballad about the miracle at the beloved Queen Dagmar's deathbed. Just as they crossed the bridge into town, Michel's voice rose dramatically, "When the King left Gulland castle/followed him a hundred knights;/and when he came to Ribe/followed him only Dagmar's squire."

They were still wrapped in Dagmar's miracle when the carriage pulled up in front of the house. Margrethe saw Dr. Nygaard's carriage at the curb and screamed, convinced that history was to be repeated and only seeing Ingrid for herself calmed the hysterical child. Doctor Nygaard suggested Karen take the children to their grandmother's house so Ingrid could 'rest.'

"She isn't resting," Jens insisted stubbornly all the way down the stairs. "All these people are running in and out of her room."

"Nevertheless," Karen said.

Several days passed before Karen found the time to write Peter of the climax to her stay in Ribe.

Ribe, March 25, 1875

Dear Peter Storkeben,

I have decided that this will be your new name. I don't think they have any storks in Australia, but if you see one, he has a message from me.

This will be my last letter from Ribe as I leave for home next week. Last Sunday, Ingrid-Fas safely delivered lovely, healthy baby Villum, named for his grandfather, and I am no longer needed here. The birth was almost anti-climactic, it happened so fast and with so little trouble after all the fuss and worry. The children and I had gone on an outing with some friends and on our return we found Dr. Nygaard's carriage outside the house. I took the children to their grandmother's house though I was disappointed not to be allowed to help, as I had hoped.

The Queen Mother was at her worst, wanting to know why we had been gone so long and irritated that the children were cross and tired. Margrethe, since she understood perfectly what was happening, was near hysteria and no one would tell us anything. Uncle Thomas was no help, being a nervous wreck himself and having been ordered out of the house. As usual, he had run home to Mama. I finally got the children settled with a card game. By suppertime, the boy Jeppe came and told us all to come home.

Ingrid-Fas was very tired and weak, but mostly from having been in bed so long. She was sound asleep when we came home and slept the rest of the evening and all night, all through the excitement of the proud father and exclaiming children. As soon as she had heard Villum's lusty cries she had closed her eyes with a happy smile, as Cook reported to me with satisfaction. She is rebounding fast, however she is still too weak to attend the baptism on Sunday. Lise has become the baby-nurse and moved into my room so she can keep the child near his mother. I do not mind at all sleeping with the children upstairs, but feel that I am no longer needed. Ingrid-Fas has plenty of help and even Uncle

Thomas has settled down and become a much gentler "paterfamilias" than we have seen in many months. The baby thrives and Margrethe dotes. Even Jens has fallen under the baby's spell, though I did overhear him complain that Villum squeaks louder than a violin and he thinks they should trade him in for a good dog!

Leaving Ribe was both harder and easier than Karen had imagined. She had become more and more homesick in the last few weeks, longing for the simpler life in Sønderho. At home, she knew everyone and everyone knew her; visitors were rare and she had known her friends her whole life. In Ribe, she had first had to adjust to living with her aunt and family, then, when she met Jesse and Michel, she had suddenly entered the adult world of relationships between men and women, a world of which she had fantasized. Forgetting how restless she had once felt, how resentful of her mother, she longed for the familiarity of home.

Yet she felt sad at leaving. She cried when she said goodbye to the baby and Ingrid-Fas and promised to come back soon for a visit. She was still sniffling when Uncle Thomas gave her a stiff hug before helping her into the waiting wagon. Svend was to have taken her in a small carriage down to the boat landing at the mouth of the Knipsaa where she could board the *Lene*. Then Margrethe and Jens had clamored to go along. Soon Jesse, Michel, and their sisters also insisted on coming. It was therefore the same group that had so recently gone on the outing that saw Karen on her way, their gaiety tempered by the knowledge that this would be their last time together.

Karen cried again at the dock as she said goodbye to her cousins. Jens tried to shake hands, but ended up throwing his arms around her neck. "Send me a drawing, and I'll write you," Karen whispered.

"I'll draw the stork on the roof," he whispered back.

Margrethe was carrying her doll under one arm. When Karen bent for a kiss, her cousin thrust the doll forward, saying, "Antoinette wants to visit Lil-Anne for a while. I don't need her any more so she feels lonely and wants to travel."

"I'm sure Lil-Anne will be honored by the visit," Karen answered gravely.

Michel looked at her with soulful eyes and kissed her hand with an elaborate bow. She wasn't sure how seriously to take him and gave him a sisterly peck on the cheek. She would have kissed Jesse as well, but he grabbed both her hands and held them, perhaps longer than he should have.

Meanwhile, Svend brought her belongings on board the *evert*. While everyone called promises to write and visit, Karen walked backwards up the dock. She would have tripped over the gangplank except that the ever-watchful Svend caught her elbow and practically lifted her onto the *Lene*. "*Farvel*—Goodbye, *Mistress Moon*," he said, trying to speak softly but only managing a hoarse bellow. Soon a chorus was calling out the refrain, while the hawsers were cast off and the *Lene* caught the outgoing tide. The sails billowed, and everyone waved and shouted. Even after Karen could no longer hear the words she could see them still mouthing "*Farvel,* Mistress Moon!"

Thirty-Four

Homecoming

Karen sat in the stern of the *Lene* until her friends on the dock shrank to blurred specks and the cathedral tower started to sink below the eastern horizon. Only then did she move forward to catch her first sight of the mill emerging on its dune, hovering above the low meadows.

"You home for good?" asked Sailor Jacobsen after he had lowered the leeboard and the *Lene* came about.

"How's that new baby?" asked one of the passengers, while another commented, "Your friends seemed sad to see you leave."

Karen remembered with a start that she was now on home territory where there were no secrets, no privacy. She tried to formulate an acceptable reply but decided on a smile and a neutral, "Yes, but I'll be glad to be home," which seemed to satisfy her curious neighbors.

She settled down between the goods and supplies stacked on the deck. Her hand automatically went to check that her headscarf was on straight enough to pass Mam's inspection and that no stray locks of hair would scandalize the Sønderho gossips. Soon

they rounded a little spit of land and the town lay before her eyes. The beach was the usual confusion of children running, hammers banging, men shouting, and women calling. Two other *everts* were pulled up on the sand and the keel of a schooner under construction was set in its massive cradle. Two retired captains sat on 'The Exchange,' as usual settling the affairs of town and world. It was good to be home.

At first Karen saw no one on the beach to meet her and she felt let down. *Well ninny, what did you expect?* she lectured herself sternly. *A reception committee as well as a farewell party? It's not as if you don't know the way to Millfarm.* But then Papa's wagon came down the road and she could see Lil-Anne eagerly bouncing on the seat.

Papa called a booming, "Welcome home, daughter," and his arms lifted her over the railing of the *Lene* with no more effort than if she had been a sack of flour. Her feet had barely hit the sand when she was almost knocked over by a catapulting Lil-Anne. "Be careful," she warned and held out the Parisian doll. "She used to live with Cousin Margrethe but has come to visit us. Her name is Antoinette—she's named for a French Queen."

Lil-Anne looked at the doll in awe. "Welcome to Sønderho, Your Highness," she said, courtseying. All the way home, she made sure that the Queen sat securely on her lap as she explained the sights. "There's the tower and our castle," she said pointing to the mill and Millfarm; then she indicated the red Danish flag silhouetted against the sky. "Mam and I put up the flag this morning—we only do that for important visitors."

Karen sighed in relief when she saw it. *Mam* is *happy to see me,* she thought.

Karen soon settled into the old routine of helping Papa mornings and going to Granmam's house in the afternoons. Sometimes it seemed that she had never been away, but although the routine was the same, she felt very different. She was content to be home, yet yearned to get away again.

One restless morning about a week after returning home, she began the next installment of her letter to Peter. By the time it could get to the Orient, the *Marianne* would have left Sidney, so she would mail this to Canton, their next port of call.

Sønderho, April 9, 1875

As you can see, I am now back in Sønderho. By Wednesday the week after the baptism of Villum, I was ready to go home. It was a quiet sail, straight across the Wading Sea in the Lene. *Papa and Lil-Anne met me at the harbor and Papa's hug nearly knocked the wind out of me. Lil-Anne kept asking if I was really home and held my hand all the way to Millfarm where everyone else waited.*

Even Mam seemed glad to see me and had raised the flag to celebrate my homecoming. Granmam had, of course, already put coffee and cake on the table. Granmam, Kirsten, and baby Frederik are all well. Please tell Uncle Paul what a fine boy he has and that he has really grown. He pulls himself up and cruises around the southroom, prattling to himself and looking for trouble.

Two days later Mam was as bossy as ever, as if I hadn't been away at all. I am Granmam's assistant midwife again, although things are pretty quiet right now. As you know, very few babies are born on Fanø until the June rush begins, that being nine months after the first ships return in the fall. Wouldn't Kirsten-Mos be shocked that I would say such a thing, especially to a man! I am hoping that soon Granmam will actually let me help, instead of just having me entertain the children while their mother is busy, but it seems all the women in Sønderho either have relatives or neighbors demanding their rights to assist. She has promised that soon she will find something more interesting for me to do. She is trying to persuade me to train as midwife and take her place someday. I do not know; the last case that I helped her with was so depressing and I do not think I want to go through anything like that again. She told me not to talk about what happened so I'll just say the family was so poor that they gave the baby to someone else to raise.

It is strange being home again. On the one hand, I have been gone less than three months and nothing much has changed, except the men have left for the summer, as usual. On the other hand, I feel so different. Everyone tells me what to do and I still cannot make up my mind about my future. Every time I see even the smallest ship set sail or the stage to Nordby drive down the road, I want to jump on and go off into the horizon. I am thinking a lot about Askov Folkschool and their summer program for women. Now that the railroad to Esbjerg has been finished, it is a short ride to Vejen, the nearest stop to the school. I hope Pastor Engel will write a letter for me—then I only have to persuade Mam to let me go. I think I'll let Papa do the persuading.

If only you were here, we could talk. I hope your next letter will arrive soon; I want to read all about the Sandwich Islands and Australia. I sent your description of San Francisco to the Fanø Weekly. *They seem to print whatever I submit, so send more great stories!*

Karen had barely put down her pen and blotted the last line when she saw Papa come padding into the southroom. She smiled at the familiar sight of his stocking feet, his wet, sandy clogs having been left in *æ frankel*. She tried to imagine Uncle Thomas taking off his boots in the foyer or paying any attention to whether he was leaving muddy footprints on the carpet for the maid to clean. So many little things had been different in Ribe, it was comforting to know that Papa was unchanged.

As if reading her thoughts, Papa said, "I really missed you. You've grown and aren't my little girl anymore."

Karen was about to protest that she was no taller than when she left, that she could tell because her Sunday skirt still reached to her ankles. Then she realized Papa wasn't talking about her height. Looking around the little office, Papa added, "I see you've succeeded in creating order from my chaos."

In her absence, Papa had been meticulous in recording all financial transactions in the ledgers, but the notes about the mill and correspondence with shareholders had piled up in wild confusion. She had spent the better part of the week straightening up and filing all the loose pieces of paper.

"Let me show you a new accounting system that I learned in Ribe. It really makes everything easier. I had to trick Assistant Lauritzen into showing me how he did it by pretending to be interested in his herb notebook. It really was very funny, me asking questions about what numbers went in which columns and him answering about the aromatic qualities of lilac and rose petals while taking every excuse to lean over my shoulder and brush against my arm! It's nice to be home where people take me and my questions seriously."

"In Sønderho, we all know what a head you hide under that scarf," Papa chuckled. He looked at the figures before them, "That does look clear. What d'you do about outstanding accounts?"

"They go on this page until they're paid, then we put a line through the item and copy it to the main page. I wanted to ask you about this letter from the bank in Esbjerg. What's this charge for? Also, has the rent for the warehouse been paid yet?"

They spent several more minutes settling accounts. Then Papa gave Karen's shoulder a squeeze, told her again he was glad to have her back, padded back through the southroom and ducked under the low lintel of the door to the hall. Karen followed him out to *æ frankel* to put on her clogs. "I'm going to Kirsten-Mos' now," she called to her mother in the kitchen.

Before going to town, she could not resist climbing up to the mill. It was the first nice sunny day they had had since her return. All week, a strong west wind had driven a pelting rain across and heath that covered the center of the island, so today's gentle breeze and sunny skies felt particularly welcome. She looked towards the east, smiling at the familiar sight of sheep and cows grazing on the spring-green meadows along the inner shore. The tide was out, so wide wet sand bars alternated with narrow strips of water, all the way to the mainland. The Cathedral tower, which yesterday had been completely hidden by a wall of rain and fog, was again a familiar bulk floating on the horizon. Karen looked up the road away from town, the road along which Peter used to stride from Nordby only a year ago. To think that he and Uncle Paul were now on the opposite side of the globe!

Karen shivered in the wool shawl that was really not warm enough in the breeze from the sea. Fortunately she had worn two wool skirts so, only briefly missing Ingrid-Fas's warm cloak, she pulled the outer skirt up over her shoulders. Charlotte should only see her now; this was not exactly the latest Paris fashion! She half ran down the hill almost stumbling in her clogs. Walking across the field, she made her way to Southhouse along the Westerlands Path. The footpaths twisting between the brick houses, hunched under their thick thatched roofs, were comforting in their familiarity, but they looked so small. In Ribe the houses were orderly, lined up along the streets; here the houses were scattered according to convenience. All the houses seemed have been built from one mold, differing only in their length, and showing their age only by how far they had settled into the sandy soil. After several months walking among three- and four-story timbered houses, it was odd to be home where the tallest building was the mill and she was eye-level with the bottom edge of the thatched roofs.

Soon she had wended her way to the front door of Southhouse. She was relieved to be out from under Mam's critical eye. Karen would still much rather help Kirsten-Mos with baby Frederik and Granmam with midwifery than do housework at Millfarm. That in Sønderho, Big-Anne's reputation for bossiness only exceeded her reputation for fussiness in housekeeping, did not bother her. Although according to the town, Lars-Anne was a close second in both departments, Karen thought she deserved first place.

"Why is it that Mam criticizes everything I do?" Karen had complained to Mette. "Granmam always seems to approve of me, even when I'm careless and she has to show me how to do it right."

Mette, showing uncommon wisdom, said, "My Mam and Grandmam are like that too—they all are."

Kirsten-Mos was different though. Growing up surrounded by strong-minded women, she had learned early to smile sweetly and comply with the wishes of others. Her calm acceptance could diffuse the worst temper and bring peace to any house, a peace that Karen particularly appreciated.

"I'm here," Karen called as she entered Southhouse, softly in case Frederik was napping. She remembered just in time to duck her head under the lintel of the front door into *æ frankel.* Since coming home, Karen had been caught in social whirlwind of friends and neighbors calling at the mill in the evening and at Big-Anne's in the afternoon to hear about her adventures in Ribe. Now that the men had gone off to sea, there was little to do except to visit and gossip. Granmam expected no births and no mothers came to consult the midwife. This afternoon, the household chores had mostly been done and the diapers had already been taken off the line and been neatly folded.

Granmam and Kirsten-Mos were sitting in the southroom and gossiping with neighbors, everyone's hands usefully occupied with knitting or spinning. Several scarf-wrapped heads turned and eyes lit up expectantly when Karen walked into the room, smiling in anticipation of what the young girl would bring in the way of stories. She helped herself to coffee and made polite conversation. No, she had brought no letters from Peter; he was sailing across the Pacific and would be out of touch for a while. Yes, everyone at Millfarm was fine.

She knew they were expecting stories from her stay in Ribe, but she found it difficult to explain just what she had done there. Attending concerts and lectures, wearing velvet gowns, viewing forests, going skating, and learning about Judaism were far removed from the experience of Sønderhonings. They related more easily to adventures around the globe than to city life on the mainland. They had enjoyed Peter's descriptions of San Francisco and Puget Sound, and the stereopticon pictures had been even more of a hit than with her cousins. Few Sønderho ships rounded the Horn, so the Pacific and the wild west coast of California were subjects of much discussion. That the city was large, civilized and had tall buildings surrounded by beautiful mountains, was a huge surprise. His description of the cable cars was met with incredulity—they could not possibly be. Peter must be have made them up!

"Did you hear the wild geese this morning?" asked Tante-Blue in her usual whiny voice. She and her twin sister were wearing identical dark headscarves, blue since they were still in mourning for Tante-Black. It was difficult to imagine that these two sour spinsters could ever have turned family and town upside down by switching identities, as legend told.

"They woke me up at dawn," Tante-Brown complained.

Karen had an idea and said, "Last spring Lil-Anne saved our gander from flying away." Sensing a story, everyone settled in to listen, knitting stopped in mid-stitch. "It was a beautiful morning like today and the geese were migrating north for the summer. They go right to the mill, using it as a landmark—just like a Sønderho captain."

Several turbaned heads nodded wisely, *æ pjægger,* the ends of their scarves, waving in rhythm. They knew about the mill, returning ships, and even geese. Karen continued.

"As the geese flew over the mill, they called loudly but were drowned out by the answering honks from our geese. We all rushed out the door to find Lil-Anne with her arms thrown around our gander to keep him from joining his wild brethren. He was honking and Lil-Anne was yelling for help at the top of her lungs while the dog pulled at his chain and barked hysterically. As she was only six at the time and not much heavier than the gander, Lil-Anne was a very brave little girl. It was only her stubborn grip around his wings that kept him from escaping. He could easily have side-swiped her and knocked her senseless across the cobblestones. As it was, it took both Papa and Christian to separate the two and lock the gander safely in the barn. From that day forward the two hated each other, the gander hissing and snapping at Lil-Anne every time she fed the poultry, and she yelling right back that he would be slaughtered for St. Martin's feast. She would scream at him, 'Just wait until fall, Martin Goose. Papa will chop off your head and Mam will roast your fat carcass. I will lick your grease from my fingers and make a pillow from your stinking feathers.' And last St. Martin's dinner, Lil-Anne ate roast goose with pleasure. She now sleeps on a new down pillow."

Everyone laughed and clapped and Karen had a new story in her repertoire.

Since there was nothing for her to do, she asked to be excused, saying she was expected for tea at Pastor Engel's. This was close enough to the truth since she had a standing invitation to the rectory.

Pastor was, as always, delighted to have a visit from his favorite student. He eagerly waved her into his cluttered study where Ellen already presided over the teapot.

"I just received a new shipment of books from my friend Sir Donald," he announced in English, as he believed frequent practice was the road to mastery. "Let us see if there is something here that appeals to you." He seemed to forget his visitor and absentmindedly piled books from the wooden box onto the little table next to his chair. "Ah yes, Coleridge," he mumbled. As he started to leaf through a dusty old leather-bound volume, his elbow almost knocked over the pile and his wife rescued his teacup just in time. Karen and Ellen smiled at each other and chatted softly, awaiting the return of Pastor's attention from another world.

"Here we are," he exclaimed. "I saw my first spring flower today. It reminded me of this poem called: 'To a Primrose.' It is so delicious," he said, licking his lips. "Well it may be a little early for primroses, but there you are, I was reminded of spring in England: 'Thy smiles I note, sweet early flower.' Isn't that perfect?"

The two women patiently listened to the end of the poem. Then satisfied that Pastor would now pay attention, Ellen said, "Dearest, I think Karen has something to ask you."

Grateful that Ellen had switched to Danish, Karen plunged ahead with her request. "I went to hear Dr. Schrøder's lecture, as you suggested."

"Well, was he all I promised?" Papa Angel said, now giving his full attention to his young friend. "Is his work at the folk school interesting?"

"I want to go there. This year," Karen blurted out, forgetting the careful speech she had prepared. "Will you write a letter recommending me? Mrs. Schrøder said that would help."

"You don't need much help from me," Pastor assured her. "They're always looking for interested, intelligent students."

"Yes, but they'll say I'm too young. Papa too, they won't let me go unless you say it's all right. Especially Mam."

"But dear child," he said, patting her hand. "I have already written. Askov is the perfect place for you to pursue your studies. Who cares about the quantity of your years? What matters is the quality of your mind. I was just waiting for you to say you wanted to go before I mailed it. Your father should write as well."

"See, I told you just to ask," Pastor's Ellen said with satisfaction and then turned to her husband. "Now tell us, how are you going to persuade her parents?"

"God will provide," answered Papa Angel.

Thirty-Five

The Message from the Stork

When I was one-and-twenty
I heard a wise man say,
"Give Crowns and pounds
and guineas
But not your heart away;
Give pearls away and rubies
But keep your fancy free."
But I was one-and-twenty,
No use to talk to me.

When I was one-and-twenty
I heard him say again,
"The heart out of the bosom
was never given in vain;
Tis paid with sighs a plenty
And sold for endless rue."
And I am two-and-twenty,
And oh, 'tis true, 'tis true.

—A. E. Housman, 1859 – 1936

AUSTRALIA, MAY 1875

By the time the *Marianne* sailed into magnificent Sidney Harbor, Peter had pushed both Lydia and Apikela to the back of his mind and taken Kelolo's advice to accept his adventures in Paradise as merely a fragrant interlude. Even his sleep was untroubled by shape-changing visions. He continued to write sketches of Maui to Karen, which he hoped she would transform into stories for the newspaper. Even with judicious censoring he had plenty of interesting characters to describe. There were, of course, the many friendly Hawaiians, but also industrious Chinese merchants, hard-working Japanese field hands, and dour New England missionaries in a remarkably peaceful blend of diverse cultures.

Captain Fredriksen and Kelolo were enthusiastic about the upcoming arrival in Sidney, both having been there before. Fredriksen's description of their destination was practical. "Captain Cook sailed into Botany Bay just south of here almost a hundred years ago, but didn't find a good supply of freshwater. Sidney is much preferable, lying as it does in the mouth of the Parcamatta River. As a deep-sea harbor it rivals that of San Francisco, though the estuary is more like that of New Orleans with a multitude of bays and inlets. It's well protected from the typhoons of the western Pacific by the narrow opening between North and South Head where we picked up our pilot. It'll be easy to arrange a profitable cargo for of iron and coal for Canton."

Kelolo was more ebullient and more interested in people than dock facilities. "Sidney is a much smaller city than San Francisco, but the nightlife is even wilder than in Lahaina," he explained. "The women are not as beautiful as at home but there are exotic Asian girls in all the bars. Be careful though, many unsavory characters hang around town. Not just sailors, but Aussies from the sheep farms and mines of the interior come here between jobs, and the stevedores are a shiftless lot. At night, the waterfront turns into one big brawl and from the whores of King's Cross one can catch a lot worse than a beating with a belaying pin. We should advise the men to be smart and stay on board ship, especially on Saturday night."

After the *Marianne* was safely anchored, Captain went ashore in the same tender that transported the pilot. Just before he went over the rail, Peter handed him his packet of letters to Karen and a thinner one to his mother for him to post. "I have my letters to Kirsten right here. I'll drop them off together," Fredriksen said with a smile.

Paul's first stop was at the harbormaster's office to register the *Marianne*. He arranged for custom inspection and for a tug to pull them to the dock, before returning with a large bag of mail. At mail call it seemed that every other letter was for Peter. Kelolo, who was handing them out with a flourish, joked, "A-n-d another fat envelope for Mate Larsen. He must have a girl in every port between here and Denmark!"

Of course, except for a few letters from his family, most were from Karen. Peter stammered, "No, just one girl." At which the crew laughed—all the hands knew about Karen.

During the rest of the afternoon, the first and second mates stayed on board to oversee to prepare for docking and unloading the cargo the next day. Peter had the evening watch and, having nothing more to do, he settled comfortably on a chair outside on the bridge to finally read his mail. It was May and, here below the equator, it was late autumn not spring. The evening was pleasant and he needed only a light jacket, it being much warmer than Denmark would have been so close to winter. Overhead, the stars covered the sky. Peter found the Southern Cross, which they had sighted a week ago, navigationally an exchange for the North Star. The lights from the city reflected in the still waters of the harbor and cast uneven blue shadows on the bridge. The sounds of wild partying wafted across the bay from the infamous Woolloomoolo Pub. Peter noticed that Kelolo hadn't taken his own advice to stay on board; neither had the crew.

Peter lit the lantern by the side of his chair and sorted the letters by their postmark, so he could read them in order. He took the first letter off the top of the pile—one from his mother, dated in February. She was not an inspiring correspondent, her style tending to be forced: "How are you, we are fine. Cousin Lone stopped by for coffee this morning and...." Yet it was nice to read the gossip from Nordby. His siblings were apparently doing well in school, though his thirteen-year old brother was not a scholar and looked forward to his confirmation next year, after which he could go to sea. The *Marianne* would be home by then and Peter would help his brother find a good berth. Peter folded the letter, neatly reinserted it in its envelope, and placed it on the other side of the chair.

The next, thicker envelope was from Karen. He leaned back, tipping his chair and put his feet comfortably up on the railing. She seemed to be having a good time in Ribe. The letter started innocently enough with Karen's encounter with an eccentric friend of her aunt's. "Mrs. Holm is the most amazing lady," he read. "She is taking me to hear Jenny Lind next week and then a reception in her honor at Bishop Balslev's house. Is that not fabulous? I will tell you all about it afterwards." Peter smiled at Karen's enthusiasm and tried to visualize her going to the Bishop's. He shook his head at the image of traditionally-dressed Karen among the glitter of such an evening. Apparently this Mrs. Holm had had the same thought, because he read on, "You should see the dress that Ingrid-Fas is lending me to wear. The fashionable ladies of San Francisco would be green with envy. It is lavender velvet and Margrethe tells me the color matches my eyes."

Peter tried to picture Karen in a fashionable dress, her blond hair free and eyes sparkling, but had difficulty as he had never seen her in anything other than her traditional Fanø costume. He smiled as she described how shocked her mother would be to see her thus. "My mam too," he thought. Then he sat upright in his chair, so violently that he almost knocked it over. He realized with a start, that his mind had called up Isabel Kensington as he had first seen her, wearing a lavender dress, the color of Karen's eyes. Isabel's eyes were much darker and the blue dress she wore that evening at Captain Bendixen's house suited her paler complexion better than the lavender morning-dress. But lavender was definitely Karen's color. That was the morning at the San Francisco post office when Peter had decided to write Karen that they should become engaged and tackle any objections to their marriage when he came home.

More thoughtfully, he read the next letter from his youngest sister, now in second grade. It was full of misspellings, but she was very proud of her handwriting, having just learned cursive writing. His mother had enclosed several issues of the *Fanø Weekly*, with what she called "your stories" although the by-line clearly also bore Karen's name.

Then there was another thick packet from Karen with clippings from *Ribe Tidende* entitled "The Wonders of San Francisco" and from the *Fanø Weekly* with an article by Karen about the folk school at Askov. A short note was attached. "I know your mam sends you copies of the weekly when one of your stories appears, but I thought these two would have escaped her notice. I forgot to tell you that I have decided to change my by-line to 'Karen Andersdatter,' as I'm tired of being a 'son'." The rest of the long letter finished with an installment written just before she returned home to Sønderho. It ended mysteriously: "I don't think they have storks in Sydney, but if you see one, he will be carrying a message from me."

Peter was glad to hear that her aunt Ingrid had had a baby boy and that all was well, but he was vaguely disturbed by the rest of her letter. It was hard enough to imagine Karen dressed up and at a fancy party, but now she seemed to be traipsing all over the countryside with 'friends' and going to sophisticated lectures. And what was the mysterious message from the stork? This was not the Karen he knew. He sensed that, like himself, she had not told all that had happened, merely enough so he could catch her excitement.

He ruminated some more on what he had read, and then decided to go to bed, leaving the rest of the mail until morning. But his cabin was stuffy and he slept only fitfully. Towards morning, he dreamt of Karen in a lavender dress, her blond hair falling to her waist and crowned with a circle of Hawaiian hibiscus, not unlike the headdress worn by Fanø brides. Her arm was about the neck of a stork who was saying, "We will live in Ribe during the summer and winter in Egypt."

"But I saw her first. She's mine," Peter mumbled as he woke.

"She's mine now—you aren't here," answered the stork.

It was still well before dawn, when he jumped out of bed to follow Kelolo's advice and finally write to Karen and propose. Lighting the lamp, he swept a jumble of charts and papers off the little table in the corner of his cabin. He opened the wooden writing desk and removed a bottle of ink and a stack of paper. Uncorking the ink, he dipped his pen and then stopped with his hand above the paper. How to begin? He sensed he could not just write as if he were an impersonal observer describing Sidney harbor. If he could only look straight into Karen's eyes and blurt out his love, all would be fine. Furthermore, even if he sent a letter today, she would not get it for weeks and he would not have an answer for weeks more. And what would she be up to in the meantime? Would she be content to wait for him to come home, perhaps a year from now or would her hunger for adventure lead her to other dance partners?

Sidney, Australia
April 21, 1875

Dearest Karen,

I heard from your stork last night. You are right, there are no storks in Australia so he had to come to me in a dream but his message was quite clear. You were there also, dressed in the lavender gown you wrote me about. I don't know what you told him to say, but he advised me we should get married as soon as I return home.

The last sentence seemed too abrupt, so he crumbled the piece of paper into a ball and started again. Slowly, the pile of discards grew on the floor and he was making no progress. He did not hear the breakfast gong and did not notice that the sun was now shining through his porthole.

There was a discreet knock on the door and Kelolo called, "First Mate Larsen is wanted on deck."

Peter jumped up with a salty exclamation, knocking over the inkwell. From the sounds on deck, it was well past the time when he should have been supervising the tugs that were to tow them to the cargo dock. Grabbing the nearest towel, he blotted at the mess and then gave up. With another exclamation that would have drawn a reprimand from his mother, he threw on his clothes and rushed out the door, tucking his rumpled shirt into his pants with ink-stained hands.

He appealed to Kelolo for help. "Have you ever proposed?" he blurted. "To a girl, I mean."

"Only in my dreams," Kelolo confessed. "But there I'm very good. Are you having girl trouble?"

Peter sighed, "How does one propose to a girl who's on the other side of the world where I can't see her eyes?"

"Ah Karen, the prolific scribbler. Why are you having a problem? I thought you were such a good writer."

"I don't know how to say all that romantic stuff."

On the way to the deck, they ran into the Captain who was helping Olaf to throw hawsers down to the waiting tug—the job that Peter should have been doing. He would have reprimanded Peter for his unusual dereliction of duty, but seeing how exhausted the first mate looked, he silently moved aside to let him take over.

It was well into evening after a busy day unloading cargo and being towed back to their anchorage before Peter could return to his puzzle of what to do about Karen. He had enlisted Kelolo's help and was reading parts of Karen's letters aloud, including the lecture by Dr. Schrøder about Askov Folkschool.

"It sounds like she is planning to attend this Askov program. I don't like the idea of her going away again," Peter said mournfully.

"Going to school sounds pretty safe," Kelolo objected. "Especially a program just for girls."

"But it's on the mainland and a very liberal place, full of socialist ideas and radical attitudes on the role of women."

"You can't expect her just to sit at home. Don't you want her to grow into a woman you can be proud to take anywhere?"

"And this mysterious message from the stork—what on earth does she mean? She sounds so restless and almost angry. At me, even. I'm really worried she will go off to Askov and forget all about me."

"You don't have a thing to say about her going to school," Kelolo pointed out. "By now, she is either going or not. Perhaps she's angry because you haven't committed yourself. You'd better propose as soon as possible! Just ask her straight out—that'll work best. I'll help you add some romantic stuff."

So the fateful letter was mailed and traveled halfway around the world to Sønderho. By the time it finally arrived, Karen had long since left for Askov.

Thirty-Six

Providence at Work

Sønderho, April 1875

Apparently Pastor Engel decided that Providence needed help in persuading Karen's parents that she should go away to school, for the following Sunday he preached on the text of Luke 10, the story of Jesus visiting Martha's house. "In Sønderho we have many Marthas who are ready to serve our Lord," he said, throwing open his arms towards the women's section, as if to embrace them all. "But we should treasure the rare Mary who is called to learn at the Master's feet."

The congregation nodded, smiling at the inspiring words, though a few whispered to a neighbor, "What's that about?"

After services, Pastor pulled Anders aside and suggested he call at the rectory during the week. Pastor's Ellen later reported the gist of the conversation to Karen. She was not usually present when Pastor met with a member of his flock, but she was asked to join the two men to contribute 'the woman's point of view.' Neither would she ordinarily

have divulged a private conversation, but in this case it was important that Karen knew what had been said.

"Miller looked nervous at first, a little like a schoolboy who has misbehaved in confirmation class and is waiting for Pastor's reprimand," she said.

Karen laughed but had a hard time picturing her big Papa as a schoolboy. Although the two men were of a height, the burly miller thought nothing of tossing about bags of flour and seldom needed to account for his actions. Pastor, on the other hand, was like a willow branch, perpetually bending to meet the eyes of his weathered parishioners; only seldom did he reprimand anyone except in the softest of tones.

Seeing Karen's skeptical look, Ellen amended her narration. "Anyway, Miller seemed puzzled that we were to talk about you. He was surprised that you would have a problem you couldn't tell him about. We explained that it wasn't really a problem but Pastor wanted to be sure he understood. He and I explained about Askov and what a great educational opportunity it would be for you. 'Our Karen is called to be a Mary,' he said. Your father smiled and said, 'So that's what you meant by your sermon!' He too admires your talents and will persuade your mother to let you go."

"Even Papa may meet his match there. She's awful stubborn."

"As Pastor said, God will provide."

"That's what Granmam always says."

That evening, when Papa had finished reading aloud from the Bible, Lil-Anne was chased to bed and Lars-Anne brought the coffee cups out to the kitchen. Papa reached up to replace the book on the beam over his chair and then bent close to Karen's ear.

"Is Askov really what you want?"

"Yes, please," Karen whispered back. "I didn't know how much until Pastor said I should go and it seemed possible. Do you really think Mam will let me?"

"I'll take care of her," Papa said firmly, winking at Karen as Mam came back to the southroom.

Persuading Mam was easier than Karen expected. Mette turned out to be God's instrument when she dropped in one evening later in the week.

"We never get to visit anymore, you're always too busy," she complained to Karen, settling down on the bench under the lamp in the southroom and pulling out her knitting. "So I thought I should come to the mountain." As it turned out, Mette really wanted to talk to Mam.

"We're always glad to have you visit," Mam said, graciously handing her a cup of coffee. "How's your mother?"

Mette changed the subject by asking about summer jobs. This would be the first summer that she was sixteen and therefore old enough to go to the mainland.

"I'm afraid that I'll be terribly homesick. Mam said you advise all the girls and I should ask you."

"You won't have time to be homesick," Lars-Anne reassured her visitor. "Even if you have a good mistress, she'll keep you busy and you'll see, the summer will fly by."

"But what is the Hiring Fair really like?" Mette said, her words tumbling over each other. "Do you just stand there until some farmer picks you? Like at a dance waiting to be asked? How can you tell if he's going to be nasty or nice? And how do you know how much to get paid?"

Mam answered in detail. Her voice droned on and on with advice about finding out from last year's girls what their wages had been and how to judge a good master. "But your mam can tell you all that, she went to the mainland for several summers before she married your papa."

"She says I won't listen to her, so 'ask Lars-Anne,'" Mette grinned.

"Notice if the farmer looks more at your figure and face than at your hands and shoulders. If his wife is along and makes him pass by the prettiest girls, you know he has trouble on his mind rather than work. If he comes straight to the group of Sønderho girls, he's interested in your reputation for hard work, not amusement."

Karen expected her to add, 'Stand tall and wear your scarf' as she had told Karen before she left for Ribe—as if that would protect against all evil. Karen also hated the idea of standing there like a cow with the herd of other Sønderho girls; she hated it even more than shy Mette. She didn't want to be sold to the highest bidder and certainly didn't want to slave on a farm all summer. Askov's beacon became dimmer and dimmer, her dream fading. She sighed and Mam read the dismay on her face but, as usual, misunderstood.

"It'll be fine, Mette will be fine," Anne reassured. "I had a bad first master, but I was younger than I should have been and didn't know any better."

Sensing an interesting tale, Mette was all-agog. "Did he try to take advantage of you?"

"Nobody takes advantage of Mam," Lil-Anne protested. "She would never be cheated out of her money."

Karen remembered the disaster of Mam's experience on the mainland from their tearful conversation in the fall. But Mam was not going to talk about that to Mette, and certainly not in front of Lil-Anne. Then Papa interrupted the unfortunate direction of the conversation by explaining what everyone knew, "Lars-Anne's next master was my Papa and she stayed several years so he must have been fair to her. Then I came home on a visit and married her as soon as she would have me!"

Karen had not noticed that Mam had only said that *Mette* would be all right until she said, "But Karen is not going to the mainland this year." Karen's heart leapt and she thought that perhaps Papa has already persuaded Mam, but then she added, "She's already been and will stay home this summer."

Karen was about to explain what she really wanted to do, but saw that Papa was shaking his head ever so slightly. He said, "My brother Niels is looking for several girls for the summer, perhaps I can arrange something for both of you, then you won't have to go to the 'slave market.' "

"I met Uncle Niels at cousin Villum's baptism," Karen said. "He seems nice enough, but if Mam thinks I should stay and work with Granmam, perhaps that would be best." She almost choked on the words.

"I thought...," Mette started, but Karen knocked her elbow so hard that she lost three stitches and had to bend over her sock to pick them up.

The conversation turned to other matters and soon Mette said good-night, thanking them for the advice. Karen walked her friend out to *æ frankel* and watched while she wrapped up in a shawl, took off her felt house shoes, and slipped into her clogs.

"What was that all about?" Mette asked. "I thought you were going to Askov this summer."

"Shh, Mam doesn't know yet," Karen whispered. "I'll explain tomorrow. If it's a nice day, meet me at the harbor after dinner."

Karen dragged Lil-Anne off to bed and then also undressed, wanting to leave Papa to his gently persuasive ways.

"Come here a minute, Karen," he called when he heard her coming back from the 'smelly place.' "Do you really want to become a midwife like Granmam?" he asked.

Karen, treading a thin line between tactics and truth, mumbled, "I like helping her more than being a milkmaid."

From Mam's horrified expression, Karen realized that bringing up the past had stirred up memories. Apparently the idea of her daughter being a milkmaid was as repellent to her as to Karen. Yet the idea of Karen studying to be a midwife, exactly what she had most resented in her own mother, was no better. Karen wondered what Mam thought Granmam had been trying to accomplish all year, having her as her helper. Wasn't the point to persuade her what an interesting profession it was? Hadn't it been Mam's idea in the first place? Karen was learning, though: people are complicated and don't always make sense. Especially Mam.

As if it were a sudden inspiration, Papa said that Pastor Engel had mentioned that he could get Karen admitted to Askov Folkschool.

"Certainly not. That's only for boys," Mam said, with longing on her face, as if this were what she most wanted for Karen, but had not thought possible. When Papa explained that there was a three-month summer program for girls only, she nodded thoughtfully.

"Three months will give her time to decide her future," Papa added. "A certificate from Askov will help her qualify as a midwife or take teacher training. Pastor thinks she would make a fine teacher. Askov has courses on bookkeeping; so if she wants, she could continue working in the shipping business."

Mam surprised Karen by saying, "What an opportunity!" and the question was settled.

The next day, Karen told Mette what had happened. "Papa just told her the facts and I never said a word. Now she thinks it was all her idea."

"What is it that she wants?" Mette said, her brow furrowed.

"Mam is determined that Christian and I never leave her and wants to keep us near where she knows we'll be safe," Karen explained.

"But she's the one who sent Christian to school in Ribe and she even let you stay there with your aunt. And now she wants you to go to Askov."

"If Christian gets a Latin diploma and passes his student exam he can go to University. I think she plans for him to become a doctor and come back to Fanø to practice. But at least he won't go to sea. As long as it's her idea, it's all right."

"And what about you? Why doesn't she want you even on your uncle's farm this summer? After all, that's where she met your Papa."

"I think she's afraid I'll marry a foreigner and never come back, even though that's just what she did and she came home anyway. In the summer Askov has only girl students, so she thinks that'll be safe."

"That doesn't make sense!" Mette protested.

"I didn't say it made sense. Mam's head is sensible enough, but she hardly ever talks about the past, so it's all mixed up in her heart. I'll never do that. I won't bury bad experiences where they'll smolder like a manure pile and stink up everything."

"And what about Peter? Doesn't she know you are only waiting for him to return so you can sail with him and make the *Marianne* a Lady Ship?"

"We don't talk about that either. She just hopes one of us will change our mind, or forget, or something. I'll worry about Peter and Mam when the time comes. Besides he hasn't asked me—yet!"

"She must be blind. Doesn't she see you're just like her? Both as willful as goats!" Mette thought for a while, and then added wistfully, "Do you really think I could get a job on your uncle's farm? At least I wouldn't be among complete strangers."

"I'm sure Papa can arrange it. He can talk anyone into anything!"

Thirty-Seven

Askov Folkschool

Askov, May 1875

At the end of April, Karen was admitted to Askov Folkschool. The program started in May, soon after her seventeenth birthday. She had not quite dared writing about it to Peter, in case the school plans came to naught. Even after being admitted, she was reluctant to tell him, sensing that he would not approve of her leaving Fanø again. Meanwhile, she had another dream-visit from the pesky stork that always seemed to want to tie her to Fanø.

She hadn't heard from Peter for a while. When she first returned home, she had received several letters from him about San Francisco and Seattle that he had mailed before leaving California. The descriptions were wonderful but he wrote nothing personal. The last letter had been mailed when the *Marianne* arrived in Hawaii—then nothing.

She wrote letters to everyone else. To Michel Mogens she sent a thank you note in awkward but readable English, since he had been her escort to Dr. Schrøder's lecture and was therefore partially responsible for her going to Askov. His reply, in the same language, was more eloquent but embarrassingly romantic. Mam immediately wanted to know who her gentleman correspondent was and frowned as if she regretted allowing Karen to go to the mainland again. The explanation that Mr. Mogens was her English teacher in Ribe mollified Mam somewhat, but Karen could tell that her mother had been reminded that traveling had already exposed her daughter to the new ways.

That's the whole point, Karen argued silently.

Jesse and Karen were more circumspect in their correspondence. They had exchanged several letters, mailed through his sister Hanna, so his parents wouldn't know that he had a non-Jewish friend. In Sønderho, the childish hand on the envelope needed no explanation beyond identifying Hanna as "a nice little school friend of Margrethe's." Jesse was to leave for Lithuania about the same time as Karen and sent the address of the Slobodker Yeshiva, the famous school he would be attending. Just wait until Mam saw her receive letters from Lithuania!

Karen wrote a long chatty letter to Ingrid-Fas, Margrethe, and Jens about her homecoming and the exciting new developments. As an afterthought, she added Uncle Thomas to the salutation, but wondered whether he would pay any attention to her doings. To her delight, both her aunt and Margrethe wrote sweet little notes and Jens sent a drawing of Ribe cathedral with a stork flying overhead. Even Charlotte added her congratulations, though Karen had the impression that the latter did not think Askov was *le dernier cri*. Best of all was the package that came a week later, which Karen fortunately intercepted before Mam knew of its arrival. She ran off to open it in the privacy of her room. Inside were several items of clothing, obviously imported by Uncle Thomas's business and the likes of which had never been seen in Sønderho. There were two French petticoats and matching pantaloons, a summer nightgown and *peignoir* trimmed with Brussels lace, and, best of all, a dress of English lawn scattered with sprigs of lavender flowers. A card was enclosed:

Dear Karen,

Happy Birthday. We wanted you to have these tokens of our affection before you leave for Askov. Charlotte insists that even there you might need a suitable summer frock for some special event. She added the unmentionables because, "one must feel beautiful from the skin out."

With love from your family and friend in Ribe

Karen opened the shutters on her tightbed and spread out her new finery. She sank down on the domed lid of the wooden confirmation chest that was the only piece of furniture in the tiny room and, with a corner of her old work apron, wiped away the happy tears that ran down her cheeks. She stared at the presents and wondered when she would ever have a use for these fancy clothes, having been warned that accommodations at Askov were primitive and most of the students of small means. It was becoming real to her that her life was about to change once more. She was suddenly not sure she wanted to leave after all.

"Why're you crying?" Lil-Anne demanded with her usual forthrightness. She had come into the room, Antoinette as usual tucked securely under one arm. Furious when Karen left her for Ribe, Lil-Anne had refused to allow her sister to move back into the room they had always shared, so since returning, Karen had taken over Christian's room where she had unpacked her presents.

Lil-Anne was explaining that Mam had gone to visit Else Jensen, when she caught sight of the clothes and stopped in mid-sentence.

"I'm crying because they're so beautiful and Ingrid-Fas is so kind to me," Karen explained. "But you have to swear not to tell Mam—on pain of death! She would not approve and say 'certainly not!'"

Lil-Anne looked at her hopelessly. "You really are leaving, aren't you?" she accused. "Mam says that you won't ever live here again."

"How can she say that? She knows perfectly well, I'll be back at the end of the summer. I'm just going away to school for a bit—just like Christian."

"He doesn't live here anymore either, but he's just a boy and you're my sister. You don't love me," Lil-Anne sobbed, sinking to the floor and putting her head in Karen's lap.

Karen put her arms around the hunched shoulders and dried first her own and then her little sister's eyes with the damp apron. "I will always love you," she murmured. Then to distract them both, she showed off the beautiful clothes.

"You have to try them on right now, so the Queen and I can see—you'll look just like a summer visitor," Lil-Anne exclaimed, brightening. She turned to Antoinette and asked, "She could even go to Paris dressed like that. Couldn't she, Your Highness?"

"I can't do that. Mam would have a fit if she saw me dressed as a foreigner," Karen said. "I may never wear this dress, but I'll know it is here. Just like your amber heart that you always wear, even though no one can see it. Now, go wash your hands and you can help me put them away before she comes home."

One by one the clothes were carefully folded. Lil-Anne handed her each piece and Karen piled the new clothes at the bottom of the wicker trunk, which would go with her to Askov. On top, they placed Karen's other treasures from her hope chest: her confirmation Bible, H. C. Andersens's *Fairy Tales*, the scrimshaw pin, and finally a bundle of Peter's letters. Her spare everyday clothes were packed last so that the treasures would be hidden from Mam's prying eyes.

Karen went into the study to write. "Dear Peter Storkeben," she started, having decided she might as well face her night-visitor head on. This was the final weekly installment of the bulky package that would be sent to Canton before she left. She wrote the story of persuasive Papa and Mam-the-goat, the pros and cons of leaving, and the good news of her acceptance. She told him about the arrival of the presents and Lil-Anne's upset at her leaving again. Although it helped to retell it all, she was left vaguely dissatisfied that her triumph would have no reply for weeks to come.

"How can I leave?" Karen wrote. "How can I not be here for the summer sunsets over the sea, the blooming of the heather, and the song of the nightingale? Is Mam right that I will never live here again? But, as H. C. Andersen said, there are all those mountains that I never saw. You tell that to your stork, but also tell him I will be back before you are."

Karen's trip to Askov was very different from her last journey away from home. The weather was good, she was well, and she finally had a chance to ride the brand new train. Papa brought her to the station at Esbjerg. After purchasing her ticket and checking her trunk, he helped her find a seat.

As he hugged Karen goodbye, Papa asked, "Are you sure that I shouldn't ride with you?"

"I'll be just fine. It's only a few stops to Vejen and they'll meet me at the station," Karen assured him. Trying to laugh away her threatening tears, she added, "I think you're just jealous that I get to ride the train!"

She lowered the window as Papa climbed down the steps. Leaning out, she waved and saw just his head and hand through the enveloping cloud of steam. The whistle blew as the train jerked to a start and she hurriedly sat down before she lost her balance. The chug of the engine and the clank of the wheels was a soothing rhythm, but Karen was too excited to even close her eyes. They stopped briefly in Bramminge, where she could have changed to go south to Ribe. Then the conductor called, "Vejen. Next stop, Vejen."

The wagon from Askov was waiting by the platform. Several of her future classmates had been on the same train or on the one that arrived from Kolding a few minutes later. They looked as bemused as she felt and the next several hours were a blur.

The school was less than two miles from the station, so soon they were going around the pond in the center of the small village of Askov. They passed a shop and a few houses, then a squat brick house was before them. This turned out to be the original 1864 building, which now housed the auditorium and classrooms. Other buildings, containing the dormitories and gymnasium, were clustered in back. There were more introductions and time for getting settled in her room. Karen had three roommates, each of them assigned to sleep on her own narrow cot against the wall. The rest of the furniture was equally sparse with two chests and a few hooks for their clothes.

Midday dinner was in a central dining room—a room filled with the noise of nervously chattering women. Most of the girls were dressed plainly in white blouses, dark skirts, and cotton aprons. Their hair was uncovered and pinned in buns at the back of the neck. Some girls wore the peasant dress of their regions, but Karen was the only Fanniker and the only one to cover her hair. She felt self-conscious in her headscarf, and decided to ignore Mam's advice and go bareheaded in the future. The rest of her everyday clothes would not make her stand out as strange, certainly not as much as the two city girls wearing what Charlotte would have called *le dernier cri.* Their noses were in the air, as if horrified by the rabble they found themselves among. Karen could just hear Michel's disdain, *They think they're being so Bohemian.*

After lunch they went to the big hall and Rektor Schrøder described the program, including the daily schedules. First thing each day, they would meet for Morning Song—a combination worship service and songfest. Then there would be smaller classes and finally a general lecture by Rektor or one of the other teachers. After lunch there would be another general lecture, and then time for individual work or meetings with teachers. In mid-afternoon, they would exercise in the gym, alternating with sewing instruction by Mrs. Schrøder. The day would end with Evensong. On Sundays they would attend the small church on the Askov Village Green and in the afternoons they could read, write letters, or take walks into the country in groups of at least three girls.

"It sounds like a lot of work," grumbled Stine, one of Karen's roommates.

"Yes, isn't it going to be interesting?" Karen replied, eyes shining and fingers itching to start.

Rector continued his introductory remarks by expounding on the value of the Living Word. Karen knew that this was a pet theory of Bishop Grundtvig, who felt students should absorb from the spoken word rather than just studying dry texts. "I see some of you are taking notes," Schrøder said and then thundered so loudly that Karen almost fell off the bench, "Put your pencils *down* and never bring them to lecture again! You must learn to listen, not just take down words."

Most of the girls had never been away from home before and some were homesick. One of the "Bohemians" was from a wealthy merchant family in Randers and grumbled that she wasn't used to sharing a room. "She should have been here when we first started," Mrs. Schrøder said. "We had so few rooms, everyone had to sleep two to a bed."

The other city girl was named Pernille and was another of Karen's roommates. She was not particularly beautiful but turned out to have a great sense of humor, and was shy rather than stuck-up. She was from Aarhus and, like Karen, had envied a brother who was attending the Latin School there. "Grundtvig's old school," Karen said.

Pernille nodded and pointed out, "The one he hated so much he had the idea for the folk schools! I think it's a little better now. Not so rigid."

Stine continued to be unhappy with all the work, but mainly the lack of men. "They're so old-fashioned, not letting us be here at the same time as the boys," she complained. "Just study, study all the time—and the teachers are all married and they're much too old." After a week, Stine and the Randers girl left for home.

Many among the remaining students turned out to be interesting. Karen soon learned that she should not judge them by appearances. Their third roommate, Elsbeth, who at first seemed flighty, was well read and had a wonderful imagination. Other girls were shy and, at first, quiet. At home, they had become used to hiding their thoughts behind stone walls of silence for fear of being teased or called "unfeminine." Now, encouraged to express their ideas, they blossomed. Three girls were from Schlesvig, south of the new border, and had come north to improve their Danish. Since the '64 war, only German was allowed below the border in the formerly Danish schools.

Karen immersed herself in her studies and reveled in being taken seriously. She was allowed to continue her reading of English literature although foreign languages were not normally part of the curriculum. However, since she had a special interest and needed little guidance, one of the teachers promised to help her find books and make suggestions. Rector said that Bishop Grundtvig approved of England—and as long as it wasn't German she wanted to study, he gave permission.

Askov kept the girls so busy that Karen only had time to write letters on Sunday, although she tried to add a few lines to Peter every night before dropping into bed, thoughts awhirl with new impressions. Before leaving for school, she had arranged with the postman to forward her mail and she started to receive many letters. A few were from family in Sønderho and Ribe, and some were from Jesse from his new school in Lithuania.

Jesse was living in the house of his teacher, the Rabbi, whom he admired as a learned and kindly man. His betrothed, Deborah, the teacher's daughter, was, "Beautiful and intelligent. She has the loveliest brown eyes. Like her biblical namesake, she is so wise that I call her, 'the judge.' She even seems to like me!" The wedding was planned for the fall, to give the young couple a chance to know each other better. Jesse seemed quite smitten with his intended and Karen was very happy for her friend.

Michel wrote almost daily and the other girls teased Karen mercilessly about all her mail from admirers. "These are just from family and friends," Karen protested. *But nothing from Peter.*

Thirty-Eight

Roselil

Roselil og hendes Moder de sad over Bord,
de taled saa mant et Skæmtens Ord.

"Før hvert Træ skal i Haven faa Blomster af Guld,
før jeg skal vorde nogen Ungersvend huld."

Hr. Peder stod paa Svalen og lytted med List,—
Den ler dog bedst, som ler til sidst!"

Og der de kom ned udi Urtegaardens Læ,
da hang der en Guldring paa hvert et Træ.

Roselille blev rød som et dryppende Blod,
hun stirred i Græsset ned for sin Fod.

Da kyssed Hr. Peder hendes Læber med Lyst,–
"Den ler dog nok bedst, som ler til sidst!"

—Folkevise

Roselil and her mother at table sat,
Speaking many a joking word.

"Every tree in the garden shall bear flowers of gold,
Before to any man I will be true."

Sir Peder stood under the eaves listening by stealth,–
"He who laughs last, laughs best!"

And when they went into the lee of the garden,
On every tree hung a golden ring.

Roselille turned red as dripping blood,
She stared into the grass at her feet.

Then Sir Peder kissed her lips with joy,—
"He who laughs last, laughs best!"

—Medieval Folksong, translated by Anne Ipsen

Finally in mid-June a letter came from Peter. It was written after they left Hawaii and postmarked from Australia. Karen read the marvelous descriptions that needed very little editing before they could be submitted to the newspaper. She laughed so much that her roommates pestered her to share the joke.

Why not? she thought. *There's nothing private here, nothing of Peter, just an amusing correspondent for the* Fanø Weekly. *I could share it with the whole school.*

Her classmates enjoyed the tales. Even her teachers were impressed to have a published writer among the students and soon she became the school storyteller. They were pleased with her byline of "Karen Andersdatter," happy that she had gone back to the old way of naming that gave equal status to sons and daughters.

A week later, Karen received yet another letter from Australia, from just before his departure. The tone was quite different, more personal but diffident, as if Peter were embarrassed. He did write how much he missed her and how he longed for a letter from her. "We are going to Canton from here by way of New Zealand to pick up timber and the Islands of the South Pacific for a load of sandalwood, so you will have time to send your reply to greet me in Canton."

He received a whole bundle of mail from me when he got to Sidney, she puzzled. *He knows that I am now writing to Canton, so why is he suddenly so impatient when he couldn't even be bothered to write me until after he left the Sandwich Islands? And what does he mean by "reply"?*

During the week the teachers kept the students too busy listening to lectures, writing, reading and doing gymnastics, for anyone to be bored. They were big on gymnastics, that and singing. No dancing though, which they thought indecent. Karen tried to tell them about the winter dances at home in Sønderho and that it was good clean fun and exercise. "It's part of the tradition," she argued with Mrs. Schrøder, since she knew the school was big on folk tradition. Mrs. Schrøder pointed out that there was no one for the girls to dance with.

On Sundays the students made their own entertainment. They were not allowed to talk to the local farm boys and the town was very small. "But there are ways to have fun," Karen wrote to Jesse, with whom she could be more open than Peter—he would be amused rather than jealous.

> *I received a letter from Ingrid-Fas that she, Uncle Thomas, and the older children were visiting my Aunt Nette and Uncle Mathias, her brother. Since Uncle Mathias's farm is only about five miles from Askov, the whole family drove up to the school and took me out to Sunday dinner in the nearby town of Vejen. Of course, I had no trouble getting permission for something so respectable. I usually wear traditional Fanø clothes, all except for my headscarf, but I decided to wear the lovely dress that Ingrid-Fas sent. I share a room with two other girls and did we have fun dressing me up and piling my hair on top of my head!*

Soon after church, two carriages drove up filled with ten cousins and two aunts and uncles—a noisy group! Surprisingly, Svend Schultz was driving one of the carriages. "Godaw *Mistress Moon*" Svend said, tipping his hat. Even more surprising was that Michel Mogens was driving the second carriage. Karen thought at first he was just one of her uncle's hands until he echoed, "Go'daw *Mistress Moon,"* with a big grin.

They had a merry dinner at Vejen Inn. Karen privately asked Michel what he and Svend were doing with her family.

"When I found out that Svend was to drive the Bangs to Mathias Andersen's farm, I asked if I could come too," Michel said. "Mrs. Andersen seems to like me," he added with a grin. "I wrangled an invitation as 'poet-in-residence' for the rest of the summer. She finds that very Bohemian, and anything is better than my hot garret in August!"

Karen couldn't help laughing. As usual, she didn't know whether Michel was kidding.

At dinner, it turned out that Uncle Mathias had been so impressed with Svend's handling of the horses that he hired him as groom for the farm. In addition, the Bang family had decided to take the train from Vejen back to Ribe. Margrethe and Jens were thrilled—Jens especially, saying, "I might just stay on the train and go on to Rome."

When Karen was dropped back at Askov late in the afternoon, she thought that was the end of the adventure. However, the following Sunday, Svend again drove up with the carriage, only this time it was empty. "Go'daw *Mistress Moon,*" he said as before, and handed her a note. The teachers assumed that it was an invitation to her uncle's farm and she never told them otherwise.

The brief note was in English. "The carriage will bring you to my magic kingdom deep in the vast forest. Come *incognito.*" She recognized Michel's style.

If Svend had not been their chaperone, Karen would not have agreed to go. Michel was very handsome and charming, but she didn't really trust him. However, she was young and it was fun to be courted, if that was what he was doing. Besides, Peter was at the other side of the world and he had not proposed—at least not yet.

She asked Svend to wait while she went back to her room.

"Are you going to wear your beautiful dress?" Elsbeth asked.

"In that dress I would be as noticeable as if I wore a Fanø scarf," she pointed out. "He said *incognito* so I'll just wear my everyday clothes and look like a local farm girl."

"Let me at least arrange your hair," Pernille giggled. "You can wear my new hat with the silk flowers."

The wagon took off. Around the bend in the road, there stood Michel with a big grin and a picnic basket. Michel behaved himself, most of the time. Whenever he seemed about to cross the line of propriety, Svend would interrupt by pointing out a bird or tree or manor house that he thought *Mistress Moon* would like. Once, when Michel started to whisper softly in Karen's ear, Svend jammed on the carriage brake so abruptly that Karen almost flew to the floor.

A couple of weeks after that, Svend again showed up and took Karen to Michel for a picnic. The next day, Karen had a letter from Jesse.

> *You speak of Michel and your suspicion of his motives. I am sure that you can trust Svend to keep him from taking liberties. I came to know him after you left Ribe and I believe his intentions towards you are entirely honorable. If I may speak like an older brother, a friend, do not trifle with his affections. I know you find this all very amusing, but he may be more serious than he lets on. It is his way to make a joke of life, but that does not mean that his feelings*

cannot be hurt. On the other hand, if you enjoy his company, do not dismiss his friendship out of hand. You are still young.

"I can't believe Michel is serious!" Karen said to Pernille. She did, however, write Michel a note declining to meet him again, suggesting that their outings were too risky. Even with Svend as chaperone, the school would not approve. Michel would immediately be fired from his fall teaching position if anyone suspected that he was meeting a female student and Karen would be sent home.

The next Sunday, Svend arrived again. This time, the note was from Aunt Nette. She invited Karen and her roommates to drive back to the Andersen farm for afternoon tea. Michel must have put her up to it. He was incorrigible! Who could resist?

Jesse continued to be Karen's confidant and she wrote,

You are so lucky that you have found your love and that Deborah will marry you. By now everyone at school knows that I am waiting for Peter to propose and that my mother does not approve. They encourage my flirtation with Michel—as if somehow Peter will know and be jealous, but I am being very careful not to give him false ideas. Meanwhile I wait and worry about Peter. Speaking of intentions, what are his?

I was becoming so cantankerous that Pernille, my friend from Aarhus, suggested that we should put on a play from an old comic folksong. The story is about Sir Peder who wishes to court Roselil. The maid vows to her mother, "Every tree in the garden shall bear flowers of gold, before to any man, I will be true." Eavesdropping, the knight schemes, "He who laughs last laughs best." Sir Peder escorts Roselil into the garden and behold, every tree bears a gold ring. Roselil turns "red as dripping blood" and Sir Peder kisses her, repeating his famous line.

Pernille said she would play Sir Peder—Peter, as she insisted on pronouncing it—and my two roommates would be the mother and the narrator. I was persuaded to join the fun and be Roselil—Papa always says it is better to have people laughing with you than at you. For the gold rings, we made chains out of yellow paper and draped them over a branch that had blown down during the night. Pernille was decked out in her exercise bloomers. Her hair was pinned up under a hunting cap, borrowed from a teacher and plumed with a pheasant feather.

The whole school came to the performance in the big lecture hall and joined in the laughing chorus with great gusto. The mother and daughter gossiped and the gold-hung branch was uncovered with a flourish. When Pernille kissed me with a loud smack, I did turn red, but from laughing at the cheers and catcalls from the audience.

It really was great fun except that now everyone calls me Roselil—even Michel who has somehow found out. I am afraid he wants the role of Sir Peder and to have the last laugh.

I seem to get in trouble no matter how hard I try to behave. Fortunately, school will be over in two weeks. I cannot believe how fast the time has flown. Although we have worked very hard and I have learned more than I can explain, it has also been great fun. It has been so nice to have Pernille for a friend. We laugh a lot, yet sometimes we stay up half the night talking about history or philosophy. If we wake Stine with our noise, she will tell us to be quiet, but sometimes she joins right in.

The Askov summer program finished in early August. Karen planned to take the train to Esbjerg, the steam ferry to Nordby, and then the stagecoach home, reversing her outbound trip. She was therefore surprised to see Svend appear several hours before she was due to leave and insist that he drive her to Esbjerg. Of course, Michel had put him up to it and was waiting at the bend in the road.

"It's not proper for you to travel unescorted," Michel said.

"Fiddlesticks," Karen retorted. "I'm perfectly capable of riding a train for fifteen miles, as I did on the way here. I have just told Svend that he could take me to the station in Vejen, but no further." Despite her continuing protests, Svend drove right past the station and continued along the road to Esbjerg. "We have plenty of time to get *Mistress Moon* on the five o'clock ferry."

Karen was furious and, blaming Michel, insisted on sitting next to Svend on the front seat. Michel spent most of the trip trying to remedy his blunder. He leaned forward so he could speak directly into Karen's ear, apologizing for not having realized that she would resent any attempt at interfering with her independence. Near the end of their trip, he succeeded in making her laugh at his silly antics and the rest of the time passed pleasantly.

They finally arrived in Esbjerg, just before the train was due. Karen saw a familiar figure walking up the hill towards the railroad station. "There's Papa!" she exclaimed.

Svend pulled the carriage over to the side of the road and introductions ensued. Papa remembered having met Svend in Ribe and was delighted that his fellow veteran of the '64 war was working at Brother Mathias's farm for the summer. If he was surprised that Michel was there, he never let on.

"I had an errand in Norby," Miller explained, "So I thought I would meet the returning scholar. Besides, the stage-driver has been very undependable and this afternoon he turned up drunk. Erik Innkeeper is furious but I volunteered to give his guests a ride to Nordby and the ferry."

"Mon he be looking for a new driver?" Svend asked. "A's done at the farm by month's end and don't have no hankering to return to Riwe."

"I'll inquire and let you know," Miller promised.

By this time they had arrived at the dock where passengers were just beginning to board the ferry. Karen was pleased that she had not just one but two chaperones to ensure Michel's behavior. His goodbye was very proper and no more effusive than appropriate between casual friends.

Papa restrained his curiosity only until the ferry was underway and the two figures waving from the dock were lost among the crowd. "You've developed quite a following on your travels," he hinted.

"Svend has appointed himself my guardian angel. He's very devoted," Karen explained. "Michel Mogens gave Margrethe and me English lessons in Ribe last winter. He's going to teach at Askov in the fall and somehow finagled an invitation to spend the summer at the farm; Aunt Nette thinks it's sophisticated to have a resident poet."

"He looks quite smitten," Papa smiled.

"He's full of romantic nonsense but he's really just a friend." Karen answered nervously. "Please don't tell Mam."

"If you say so," Papa agreed and flicked the reins of the horse to go down the road to Sønderho.

Thirty-Nine

The Fateful Letter

Sønderho, August 1875

A festive welcome greeted Karen even before she and Papa reached Millfarm. Lil-Anne and Christian were waiting for them by the side of the road a mile from home and climbed on board with pails of blueberries they had picked for supper. Lil-Anne nearly knocked Karen out of the carriage with her hug and wouldn't stop babbling the rest of the way. Granmam, Kirsten-Mos, and little Frederik were all waiting in the courtyard and Mam came to the kitchen door as soon as she heard the commotion. Lars-Anne stood in the doorway as if she were welcoming any supper guest, but Karen noticed that the flag was flying from the mast.

Karen felt strange to be home at Millfarm after three months away. She kept expecting to be reminded of a lecture or asked to listen to someone's composition, but instead found herself in the way as Mam or Girl-Ellen bustled about with household chores. The grain harvest was in full swing so tomorrow she would help stack the bundles, but today, as Mam reminded her, she would be expected to call on friends in town. Her first stop was

at the parsonage. She stayed only long enough to tell Pastor Engel and his wife that she was home and thank them for helping her get to Askov. "I have so much to tell you both," she said and promised to come for tea Sunday afternoon.

She dropped by Emma Hansen's house at the east end of town to say hello to Mette's mother. Her friend was still working on the mainland at Uncle Mathias's farm and she missed her familiar round face. Emma was in the back taking laundry off the line and Karen stopped to help her while they chatted.

"Home for a visit?" Emma teased. "Where are you traveling to next?"

"Oh, I plan to stay a spell," Karen retorted. "You have to tell me the latest gossip. You know Mam, she tells me nothing."

"Things are pretty quiet here, what with the men gone and the girls on the mainland for the summer. Mette certainly is grateful to your papa for arranging her job with Mathias Andersen. She's a good girl but awful shy."

"Uncle Mathias is a decent sort though Aunt Nette is a bit pretentious. I saw Mette a couple of times this summer; the farm is so close to Askov. Once she got over being homesick, having a job seemed to give her more confidence."

Emma smiled, happy that her daughter was doing well. Having finished folding laundry, she suggested that Karen go down to the harbor. "The *Lene* just brought in a load of peat, so everyone will be there, and you can show them that you're back."

"I need to go and help Kirsten-Mos," Karen said, departing hurriedly.

As she dashed off, Emma called after her, "Come for coffee some afternoon and we'll talk. I want to hear what you did at school."

Down at the harbor, the flat-bottomed *evert* was pulled up on the low-tide beach. Kirsten-Mos, her skirt girded and pulled up around her thighs, was sloshing around in the wet sand, loading blocks of peat onto a wheelbarrow. Frederik, chortling with glee, was practicing stomping in the puddles with his bare feet. Having only recently learned to walk, the toddler was not very steady and periodically tumbled over, much to his further delight. His no-longer-white shift was soaked and he was covered in wet sand from his hair to his chubby toes.

Karen had forgotten to wear her work clogs so she took off her shoes and socks and waded into the water to help her aunt. *I've become a regular city girl*, she chided herself. *A foreigner who doesn't even know how to dress!*

"I'll help you to get this happy sailor home for a bath," Karen said to Kirsten-Mos. Her aunt gave her a welcoming smile and stretched a kink out of her back. Tucking a stray lock under her scarf, she left a smudge along her cheek. Karen scooped up her nephew and piled him on top of the barrow with peat. "Boy, are you wet," she said to the toddler. "Vet," he echoed enthusiastically.

On the way home they talked of Frederik's latest words, then of their absent loves.

"What do you hear from Peter?" Kirsten-Mos asked with an innocent smile. "Paul thinks he's asked you an important question."

Karen looked perplexed. There had been no letter like that, even waiting for her when she came home. Only a stilted note from Singapore, talking about a minor South Pacific storm they had had to ride out on the way. "Whatever could Uncle mean?"

"Perhaps he was mistaken, I'm sorry if I spoke out of turn," Kirsten-Mos apologized.

"Well in any case, don't say anything to Mam about this. She still gets hysterical if anyone hints there is more than storytelling between us."

"I wouldn't think of mentioning it. If there is something Lars-Anne needs to know, you'll be the one to tell her."

Now Karen was really confused. What was Peter up to? Had Uncle Paul mistaken her for some other girl of Peter's who was being asked an important question? She could hardly concentrate enough to give Frederik his bath. Kirsten-Mos had had the foresight to leave the tub outside in the sun so the water was comfortably warm. The little boy enjoyed splashing here, as much as he had at the harbor, until Karen was as soaked as he.

During the next few days, Karen helped with the harvest in the mornings and in the afternoons she worked on the books. The mill ledger was reasonably up to date since during harvest there was little grain to be ground, but the shipping ledger was way behind. Papa had barely kept up with the various warehouse and other bills and there was a pile of bank deposit slips to sort through. One of the subjects at Askov was bookkeeping for small business and Karen thought she could adapt what she had learned for the shipping company. The books would have to be completely redone though, not a project for one day.

The next afternoon she finally found time to unpack. While Christian was home for the summer, Karen shared Lil-Anne's room and had been living out of the wicker trunk that she had taken to Askov. She wanted to put away her papers from school, the bundle of letters from Peter, and especially the lavender summer dress at the bottom of her confirmation chest away from Mam's prying eyes. She had Christian carry the wicker trunk into his room where the wooden chest was and opened the lid. There on top was a thin letter from Peter, postmarked from Sidney and dated in May.

She confronted Mam and shouted, "What's this letter doing here? Why didn't you tell me the minute I got home?"

"It arrived a week or two before you were due back, so I put it in your chest and forgot about it," Mam explained off-handedly.

"How could you forget?" Karen screamed, her voice rising on the word 'forget.' "Why didn't you forward it to school?" Her voice was now icy-cold.

"I thought there wouldn't be time," Mam replied. "Besides, if you'd unpacked and put your things away as soon as you came home, you would've found it right away."

That's right. Blame me when it's all your fault! Karen thought and stormed out of the house, leaving the rest of her things on Christian's bed. She ran up the dune to the mill and sat down on the steps. Ripping open the letter, she hurriedly scanned the contents. It was all that she could have hoped for; here was the important question that everyone knew about but she. Peter, declaring his love at last. He swept aside all problems of her youth and parental approval and proposed that they be married as soon as he returned. "Now that you are seventeen, getting a King's permission letter should not be difficult," he wrote.

Not as hard as getting the goat-Anne's permission, Karen thought.

His letter continued, "As soon as I hear from you that you agree, I will write your parents and ask for your hand."

That's easy enough for you," Karen mumbled. *You won't be here for the typhoon.* Then she realized that poor Peter had been waiting all this time to hear her answer and had received nothing but chitchat and girlish nonsense. No wonder his letters were so distant! She read the letter for the third time and it was fortunate that she already knew the words by heart for her tears blurred the page.

Papa's voice interrupted the fourth reading. "What was all the shouting about?"

"Mam was keeping a letter from Peter. She says she 'just forgot' to give it to me, but I don't believe it. She just won't take him seriously. How can she be so mean?"

"How can she take him seriously when you never tell her how you feel?"

"She won't listen. She just doesn't understand anything! And now Peter wants to write you for permission to get married when he returns."

"That's good news. Isn't it? Isn't that what you want?"

"She'll never agree. Can't you talk to her?"

"We have time. You tell Peter to write and I'll see what I can do in the meantime."

Karen hurried back to the office to write Peter. She could not think of what to say and finally decided to fill a page of her best letter paper with "YES!" written with a brand new steel nub and dipped in her best blue ink. Explanations and problems could wait, her answer could not.

"I don't believe for a minute that she forgot," Karen repeated to Kirsten-Mos that afternoon. She had dropped off her all-important reply at the post office addressed to India, the *Marianne's* next port. Then she rushed over to Southhouse. "She thinks that by not talking about Peter, he'll stay away. And now she is sulking, waiting for me to apologize—she does that, gives me the silent treatment until I can't stand it any more and say I'm sorry, even if I can't remember what I've done. It seems to me she's the one who ought to apologize. Papa thinks she'll come around, but it'll never happen."

"I'm sure she did just forget," said Kirsten, ever the peacemaker, but even Kirsten had talked about her sister as "she," as if the conversation were about Big-Anne.

"She'll never trust him." Karen burst out vehemently. "He's a seaman like her Papa and her brother. She trusted them to come home and they died and left her. It's not fair, my Peter isn't her brother and he's not dead."

Karen wished she could take back the words but it was too late. However, if Kirsten was hurt by her outburst, she didn't say, but quietly continued to fold diapers.

Forty

Stormy Passage

I stood on the forecastle, looking at the seas, which were rolling high, as far as the eye could reach, their tops white with foam, and the body of them a deep indigo blue, reflecting the bright rays of the sun.

Our ship rose slowly over a few of the largest of them, until one immense fellow came rolling on, threatening to cover her...I sprung upon the knightheads, and seizing hold of the forestay with my hands, drew myself up upon it. My feet were just off the stanchion, when she struck fairly into the middle of the sea, and it washed her fore and aft, burying her in the water. As soon as she rose out of it, I looked aft, and everything forward of the mainmast, except the longboat, which was griped and double-lashed down to the ring-bolts, was swept off clear.

The galley, the pigsty, the hencoop, and a large sheep pen which had been built upon the fore hatch, were all gone, in the twinkling of an eye—leaving the deck as clean as a chin new-reaped—and not a stick left, to show where they had stood.

Two Years Before the Mast
The Pacific Ocean, June 1836
Richard Henry Dana, Jr.

The Indian Ocean, August 1875

The fifteen-hundred-mile passage of the *Marianne* from Canton to Singapore was as troublesome as her crew had seen since leaving California's shores in the spring. First they were nearly becalmed, the winds so light and variable that every watch was spent aloft taking in and then making sail, so as not to lose a single breath. Then, five hundred miles northwest of the Portuguese port, they were overtaken by the last of a typhoon and blown three hundred miles back the way they had come. Fortunately, after having cut loose a few spars and a shredded mainsail, the damage could be repaired at sea from ship stores, and the precious cargo remained high and dry.

They stopped in Singapore only long enough to replenish food, water, and marine supplies so there was no chance to sample the infamous night-life of the town. The mailbag waiting for them was light because they knew they would stay there only briefly. Peter did receive a short note from Karen full of her usual chitchat, including the excitement of being a student at Askov, and an issue of the newspaper with his story about Hawaii. He could not understand why she had not answered his marriage proposal; it was not like her to ignore him. Perhaps she was so full of adventures at school that she couldn't think about the future. Could it be that her letter had been lost? But surely she would have said something in the subsequent one! All sailors knew about the uncertainties of mail on the seas, but only during the darkest hours of the night did it occur to Peter that *his* letter might have gone astray.

It was late August by the time the *Marianne* left Singapore, tacking against a contrary wind through the Straits of Malacca between the Malaysian peninsula and Sumatra. They bypassed the Nicobar Islands, famous for their valuable coconut plantations and infamous for their pirates. Malaria had destroyed one Danish colony after another until the government abandoned its presence there in 1848. The English had finally taken over six years ago, but the Nicobar fever was still such a deadly threat that Fredriksen decided to forgo the islands and the potential profits to be made there. Their next port was therefore the former Danish Colony of Tranquebar at the southern end of the Coromandel Coast of East India.

Peter paced the deck. All day and every evening, he paced up and down, sweating in the tropical humidity. So certain had he been of Karen's answer that he had broadcast his impending engagement to all and sundry on board. Now he was sorry because he had become the brunt of endless kidding and sly remarks at his glum face after mail call in Canton and Singapore. He hardly dared hope that an answer would be waiting for him when they arrived in India.

Captain Fredriksen couldn't help noticing that something was on Peter's mind. Over chess one night, he therefore broke their shipboard protocol and asked what was troubling him. Captain did his best to comfort the young man; he was certain that Karen would say yes and that there was a perfectly good explanation for her silence. Kelolo was more skeptical. From his self-proclaimed vast experience with women, admittedly mostly one-night stands in the South Seas, he found nothing strange in a *wahini* not wishing to commit herself to one *kanaka*, especially if that man were halfway around the world. "You really can't expect her to jump at the chance," he said. "There must be plenty of interesting men to entertain her at home."

Peter looked even more glum as he paced through the long nights. When they finally arrived in Tranquebar, the soles of his boots were worn through, as if he had walked the whole two thousand miles. It was a pale and anxious young man who waited on deck for the mailbag. He barely had the presence of mind to excuse himself as he rushed to his cabin, arms full of his share of letters, the whistles and catcalls of the men ringing in his ears.

Karen's name stood out in flames as he sorted the envelopes. Soon there were two neat stacks on the floor to the left of his chair: 'Karen' and 'others.' Most of the envelopes from her were thick, but there was one very skinny one. Instinctively guessing that this was what he was looking for, he ripped open the envelope and unfolded the single page. It was completely covered in rows and rows of large letters. At first, in his nervousness, he could not read them.

Then, "It says YES!" he shouted, jumping out of his chair and knocking over the neat stacks on the floor. He stumbled up the stairs to the quarterdeck and ran to the railing overlooking the scattering of sailors on the deck. "She said YES," he repeated, waving the fateful piece of paper. The crew cheered.

After his watch that evening, Peter went to his cabin to write to Mr. and Mrs. Andersen requesting Karen's hand in marriage. Later he would wonder whether it would have been better or merely discouraging if he had first taken the time to read Karen's other letters that made it only too clear that whereas permission from Anders was forthcoming, the young people's plans might founder on Lars-Anne's granite.

In any case, Peter finally decided he could not compose a more persuasive letter if he struggled for several more nights. He had described the success of their voyage in the most glowing terms, knowing full well that his future father-in-law would already have the figures to the last penny. He had described his rosy future and Captain Fredriksen's promise that he would soon rise to become the *Marianne's* skipper. "In a few years," he explained, "a captain's share of her profits would enable us to buy a house in Sønderho or Nordby, as Karen wishes." Knowing Lars-Anne's fear of the sea, Peter declared that he would soon be in a position to give up the sea for a safer profession, the nature of which was yet to be determined. As for Karen, he praised her beauty, intelligence, and character. "Together we will bring wealth and respect to our families and towns."

The masterful letter took all night and a whole box of paper to compose and Peter was at the door of the Tranquebar post office as soon as it opened the next morning. He had done his best—the rest was up to the vagaries of the fates.

Peter's buoyant mood carried him through the rest of the day, but it flagged somewhat when he read the rest of Karen's letters and understood the obstacles ahead. More uplifting, the bundle also contained several issues of the *Fanø Weekly* with his stories from Sydney and Canton and a copy of one of Karen's own unpublished stories. She had written a moving composition at school about a servant girl who had been fired when a shop assistant had tried to "take advantage of her."

"Everyone at school liked it and said I should send it to one of the big city newspapers. I don't dare because Mam might find out and be furious that I wrote about her experience—even though I changed the setting and the names. I heard similar stories here at school so I think that outrageous treatment of country girls is very common and should be talked about more."

Peter was fascinated by the formerly Danish Colony of Tranquebar, bought in 1620 to allow Denmark to take advantage of trade opportunities in India.

Despite the sale of the town to England thirty years earlier, The Danish East India Company continued their important presence and Captain was expecting to pick up some fine cargo for the final leg of the *Marianne's* journey home. He and Peter were soon swept up by the generous hospitality of their fellow countrymen.

Although they only had a few afternoons free, Peter and Kelolo explored the old Dansborg fort that still lay along the beach. Peter described it in his next installment to Karen. He also thought she would be interested in the mission school in town, which was founded according to the same Grundtvigian principles as Askov. Instead of just trying to convert the natives, these missionaries taught life-skills and provided the only educational opportunity for the area's "untouchable" boys and girls.

The *Marianne* stayed in Tranquebar only long enough to lay on fresh food and the final cargo. Her holds were now loaded to capacity with sandalwood, rice, China silks, India tea, and spices for the lucrative European markets. The livestock pens were replenished with pigs and poultry, and they had enough fruits and vegetables for the passage to Cape Town, their final port before the trip home.

Peter was sad to leave Kelolo behind in India, and hired a young Dutchman, Han van Dam, to replace him. Peter and Captain had tried in vain to talk the Hawaiian into signing up for the rest of the voyage, but he refused, saying Europe was too cold for his thin blood.

"At least come with us to Cape Town," Peter had argued.

"Africa is not a good place for dark-skinned men," Kelolo said firmly. "Anyway, all this talk of engagements has made me decide that it is time for me to return home and settle down."

The two men had a farewell lunch near the old fort. In their reluctance to say a final goodbye, the two friends were kidding around, fantasizing about Kelolo coming along.

"Now, if you were going the short way through the Suez Canal…," Kelolo quipped, knowing full well that it was prohibitively expensive to tow a sailing vessel for 100 miles on the canal, through the Egyptian dessert.

"We'll talk Fredriksen into installing a steam engine in the *Marianne* at Suez," Peter added, caught up the fantasy. "Karen will take the train to

Marseilles on the warm Mediterranean." Recalling Elisabeth Bendixen's parting advice in San Francisco, he said off-handedly, "We'll set out to sea and Captain Fredriksen can marry us, with you as best man!"

The friends looked at each other, laughing. Kelolo said, "In your dreams!"

"Seriously," he added. "Are you not worried that Karen's mother will win? Karen has agreed to an engagement, but her family will have the final say until she is of age. Unless you want to wait until May, you'll need something very romantic to sweep Karen off her feet and persuade her to elope with you."

Peter looked morose—Kelolo was expressing his worst fears. Lars-Anne was a formidable foe and he saw little hope of persuading her to allow her daughter to marry a seaman. How could he get Karen out of her clutches? Squaring his shoulders he said, "I am determined to have the last laugh."

The germ of an idea tickled the back of his mind. Fortunately, he would have time on the long journey home for the seedling to mature.

Forty-One

Dancing Sønderhoning

A haar hørt tæ dæ sku' væ' Fæst
aa dæ sku' væ' i Javten.
A vel daans mæ Mett' Mari
aa saa mæ lille Ane.

Himmel, Jord aa Fanøkroer
aa sejsten elementer.
Sytten tunte Fanniker
de danser i dær Træsker.

Nær de haar dær træsker slidt
de daanser i dær sokker.
Nær de hær dær sokker slidt
de daanser i dær flapper.

Sønderhoning Sang
per Johannes Ipsen

I have heard about a fest
an' it will be tonight.
I will dance with Mett-Marie
An' then with little Ane.

Earth an' sky an' Fanø Inns
an' sixteen elements.
Se'nteen weighty Fannikers
are dancing in their cloggers.

When they've worn the cloggers out
They will dance in th'r sockers.
When they've worn the sockers out
They will dance in the flippers.

Traditional Sønderho Song
Translated by Anne Ipsen

Sønderho, October 1875

In **October, harvesting potatoes and other fall crops was** hampered by an onset of wet and blustery weather. Despite the misery, preserves were made, honey collected, fish salted, and hams smoked, all in preparation for the coming winter. Anders Miller and Apprentice-Erik threshed and ground grain whenever the weather permitted. Only a few of those Sønderho girls who had gone to mainland farm-jobs for the summer had yet returned home and therefore the bulk of the work still had to be done by the older women. Karen energetically pitched into the work, buoyed by Peter's proposal. Soon he would be home and all would be well. Now if Mam would only agree. Then she could announce the joyful news to everyone.

Lars-Anne brooded about the house in silence. A tragic telegram had been delivered to a house in the Fuzzy Mountains announcing a shipwreck, though fortunately with little loss of life, and Mam had been reminded that it was twenty-three years ago that the *White Karen* had been lost. Although Karen now understood the reason for her mother's depression, she felt unable to help her through the difficult fall months. During the next few weeks, while the town waited for the ships to return, Karen stayed out of her mother's way as much as possible.

When Peter's letter to her parents arrived in early October, it did not seem a good time to give it to Lars-Anne, and Karen kept the letter from her. Finally, Papa said it would not do to wait any longer and suggested that he share Peter's proposal with Anne next Saturday evening after the house had settled for the night. That way they could all discuss it calmly on Sunday morning and give Mam a chance to find her peace during church. "I've broached the subject with her a few times in the last month," Papa said. "I'm sure she'll come around in time."

Karen lay tense in her tightbed that night, hoping for the best and fearing the worst. Her parents' voices came through the door, but not the words. Then she heard Mam's "Certainly Not!" followed by, "Let them wait until May when she's eighteen."

I knew it, Karen thought. *She probably hopes Peter will change his mind by then—she must know that I won't.*

After a sleepless night, she finally mustered her courage and faced the family at breakfast. Papa looked less optimistic than the night before and Mam's face was as dark as the morning sky. Impatient, Karen was about to pull the problem into the open when Papa stopped her. "Give her more time," he whispered while Mam was in the kitchen to fetch more butter. Lil-Anne, sensitive as always to everyone's feelings, was looking from one face to another for clues about what was going on. She too decided that silence was wisest. Only Apprentice-Erik seemed oblivious to anything other than the large bowl of oatmeal before him.

The following week, bad weather kept Karen close to home. She and Mam spoke only as necessary about daily chores and the atmosphere continued to be tense, so she tried to focus on her work. She couldn't even use her usual excuse of helping at Southhouse to escape because Kirsten-Mos had found a girl to help her in the mornings. Karen therefore stayed home working on her writing and on the sadly neglected books well into each afternoon. As the ships returned and anchored for the winter, the pile of bills of lading and sales invoices accumulated and needed to be unraveled and entered in the ledgers.

She wrote to Jesse and Deborah in Lithuania to congratulate them on their wedding and express the hope that the three of them could someday meet. She wrote in Danish, not trusting her German to convey her emotions and knowing that Jesse would translate. She went on to describe her continuing troubles and despair at finding a good resolution. "Short of meeting the *Marianne* in Holland and eloping with Peter, I can see no hope," she wrote. "Mam will never agree. She just will not see that we love each other. She says, 'Marry a sailor and weep at his grave.' But just because so many in her family stayed out there, doesn't mean that Peter will."

Jesse replied almost immediately, thanks to the miracle of the new trains. It was amazing to write to someone in another country and have an answer so quickly. He counseled patience. "There's nothing you can do right now. When the time comes and Peter returns, you'll know what's right."

Deborah added a note in German, written simply enough for Karen to understand. "Jesse has told me of your troubles. It must be difficult to have your Peter so far away when you need his strength most. If you elope, will your family disown you?" she asked. "That is what would have happened to me. I had met a young man that wanted to marry me, but I'm so glad I waited for Jesse. My Tzaddik is my true love and my parents did know what was best. Tzaddik is my pet name for Jesse; it is Hebrew for a 'righteous man,' but I like to think it also means a wise man."

"That's no help!" Karen exclaimed frustrated, "Everybody says 'be patient' but nothing happens."

Deborah continued, "If your marriage to Peter is meant to be, it will happen. Be careful that you don't lose your mother in your haste to marry Peter. We continue to need our parents' wisdom."

Karen and Papa made a trip to meet with stockholders and inspect the warehouse in Esbjerg. "If business continues to grow, we'll need to open an office here," Papa said, planting a seed in her mind.

Taking the stage with Svend as driver, Karen even went to Nordby by herself to visit the newspaper editor about an idea she had had for a series of interviews with seamen that were home for the winter. They had a well of stories from their travels in the Mediterranean and Africa that she thought deserved larger audiences than could fit into a neighbor's southroom, and more permanence than a yarn spun on a cold night.

While in Nordby, she also called on her future mother-in-law. After an initial awkwardness, each wondering what the other knew about Peter's intentions towards Karen, they became friendly, sharing a consuming interest in their wandering seaman. Bodil Larsen proudly showed Karen around her home. The house was built in traditional Fanø style with bedrooms at the west end and stable at the southern. The stable contained only one milk cow and a few chickens while the town shepherd cared for her sheep on *Grønningen,* the lush meadows at the northern end of the island known as the 'Greening.'

When they climbed the stairs to the loft, Bodil showed Karen the studs that outlined an additional bedroom she was having built. Her face was without guile as she explained, "I thought Peter should have his own room away from the younger children when he comes home. Now, of course, he has other plans …."

Was that a hint? The new room was certainly large enough for two and only a short ferry-ride away from Esbjerg. Karen ruminated on a plan. The *Marianne* was to make landfall in Holland, next month. She could take the train and meet Peter there and perhaps they could find a way to be married. Rather than following the Fanø custom that a young couple live with the bride's family while they saved up for their own house, she and Peter could move in with Bodil Larsen. Perhaps Papa would let her open the office in Esbjerg. Then when Peter became *Marianne's* Captain, they could sail together. The plan would work, so why was her heart so heavy? Karen wondered if she could live in someone else's house. Mam was at least a familiar problem, but could Karen stand being told what to do by a stranger? Would she be allowed home to see her family? Would Mam ever speak to her again?

Karen made a furtive trip to the ticket office to find out about trains to Holland. If the man at the desk thought it peculiar that a Fanniker girl would plan such a long trip, he hid his curiosity and helped her figure out the schedule and the fare. She would take the same train that had brought her to Askov, but go through Vejen and on to Kolding. There she would have to change trains and take the overnight express to Amsterdam. Karen had just enough money saved up from the allowance that Papa had sent her during the summer to pay for a third class seat to Amsterdam, but then what? It was very frightening to think about being on her own in a foreign country.

Mette returned from Uncle Mathias's farm and Karen shared the sequence of letters, including the one from Jesse. "So much for wisdom from the East," she moaned. "It's easy for them to advise being patient—they're safely married and already have a baby on the way."

"There's a thought," Mette said with a wicked gleam in her eyes. "Then Lars-Anne would have to agree."

"We're not that stupid," Karen retorted. "A baby just makes everything more complicated—I've learned that much from helping Granmam."

The continuing drama of Karen and Peter was much gossiped about in town, there being much speculation though little in the way of hard facts. Then the attention turned to Lone Thatcher and Thomas Jensen. Thomas lived on his parents' substantial farm off the road to Nordby, about two miles north of the mill. Lone had worked there during the summer and the two young people had decided to marry. The banns had been read and the prospective bride was proudly showing off her left hand to all and sundry. The gold ring would be switched to her right hand during the wedding ceremony, scheduled for late October.

Lone still lived at home but Thomas had been seen leaving her house early one morning and everyone assumed that, according to Sønderho custom, he was sharing her tightbed.

"They seem to be in an awful hurry to marry," whispered Tante-Blue to Karen in front of Brinch's store. As usual, Tante-Brown finished for her, "No one marries in October. It just isn't done—unless...," She smirked and her voice trailed off.

Karen didn't deign to answer. She was to stand bridesmaid for her friend and wasn't going to add to the gossip—if she knew anything, she did not let on.

Sunday evening dances started again and were well attended by young and old seeking to escape the fall doldrums. The prospective bride and groom diligently came to practice the wedding march, a variant of that most difficult of local dances, the *Sønderhoning*.

Karen was a skillful dancer and, since it was considered bad luck for the couple to practice with each other, she was often called upon to partner with the blushing groom while Papa escorted the intended bride. Karen was looking forward to the festivities but found it difficult to watch the happy couple. Like most young girls, she had dreamt of the day she and Peter would stand before Pastor Engel. Papa Angel would smile benignly at them over his white clerical ruff, Peter would be tall and handsome, and Karen would be beautiful in her white shawl and flowered crown. All she knew of Holland was that it was as flat as the land around Ribe. What kind of celebration would they have if they married among strangers?

The week before the wedding, Lone's two younger sisters came to Millfarm to issue the invitation. "And bring soft shoes," they ended. After being given a treat they scampered off to the farm next door to repeat their singsong message.

That night as they were preparing for bed, Lil-Anne recited the invitation again, letter perfect, except with Karen's name as bride. "I've been practicing so I'll know how to do it when Peter comes home," she said.

Karen's heart sank. Lil-Anne would not be reciting invitations for Karen, the dividing walls would not be removed to make room for a celebration, and no soft shoes were needed for dancing that would not take place. "Why are you crying?" Lil-Anne asked, but Karen pretended that she had something in her eye.

On the day of the wedding, Mam looked glum as if she, too, knew that Karen's wedding would not fulfill her own dreams for her daughter. Frowning, she ordered everyone about to prepare for the day. "Anders, make sure that Lil-Anne is ready on time and bring her to the church. Karen, go to Southhouse and have Kirsten help you with your bridesmaid crown."

She disappeared out the door to go to Lone's house. Both Lars-Anne and Kirsten were skillful at sewing the crowns of dried flowers into the hair of the bride and her attendants. As was often the case, they had been asked to help with Lone's wedding to ensure that the crowns would not come loose during the dancing.

"I know where to go, you don't always have to tell me," Karen mumbled resentfully as she trudged down the Westerlands path.

The wedding was all that anyone could wish. The bride and her attendants were beautiful, the groom handsome, and Pastor beamed benignly. This was Karen's first experience as bridesmaid, but she could hardly concentrate enough to follow the ceremony that she had watched from a pew so many times before. After church, the congregation paraded to Lone's house to celebrate and dance. A long line snaked through the town, led by the bridal couple, attendants, and families, and followed by the guests. Those not invited to the party stood in their doorways to applaud the procession.

At the house, they were greeted by a generous punchbowl and many toasts were proposed, until Musicmaster played the introductory strains of Sønderhoning. Jeppe, one of the groomsmen and Girl-Ellen's brother, was Karen's partner in the march. He was a clumsy oaf with none of Peter's elegance. At the end of the promenade section, he let go of her hand as they came about and then put his arms around her, clasping both her hands in his rough paws. Karen closed her eyes and imagined he was Peter, feeling the warmth of his hands, and of his long body against hers.

The pain of a not-so-soft-shoe on her instep jarred her awake. Looking at Jeppe for the first time, she almost laughed at the befuddled look on his face. She had heard the veiled whispers at dances, teasing the young men about how much they liked this part of Sønderhoning. Mette had confided once that one of her partners had been so overcome, they had to drop out of the dance. Was Jeppe merely embarrassed to have stepped on her foot, or about something else? She smiled stiffly in response to his mumbled apology and was relieved that the next dance pattern was less intimate and they could walk side-by-side.

Karen went back to her daydream, thinking about meeting Peter in Holland. She would need to invent an excuse for leaving Sønderho. Perhaps she could tell Mam that she was going to visit Ingrid-Fas in Ribe, but instead of taking the train to there, she would go overnight to Amsterdam.

The pattern switched back again as Karen came about. Jeppe put both his arms around her once more and the music became faster and faster, the couples twirling around the floor with feet intermingled in a competition of endurance and skill. Miraculously, practice paid off, and Karen and Jeppe survived to the end without tripping over each other's feet. At the final chord they stopped, breathless and red in the face, this time from exertion. Jeppe slapped Karen's hand in the traditional gesture of thanks for being his partner, hitting with more enthusiasm than was necessary. When Karen hastily withdrew her stinging hand, he blushed again and rushed to the punch table to fortify himself with a healthy slug of rum. Surely, Jeppe knew better than to imagine that Karen would ever…? Did he really think she was dreaming of him? Would the evening never end?

The rest of the party, she tried to avoid Jeppe's dogged attentions and was relieved when Papa led her onto the floor. They did not speak, merely enjoying the slow dance. "Soon it'll be your turn," Papa whispered and patted her hand encouragingly as he escorted her back to their seats. Karen mumbled a response, wishing that it were so. Then her parents were out on the floor. Watching them, Karen marveled at how Mam, who had said little all evening, melted into Papa's arms. Her face relaxed, her mouth curling into a soft smile. Karen closed her eyes and melted into Peter's arms and suddenly felt as flushed as if she were dancing the wildest dance. *What's the matter with me tonight?*

Her parents returned to their seats and Musicmaster announced a round dance. Svend Schultz came over and bowed first to each of her parents, then to Karen. He stretched out a white-gloved hand in mute invitation. Svend was now installed at the Inn as the regular stage driver. He had been watching the Sønderhoning dancing without being able to participate, and now saw his chance with the familiar off-island dance. Although usually scruffy looking, tonight his clothes were carefully brushed and his unruly hair water-combed to one side. He led Karen out on the floor, his squat body stiff and formal. Then he grinned up at her, bristling with curiosity, but confined his remarks to a polite, "Æ first mate'll be home right quick, A expects."

The music relieved Karen of needing to reply and she gratefully turned to her next partner in the round. When the women went to the center of the circle, Mette grabbed her hand, squeezing extra hard. "Practicing?" she teased. Then it was the men's turn to go to the center and, instead of clapping her hands, Mette pointed to the flowers in Karen's hair. "Next it'll be my turn to stand up for you."

If everyone expects a wedding, Karen thought, *they should tell Mam.*

She met Svend again at the end of the dance when his shy slap barely touched her hand and he escorted her back to her seat. He repeated his bows and thanked Papa for allowing him the honor.

It was then time for the bride and groom to depart to a chorus of well wishes, some bawdier than others. But the party went on and it was almost dawn when the last stragglers left and Karen gratefully sank into a chair. The musicians packed up their instruments, promising to come back in the evening for the second day of festivities. A lighthearted banter began as groomsmen clumsily untangled flowers from the braided locks of the bridesmaids. The teasing, well lubricated by the leftovers of the punch table, became more and more suggestive as sea-worn hands fumbled with hair which they had heretofore only seen on their mothers and sisters and never been allowed to touch.

Suddenly overcome by the intimate feel of Jeppe's fingers, Karen jumped up from her chair and, pleading exhaustion, dashed across the room. She barely glimpsed a sea of surprised faces and a dejected Jeppe as she slipped out the door and half-ran home through the dawn. She stumbled up the path to Millfarm in her sodden dance-shoes, having forgotten to change to her boots. Looking back over her shoulder as she pushed open the door into *æ frankel,* she saw the sun coming up over the horizon. The houses of the town lay huddled under thatch that glowed in the soft rosy light. Seagulls, silhouetted against the billowing white clouds, screeched, announcing a new day.

Karen kicked off her shoes and crept to her room. Still half-dressed, she crawled into her cold tightbed. Despite leaden legs and sore feet, she tossed sleeplessly. Then a tall figure in a black frock coat and red silk stockings lifted her and carried her towards a full-rigged ship. Mam grabbed one of her arms saying "certainly not" and Kirsten-Mos pulled the other saying "nevertheless." Peter wrenched her free and announced, "She's dancing with me." He carried her across the gangplank and placed her gently on his bunk. Lulled by the motion of the ship as it sailed away towards the dawn, she was finally overcome by dreamless sleep.

It was well into the afternoon before a scarfless and bleary-eyed Karen emerged from her room. She carried a cup of coffee into the southroom and huddled next to the warm stove, regretting drinking so many toasts last night. Girl-Ellen appeared and announced that Jeppe was in *æ Frankel*, come to call.

"I can't see him. I'm not dressed," Karen whispered in panic. "Tell him I'm not here. Tell him anything—a stork carried me away—I've gone to sea—anything."

"Un don't need to carry on so," Girl-Ellen muttered. "He only come 'cause Mam told him it be proper. He don't look no better than unself and will be glad to go home to sleep it off. A'll just tell him to come by later, when it be time to escort un to the second-day party."

Forty-Two

The Lilies of the Field

Behold the fowls of the air: for they sow not, neither do they reap, nor gather into barns; yet your heavenly Father feedeth them. Are ye not much better than they?

And why take ye thought for raiment? Consider the lilies of the field, how they grow; they toil not, neither do they spin:

Take therefore no thought for the morrow: for the morrow shall take thought for the things of itself. Sufficient unto the day is the evil thereof.

—Matthew, 6: 26, 28, 34

Cape Town, October 1875

Captain Fredriksen and Peter were having their customary beer at a dockside bar in Cape Town. They had made good time on the 5,000 mile journey through the Indian Ocean but the *Marianne* wasn't close to beating the speed records set only a few years earlier by the bigger and faster clipper ships.

"Can you imagine the sight of the *Thermopylae* and the *Cutty Sark* racing off these very waters in '72!" Paul was saying, eyes shining.

"I'm afraid that the opening of the Suez Canal has finished the glory days of the tea clippers for good," Peter replied regretfully.

Peter pulled out Karen's letter and read aloud about the continuing impasse with her mother, referred to only as 'She,' 'Her,' or a very formal

'Lars-Anne.' He also shared an awkward note from Anders, who attempted to reassure Peter that all was not lost and that he would continue to work toward an eventual resolution. The two men discussed the depressing news, looking at each other in despair and searching in vain for some overlooked piece of paper with better news.

"Why does Lars-Anne dislike me so much?" Peter asked. "Am I really so bad?"

"Not at all. Not at all, my dear boy," Frederiksen replied in his most reassuring uncle voice. "She mistrusts all sailors. You should have heard her when Kirsten and I were engaged! Her shouts carried all the way from the mill to Southhouse. Fortunately, Big-Anne was on our side and Kirsten, for once, could not be swayed. By the time of the wedding, Lars-Anne had bowed to the inevitable and was even gracious about it."

"So, you think that she'll accept me, if the wedding is inevitable?"

Captain Fredriksen nodded and said, "With all of Sønderho telling Lars-Anne what a fool she is, perhaps she will greet you with open arms when we return."

"I wouldn't bet the cargo on that," Peter responded glumly. "You should know by now that the women in that family, from Big-Anne on down, are so stubborn they have iron spars for spines. And Lars-Anne is the worst. You're lucky to have married the sweet one."

"Amen to that," Paul agreed. Then he had an idea, "I wonder if Kirsten would help you," said Paul. "As Captain, I could...."

Peter didn't even let him finish, but eagerly told him what he had been thinking. Soon the two men had hatched a plot.

"Do you really think that Kirsten will do this?" Peter asked. "Will she be able to persuade Karen?"

"Kirsten will do it to please me," Paul answered. "In her sweet way, she can be very persuasive."

Van Dam, the new bosun, happened by, and Paul invited him to join them for another beer, saying, "Han, don't you have family in Rotterdam? We need to ask them a favor...."

Pleased with their cleverness, they composed the letter to enlist Kirsten's help. They would mail it in the morning before leaving Cape Town. Not until they docked in Rotterdam would they know whether their plan had worked.

Sønderho, October 1875

Meanwhile, Karen tried to be patient as she awaited Peter's return, but the rest of October moved as slowly as a ship becalmed in the doldrums of the Pacific. She had sent off her last letters to Cape Town, but then could write him no longer since they would not make landfall until they reach the North Sea and she was not yet sure just where that would be. She received Peter's letter from India, containing rich material from which to write more articles. Although his letters were warm and full of confidence, he did not mention the wedding directly and their future only vaguely. It was as if, even at the opposite side of the globe, he had heard the same flood of advice and taken to heart that they only needed to be patient. *Does he expect me to make it happen? Is it all up to me?* she thought crossly, irritated by his passive optimism.

Before long, another complication intervened in the form of Michel Mogens. Unaware of his disastrous timing, Michel arrived in Nordby one Saturday with the late ferry and was driven to the Inn by Coachman-Svend. He breakfasted early Sunday and walked through town in good time for the church service. Presuming that the spaciousness of the nave would provide anonymity, he decided to wait for Karen in a back pew nearest the door. Little did he realize that, in Sønderho, a foreigner was as conspicuous as a strange ship in the harbor. The congregation was already abuzz with speculation as to his identity when Karen arrived. Michel's discreet nod as she passed by on the way to the women's section of pews did not go unnoticed, and Karen's surprised recognition immediately doubled the volume of gossip.

"That's one of the men that saw her to the *Lene* when she came home from Ribe," said one, and another whispered, "He was with her in Esbjerg when she came back from school!" "Oh-oh," Tante-Blue said and Tante-Brown completed her sentence, "Young Peter had better hurry home!"

Papa raised his eyebrows at Karen from the men's section across the aisle. "I don't know," she mouthed back. Mam had not missed the by-play. She had a speculative look on her face—what was she up to?

Speculation would have continued about this latest development in the Karen-Peter saga, if Pastor had not interrupted by announcing the opening hymn. He looked at Michel and then in Karen's direction, as if he had caught the murmurs of the congregation and was also speculating about the connection between them.

Unfortunately, he had chosen Matthew 6 as text for his sermon. Karen's mood was not helped by his eloquent words on patience and the lilies-of-the-field, accompanied by waving arms. It was fine for Papa Angel to advise her not to worry, but the situation was getting much too complicated and her faith in Papa's ability to find a way out was fading fast.

Finally the interminable service concluded. Of course, Michel was waiting outside the door afterwards and introductions could not be avoided. Papa remembered him from Esbjerg and Mam, all smiles, extended a warm invitation to dinner as if he were an old family friend. Michel maneuvered Karen to walk with him, dropping behind the family far enough speak privately to her on the walk back to Millfarm.

"What are you doing here?" Karen hissed, keeping her mouth in a neutral half-smile so as not to provide fodder for more gossip.

"I wanted to meet your family in the hope that they would like me and that you would agree to have me speak to them about us getting married next spring. Now that I have a secure job at Askov, my prospects have improved and make it possible for me to ask you to share my life. Indeed, Dr. Schrøder encouraged me and I know he would welcome your return as part of the teaching family."

"You mean you spoke to Dr. Schrøder before you asked me?" Karen whispered, trying to control her anger.

"Only in very general terms, but he likes you and so does Mrs. Schrøder," Michel soothed. Then apparently sensing that Karen was not as receptive to his suggestion as he had expected, he hastened to add, "If you need to think about it some more, I won't speak to your parents just yet."

"No, please don't say anything to them. Especially today," Karen answered weakly but was too stunned to say anything else. This was the situation that Jesse warned her about. She thought she had made it clear to Michel that they could be friends, and no more. *Did I really lead him on without meaning to?* One tiny corner of her mind imagined her returning to Askov as his wife, and becoming a teacher. It would be a good life, one that suited her. Then her heart cried, *But he's not Peter! Peter, where are you?*

It was a strange dinner. Michel was charming, Papa his quiet but observant self, and Mam unusually sociable. Even Lil-Anne fell under his spell and only Karen withdrew into her conflicting thoughts. Fortunately, the guest excused himself right after the meal, pleading the need to catch a train back to Askov.

Karen saw Michel properly to the door, avoiding his fumbles to embrace her.

"We'll talk again soon," he promised.

"I'll write," Karen responded, thinking that in a letter she could say 'no' more firmly, yet more kindly.

"What a nice young man," Mam said when Karen returned. "You two make a lovely couple and he seems to have a good future in teaching."

She can't wait to get rid of me, Karen thought. *She's abandoned her plot to have me marry a miller and stay in Sønderho. I guess having me as a close-by-landlubber is preferable to my marrying a seaman and sailing around the world.*

"But what about Peter!" Karen burst out before she could stop herself.

"Wed a sailor and weep at his grave," Mam said. She would have continued with her usual litany about how seamen in general, and Peter in particular, were undependable but was interrupted by a knock on the south door, the door that only a stranger would use.

Bodil Larsen had come to call. Peter's mother had received a letter from her son about his plans and after thinking about it, she had decided to grab the bull by the horns and take the afternoon stage to Sønderho. She liked Karen and had always admired Anders Andersen. She appreciated Karen's help with publishing Peter's stories and had been pleased by those contributions to the paper written by Karen alone. Her son had warned her that his future in-laws were not enthusiastic about a match and had explicitely requested that she stay out of the discussion. But, she thought, she might be able to further her son's suit in person. Perhaps, in lieu of the customary appearance of the fiancé with the bride's family at church, they could arrange for her own symbolic presence next week and a little collation at the mill afterwards to make a tasteful announcement. The Yes-party and the banns could follow the *Marianne's* return and the wedding be held before Christmas.

Little did she expect the frigid reception that awaited her in Lars-Anne's southroom when she stated her mission. "I'm afraid that we consider your son totally unsuitable for Karen and will not grant permission for her to marry him. Besides she has a wonderful opportunity from a famous poet, a close relative of Bishop Balslev's."

Karen was appalled at Mam's rudeness. "I won't have Peter's mam treated this way," she exploded. Turning to Mrs. Larsen, she took her arm and said, "We are leaving. I'll walk you back to the Inn and Svend will see you safely home to Nordby." With that she propelled the surprised visitor out the door and down the road. They waited in awkward silence in the courtyard of the Inn, until Karen could deliver her future mother-in-law into Svend's competent hands.

Unable to face Mam, Karen took a long walk, eventually reaching the beach on the west coast. She sat down in the sand just above the high tide line, idly playing with a seashell. Watching a sandpiper running up and down looking for tasty morsels trapped in the wet seaweed, she thought of Granmam. She would know what to do; she and Kirsten-Mos would let Karen stay with them so she wouldn't have to go back to Millfarm. She rose and absently brushed sand off the back of her skirt and all but ran back the beach road towards town.

At Southhouse, Karen blurted out her complicated tale to Kirsten-Mos and Granmam. "I won't live in her house until she comes to her senses," she raged. Granmam was at a loss at what to say but reluctantly offered her angry granddaughter the northroom bench for the night.

Everyone tried unsuccessfully to mediate between mother and daughter. Anders used all his persuasive skill to get Anne to admit that Peter was dependable and Karen to accept some compromise; Lil-Anne shed tears, mimicking Papa's words; Kirsten-Mos used every soothing infusion she knew, and Pastor Engel counseled everyone on the grace of forgiveness. Lars-Anne was unyielding. "Wed a sailor and weep at his grave," she repeated and Karen stayed on the bench at Southhouse. Only Big-Anne remained unusually silent.

Karen did go to Millfarm every morning to work in the office but avoided everyone by sneaking in the south door. She wrote to Bodil Larsen, apologizing for the lack of Sønderho hospitality and tried to explain her mother's problem and her own determination to marry Peter. To Michel she wrote: "You are a wonderful friend and I adore your company, but much as I am flattered by your offer, I have to decline. You will perhaps not be too surprised to learn that Peter Larsen and I are engaged and plan to marry as soon as he returns." Since she could not write to Peter, she poured out her soul to Jesse: "What a mess I am in. I wish you were here. It must be wonderful to have a marriage approved and blessed by everyone." A year ago, she had promised, "Karen-Mos, I'll make you proud. I'll be somebody for us both." She had not realized then how complicated it would be to become "somebody" and how frightening the road to independence.

One day, Ellen Engel called on Big-Anne at Southhouse. "How are we to heal this impasse?" she asked over a cup of coffee.

"I feel so helpless," Big-Anne confessed, relieved to share her distress with a sympathetic ear. "I've prayed for guidance," she said. "Perhaps you are God's answer. I haven't wanted to make matters worse with my bungling interference. My daughter is impossibly stubborn and never listens to me. She thinks I failed her when she was a child and perhaps I did. Karen is being just as stubborn, and I don't know what to do."

Just then Karen came in. "I've finished folding Frederik's dia—Oh hello, Ellen; I didn't know you were here."

"Don't leave," Granmam said. "We were just talking about you."

"Remember Pastor's sermon: the lilies of the field don't spin." Pastor's Ellen said. Granmam added, "God moves in mysterious ways, little sparrow."

I wish He would let me know his plan soon! Karen grumbled, and would have said so out loud when there was a fortunate intervention in the form of the mailman.

"I have letters for both Karen and Mrs. Fredriksen—from Africa," he announced cheerfully. "I knew you were here, so...."

Karen snatched the letters from his hands thinking resentfully, *I'll bet the whole town knows where I'm living!* But aloud, she managed a polite "Thank you."

Kirsten-Mos came running when she heard the voices. She grabbed her letter and devoured the contents. Karen went off to the northroom, ripping open her envelope on the way. The news was better than she had hoped. Peter said they were expecting to land in Rotterdam in about three weeks. The *Marianne* would sell most of her cargo there and load coal and arrive in Esbjerg harbor about two weeks later. Again there was no mention of their impending marriage, only a mysterious postscript advising her to "listen to your aunt Kirsten."

Karen was very fond of Kirsten-Mos. "One of God's Peacemakers," Papa Angel called her. But since when did Kirsten-Mos become a fount of wisdom? Did Peter have some plan that Kirsten-Mos was supposed to tell her about or would there only be more advice about patience? What about her own plan? What if Peter thought her too bold in coming to meet him? What if he rejected her plan to elope? Going all that way on her own, only to be refused, would be humiliating. She needed a fallback plan. She decided to write Ingrid-Fas and take her up on her invitation to visit. This was better. Karen would have an excuse to get away from Fanø and also be able to go Ribe if Peter didn't want to elope. *I won't tell Ingrid-Fas about the complicated situation, but just ask if I can visit for a few days in a couple of weeks.*

When Karen returned to the southroom, Kirsten-Mos announced with a determined look on her face that she was going to Millfarm to speak to her sister. Alone. This was so uncharacteristic that the three women looked at each other in surprise as Kirsten hurried out the door without so much as a request for someone to look after Frederik until her return.

A half-hour later, Lil-Anne arrived at Southhouse, the doll, as usual tucked under her arm. "What's going on?" the child asked. "Kirsten-Mos came to Millfarm and said she had to see Mam. Right away! She told me to leave the house!"

Karen and Big-Anne questioned the child. She reported that while she was putting on her boots, she had heard voices rising and falling through the door, but no words. "Her Highness who, being a Queen, is allowed to eavesdrop, told me that Mam said 'certainly not' and 'nevertheless.'"

When Kirsten-Mos returned, she looked excited and determined but not glum. Karen was dying to find out what was up but knew it would do no good to rush her aunt—she would speak when she was ready.

Finally, after supper she made her surprise anncuncement. Speaking only to Karen, as if Big-Anne were not there, she said, "Paul wants Frederik and me to meet him in Holland. He wants to see his son as soon as possible."

She paused as if to muster her argument, while Karen said politely, "That's wonderful." Then she realized the implications. This ruined all her plans. Now she wouldn't be able to meet Peter in secret.

"I can't possibly go alone," Kirsten-Mos continued, waking Karen abruptly from her daydream. "I don't know anything about trains. My school-German is rusty and I don't speak any English," Kirsten wailed. "But you do...." Her voice trailed off, only her pleading eyes finishing the sentence.

Suddenly Karen realized the opportunity. "And Mam agreed to have me go?" she exclaimed incredulously. She could hardly believe it. Was this Peter's idea? Had he persuaded Uncle Paul to ask Kirsten-Mos to come to Rotterdam? What on earth was he plotting? "Yes. Yes, of course I'll go with you," she said impatiently.

Kirsten-Mos was grateful. "I miss Paul so," she whispered, her eyes filling with tears. Neither of them mentioned Peter, and Karen wondered if Kirsten-Mos was so naïve that she did not understand what everyone would say if Karen went to Holland. *Doesn't she know that it would be tantamount to a Yes-party?*

Forty-Three

The Amsterdam Express

DENMARK, NOVEMBER 1875

The night before they were to leave, Karen went to Millfarm to pack. Lil-Anne and Antoinette came into her room to help, looking very solemn. "Her Highness has decided to accompany you on your travels," the child said formally.

Trying not to hurt her sister's feelings, Karen curtsied to the doll, "*Madame*, I am afraid it will be much too long and uncomfortable a journey for a Queen."

"I told you…," Lil-Anne whispered to her companion, then changed the subject. "Why aren't you taking your pretty clothes?"

"The dress Ingrid-Fas gave me is much too summery for November," Karen answered regretfully.

"Her highness says to bring it anyway—you never can tell if you'll meet the King of Holland—and you have your lovely shawl."

So Karen placed the lavender dress and petticoats under the bundle of Peter's letters. "I don't have room for everything," she despaired. "I need more stuff for just a couple of weeks than I took to Askov for the whole summer!"

Hearing voices, Lil-Anne went to investigate and returned with the surprising news that Svend Schultz was in *æ frankel.*

Sure enough, there he stood, hat in hand, talking to Papa. "The stage be more comfy than æ hay wagon. If'n Miller comes along, him can bring it back to the Inn."

Papa turned to Karen and said, suppressing a grin, "Svend tells me he has always wanted to ride the train and has decided to take a vacation to Holland. It just happens that he plans to leave tomorrow and will be pleased to be your escort."

"A'll pick up Mrs. Fredriksen and Master Frederik in the morning and then swing by here for *Mistress Moon* and Miller," the indomitable Svend announced as if it were decided.

Karen shrugged resignedly—this whole trip was out of her control. She didn't think she needed help, but she accepted the offer politely. Shaking her head, she returned to her packing. At least Svend's German was better than hers! Between that and English, they could make themselves understood.

As promised, the stage drove into the courtyard in the morning, Svend at the reins and a very excited Frederik sitting next to him on the high seat. Kirsten's pale face peered out the window.

Lil-Anne gave Karen a subdued hug and retired to the stoop to watch. "She'll be back in a few weeks," she comforted Antoinette.

If Lil-Anne looked unhappy, Lars-Anne was positively grim. Ignoring Karen, she went to the carriage to say goodbye to her sister and handed her a food basket. Papa climbed up next to Svend, commenting cheerfully, "I always wanted to be a coach driver!" And off they went.

Papa came with them on the ferry to Esbjerg and bought the train tickets. He insisted on paying for Svend, and Svend let him as long as his was for a third class compartment. Svend brought the bigger luggage to the baggage car and stowed the smaller bags over their seats.

Papa gave Karen instructions as if he were an experienced world traveler. "Here are your tickets and the bank draft. Deposit it as soon as you can so you'll have Dutch money. Don't trust anyone on the street to exchange. Don't forget to change trains in Kolding and check which platform is for the express coming from Copenhagen—you don't want to get on the wrong train and end up there! Once you get to Amsterdam, you'll have to find out when the train to Rotterdam leaves, but the tickets are for the whole way—out and return." At the last words, he gave Karen a meaningful look. She hurried up the steps so he wouldn't see her blush. Papa followed her to the seats that Svend had claimed. Kirsten was sitting primly, an anxious frown on her face, while Frederik bounced up and down on the floor wedged between her legs. Svend was across the aisle, hat in his lap; this was also his first train trip. Papa hugged Karen one final time, the expression on his face switching between envy and worry, envy that his daughter was going on such an adventure without him, worry that she was traveling into the unknown.

"Look after your aunt and don't run away with a sailor," he teased, coming uncomfortably close to the truth, as he turned to go down the steps.

Karen lowered the window and called, "But you ran away with the milkmaid."

"Best thing I ever did!" he cried from the platform, disappearing in a cloud of black smoke.

"Algone," said Frederik, waving. The train started with a jerk that sent him flying to land on his seat. "Boom," he said cheerfully, but did consent to sit beside his mother on the wooden bench. Knowing how nervous Kirsten-Mos was, Karen made sure she had a window seat and was sitting facing forward.

"It helps to look at the head of the train on the horizon, it will steady your stomach," Karen, the experienced traveler, explained.

"But the horizon keeps rushing by," Kirsten-Mos complained.

"Nevertheless. We can open the window just a bit, the fresh air will also help."

Little Frederik was made of sturdier stuff and was perfectly happy to explore the car, Svend firmly grasping his hand. He babbled his baby-thoughts to anyone who smiled at him and was not at all daunted when a curve in the road tumbled him into the arms of a stranger. "Oops," he cried enthusiastically and added, "Choo-choo" as if to explain the reason for his mishap.

He was in his element and wanted to talk to every passenger, explore every car. He dragged Svend all the way to the front of the train and tugged at the sign suspended from a chain across the door.

"No. No further," Svend explained. "The sign says '*Adgang Forbudt.*' That means un isn't allowed. That's the way to æ engine—æ conduct'r don't want us there." Just then the conductor appeared to check their tickets. Seeing the uniform the little boy inquired, "Capt'n Papa?" and was halfway up into the startled man's arms before Svend could catch him. When he was firmly returned to his mother's side, he had one of his rare but powerful tantrums. Inconsolably he sobbed over and over, "Capt'n Papa!" Having been born six months after the departure of the *Marianne*, he had little concept of what it meant to have a father but understood clearly that one had been promised him and was now denied. Karen's reassuring "later" was beyond his comprehension. Finally he fell asleep, hiccupping moistly into Kirsten's chest.

Karen looked out the window as they stopped at one station after another. She had a moment of longing when they paused briefly at Vejen—it would be so much safer to simply get off there and visit her friends at Askov than to hurtle into the uncertain future.

The forty miles to Kolding went quickly and without problem. The station, although small by international standards, was overwhelming with crowds of people running up and down stairs. They all seemed to know where they were going and were too busy to answer questions. Karen went to find out about their train to Holland while Svend checked that their baggage was transferred to the express. Kirsten-Mos remained sitting on a platform bench with Frederik and the hand luggage. Karen followed the crowd up a long flight of stairs to an even busier and noisier great hall. Finally she saw a sign that pointed the way to an information desk manned by a harried clerk. Noticing that people were waiting their turn in a queue, just like at the grocery store in Ribe, she went to the end of the long line, hoping that her aunt would not think her lost. Finally, it was her turn and the clerk looked up and down at her folk costume. He said a chilly, "May I help you, Miss?" and seemed ready to pass on to the next in line. Karen looked down her nose at the little man and, copying the nasal tone that Charlotte used with recalcitrant shopkeepers, she informed him that she had a ticket for Amsterdam but did not know when the train left or how to find the platform. Armed with his reluctantly given instructions, she went back to find her aunt. "My Good Man," she muttered to herself, "If everyone knew their way around, one wouldn't need to ask, and you would not have a position. So there."

Coming down the stairs, she saw the droopy *pjægger* on top of Kirsten-Mos's headscarf. Sitting completely still on the bench, surrounded by baskets and with a squirming Frederik securely held on her lap, she looked near hysteria. The crowd, glancing curiously at the strange figure as they flowed by, might have been the incoming tide eddying around an abandoned rowboat.

Karen herself felt overwhelmed by the crowds. Looking down at the dejected figure she suddenly realized how much more difficult this must be for quiet Kirsten-Mos and her heart went out to her. Her aunt had braved a strange train and foreign lands, all for love of a man she had not seen in nearly two years. Kirsten had persuaded Mam out of her own need, not just to facilitate Karen's plans. Just then Svend returned and Kirsten looked less forlorn. His invention of a trip just so he could help them was a kindness beyond measure. Karen realized now how reassuring it was to have his sturdy figure along.

The train did not leave for another hour so they sought refuge in the station restaurant. Svend could barely be persuaded to join them at the table but finally agreed to sip a cup of coffee, perched at the edge of a little chair. By this time, Frederik, over-stimulated and upset by his mother's anxiety, was a handful. It was a relief when Karen could settle them all in the express train. Svend helped her find their seats in the sleeping car before going back to his place in third class. "Come and get us when it's time for dinner," she said.

"A could make do with the leftovers from æ basket," Svend argued, but Karen insisted he join them for a hot meal.

The train had hardly started when they crossed the border into Germany, that much disputed border established after the '64 war. More passengers came on board but they continued to speak mostly Danish, even the conductor who told them he was from just north of Schlesvig. When they passed through Flensborg, Svend came by and pointed out the window at the fertile fields dotted with fat black and white Holstein cows.

"Ma brother's horse farm be over that hill," he said and added sadly, "He writes me that his chillun nu have to speak German in school."

"You should visit them on the way home," Kirsten suggested.

"A'll think on that."

In the dining car, their waiter turned out to be a classmate from Svend's elementary school. Karen had always thought that he spoke Danish with a strong regional accent, but now he and his old friend chatted away in South-Jylland dialect so thick she could not follow the conversation.

Soon they passed Schlesvig Fjord. "Dannevirke starts here," Svend reminded them, referring to the dirt fortification that Viking kings had built across the Jylland peninsula in the ninth century. "Much good it be in '64."

Back in their seats, Kirsten settled with a droopy Frederik on her lap and closed her eyes. Karen leaned her forehead against the windowpane and watched the hills flow by, still green despite the chilly November wind. The sandy moors of home hardly compared with these lush fields; it was no wonder that Bismarck and the Kaiser wanted the land for their German empire. *But the sea is still ours,* she thought. *They can't steal that.* Silhouetted against the sky, a V of geese pointed south along the railroad tracks. She could not hear their calls over the noise of the train but felt them in her bones. "Peter, my love; we're coming, we're coming; at last, at last," called the birds while the wheels beat the rhythm, "Peter Larsen, Rotterdam; Peter Larsen, Rotterdam."

She must have fallen asleep because she almost didn't catch the words when Kirsten-Mos touched her arm and whispered, "Don't do it. I know your plan. Don't do it, it's a big mistake."

"What are you talking about?" Karen whispered back so as not to awaken the boy. How could Kirsten-Mos know?

"About Paul marrying you and Peter at sea. He wrote me. That's why he insisted I bring you to Holland. Not just so he could see Frederik sooner. Don't do it," she repeated.

"If that's the plan, no one told *me*," Karen said irritably. How dare they all plot without her? If they were using Kirsten-Mos's innocence and Karen's ignorance as a strategy to fool everyone, they had failed, judging by Mam's glum face when she said good-by. "What did you tell Mam? You couldn't have told her about our being married on the *Marianne*. She'd never have allowed me to go."

"I couldn't lie to my own sister. She'd never talk to me again. Besides she guessed right away that something was up. So I told her the whole story."

"But if she knew, why did she let me go?"

"Because I begged her, I wanted to meet Paul. Then I told her you would go anyway, that she couldn't stop you. I also told her that her only chance to not lose you completely was to let you go. She agreed but made me promise to persuade you to wait."

"Peter and I don't want to postpone getting married for another six months! It's been almost two years already!"

"Not six months, just two. Then Anders and Anne will give their blessing and meanwhile Pastor Engel will write for King's permission."

"What difference will two months make? It's easy enough for everyone to say 'wait, wait.' You should know how I feel. You didn't even want to wait two more weeks for Paul to come home. You all think I'll change my mind, don't you?"

"You were just a child when Peter left, and he's seen the wonders of the world. You may feel certain now, but you need a little time to get to know each other again."

"I know all I need to know from Peter's letter," Karen insisted. Suddenly, she realized what Kirsten-Mos had said. "How did you persuade her? What finally changed her mind about Peter? She doesn't like him, just because he's a seaman. Two months isn't going to change that and she should know that my mind is made up."

"It isn't really about Peter, anymore. She realized that she was more afraid of losing you than having you marry him."

"Why couldn't she just have talked to me—explained how she felt and that she would give her blessing? Is she really so stubborn she can't admit she changed her mind?"

"She *is* stubborn, but she was afraid to talk to you. Every time she tried, you would find something else to do and then you moved to Southhouse. She was afraid that you're so stubborn you would do the opposite of what anyone said."

"Stubborn! Look who's calling the kettle black! But I still don't understand how you persuaded her."

"I reminded her of when she married Anders."

"What do you mean?"

"Big-Anne didn't approve of Anders and refused to have the wedding at Southhouse. He was not a Fanniker but a foreigner and he was not what she'd planned for Lars-Anne. They were going to elope as soon as Lars-Anne was eighteen. Anders already had his journeyman papers and was talking to a miller on Vejle Fjord about a job, so they could have managed on their own. Then Granpapa decided he was getting too old to manage the mill. He offered to have Anders take over and to hold the wedding at Millfarm. Lars-Anne lived there anyway whenever she was home so it was not supposed to be strange that the wedding would be there, but it caused a scandal anyway."

"I knew she lived at Millfarm when Granmam went to the mainland to become a midwife, but I forgot that she stayed there even after she came back," Karen exclaimed, caught up in the story. "You can't have been very old when she married Papa. Are you sure you remember it right?"

"Oh, I remember all right. I may only have been six, but I'll not soon forget the shouting matches between them. That's why Lars-Anne lived with our grandparents at Millfarm. She and Big-Anne never did get along and it was much better for them to live in separate houses. Then they stopped talking altogether. I used to run back and forth between Southhouse and Millfarm with messages. You could take lessons in stubbornness. Those two are masters; but I guess you know that. Big-Anne refused to attend the wedding and it was not until you were born that the two of them would even talk to each other."

Karen was speechless. Why did it all seem so familiar: stubborn mother and stubborn daughter and Kirsten the peacemaker? Were they all caught helplessly in a chain of fate, generation after generation? This is what Deborah warned of; Karen could lose her mother if she insisted on going her own way. At least they didn't usually shout at each other. Two months didn't seem so long, but would Peter agree to wait? She was still convinced that Mam had some unspoken hope that all would blow over. It might be best to come home with a *fait accompli.*

The conductor interrupted, and while their bunks were made up they went for a walk. Karen took some blankets back to Svend, feeling guilty that he would have to sleep on a hard wooden bench while they had comfortable tightbeds, but he seemed content, chatting and smoking with new friends. She walked back to their sleeping car and helped Kirsten and Frederik settle in their lower bunk. Finally she climbed up the ladder to her own. She thought she would never be able to sleep for excitement, but soon the rhythm of the wheels clanking along the rails lulled her away to a green hillside with sheep and cows.

"Hamburg next; Hamburg," a voice announced in the distance, first in Danish, then in German. They must be crossing the Elbe River, the old pre-war Danish border with rapacious Germany.

The next morning, Frederik awoke early and Karen took him to breakfast, letting Kirsten sleep. At the table, he crawled onto Karen's lap by the window and pointed at a yellow sparrow sitting on a branch with red berries. "Bird," he said. Then it flew away. "Bird gone."

"The train made too much noise, " Karen explained.

When they crossed over a canal, he saw boats. "Ships," he exclaimed. "Papa! Capt'n Papa!"

"Soon, soon," Karen soothed feeding him bits of a roll softened in milk.

Back at their seats, Kirsten was dressed and breakfasting on stale bread and chunks of cheese from Mam's bottomless basket. Karen tried in vain to persuade her aunt to remove her headscarf, as she had done, so they would be less conspicuous.

"I'd feel indecent," Kirsten said, horrified. "Unclothed. It's fine for foreigners or even you, to have everyone see your hair, but Paul wouldn't approve. I wouldn't feel like myself."

"Uncle Paul won't even arrive for several more days and when we meet the *Marianne*, we can both dress as Fannikers," Karen said but gave up the argument.

They whizzed through a local station without stopping. Several Dutch women, waiting on the platform, were colorfully dressed in snowy white aprons and even whiter caps whose wings made them look like they were about to fly away. Frederik pointed enthusiastically and Kirsten, pulling down his hand, looked meaningfully at Karen; if the natives could dress peculiarly, she could certainly wear a proper Fanniker headscarf.

"Amsterdam next. Amsterdam," called the conductor in Dutch, and then in German.

Svend materialized to take charge of the hand luggage. "Æ train to Rotterdam be on the other side of æ platform," he informed them, having asked his friend the conductor. "Un leaves in a quarter hour."

Karen stood on the platform at the Rotterdam station, not sure where to go next. A tow-headed youth approached and bowed politely, saying in halting schoolboy German, "I'm Willem van Dam. My brother, Han, is officer on the *Marianne*."

That much Karen understood—that and something about a telegram. It took her a minute to figure out the 'Han' because Willem pronounced it as if he were trying to dislodge a fish bone caught in his throat. Then she remembered that Peter had written that when Kelolo left the *Marianne* in India, Han van Dam from Rotterdam became the new bosun. Svend nodded encouragingly and explained to Kirsten and Karen that Miller had sent a telegram to the van Dams naming the day they were to arrive. The lad had met every train from Amsterdam since early morning and was there to take them to an inn near the harbor.

Svend and Willem chatted while they retrieved the baggage. Between them they carried it out to the curb where Svend grandly called a cab. Karen wondered how they would pay for this extravagance since she had no Dutch money, having been afraid that the money exchangers on the train might cheat her. Svend reassured her that Willem had brought some coins and they could repay him later.

"*Wo ist der bank?*" she managed to ask.

"*Der Nederlansche Bank?*" the boy asked, followed by some words that she didn't catch. When he pointed to an imposing building on the other side of the square, his meaning was clear and she nodded. Svend explained that their inn was just down the street, so Karen could easily walk up later and deposit the bank draft Papa had given her. He also said that he would share Willem's bed at his home, so he would not be staying at the hotel.

The Rembrandt Inn was in an old but attractive brick building on a canal. The Lek River, where the *Marianne* would dock, was just around the corner. Karen was relieved that the clerk spoke English as well as German. She let Svend and the boy take care of registration, while she and Kirsten-Mos were shown upstairs to a lovely sunny room.

Karen looked out the window at the beautiful tree overhanging the canal. *I can't believe that we're here*, she thought.

Forty-Four

The Last Laugh

ROTTERDAM, NOVEMBER 1875

Karen, Kirsten, and Frederik settled into the Rembrandt to await the arrival of the *Marianne.* Away from the critical eyes of her mother and sister and the curious noses of the Sønderho gossips, Kirsten became a much younger, gayer person, the years dropping away until she seemed hardly older than her niece. Karen realized that her aunt was less than ten years her senior and increasingly thought of her as a girlfriend, more serious of nature than Mette but good company and a trustworthy confidante.

At first they only explored the sights near the inn, feeling more comfortable by the Lek River than in the busy city. Accustomed as Rotterdam was to people from around the world, the two women with the little boy were hardly noticed. The little canal by the hotel went down to the Lek River, filled with sailing ships at anchor, and they found out that the river was really part of the Rhine River Delta, whose vast waterways coursed through the Low Countries of Holland and its neighbor, Belgium.

The day after they arrived, Willem van Dam dropped by to make sure they were comfortable. He delivered an invitation from his mother for dinner that evening. He came back later in the afternoon to conduct them through the center of town to his family's dairy store, above which they lived. The widow van Dam greeted them in a flurry of Dutch at the door. Her friendly, smiling face was as round as one of the Edam cheeses behind her on the store shelves, and her dimpled hands stretched towards them in welcome.

They were immediately asked to sit down while their hostess carried in one steaming dish after another from the kitchen. A whole staircase of blond-haired van Dams grinned at them from around the table, all looking exactly like their mother, from Willem on down to the youngest toddler. The eldest son, the Han that was second mate on the *Marianne*, had been away for three years, so the family was as anxious for news of the bark's arrival as Karen and her aunt. Mrs. Van Dam spoke only Dutch, so throughout the meal Svend and Willem translated and haltingly they were able to exchange what limited information they had. The van Dams had apparently received a telegram a few days ago, announcing that they could expect the *Marianne* to arrive in a week or so. A Captain Villiers, a name not known to any of them, had sent the telegram from Le Havre. They guessed that, by common courtesy of the sea, the two ships had crossed and Villiers had been asked to relay the message.

Every morning, the two turbaned women, attended by faithful Svend carrying an enthusiastic Frederik, were at the door of the harbormaster hoping for word, and every afternoon before he closed his doors, they appeared again. The rest of the time they strolled along the twisting streets, venturing further and further from the Rembrandt Inn. The Baroque houses looked a little like those in Ribe, except they were larger and closer together. The city was much bigger and looked impressively prosperous. They imagined going to balls and theatres dressed in the luxurious silks and velvet displayed in the windows of the dressmakers, and wondered how their handsome loved ones would look in the English tweeds or herringbone woolens at the haberdashers. They dared spend only a few of the coins in their reticules as they didn't know exactly when the *Marianne* would arrive, however they could not resist a sailor suit for Frederik to wear to welcome Capt'n Papa. With that promise as motivation, the little boy patiently stood still while the short trousers were measured for length.

"We need not worry," Karen reassured her aunt. "The draft we deposited in the bank is large enough to take care of us for a long time." Nevertheless, they were not used to the high finance of world travelers and allowed themselves few indulgences.

They were drawn to the waterfront, little Frederik tirelessly walking to the ends of each jetty and inspecting every arriving or departing ship. Although he could not say the words, he would point confidently at the right vessel when asked to find a brig or bark and he knew the difference between a square and a schooner rig. One gray morning, he was confused by one ship, newly arrived from New York, that seemed to be neither. "That's a *hermaphrodite brig,"* his mother explained. "The foremast is square-rigged while the aft looks like a schooner."

"Her-brig," Frederik tried, to the amusement of an American sailor hauling a large hawser onto the pier.

"Ya got it mate," he said hoisting the crowing boy onto a coil of rope as tall as the child. He then went on to explain some of the fine points of his ship. Neither man nor boy was bothered by the fact that they did not speak the same language. Frederik manfully echoing, as best he might, the rich array of nautical terms the sailor carefully enunciated to further his education.

Frederik slid off his perch when he caught sight of an impressive frigate, anchored out in the bay. Even from land it was evident that the gleaming ship was spruced up for company. Every brass fitting was polished, every porthole washed, the decks scoured to shining whiteness, and the gold paint on the bowsprit fresh and gleaming. The boy's body vibrated in excitement when he saw officers in full dress uniforms, beribboned and with gold epaulettes on their shoulders, escorting elaborately gowned ladies to a launch. He knew better than to think he could board such a fancy ship, but he waved to the departing boat with such longing that the admiral in the bow could but smile and touch his plumed hat in a salute.

When they returned to the inn for lunch, the cloud-filled sky became a drenching downpour. Happy to have avoided all but a few sprinkles, Karen and Kirsten were chatting about the morning's sights and looking forward to the Rembrandt Inn's generous table when the desk clerk ran forward with a message. The harbormaster had sent word that a three-masted bark had heaved to at Hoeck van Holland and signaled for a pilot. He estimated that it would be late afternoon before they could expect the *Marianne*, if so it were, to negotiate the river from the North Sea and drop anchor.

Svend was dispatched to the van Dams to spread the news. Kirsten and Karen could hardly eat their bread and cheese for excitement. Fortunately they managed to conceal the imminence of the arrival from Frederik and he contentedly went to his little cot for a nap.

In whispers, the two women fussed over their dress. Because of the weather they did not wear their best silk blouses and aprons but did change their scarves to some with bolder red stripes and put their oldest green flannel skirts over their second best.

"I can't make these stupid *pjægger* lie right," Karen hissed in frustration. "Peter always brags about how well his mother ties her scarf."

Kirsten offered to help. "Your mistake is looking in the mirror. There," she added with satisfaction. "Now Peter will have to admit that Sønderhonings can tie as well as anyone from Nordby."

Kirsten completed her dressing by tying the ribbon of her *bul*—vest, across her chest and fastening her amber pin on her neckscarf. Karen wore the whalebone scrimshaw that Peter had sent her and looked nervously at Kirsten.

"Don't look so defiant," Kirsten chuckled. "Your disagreement over wearing that pin is with Lars-Anne, not me. Besides, meeting him at landfall speaks louder of an engagement than a simple brooch ever could." So, Kirsten *did* understand that she and Peter would be the talk of Sønderho regardless of when or how they returned to the island.

Frederik awoke from his nap and all that remained of their preparations was to put on his new suit. Again, the promise of "Capt'n Papa" was the key to his cooperation.

It was still pouring. Without noticing the shocked glances of the other guests, Karen and Kirsten automatically threw the backs of their topmost skirts over heads and shoulders to protect their finery from the rain. Kirsten had picked Frederik up and tucked him inside her up-ended skirt when the horrified desk clerk came rushing outside and handed each of them an unfolded umbrella. "Ladies, please accept these, compliments of the Rembrandt."

Karen was familiar with this British invention and thanked the obliging clerk. Kirsten, by now immured to the strange customs of this peculiar place, merely shrugged. With some awkwardness she proceeded down the street, juggling the sturdy boy on one arm and the umbrella with the other. When Karen tried to tell her that she should pull down the skirt, her aunt pointed out, somewhat huffily, that Frederik would be cold. "I have my good skirt on underneath so I don't see what all the fuss is about." Then handing Karen her umbrella she added, "This fancy contraption is more of a hindrance than a help."

The rain changed to a light drizzle while the two women and little boy kept soggy vigil on the quay. Frederik, tired of being carried, wriggled out his mother's grasp and entertained himself by stomping in nearby puddles and admiring the spouts of water around his feet. Finally the *Marianne* rounded the point, most of her canvas furled, leaving only enough staysails to help steer through the ships of the busy harbor.

"Capt'n Papa," Kirsten said pointing to the shorter of two figures standing on the bridge.

"Capt'n Papa?" the little boy whispered, awestruck.

Karen's gaze riveted on the taller of the two men and her eyes refused to move. *My, he's big*, she thought and then as the ship drew closer and dropped anchor, *Oh, my!* It wasn't that she had forgotten how tall he was or that he had grown, but the gangly figure of two years ago was now an impressive man and a very handsome one at that.

The men aloft had caught sight of the watchers on the quay the minute the *Marianne* rounded the point. The two distinctive silhouettes were an unmistakable symbol of home, and loud cheers and whistles spread through the Danish crew. The two officers on the bridge were a little more dignified, but only a little, as they waved their tall black hats from side to side and grinned from ear to ear. Peter almost forgot protocol in his eagerness to make his way to the tender that met them even before the anchor had found bottom. Barely had the Pilot and Captain descended the companionway before the first mate transferred command of the vessel to Mr. van Dam and leapt down to the main deck, guided only by his hands on the side rails, feet not touching the steps. He would have catapulted over the railing and into the tender, if experience at sea had not restrained his impulse. Neither he nor the Captain could bear to sit calmly while they were rowed ashore but stood on practiced sea legs, grinning and waving all the way.

Leaping ashore, Peter wrapped his long arms around Karen's soggy shoulders. "You really came," he murmured into her *pjægger*.

"Oh my!" was all Karen could say, her knees week.

Peter tipped her head up to meet his lips and Karen went limp. The crew cheered even louder and one of the men called for a nine-fold Hurrah.

Karen finally found the breath to whisper, "You're wet."

"Not as wet as you," Peter laughed, and then added regretfully, "I have to go right back onboard while Captain Fredriksen clears our papers with the harbormaster. Today and tonight are his and Kirsten's, but tomorrow is for us. Please come onboard in the morning, I have something to show you."

Reluctant though she was to see Peter return to his duties, Karen realized that Uncle Paul and Kirsten deserved this time alone. Besides, someone had to watch little Frederik. That is, if he could be separated from his Capt'n Papa. Uncle Paul gravely shook his son's hand and then, to the child's delight, lifted him onto his shoulders. From his high perch the boy was making a noise suspiciously like that of a rooster as he patted the top of his father's tall hat.

Finally, duty called and the Captain picked up his pouch full of papers and bills of lading while the first mate returned to the ship. Uncle Paul escorted the ladies back to the Rembrandt Inn and proceeded to the harbormaster's office with a promise to return as soon as he had made arrangements for the cargo.

Supper was a family affair, with Frederik insisting that he sit on his own adult chair, as close to his father as possible, though his eyes were just level with the table top and he could barely see the food on his plate. Finally, he was persuaded to let Capt'n Papa take him upstairs to bed. His cot and Karen's belongings had already been moved to another room, and the distressed boy insisted this was not where he slept. Only when Papa promised to tell him a story about the *Marianne* and sit with him a while did the boy agree to be tucked in. Karen retreated to a corner out of the lamplight and watched father and son. Eventually, the boy's eyes drooped close, but they flew open every few seconds to reassure himself that Capt'n Papa was still there. Finally the lashes fanned over his rosy cheeks and Uncle Paul tiptoed out. Karen heard his soft knock on Kirsten's door, quiet voices, and then silence.

She thought she would never be able to go to sleep. What would happen tomorrow? What could Peter have to 'show' her? Did he mean 'ask'? She replayed the scene at the dock and felt the strange sensation of floating that had made her knees go limp. Was this why Mam smiled whenever she danced with Papa? Surely not after all these years? Not at her age!

The morning dawned dry and a brisk wind chased the gray clouds across the sky. Karen was taking Frederik downstairs for breakfast, but as they passed his parents' room, he escaped. Unable to manipulate the handle, he pounded on the door and called "Mam" and "Capt'n Papa." A rosy cheeked, smiling Kirsten let him in. She was still in her nightdress but the remains of breakfast were on the table by the window.

"Come in," she invited. "There's plenty more food for you. Paul's already left for the *Marianne*. We're to meet there as soon as we're ready. Peter wants you to go straight to his cabin."

"He said he had something to show me," Karen answered.

"Just remember what I told you. Trust your good sense and don't let him talk you into anything you don't want to do."

The *Marianne* was being unloaded when they reached the wharf. Frederik watched the cranes lifting big nets filled with cargo out of the hold, and explored the piles of wooden crates and barrels already on the quay. Kirsten pulled him to a safe distance and whispered to Karen that she should go on board. Catching sight of her, Peter bounded down the gangplank and, taking her hand as gallantly as if he were escorting her onto the dance floor, he led her to his cabin, a big grin on his face.

The tiny floor was completely filled with buckets of sand from which sprouted tree branches winter-bare of leaves. From the twigs hung golden bangles, softly jingling with the movement of the ship. Karen didn't know whether to laugh or cry as her hands flew to her blushing cheeks.

Peter knelt at her feet. "The African bangles are just of brass; but these are gold," he said, holding out a little box with a pair of wedding rings, gleaming against the black velvet.

"Yes; yes," she whispered before he could ask. She could not resist adding, "Sir Peter."

"I was hoping you would say that. Otherwise a perfectly good feast would have to be canceled." Gently he slipped the smaller ring on her left hand and the other on his own.

Peter rose from the floor and, as he had on the dock, he lifted her chin so he could reach her mouth. Then he kissed her.

Feeling light-headed, Karen parted her lips to breathe. His tongue took her open mouth as an invitation to explore. Never had she felt like this, her body light as the breeze coming through the porthole, her ears ringing as if they were the golden bangles.

When Peter finally let her go, she sank slowly to the floor, her legs unable to support her. He turned the cabin's only chair away from the corner desk where he had written her so many letters, and sat down. Taking her hands in his, he explained the plan that Kirsten-Mos had warned her about. "As soon as we've loaded our new cargo, we'll sail out to the Hoeck and into the North Sea. Captain Fredriksen will marry us. Then you and I will sail the *Marianne* home while Captain and Kirsten return by train."

Karen's heart sank. It was happening too fast. Kirsten was right; she couldn't do it this way. She needed her mother and father to be there and Peter's family too. Mette should be her bridesmaid and Mam should sew the bridal crown on her head.

Two fat tears dripped onto Peter's hands still enveloping her own. "Whatever is the matter?" he exclaimed. "It won't be as bad as all that to be married to me!" he chided. He sat down to the floor next to her, overturning a bucket, and wrapped his arms about her.

Karen, head buried on his shoulder, mumbled, “It’s too sad, I can’t do it.” She tried to explain between sobs. “Just two months. That’s all she asks. She may think we’ll change our mind, but two months is a short time. Then we can do it right and stand tall before Papa Angel.”

It took Peter a while to understand what she was saying. Undone by her tears he murmured, “I never thought you’d cry! All the way home, I saw this day in my dreams but never did you cry.” He pulled a large handkerchief out of his pocket and dabbing awkwardly at her damp face, added, “But Roselil, if that’s what you want, that’s what we’ll do. Bridal crown, Sønderhoning, and all. You’re right, two months will go quickly.”

Then with a gleam, he added, “But tonight we’ll have the biggest Yes-party the *Marianne* has ever seen.”

“There has never been a Yes-party on the *Marianne*,” she objected.

“Nevertheless,” Peter laughed and kissed her again.

Peter adjusted his back more comfortably against the railing of his bunk and stretched his legs against the over-turned bucket. Karen snuggled into the warm nest of his arms.

“You smell of Yardley shaving cream,” she said and reached a tentative hand towards his face. She traced a brushy side-whisker with her finger. “When did you trade your mustache for *Piccadilly Weepers*?”

“Everyone said a mustache made me look like a pirate. *Side-Burns,* they call them in San Francisco. They’re all the rage and the ladies swoon over them. You’ll like San Francisco—it’s a fascinating city.”

“Are we going to San Francisco?”

“This summer, as soon as my captain’s papers are in order, we’ll sail the *Marianne* to ports in the North Sea; Norway, Holland, England, France—wherever we can arrange good cargo. Then in the fall, we’ll sail down along Africa and around the Cape, through the Indian Ocean and across the Pacific. You *do* want to come and make the *Marianne* a Lady Ship?”

“Oh yes. Oh my, yes,” Karen mumbled.

“You’ll like Hawaii too, and Canton is fascinating.” He buried his face in her scarf. “You smell good. Like roses. Maybe I really should call you Roselil.”

"That was my nickname at school—to tease me about you," Karen said. "We even did a play from the song. How did you know? Did I write you about that?"

Peter looked at her in surprise. "I didn't know. You didn't tell me. I was afraid that you might need persuasion because of your mother. Making 'every tree bear flowers of gold' was the most romantic way of proposing that I could think of."

"Mmm," Karen murmured and snuggled closer, liking the way it made her body tingle. "My fragrance isn't roses though. It's lavender—to go with my eyes—and my dress. I have a real dress with lavender flowers, but it's for summer and too cold for now."

"I remember seeing that dress," Peter said and then corrected himself, "You wrote me about it. Wear it tonight for the party. I promise, you won't be cold."

Both fell silent. Finally Karen sighed, "I suppose we should go. The crew must be wondering what we're up to."

Peter grinned. "Let them think what they will!"

They rose stiffly from the floor and helped each other brush sand off their clothes. "I don't think Roselil's garden had willow bushes," Karen teased. "Wherever did you find them?"

"I wanted flowers but it's too late in the year. The harbormaster was very helpful and offered anything in his garden. No, don't try to clean it up; the cabin boy'll do that."

"Yes, Sir Peter." Karen said. Poking at some stray locks of hair, she added, "I must look a mess."

"You never could keep that headscarf on straight," Peter agreed affectionately. "I think we need to start over." He pushed her onto the chair and, with surprisingly nimble fingers he undid her scarf and took off the under-bonnet. "I used to help my little sister when she was learning to tie but I'm out of practice," he apologized. He ran his fingers through her braid so her hair rippled down over her shoulders. "I knew it would be long and silky. Just like this it looked when I dreamt of you."

"Mmm," Karen sighed, moving her head, like a cat begging to be petted.

Coming to her senses, she pushed his hands away and automatically re-did her braid. Replacing the bonnet, she re-wrapped the scarf and knotted *æ pjægger*.

Peter looked on with approval. "Almost good enough to pass my mam's inspection," he teased. "But I like it better uncovered, so I can play with your hair."

As they went out the door, Peter leaned down and whispered the last line of the folksong in her ear, "He who laughs last, laughs best." Then he added with a phony leer, "You know what a Fanniker couple does after their Yes-party?"

Karen was at first puzzled. Then she blushed and laughed, "Yes, Sir Peter." Her knees buckled and Peter grabbed her elbow. Together they faced the cheering crew.

Fanø

Fanø, oh Fanø, how beautiful you are,
White is your beach, your waves so green.
Where are the dunes, and where the breakers,
Where is the blowing sand whiter than here?

Ask the bird that leaves every year,
Only to return each spring,
Would it do so if not pleasure
Drew it to our sandy coast?
Fanø, oh Fanø, how beautiful you are,

White is your beach, your waves so green,
Home, oh home, my heart tells me true,
You are the fairest place on earth.

Henriette Nielsen

Translated by Anne Ipsen

Notes

What's Real and What's not.

K*aren from the Mill* is a work of fiction and all of the characters are from the author's imagination, except for a few historical people. Hans Christian Andersen (1805–1875) and Bishop N.S.F. Grundtvig (1783–1872) are cultural giants of eighteenth-century Denmark; errors in interpreting their influence, ideas, and writings are unintentional. Dr. Ludvig Schrøder (1836–1908) founded Askov Folkschool in 1864; the school is still active today and continues to be inspired by his vision for adult education. Carl Frederick Balslev (Bishop of Ribe, 1867–1895) would have been surprised to find that he had a poetic nephew called Michel Mogens and should not be held responsible for his antics. The singer Jenny Lind (1820–1887) was known as the Swedish Nightingale, but there is no record that she gave a concert in Ribe in 1875.

The town of Sønderho and the island of Fanø of the mid-1870s have been described as accurately as possible, but liberties have been taken with its people and houses. It is hoped they will forgive the artistic license and understand that Karen and her family are fictional characters, invented to tell a story, not history. The Sønderho mill and its farmhouse inspired Millfarm. The real stumpmill was built in 1770 and was replaced after an 1894 fire with the more modern mill that is today a town museum. In 1874, it was owned by a consortium of Sønderho families and operated by a master miller from the mainland. Any resemblance to Karen's father is coincidental. Jørgen Lind drew the cover picture of the Mill and Møllegaarden as they probably looked in 1870. He lives in present-day Møllegaarden and is an architect, specializing in restoring old houses. Jørgen also serves as the town archivist and is a valuable resource on its history and spirit.

According to a tablet inside the church, Jørgen Lytte Staarup Hilde was the 18th Lutheran Pastor of Sønderho from 1863 to 1879. The name of Pastor Johannes Engel, Karen's otherworldly 'Papa Angel,' does not appear. The town's real Smith was Andreas Sørensen (1831–1891). He was born on the mainland but his wife, Anne Mejnertz Sørensen, was a Fanniker. Their fictional 'foreign' counterparts are Smith and wife Lone Smith. A gravestone in the cemetery names H. K. Kristensen (1845–1911) as Sønderho's teacher for 35 years. The misogynist schoolmaster, Madsen, was created to facilitate the plot and would not have merited such respect.

Most chapters begin with small pictures from various sources. Each illustrates an image in the chapter and gives a visual impression of Fanø and the neighboring countryside in the nineteenth century.

The pictures for chapters 1, 3, 5, 7-10, 12, 14, 16-19, 21-23, 25, 28, 33, 36, 37, and 39 were scanned from *Dansk bondeliv i forrige århundrede (Danish Farm Life During the last century)* by Gunnar Knudsen, Chr Ericksens Forlag, 1975. The originals are xylographs, lithographs, and ink drawings from the second-half of the nineteenth century. Although only a few are from Fanø, all are evocative of contemporary farm-life and mostly self-explanatory. Three xylographs are particularly interesting but need a title: Fanø Girls at the Ribe Hiring Fair (1876, Chapter 36), Women Students at Askov (1885, Chapter 37), and Unloading a Boatload of Hay on the Norby Beach (1881, Chapter 39).

Dr. Johannes Ipsen was Jørgen Lind and the author's grandfather. A surgeon by profession and an amateur artist, he spent summers in Sønderho. His vacation home was the model for Southhouse, where Karen's grandmother, Big-Anne and Aunt Kirsten live. Five of his sketches, signed II, grace chapters 13, 15, 34, 43, and 44.

The *Marianne*, First Mate Peter Larsen's ship, is a three-masted bark, as illustrated by Richard Dana, the author of *Two Years before the Mast (1836–Chapter 2).* The Danish artist Julius Exner sketched the little girl in the Fanø bonnet in 1884 (Chapter 3), and Erik Henningsen drew his vision of Sønderho the previous year. The illustration of the first San Francisco cable car (Chapter 26) appeared in *Harper's Weekly* soon after 1873 when they first began to transport passengers 3000 feet up and down Clay Street Hill (elevation 307 feet).

Four twentieth-century photographs are included. Two of Fanniker costumes are pictures of the author (back cover) and the author with a friend (Chapter 4). Today, fifteen model ships hang in Sønderho church, more than any other nave. One of these is the *Maria*, photographed by the author for Chapter 11. It was reputedly built by the captain of the *White Karen,* which inspired the story of Karen's grandfather's tragic ship. The 1930s photograph of the centuries-old Ribe pharmacy, on which Uncle Thomas's house and import business is loosely based, appears in Chapter 24.

Quotations of poems and other writings from the nineteenth century introduce eleven chapters. Two of them are Danish folksongs, translated by the author. Translations of other brief passages are in the text.

Innumerable sources were used to research *Karen from the Mill.* In addition to the book by Knudsen, cited above, the most valuable were: Andreas Sørensen's memoir *Ved det yderste Hav (By the Outermost Sea),* Gyldendahl, 1953; Sønderho, *En skipperby i Vadehavet (Sønderho, A Seaman's Town in the Wading Sea)* by Niels Frederiksen, Fiskeri og Søfartsmuseum, Esbjerg, 1989; and the ineffable *www.google.com.*

About the Author

Anne Ipsen was born in Copenhagen, Denmark, and came to the USA with her parents soon after World War II. Since then, she has often visited family in Sønderho on Fanø, off the west coast of Denmark. The picturesque town and the island's fascinating seafaring history inspired *Karen from the Mill.* In the photograph, Anne is dressed in the local folk costume and stands by the garden door of her grandfather's vacation home, the model for Southhouse in the novel.

Anne has written two memoirs: *A Child's Tapestry of War* and *Teenage Immigrant. Karen from the Mill* is her first novel. She and her husband live in Minneapolis and have three grown children. For more information visit the web at *www.ibusgroup.com*